KISS MY GIRAFFE

BOYS OF THE BAYOU GONE WILD

ERIN NICHOLAS

ISBN: 978-1-952280-29-0

Editor: Lindsey Faber

Cover photo: Wander Aguiar

Cover design: Najla Qamber, Qamber Designs

THE SERIES

Boys of the Bayou-Gone Wild
Things are going to get wild when the next batch of bayou boys falls in love!

Otterly Irresistible (Griffin & Charlie)
Heavy Petting (Fletcher & Jordan)
Flipping Love You (Zeke & Jill)
Sealed With A Kiss (Donovan & Naomi)
Say It Like You Mane It (Zander & Caroline)
Head Over Hooves (Drew & Rory)
Kiss My Giraffe (Knox & Fiona)

Connected series...

Boys of the Bayou
Small town, big family, hot-country-boys-with-Louisiana-drawls, crazy-falling-in-love fun!

My Best Friend's Mardi Gras Wedding
Sweet Home Louisiana

The Series

Beauty and the Bayou
Crazy Rich Cajuns
Must Love Alligators
Four Weddings and a Swamp Boat Tour

Boys of the Big Easy
Hot single dads in the sexy city of New Orleans

Easy Going (prequel)
Going Down Easy
Taking It Easy
Eggnog Makes Her Easy
Nice and Easy
Getting Off Easy

MAIN AND RECURRING CHARACTERS

Bennett Baxter: partner in Boys of the Bayou, married to Kennedy. (Crazy Rich Cajuns).

Caroline Holland: heiress, wildlife animal advocate, FBI consultant. Engaged to Zander. (Say It Like You Mane It)

Charlotte (Charlie) Landry: engaged to Griffin. Marketing director for Boys of the Bayou Gone Wild. Granddaughter of Ellie and Leo. (Otterly Irresistible).

Cian (pronounced KEE-an) O'Grady: Fiona's younger brother.

Colin Daly: Fiona's friend and bodyguard.

Cora Allain: Ellie's best friend, works as the head cook at the bar, Maddie's grandmother.

Declan O'Grady: Fiona's oldest brother.

Diarmuid (pronounced Deer-mid) **O'Grady:** Fiona's grandfather.

Donovan Foster: Griffin's brother. Wildlife rehabilitation expert. Former TV star and current internet sensation. In love with Naomi (Sealed With A Kiss).

Ella Landry: Josh and Tori's daughter, Ellie and Leo's great-granddaughter.

Ellie Landry: Zander's grandmother, owner of Ellie's Bar, matriarch of Landry family, married to Leo.

Fiona Grady: heroine. Runs an animal park in Florida, exotic animal supplier for the Boys of the Bayou Gone Wild.(Kiss My Giraffe)

Fletcher Landry: Married to Jordan. Cousins-Charlie, Owen, Sawyer, Kennedy, Josh. Third grade teacher. Zeke and Zander's older brother. (Heavy Petting).

Griffin Foster: engaged to Charlie, wildlife veterinarian, business partners with Tori Landry, brother-Donovan. (Otterly Irresistible).

Henry: Cian's bodyguard

Jacob: Saoirse's nemesis/ then friend. (9 years old)

Jillian (Jill) Morris: wildlife veterinarian, specializing in penguins. From Bliss, Kansas. Married to Zeke, twin daughters Poppy and Allie. (Flipping Love You)

Jonah: Torin's bodyguard

Jordan Benoit: married to Fletcher, from Autre, educational director for Boys of the Bayou Gone Wild. (Heavy Petting)

Josh Landry: Zander's cousin, partner in Boys of the Bayou, married to Tori. (My Best Friend's Mardi Gras Wedding)

Juliet Dawson Landry: Zander's cousin-in-law, lawyer, married to Sawyer. (Beauty and the Bayou)

Kennedy Landry-Baxter: Zander's cousin, Josh and Sawyer's sister, married to Bennett, Mayor of Autre. (Crazy Rich Cajuns)

Knox: hero. Autre city manager, friend of family. (Kiss My Giraffe)

Leo Landry: Landry family patriarch, founded Boys of the Bayou, married to Ellie.

Maddie Allain Landry: partner in Boys of the Bayou, married to Owen. (Sweet Home Louisiana)

Mitch Landry: Zander's cousin, works for Boys of the Bayou, dating Paige Asher. (Four Weddings and a Swamp Boat Tour)

Naomi LeClaire: friend of the family, grew up in Autre, girl-friend to Donovan. (Sealed With A Kiss).

Oisin (pronounced Osh-een) **O'Connor:** Diarmiud's right hand man, advisor, best friend.

Owen Landry: Zander's cousin, partner in Boys of the Bayou, married to Maddie. (Sweet Home Louisiana)

Paige Asher: dating Mitch, from Appleby, Iowa. (Four Weddings and a Swamp Boat Tour)

Saoirse (pronounced Sear-sha) **O'Grady:** Fiona's daughter.

Sawyer Landry: Zander's cousin, partner in Boys of the Bayou, married to Juliet. (Beauty and the Bayou)

Tadhg (pronunciation: Tige) **O'Grady:** Fiona's great-great-great grandfather

Tori Kramer Landry: local vet, married to Josh, Ella's mom. (My Best Friend's Mardi Gras Wedding)

Torin O'Grady: Fiona's second oldest brother.

Zander (Alexander) Landry: town cop, Zeke and Fletcher's brother, engaged to Caroline (Say It Like You Mane It)

Zeke (Ezekiel) Landry: Zander and Fletcher's brother. Owns local construction company (also works as family accountant). Married to Jill. Twin daughters, Poppy and Allie (Flipping Love You)

ABOUT KISS MY GIRAFFE

Enemies to friends to almost lovers...then back to kind-of enemies... to lovers. For a guy who wanted to keep things simple this is anything but.

Fiona knew Knox would be mad when she moved in next door.

And not because she brought a collection of wild animals with her.

And she was right.

So she intended to leave him alone. Mostly.

But *he's* not ignoring *her*. He's actively working to send her and her "ridiculous menagerie" (rude) right back out of town.

Still, as hard as she tries, it's impossible to stop thinking about the small town grump's long hair and tattoos and that *mouth*.

Not the one that's almost always set in a grim line and says things like, "you got a permit for that?"

Nope, the one that kisses her like she's everything he's ever wanted and says *very* dirty things in her ear. And sweet, protective, supportive things. Sometimes.
Accidentally. When she catches him off-guard.

The one that also says he only wants a long-distance fling with her. Nothing serious. And that he never dates women he sees every day. Like his *neighbor*.

Well, fine. If he doesn't want her—and her unbelievable past and that-can't-be-real *future*—then she doesn't want him either. He can just kiss her...giraffe. (Yeah, she actually has a couple of those.)

Now she just needs to convince her heart to give him up.

PROLOGUE

Be sure you've read the prequel to Kiss My Giraffe, **Otterly Into You!**

1

"Oh...um..." Fiona coughed. "I...*damn*."

Knox blinked at the petite brunette on his front porch. She was staring up at him, her eyes wide.

"Are you okay?" he asked. She looked nervous and a little dazed.

He was stunned to see her, but he was also immediately concerned. Confident and flirtatious was Fiona Grady's default mode. Anything else made him worry. As much as he *really* didn't want to.

"You just look so hot in those glasses." Her gaze tracked over him, from his untucked button-down shirt to his blue jeans, to his bare feet. "I wasn't expecting that," she told him when her eyes returned to his.

And *she* was not what he'd been expecting when he'd heard the knock on his door at nine o'clock at night. Now, having her in front of him suddenly after three months of no contact, he had a mix of emotions swirling through his gut. One, of course, was exasperation. That was always one of the primary things he felt when Fiona was involved.

He pulled his glasses off. "What are you doing here?"

She shook her head. "Sorry, that whole hot-nerd thing was really distracting. I always think about your long hair and tattoos and muscles and how *big* you are." Her gaze traveled over him from head to toe again. Slowly. She met his eyes and grinned. "I forget that you're a geek underneath it all."

He sighed. He'd missed her. Fuck. He didn't want to miss her. He didn't want to know what had kept her away from Autre, Louisiana, for the past three months when she'd been making trips to his little town at least monthly ever since the petting zoo-slash-park-slash-sanctuary had started growing.

"I didn't know you were in town," he said, trying for nonchalant.

"Just got here. Came straight over."

"Why?"

He liked that she'd wanted to see him first thing when she'd hit town.

But he didn't want to like that. He hated that he'd missed her, worried about her, actually felt hurt that he hadn't heard from her.

He did *not* want to be wrapped around this woman's little finger.

Yet he felt a distinctly unpleasant sensation of *twisting* whenever she was here.

"Oh." She frowned. "Right. There's a reason I came straight here. An important one."

He crossed his arms and propped a shoulder against the doorjamb. He should probably invite her in, but that was trouble because he wouldn't want her to leave. "I'm waiting."

And fucking worrying. She looked nervous. Fiona Grady *never* looked nervous. She was a ballsy, bold, do-gooder who always thought she was right and was willing to risk huge fines, jail time, and even bodily harm to save the animals she was so passionate about.

But she always knew what she was doing. She seemed to

charge into situations, her passion turned up to max-level, her sassy tongue lashing whoever was in her way with statistics and laws and the names of people very high up in law enforcement and politics. But in the time he'd known her—almost two years now—she'd never looked nervous.

She absolutely twisted him up.

She wet her lips. "Okay. Remember that thing we talked about at Christmas?"

Knox felt his gut clench. They'd talked about sleeping together. And him becoming the *temporary* foster dad to three baby otters.

And they'd kissed for the first time. A kiss that had been causing annoying, unwelcome, frustrating dirty dreams for *three fucking months.*

"About having a salacious affair where we sneak around behind our friends' backs and sleep together whenever I'm in town?" she pressed when he didn't answer.

"Yes. I remember." Too well. He was incredibly pissed about how often he'd replayed that conversation and how restless he'd been waiting for her to call or come back to Autre.

He didn't *pine* for women. Ever. He did the opposite of that.

But now she was here. And Knox wasn't sure what he was feeling. Her showing up unannounced wasn't unusual. Fiona Grady rolled into Autre without warning more often than not in her grape-soda-purple truck that sent his heart hammering and cock hardening.

But it had been three months since he'd seen her. Since they'd talked. Since he'd had any clue what she was doing, where she was, *how* she was.

Suddenly, she was on his doorstep asking about their plan to bang whenever she was in town for a couple of days?

"Okay, well, there's something I need to tell you that will make you *not* want to do that anymore," she said. "So I was wondering if maybe you wanted to get naked together once before I tell you and ruin everything?"

He opened his mouth to reply. Then shut it without a word. *What the hell?*

He glanced over his shoulder. Three minutes ago, he'd been sitting at his kitchen table doing paperwork with a cup of coffee and listening to a podcast about new creative urban development ideas.

Now the woman he was low-level obsessed with was on his porch asking if he wanted to have sex before she told him something that would make him not want to have sex with her anymore.

He ran a hand through his hair. *This* was why Fiona Grady was no good for him. She came into his carefully controlled and organized life and made things chaotic and messy.

"Are you sick?" he asked.

"Sick? No."

"Dying?"

"*No.*"

"Is anyone dying?"

"No."

"Are you married?" He braced himself. He knew very little about this woman, actually, and if she belonged to someone else, he'd...leave her alone. And hate that man. And never forgive her for stirring him up like this.

"Absolutely not."

"Engaged?"

"No."

Okay, that was all...way too much of a relief. He should not be this happy to hear that.

"Did you kill someone?" he asked.

She tipped her head, her mouth curling. "Is that a definite deal-breaker?"

No, probably not. Knox narrowed his eyes.

6

"No, I haven't killed anyone."

"Are the Feds looking for you? Or will I be implicated in some kind of crime if I let you in?"

"Not that I'm aware of."

"That's not a no."

"I'm just being honest."

Fair enough. Fiona was a wild animal advocate. The type of person to show up at roadside petting zoos and "circuses" to monitor how the animals were treated and hand out literature to people attending the events, raising awareness about the poor conditions and treatment of those animals. She showed up to help rescue and care for animals, wild and domestic, after natural disasters such as hurricanes and wildfires. She regularly lobbied local, state, and even the national government for animal protections.

The chance that she could have done something in the "gray area" for one of her causes was pretty good.

The problem with *that* was he knew that wouldn't keep him from wanting her.

She was precisely the kind of woman he should be avoiding.

He studied her face for another long moment, then gave in to the inevitable. He pushed his door open.

"Yeah?" she asked.

"Yeah."

She wasn't dying, wasn't married, and hadn't killed anyone. And he wanted her more than he'd ever wanted another woman in his life. So how was he possibly going to shut the door on her? After three months of missing her? He wasn't that strong. Or stupid.

But what the hell did she have to tell him?

He ignored that question. As she stepped across his threshold, her body brushed against his, and her scent—a fragrance that was sweet but tart at the same time, like citrus and

7

sunshine—floated up to him. He had to clench his hand into a fist to keep from reaching for her. He wanted to bury his hand in the thick, dark strands that fell to her shoulders, gather it in one fist, tip her head back, and hold her still as he kissed her the way he'd imagined for months.

The kiss in his office at Christmastime had been a mistake.

It had given him a taste of a drug he was already addicted to. He felt like his body *needed* her. And he was pissed at himself, not for taking that taste, but for not taking *more* of it. He'd been the one to pull back. She'd been ready to go back to his place. Hell, he was sure he could have gotten her naked right there on his desk. But he'd pulled back, teasing her that she'd have to return to Autre and get the baby otters she'd dropped in his lap—not quite literally, but almost—if she wanted more.

He'd been so sure she wanted more. That she'd be back. Sooner versus later, as arrogant as that sounded.

That kiss had been a soul-rocking-never-leave-his-thoughts kiss. He'd been *sure* she felt the same way.

Worse than the best damned kiss of his life, at that point, he'd been certain Fiona Grady was exactly the right woman to have an affair with. He'd been all in.

And then three months had passed with barely any contact at all.

She'd answered a couple of texts when he'd finally sent them.

He'd started with *you lose your map to Autre?*

Her response had been *still at home.*

Before Christmas, he'd thought the wildlife sanctuary and giraffe ranch she ran in Florida was home. Turned out she was from somewhere in Europe and had been heading there for the holidays.

He hadn't asked for more details. He'd been stupidly telling himself for almost two years that the less he knew about her, the less fascinated he'd be.

He'd been dead wrong, but that's what he'd told himself.

His next text had been, *you ever comin' back?*

He'd also lied to himself about how vital her answer to that question was to him.

Of course, had been all she'd replied.

No further detail. No flirtation.

He'd let almost an entire day pass before he texted again. But he couldn't *not* send that next one.

You okay?

He'd included another lie to himself about how much he needed an answer to that.

Yes.

No elaboration. No emojis. Nothing else.

So he'd let it go. He hadn't texted again.

And now here she was *in his house*, and she had news that she knew he wouldn't like.

But she'd also offered something far more dangerous.

"Fi."

The gruff single syllable form of her name that only he and her best friend, Griffin, ever used made her spine straighten, and she turned to face him. He closed the door but didn't move away from his spot.

"Yeah?" she asked softly.

"Are you okay?" He needed that answer as much now as he'd needed it two months ago in that text.

She studied him. Then shook her head. "Not completely."

She *had* to be okay. He *needed* her to be okay. Because yeah, he loved her long, dark hair, big blue eyes that seemed to twinkle constantly with mischief, tight body, and sassy mouth. But above all else, what he liked about her was that she was perpetually even better than *okay*. And she never asked him for a damned thing. Until those baby otters. And those were half a joke...and entirely temporary.

Or so he'd thought.

"Fi, I—" he started

But she cut him off. "I missed you."

He looked at her. She didn't seem on the verge of tears or like she was about to tell him all her problems. "I missed you too," he said, deciding to be honest.

"So we should take our clothes off."

Yes, they should. They should get naked and have hot sex, and then he could walk her to the door and say, *You know what? I don't need to know your news. Let's just keep doing this.* If he didn't know the reason that would make him *not* want to have sex with her, he could keep wanting that, they could keep doing it, and everyone would be happy.

He liked life organized and things put into tidy boxes—literally and figuratively. He loved to be decisive, to act, and to take charge. Women like Fiona, who were bold and driven and didn't let anyone intimidate them, and who would tell him to go to hell when necessary, were perfect for him. As long as they didn't live within a 100-mile radius of him. A buffer zone was critical.

He realized neither of them had said anything for several long seconds after she'd said they should get naked.

"Knox, you should know—"

He covered the space between them in two long strides, cupped her face, and covered her mouth with his.

He didn't want her to tell him anything. He didn't want to know whatever was going to change this thing between them. He wanted her. The self-assured, kickass woman he'd gotten to know. Who lived seven hundred miles away.

He did *not* want whatever chaos or craziness she'd brought with her.

That probably made him an asshole.

But he'd make it up to her with orgasms.

She gave a needy little whimper against his lips as her hands came up to grip his wrists as if holding him close, urging him to keep going.

Taking his time to taste her, to relish this, to drink her in, he walked her back until she bumped into the wall behind her. Then he slid his hands down her body, loving how she shivered and arched closer. Finally, he cupped her ass and lifted her. Her legs went around him, and he pressed her into the wall.

She was small. She stood barely above five-feet and weighed almost nothing. He was a big guy, six-four, and 'brawny' as his mother described him. He'd played football—very well—and he knew his size helped him get stuff done. People didn't argue with him when he confronted them over property line disputes or told them they had to clean up their empty lot. Sure, some of it was his growly attitude and lack of patience, but his size helped.

It was undoubtedly an advantage when it came to putting Fiona up against the wall so he could settle his aching cock into the notch between her legs.

She gave a little gasp that turned to a groan, and her hands slid into his hair. He wore his long too, and as her fingers curled into his scalp, seeming to pull him in even closer, he relished how she gripped him.

He kept one hand on her ass and palmed the back of her neck with the other, tipping her head slightly. He stroked his tongue over her bottom lip, then delved inside to taste her fully. He gave a low growl as she met his strokes with her own.

They kissed, pressing against each other, their gasps and groans filling his foyer until he finally pulled back. He stared down at her, his gaze burning into hers.

"Right here or bedroom?"

She swallowed, her breathing ragged. "Bedroom. I want you all stretched out."

A surge of heat went through him. He wanted that too. Plenty of room to move, change positions, and get at every inch of her.

He pulled away from the wall but kept his hold on her.

She laughed slightly. "I can walk."

"Now that I've finally got you here—" He pressed her against his painfully hard cock. "I'm not letting you go."

She gave a delicious little groan. "Yes." That was all. A simple agreement.

He carried her up the stairs to his second floor and headed for his bedroom. He'd lived in this house for years. Ever since he'd come back to Autre after college. This town had always been his plan. This was home, and he wasn't leaving.

Knox strode across his bedroom, an enormous space that had once been two smaller bedrooms. His bed was near the windows on the south side of the room. He could see the back of the enclosure from that window where Autre's big cats, a young lion and an old-man tiger, lived. Fiona would love that.

Knox lowered her to the mattress, following her down. His hands were now free to roam, not needing to hold her up. He ran his palms up and down her sides as he kissed her deeply. She lifted her hips, pressing into him, wrapping one leg around his waist, so they fit perfectly.

She was small, but she was strong. Not just in spirit, though certainly that, but physically as well. She ran a wildlife sanctuary. She threw hay bales and gigantic hunks of meat around and helped herd animals for veterinary checks and transport. He didn't have to worry about hurting her. He could trust she'd tell him to back off if he was too much. God, he needed that almost as much as he needed her bare skin and hot, warm body around his.

So he unleashed his need for her.

He pulled back just enough to unbutton his shirt and yank it off. Her gaze and hands were hot as she ran her palms over his bare skin, and Knox shuddered. "Fuck, I love your hands on me."

"Me too. God, how have we waited this long?"

That was a great question. When he'd first met her, he'd known she was trouble. He expected that she'd drive him crazy and that they'd clash whenever she came to town. He'd been right. But those clashes had been foreplay. He'd acknowledged that to himself only, the second time she'd come to Autre. But he'd started feeling respect for her right away. Not only the work she did but the way she treated the people he loved most.

He'd quickly realized Fiona was pushing the Boys of the Bayou Gone Wild petting zoo toward becoming a sanctuary. She'd seen their potential before they'd understood it themselves. And she'd been right on. She'd given the animals a loving place to go, and she'd given the *people* a purpose that they'd all embraced and grown from.

He was crazy about her for that alone.

Anyone who loved his people as much as he did would be able to get past a few of his walls. So he'd resigned himself to liking her. Admiring her. Enjoying their banter and her sass.

But damn, he hadn't expected the physical desire to be so strong.

He just couldn't fight it anymore.

A long-distance, no-strings-attached fling with this woman was perfect.

So no, he did *not* want to know whatever she thought would change his mind about that.

"We waited because I didn't like you for a long time," he said, leaning in to run his mouth down the length of her throat.

"Liar," she said with a breathless laugh. "You liked me as soon as I brought swearing parrots to town."

He groaned. Those parrots had caused him all kinds of headaches with the locals. "No."

She wiggled underneath him, pressing up against his fly. "Yes."

"I *wanted* you, but I didn't like you."

"Oh, you *wanted* me the very first time we met." She grinned up at him. "Just like I wanted you."

"I wanted to paddle your ass."

Her eyes went wide but not with shock. Heat. There was heat there. "I know."

He narrowed his eyes. "Yeah? But you kept poking me."

"Yep."

He ran a hand down her side to her butt and cupped a cheek, squeezing firmly. "I still want to regularly."

She gave him a sly grin. "I know."

He shook his head. "I'm going to get to be really dirty with you, aren't I?" Fiona was the perfect type to push and play with. She would never let him overstep, and she would give as good as she got.

His cock pulsed with that knowledge, and his body heated. The things he wanted to do to this woman. With this woman. He knew she'd meet him head-on, fully participate, make him beg if she wanted to. But if she let him push *her* to the point of begging, that would be...amazing.

"You can be however you want to with me," she told him softly.

As she answered, something in her voice or her eyes made him pause. That was so sincere. So...heartfelt.

She meant it, and he sensed that she was referring to things beyond sex.

Instead of pulling away as he probably should have, he lowered his head and kissed her hungrily. She wrapped her arms around his neck, pulling him down more firmly against her body. She kissed him back, her hands going to his ass, pulling him into her. She felt like heaven.

"More," she said softly against his lips. "Please."

He dragged his bearded jaw over her cheek and down her neck. "We're going to do this, Fi," he said roughly against her ear. "We're going to have this wild affair. We're gonna fuck each other senseless." He lifted his head to pin her with his gaze. "And you're going to keep your news to yourself. I don't wanna know. When you come to Autre, you're going to be in my bed. When you're not here, you're gonna answer my fucking texts. But I don't need anything else."

And he meant that. The long-distance relationship would work. People thought those were hard, and he was sure distance was tough for some. But he knew well that long-distance was perfect for some couples. Like him and Fiona. Two independent people didn't need to be all wrapped up in each other.

He moved to unbutton her jeans, *needing* desperately to see —and lick—the tattoo on her hip. He'd seen it when he'd needed to do first aid on the ostrich bite on her lower back a few months ago. The tattoo curved over her left hip bone and read *All great changes are preceded by chaos.*

That was Fiona. She had the potential to turn his world upside down.

Unless he kept that under control. Kept her in the little "fuck buddy" box in his life. Didn't give in to his urges to know more about her and get involved in every little bit of her life.

He popped the top button on her jeans, and she shifted. At first, he thought to give him better access to lower the jeans. But a second later, he realized she'd unwrapped herself from his body to move away and now had a hand resting on top of his. Stopping him.

He lifted his gaze.

She looked torn.

He didn't like torn. He liked decisive, and he knew exactly what he wanted her decision to be here.

"Don't," he said simply.

"I have to tell you."

"No, you don't."

"I do. And..." She sighed. "Dammit. *Before* we do this."

"*No.*" She really didn't need to tell him at all. But he believed her when she said it would change his perspective on things.

"There are a few things I think you should know, but there is *one* thing you for sure need to know. Before we get naked. As much as I would love to just strip you down and ride you 'til sunrise, you'll be mad after."

Despite his brain saying *yeah, now I do need to know whatever the fuck this is,* his body was still *really* into the idea of naked now, consequences later.

"What makes you think you'll be riding?" he asked, lowering his voice as he squeezed her ass again. "I like being in charge. I planned to start with you spread out, taking me deep and slow, then finishing with you on your hands and knees, coming hard and fast as I pound into you."

"Oh my *God*," she groaned. Then she pushed him back and scrambled up the bed, out from underneath him. "Stop." Her gaze traveled over his bare shoulders, chest, and abs. Finally, she tipped her head back. "*Fuuuuck*," she said to the ceiling.

"You okay?"

"No. I'm here in *your bed* with you half-naked, looking like..." She waved her hand. "*That.* It's making it *very* difficult to do the right thing here."

"The right thing is taking your clothes off and putting that mouth to better tasks than talking."

"No." She sighed. "Unfortunately, it's not. Because if we're as hot together as I expect and you give me the orgasm that I'm betting you're going to, I will be even *more* upset when you're pissed at me later. It's better to not know how good this could be if I can't have it again."

"We're absolutely going to be hot together and I'm gonna give you more than one orgasm and I've decided I don't care if you're keeping some animal abuser in a cage in your basement and are treating him the way he treated whatever animals you rescued from him."

There was definite heat in her gaze even as her lips curled. "I've had that happy daydream more than once."

"The multiple orgasms?"

"The abuser in a cage. But orgasms are really good too."

He gave a soft snort. He started to crawl after her. "Fi—"

"I'm moving here," she blurted out.

He froze.

And *dammit*, she'd done it.

She'd ruined everything.

2

Yeah, that look on his face was exactly what she'd been expecting.

Dammit.

Fiona scooted up until she was propped against the headboard. He was still on hands and knees and she saw one hand curl into the duvet.

"What did you say?" he finally asked, in a low growl.

"I'm moving here. I've...moved here." As of tonight. When she'd driven past the sign on the edge of town, she'd officially been home. "That's what I came over to tell you. One of the things. Probably the most important one right this minute."

God, there were so many things she needed to tell him. Or that he was going to find out whether she told him or not. She'd been thinking about him on her long drive from Florida. Not her grandfather, or the rest of her family, not her animals or her business. Knox. And how this move could end everything before they'd even started.

She should have told him everything before this.

But he hadn't wanted to know.

Over the almost-two-years that she'd known him, they'd

gone from adversaries to sort of friends to more-like-real-friends to it-feels-like-we're-going-to-end-up-naked-together to making an actual plan to have an affair they were going to keep secret from all their friends.

Who *planned* something like that?

Knox.

The small town city manager absolutely loved a plan and knowing what was going to happen and having control over it. He was definitely the type to have to think it over, then talk it all out, lay out every expectation, hell, maybe even sign some official rules. So, she'd expected to come back to Autre and sit down with a beer and hammer out the details. She was fine with that. But she would have worn her skimpiest bra and underwear and been ready to start *that night.*

She didn't come to Autre often. They had to make the best of the time they had.

Until her grandfather had messed everything up.

She'd spent two and a half months at home for Christmas. Then she'd returned to Florida and arranged to move her animal sanctuary to Autre and blend it with the one here. And blend her life with the one the people here were living.

But now that she was going to be here, all the time, she knew that the chances of Knox ever seeing her favorite thong were much, much smaller.

Knox had made it *very* clear that he didn't want to get personal. Naked sure. Personal no. But living in the same town, spending time with the same group of people, and moving her work here, meant that sleeping together had the potential to turn into more. And Knox didn't want more.

She hated how much he'd been on her mind. She couldn't *not* make this move because of the grumpy, nerdy, sexy city manager who was so hot and cold with her, she never really knew what he was thinking or feeling.

Fiona grabbed a pillow and clutched it against her chest, feeling the need for some barrier.

At first it had been fun not really knowing how Knox would react to her each time she came to Autre. She didn't mind being kept on her toes. She rarely planned or got worked up about details. She just went with the flow and did what needed to be done.

Not being able to figure Knox out had been a fun challenge. Poking at the grumpy bear who had long hair and tattoos but also kept perfectly sharpened pencils in a pencil cup on his desk and who clearly hated surprises had been a good time.

And then she'd done something really stupid.

She'd fallen for him.

And now, they were over.

Finally, Knox pushed back to rest on his heels and asked simply, "What the fuck for?"

God, he was hot. Broad chest, massive shoulders and arms, a tanned hue to his skin that spoke of time in the sun without a shirt, tattoos over one shoulder and down his upper biceps to his elbow. Nothing that would go below the edge of a shirt-sleeve though, of course. He had to keep up appearances as the buttoned-up, serious city employee.

Fiona took a deep breath and blew it out. Her answer to the question was simple. But the consequences of the decision were not. "I want to live here. Autre is amazing and the people here with the animal park are exactly the kind I want to work with."

"You have an animal park."

"I do. And I have a bunch of really wonderful employees and a great network of people. But it's nothing like here. Working here with Griffin and Donovan and Naomi and Jordan and Charlie..." She sighed. "They're my people. They have the same hearts that I do. I've seen the way they've grown along with the park over the past couple of years. They've all taken their passions and their intelligence and their huge hearts and turned it all toward this amazing cause that is such a part of me. The idea of getting to work with them every single day and turning this place into an even bigger wildlife sanctuary is a dream come true."

She was proud of her own sanctuary in Florida, of course, but the chance to have the camaraderie she'd found here every day was too tempting to pass up. She rescued and cared for abused and neglected animals. She helped rescue and rehome animals displaced by natural disasters. She lobbied and educated and preached and fought to protect endangered animals and to strengthen protections around all animals. And she would not apologize to anyone, including the big, hot, broody man she wanted more than she wanted another piece of Ellie Landry's pecan pie.

It was her calling. Her passion. And to share it with a bunch of people who she'd seen find the same calling and want to turn it into more was amazing.

Besides, she *had* to know that the animals and the cause were in good hands if and when she had to go home. To her *real* home. Thousands of miles away with an ocean between here and there.

Knox shoved a hand through his hair.

He couldn't be *shocked*. Griffin Foster, one of the town's vets, had been Fiona's friend for years. They'd worked in Zambia before they'd both returned to the states. It was how Fiona had known about Autre and their petting zoo to start with. Now Griffin was engaged to Charlie Landry, the woman who was hell-bent on turning the petting zoo into a major tourist attraction. Together they had big dreams.

Fiona pulled her bottom lip between her teeth and watched Knox for several long moments. Finally, she said, "I know this complicates things between us."

He blew out a breath and turned so he was sitting on the edge of the bed, his back to her. "Yeah, it does."

"I know you're not looking for a girlfriend."

He didn't reply immediately. After a few beats, he said, "I don't date women I have to see every day."

Fiona felt her brows rise. Well, that was kind of an asshole thing to say. But it fit. And at least he was being honest.

"Okay, then," she said. She didn't have to like it, but she had to accept it. Besides, she wasn't in a position to push for a relationship. She came with a lot of baggage. Literally and figuratively. Her truck was packed full of *stuff* and hers was just the first truck that would be rolling into Autre.

Plus, she'd been lying to him for almost two years.

Okay, technically, she hadn't told any *lies*. She'd just been purposefully leaving out details of her life. But that had been easy with Knox. He had never wanted to know personal information about her. When their conversations started to go there, he'd pull back. He hadn't even wanted to know where exactly she was going for Christmas. He'd been surprised to learn it was another country, but he'd quickly shut down further conversation about it. He didn't want to get closer to her in any way other than physical. He'd made that clear all along.

But now, he wasn't going to be able to avoid knowing those details. A couple of them would be quite obvious. The others would be kept within the tight circle of friends she had here. But Knox was in that circle. There was no way the Landrys would know something Knox wouldn't find out.

"There's more," she said.

"I'm not interested," he said. He glanced at her. "You moving here changes everything. I don't need to know anything else."

But he did need to know it all. He just didn't realize that yet.

"So we're just going to be friends?" she asked.

They had a lot of friends in common and there would be no way he could completely avoid her if she was living in this little town, even if it was only for the next few months, but somehow "friends" seemed like a strange descriptor.

They'd butted heads over her contributing animals, resources, and knowledge to help build the animal park he hadn't wanted in his town from day one. Then he'd gotten almost protective of her when he'd learned some of the other things she did—confronting abusers, protesting, showing up in the aftermath of hurricanes, earthquakes, and wildfires. Then he'd unexpectedly asked her out for ice cream on one of her visits.

She knew their friends all thought they'd done more than eat ice cream.

And they had. But not like that. They'd talked. She'd told him more about what she did and he'd explained how the animal park was making his job harder and they'd inevitably started understanding and respecting one another more.

And then they'd kissed at Christmas.

Man, that had been a mistake. Because it had been the best kiss of her life. That kiss had been better than a lot of the sex she'd had. And it had started an ache in her she'd been feeling for three months. Not just a physical ache for him, but an ache to be closer to him, to know him better. To tell him *all* her secrets. Secrets she'd kept from nearly everyone in her life for a decade. Secrets that were about to get spilled out all over the streets of Autre. The streets Knox worked to keep repaired and clean and orderly.

He was really going to hate her now.

"Sure, we'll be friends." He didn't sound enthusiastic about it.

"You're going to find out about the rest of it," Fiona said. "You sure you don't want to hear it from me?"

He shoved up from the bed and reached for his shirt, shrugging into it but not fastening any buttons. "Nope. If we're not involved, it doesn't really matter to me what's going on with you."

Well, ouch. She didn't totally believe him, but the words stung a bit nonetheless.

"It might make things even more...annoying for you."

He turned and pinned her with a frown. "It better not."

She rolled her eyes. He didn't want to know what it was, but "it better not" annoy him. He was such a pain in the ass.

The shirt didn't cover his chest or abs, and *she* felt a prickle of annoyance. Dammit. She was going to forever regret not letting this go the rest of the way before she opened her mouth. But she couldn't have slept with him without him knowing this very important fact.

Still, him just shutting down and turning away—literally, he'd turned his back and had paced to the window—rather than asking what was going on and delving into her answer about not really being okay and asking how he could help, was more of a dick move than she would have expected.

"Knox—"

"You should just go."

She stared at his back. He was going to kick her out? He'd just been running his hands all over her, talking, saying deliciously dirty things, and making it very clear that he wanted her as much as she wanted him. Now, just like that, he was dismissing her.

"Fine." She scooted to the edge of the bed and stood. She straightened her clothes.

He wasn't even looking at her.

Knox was very open and honest about what he wanted and expected from the people around him. And mostly that was to keep things simple and upfront as much as possible.

She liked that. Usually.

She'd not only seen it in how he did his job, but also in his personal relationships with their mutual friends. Knox was straightforward and even blunt at times, but everyone knew where he stood.

There were a lot of secrets in her life along with complicated relationships and roles for her and those closest to her. Knox was a breath of fresh air. She didn't always agree with him, but she always knew what he was thinking and feeling.

Like right now.

He was done with her. Done with this particular interaction and more, done with pursuing anything else.

Well, she had to accept that.

Just like she had to accept that hurricanes were real and made a hell of a mess. She didn't enjoy them and she sure as hell couldn't prevent them. She just had to deal with their consequences. Go in and do her best to clean up as much of the wreckage as she could afterward.

Looked like tomorrow she was going to have some work to do. Because whether Knox saw it coming or not, it *was* going to be messy.

"Okay then. I'll see you tomorrow."

He turned. The muscle along his jaw tightened for a moment, then he said, "My answer will be the same tomorrow, Fiona. I'm not interested."

She lifted her chin and met his eyes. "I don't think it's going to matter if you're interested." She started for the door of his bedroom. "Oh, and if you see me on my back patio tomorrow morning having my coffee and breakfast before heading to the meeting, you better stay on your side of the property line. I don't share my *muffins* with grumpy assholes."

"What do you..." He didn't finish the question.

She didn't know if it was because he told himself he didn't care about *any* of her muffins, or because he'd remembered the house behind his had been for sale.

"Fucking son of a bitch," she heard him swear when she was halfway down the staircase.

Ah, he'd remembered.

He could sure try to avoid and ignore her. But, for once, Knox wasn't going to get his way.

A sly smile curled her mouth as she left his house through the backdoor and turned to walk across their shared backyard to her new house.

———

Knox's first sign that his day was going to be complete shit was when Zander Landry met him on the steps of city hall with a large cup from Bad Habit, the quaint little coffee shop in the next town.

The shop was painted a sunny yellow and had white wooden shutters and a white wooden front porch and oozed *happy* and *welcoming* and *charming*. It was a place no one would think to look for either him or the grumpy, put-upon town cop. Neither of them really did "quaint" or "sunny". But they both loved to be left alone, so when they needed an escape from their hometown, where no one was ever really alone, they headed for Bad Habit and the table nestled in the corner of the upper loft at the back of the shop.

He didn't feel particularly sunny or charmed as he accepted the coffee from Zander this morning either. "Who'd you arrest and for what?" Knox asked, noting the scrawled words on the side of the cup that read *two shots butterscotch*. Shit, this was a butterscotch latte. Not just a plain old cup of coffee. Something big was going on.

"No arrests," Zander said with a grin. "Just thought you could use this for the meeting." He pulled the door to city hall open and gestured for Knox to step through before him.

Dammit. Whatever was coming was going to suck.

"What meeting?"

"Our meeting with the mayor," Zander said, lifting his own

cup. Likely a cinnamon dolce latte, Zander's favorite from Bad Habit.

"We have a meeting with the mayor?" That wasn't on Knox's calendar. Meetings with the mayor and the sheriff were something he generally knew about ahead of time.

"We do." Zander gave him a puzzled look as he pulled the door open to the mayor's office. "We need a plan, right?"

"A plan for wh—" Knox didn't finish his question as his eyes landed on the woman sitting in front of the mayor's desk.

Sonofabitch, he'd *known* this would happen. He'd just hoped he'd make it 'til lunch time before he had to actually face the fact that Fiona Grady was now living in Autre. In the house right behind his. The house he'd stoically avoided looking at that entire morning as he got ready for work—despite the wide windows on the east side of his bedroom that looked out over her backyard and the back of her new house.

He hadn't been quite as stubborn about it last night as he'd paced his bedroom and gone over their conversation and the news about her moving in right behind him. He'd looked out that window repeatedly. Noted the lights shining in the windows. Wondered which bedroom she'd chosen. Wondered just how in the hell he was going to ignore her and not watch her house like a fucking stalker, making note of her comings and goings, who came over to visit, and if they were male, her age, single, and handsome.

This was going to be *hell*.

And now she was sitting in Kennedy Landry's office looking gorgeous...and well rested. Though not at all pleased to see him.

Her hair was in a braid at the back of her head and she was wearing jeans and a red V-neck t-shirt. Nothing special. Nothing sexy. Nothing that he didn't see dozens of women wearing every day. But she looked absolutely amazing and everything in him seemed to strain toward her.

Of course, the look on her face would have kept him as far across the room from her as he could get even if he hadn't declared—to himself and to her—that he had no interest in or intention of pursuing any kind of relationship with her.

She was pissed. And not hiding it.

"Morning, Knox," Kennedy Landry, Autre's mayor and his boss, greeted. "Have a seat. We're ready to start."

"Hi, Knox," Charlotte Landry said from where she was leaning against the far wall.

Charlie was the marketing director for the Boys of the Bayou Gone Wild animal park and general spokeswoman for the family when it came to the animals. She was engaged to Griffin and related to all of the owners and, well, basically had made growing the park her mission in life. Plus, when Charlie had an opinion about something, everyone knew it and she did *not* like to be left out of things. It was just easier to include her on meetings from the beginning.

"Mornin'," he returned. "I wasn't aware we had a meeting planned for today."

Kennedy knew how much he liked a schedule and a plan.

"You didn't think that we would need to talk about this?" Kennedy asked. "Or did you two already come up with a plan?"

She was clearly including him and Fiona in the "you two".

Knox frowned. "I don't even know what we're talking about."

Kennedy, dressed as usual in mostly black, including her darkly dyed hair, eye makeup, and fingernails, glanced at Fiona. "Obviously Fiona's situation."

Fiona shook her head. "He wouldn't let me tell him the details."

Kennedy frowned. "So what does he know?"

"That I've officially moved here. And that I'm his backyard neighbor." She sent him a smirk. Then she turned back to

Kennedy. "But let's just say that I won't be going to his house if I need a cup of *sugar.*"

Kennedy frowned at Knox. "You kind of need to know the whole thing. And to not be an asshole."

"Is it cool with HR that you call your employees assholes?" Knox asked.

"Is it cool with HR that my employees *are* assholes?" Kennedy asked. "Let's go ask her together."

Lydia, their HR director, was part time. And a long-time friend of Kennedy's. Just as Kennedy was related to all of the Landrys in town—the biggest and most influential of the founding families—Kennedy had history with everyone who worked for City Hall.

Okay, they *all* had history with everyone who worked for City Hall. And any other damned place in this tiny town.

Knox sighed. "Fiona is moving to Autre. Why does that deserve a special meeting with the mayor, city manager, Boys of the Bayou, and sheriff?"

"Well, obviously I need to be up to speed when it comes to hosting this thing. Zander needs to be involved because of security. One of the main focuses is the animal park. And you have a number of projects to oversee," Kennedy said.

Knox took a deep breath and blew it out. Of course, Fiona being here was going to be a headache. He didn't even know the details and already he felt the need for the bottle of ibuprofen he kept in his top desk drawer.

Kennedy had to host something? There would be security concerns? Ibuprofen might not be strong enough.

Zander dropped into the chair in front of Kennedy's desk next to Fiona and propped his ankle on his opposite knee. "I think we might be here for a while." He lifted his cup for a sip of coffee.

Knox clenched his jaw and then leaned against the bookcase along the wall across from Charlie. "Let's hear it."

"Well, the first order of business, of course, is getting Autre ready for the visit. All of the formalities and security around having them here can come a little later. But there're a lot of projects to get started as soon as possible."

"He doesn't know *anything*," Fiona interjected. "I only got as far as telling him I'd moved to town. He doesn't know anything about my grandfather or anything else."

Knox scowled at her. Even her voice made his gut clench. It was simply a matter of wanting what he couldn't have, he was sure. But he hadn't slept worth a shit last night and had planned on using his extra grumpy mood to go confront Bill Robleau about tearing down the ramshackle shed behind his house that was not only an eyesore but had turned into a breeding ground for rodents, which was a major problem for his neighbors.

Instead, Knox was facing *his* new neighbor and was very afraid that he was going to be anything but gentlemanly in the upcoming interaction.

"Well," Kennedy said, sitting back in her chair and crossing her arms. Suddenly, she looked amused. "Why don't you bring him up to speed right now?"

Fiona rolled her eyes. "He definitely needs to be involved?"

"Oh, absolutely. We're going to have to push the sewer line project back, and he's going to have to organize getting Main Street cleaned up and several of the business storefronts repainted. Not to mention that the town square needs to have some landscaping done." Kennedy gave Knox a grin as his scowl continued to deepen. "He definitely needs to be fully informed."

"We're pushing the sewer line project back?" Knox asked. "That's unacceptable. I just got everybody on board with having their streets and yards dug up. We have a very tight timeline for getting everything done and we have contractors ready to go."

"Well, we can't have dug-up sewer lines and torn-up streets when Fiona's grandfather comes to town."

Knox looked from Kennedy to Charlie to Zander. "Why does it matter that Fiona's grandfather is coming to town?"

Was it rude to talk about her as if she wasn't there when she was sitting right in the chair in front of him? Probably.

"Well, since Fiona's grandfather has to approve of wherever she's going to be living, of course we want Autre to make a great impression," Kennedy said, as if that were obvious.

Knox lifted a brow. Fiona's grandfather had to approve of where she lived? No. That made no sense. Even if she wasn't a total ballbuster. "Now I know you're fucking with me."

"No. She's serious. It's in the Constitution," Fiona answered.

Finally, Knox looked at her again. "It's in the Constitution that your grandfather has to *let* you live in certain places?"

"Yes." Fiona met his gaze directly. "He has to approve of anywhere I consider a permanent residence."

"Babe, I don't know who convinced you of this, but that ain't how the Constitution works."

She gave him a cool stare. "Are you referring to the United States Constitution?"

"Of course."

"Are you aware there are others?"

"So what constitution is this?"

It hit him as soon as the words were out of his mouth. Dammit. He sounded like a dumbass. Of course there were other Constitutions and he knew Fiona was from another country. He'd only found out at Christmas, when she'd told him she was going "home" to visit her mother, that she wasn't American, but that still should have saved him from sounding like a completely uneducated dick.

Was it possible there was a country in the world that required grandfathers to actually approve of where their grand-daughters lived? Sounded like crap to him. Also sounded like something that the Fiona Grady he knew would never stand for. She was fiercely independent, incredibly intelligent, and pretty much did whatever the hell she wanted. All of which was hot as hell and wildly attractive to him.

Her chin tipped up slightly. "The Constitution of the Kingdom of Cara."

"What is the Kingdom of Cara?"

Fiona took a deep breath and turned in her chair. "It is a small island nation south of the Faroe Islands, about halfway between Norway and Iceland. It's just a bit bigger than Rhode Island and was given to my great-great-great-grandfather by the King of Denmark after my grandfather saved his life when the ship they were sailing was sunk by pirates."

Knox blinked at her.

Um...*what*?

Kings and pirates and island nations? But she looked completely sincere.

"My grandfather pulled him and three other men to safety. Fifty other people perished. The King of Denmark was so grateful that he awarded my grandfather the island. My family has ruled Cara ever since."

Knox rolled his eyes "Come on."

"She's serious," Kennedy said. "It's all real."

Yeah, there was a niggle in Knox's gut that told him it was all true. Fiona Grady was unpredictable and bold and fierce and compassionate to a fault. But she wasn't a liar.

And, if anyone would have a you've-got-to-be-fucking-kidding-me backstory like this, it would be her.

"You're telling me your grandfather is president of another country?"

"King, actually."

King. Right. Of course, he was. Fiona wouldn't just be the granddaughter of a politician. She'd be fucking royalty.

Knox waited for a heartbeat, wondering where the wave of

shock was. But, after witnessing Fiona bringing red pandas and a tiger and a zebra to Autre, Louisiana, seeing her rescue animals in the aftermath of a hurricane, and watching her marching herself and a pack of other Autre ladies to jail to protect one of them from being arrested alone, he knew anything was possible with this woman.

"So your grandfather is the *king* of a Danish island nation across the Atlantic Ocean—"

"Not Danish. My great-great-great-grandfather was an Irish sailor who happened to be taking the Danish king and his entourage between the Faroe Islands."

"So you're Irish?"

"We're descended from the Irish and immigrated to Cara from Ireland, but we are our own country."

"And that makes you what? A princess?"

Fiona lifted a shoulder. "Well, it would, except that I abdicated my claim to the throne when I was eighteen."

Okay, there was a little bit of surprise. Good to know he could still feel that emotion. "You gave up the throne?"

"Yes. So did my brothers."

"Why?"

"Because we don't think the country should be ruled by a monarchy. We want Cara to become a democracy."

"And..." He shook his head. He was actually talking about this seriously? But he was fascinated. And he was going to have to look up a whole bunch of shit about Denmark and Ireland and the Faroe Islands and Cara and...everything else.

"My grandfather and his advisors don't agree. We've been in a stand-off for about a decade. But anyway, no, *technically* I'm not a princess."

"But your grandfather *is* a king?"

She nodded.

"I suppose your mother or father is next in line?"

"My father was my grandfather's son. He died when I was

nine. My mother has no claim to the throne because the ruler has to be a blood descendent."

Knox was still grappling with all of this information. "So your grandfather's coming to Autre? And he has to approve of it before you can officially live here?"

Her eyes narrowed, but she nodded. "Yes."

Those narrowed eyes told him how well she knew him. She knew that he was already realizing that if he didn't want her to live here, all he had to do was make Autre unappealing to her grandfather.

How hard could that be? Knox loved his little town and had no intention of ever leaving it, but he wasn't sure that the things he found charming were actually royalty-level impressive. He couldn't imagine an actual king loving a tiny town along the bayou filled with blue-collar workers and people who spent their Friday nights sucking the meat out of things that crawled around in muddy water, and who thought the epitome of fancy was drinking their moonshine out of glass instead of plastic.

He was as fascinated by this as he was about everything he learned about Fiona Grady, but he definitely didn't want to be and this was right on schedule for incredibly-chaotic-and-fuck-up-his-life messy. Leave it to Fiona to take holy-shit-you're-never-going-to-believe-this to the next level after being an Autre local for less than twenty-four hours.

"So what does all of this actually have to do with me?" Knox asked, addressing Kennedy.

"Well, like I said, we have some cleanup and improvements to do around town to get ready to impress the king," Kennedy said as she leaned in to rest her elbows on her desk. "This is pretty cool for Autre. It's not like we have a king come to town very often. Oh, and you need to rush the building permits for Zeke. He's going to be renovating and adding onto her new house."

"Zeke's building a castle?" Knox asked dryly.

"I've actually never been a big fan of castles. Too big and cold and imposing," Fiona told him.

He rolled his eyes.

"The house she bought needs some definite fixing up. And he's adding an...apartment on for Colin," Kennedy said. Her smirk said that she knew how *that* name would affect him.

Knox's brows slammed together. "Colin is coming here too?"

"He's her bodyguard," Zander said, lifting his cup for another casual sip of coffee.

Knox focused on Fiona. Colin was someone he'd been hearing a lot about and had never met. He was her business partner and "close friend".

Yes, Knox had been very fucking jealous of Colin.

"Your bodyguard?"

Fiona nodded. "We used to tell people he was my boyfriend and my business partner because that made it make sense why he lived with me. I don't tell people about my family or that Colin is a bodyguard."

"He's *not* your business partner?"

"He helps with the animals, but only because he likes it. He's actually private security paid by my grandfather."

"But he's not paid enough to buy his own house?"

"We both prefer he have a space that's as separate as possible, but he has to live on the same property."

"Let me guess, that's in the Constitution too."

"That's just my grandfather's rule. But...he's the king."

Jesus. Knox shoved a hand through his hair.

"So, Fiona is our friend and we're *thrilled* she's decided to move here, even if it means we have to do a little bit of extra work. Whatever she needs from us we'll do a thousand percent. Right?" Kennedy asked. The question was clearly directed at Knox.

Whatever Fiona needed them to do. Right.

What Fiona needed was to head right back out of Autre and back to Florida, where, apparently, her grandfather already approved of her living. She could have her animal park and her animal causes and her friendships with everyone here in Autre. And Colin. Just as she always had. She didn't fucking need to be in Knox's backyard.

He nodded. "I agree that I need to give my part of this project a thousand percent."

Fiona was watching him with suspicion.

Uh-huh. She was sharp. And knew him. So she was catching on that *his* view of this project was not in perfect alignment with hers.

Well, she wasn't *technically* a princess. So she didn't need to be treated like one.

3

"Wow," Kennedy said as the door shut behind Knox. "He's not very happy."

Fiona sighed and slumped back in her chair. "Did you really expect him to be?"

"I expected him to be annoyed, but I thought you two were getting along better."

Fiona shook her head. "You know that Knox has very specific ideas about how things should go. He was fine with me when I was only here once in a while, *temporarily*, and seven hundred miles away the rest of the time."

Kennedy lifted a brow. "You really didn't tell him about any of this?"

Fiona lifted a shoulder. "It was a moot point before. If it had ever gotten to the point between us where it mattered who, what, and where my family was, I would've told him. I didn't intend to just show up here in Autre and spring this all on him. But I didn't expect to be doing any of this."

Charlie leaned forward in her chair. "I promise that we're going to make this move wonderful. Your grandfather's going to love Autre."

"As long as Knox doesn't get in the way," Zander said.

Kennedy frowned. "Knox isn't going to get in the way. He'll do his job. He might be grumpy about it, but this is the perfect chance for Mr. Perfection to get Main Street cleaned up and the town square looking impeccable. Those storefronts and flowerbeds have been bugging him for months."

Fiona glanced toward the door where Knox had disappeared. She really hated how everything had ended between them last night and in the meeting today. They'd always poked and teased, and she knew that a lot of the time he was genuinely frustrated or irritated with the animal park, but she knew he was a good guy. He truly loved this town and the people in it. As did she. It was one of the main things they had in common. She'd hoped that he would see that.

She'd also hoped that he would understand what a big deal it was for her to choose Autre as her new home. That he would get *why* she'd chosen Autre. Even if he didn't know that she only intended to be here for six months—long enough to get her animals settled and the Gone Wild people all trained in animal rescues and hooked up with her network of other rescuers. He knew how important her work was to her and that these people shared her passion for that work. Surely Knox would understand that the idea of being here in their midst every day, sharing her resources, training them to do rescues with her, caring for the animals together, had implanted itself and she'd been unable to shake it.

Of course, he would have to see past the surprise about her background and family, not to mention the fact that she'd kept it from him.

But why would she have told him all the secrets about her family? "Hey, I grew up in a castle!" wasn't something she told people often. Or ever. And certainly not people like Knox.

He wasn't a friend. Exactly. They weren't confidants. Because he never wanted to know anything personal. They weren't lovers. They unfortunately hadn't made it to that point. And they weren't really colleagues. Sure, she was helping build an animal park in the town where he was the city manager, but the Landry family owned the park and ran it. She was more of a resource than an employee. So yes, their professional paths had crossed but they had no obligation to actually cooperate or get along.

Knox was probably the first person in her life that she hadn't been able to specifically define. But she did know that he was important. His opinion was, anyway.

She liked the idea that she had won him over in the time they'd known one another. She'd gone from general annoyance to someone he respected. She knew he even felt protective of her at times. He'd seemed genuinely concerned when he found out that she worked in the aftermath of natural disasters, and had been downright riled up when she returned with the crew from the cleanup of Hurricane Clare in Alabama last year.

Still, he had absolutely kept her at arm's length. She shouldn't have been surprised about his reaction to any of this. More, she shouldn't be upset by it.

"So, let's dig in," Charlie said. "Obviously general town cleanup and telling everyone to be on their best behavior does need to be the top of the list. But what else do we need to do? Is there some kind of formal ceremony we need to prepare for?"

Fiona tuned back into the conversation and focused. *These people were her friends.* They wanted to make this work for her and she was incredibly grateful. She needed to put Knox out of her head.

"No, nothing formal. My grandfather's going to be concerned with whether Autre is safe far more than whether the town square is cleaned up."

"That is not a problem," Zander said firmly. "You'll be safer here than you were in Florida."

Fiona turned toward the town's cop. "He'll be concerned

about how small the town is. And that everyone will know the family's business. And the bayou. He's going to see that as an unsecure border."

Zander shook his head. "Smaller is better. I know everybody in this town and can give a thorough background report on each one of them. The bayou is actually a very secure border. Not just anyone can come through there. You know how to handle yourself and how to get around. And no one knows the bayou better than me and my cousins and friends. Besides my deputies, I have some friends who help me keep track of what's going on in or around Autre. Keeping this town and everyone in it safe is personal for us."

"Want to fill the mayor in?" Kennedy asked with a little frown.

Zander shook his head. "Got it covered. But I'll just tell you that Spencer, Wyatt, and Theo are part of it."

Kennedy studied him for a moment then nodded. "I definitely feel safe with you guys in charge."

Fiona looked back and forth between the two cousins. "I met Spencer. Who are Wyatt and Theo?"

"Wyatt is Spencer's brother. He's in the Coast Guard and has personal ties to Autre. Theo is one of the game wardens. Good friend of mine and very protective of the town."

"Why haven't I met Theo before?"

"He stays to himself. Not really a people person. But he's an ex-Navy SEAL who takes Autre's safety very seriously."

"Okay," Fiona said. "I totally trust you, Zander."

"I can convince your grandfather that you're safer here with people meddling in your life every single day than you ever were in Florida."

She laughed. "People meddling in my life makes me safer?"

"Absolutely. My family will notice the moment you're five minutes late for something, or feeling a little under the weather, or have an extra worry weighing you down."

Fiona thought about that and about the Landry family. She believed every word.

"I can probably even convince Spencer, Wyatt, and Theo to stop down to meet your grandfather if needed."

Fiona shook her head. "Really the only person you'll need to convince is Colin. My grandfather totally trusts him for anything having to do with safety and security."

Zander nodded. "Sounds good. When can *I* meet Colin?"

"He'll be here later today."

"Okay then, we have the safety part taken care of. What else will your grandfather care about?"

"That will be the main thing. I, however, can't wait to show off the animal park. When I left home originally, I did it with a lot of...drama. I declared that not only should the country be ruled by representatives democratically elected by the people, but that we should be expanding our influence and making the world a better place. Cara is very isolated and we interact almost exclusively with the Republic of Ireland. I would love to see Cara have more international relationships."

"And our animal park is going to help with international relations?" Charlie asked, her eyes wide.

"It's complicated," Fiona admitted. "More so than I realized at age eighteen, of course. My goal has changed a bit since I left home. I've grown up and learned a lot. Now what I want to do is take what I've learned and bring it back to Cara."

"What does that mean?" Charlie asked. "There's something that you've learned being in Zambia and the United States that you think Cara needs?"

Fiona looked around the room. She had a big plan that so far had met with nothing but resistance from her grandfather. But these people were her friends and she knew they would be supportive.

"I want to turn half of our island into a wildlife preserve. There are a number of endangered animals around the world that need a place that can truly protect them and increase their numbers. Cara is perfect. It's an island, so we can completely control what and who come in and out. There would be no poachers, no one capturing animals for zoos or circuses or to keep as pets. And my family is solely in charge of how the money is spent and the laws that are enacted. The animals could be absolutely protected. The isolation that always drove me crazy could now be the number one asset in doing something that could make a huge impact on the world."

She realized that it all meant that she would have to admit that her grandfather had been right in keeping Cara solitary and under his rule. And she *really* hated admitting her grandfather had been right about things. He gloated. It was *not* very king-like in her opinion.

"And your grandfather's open to this idea?" Charlie asked.

"No. Not at all. But he also hasn't been here to visit in about five years. I'm hoping to show him how I've helped you build this sanctuary and what I've taught you, and that it will prove that I know what I'm doing and that he should trust me on this. And…" She took a deep breath. "I have more to negotiate with this time."

She wasn't ready to tell everyone in Autre about *all* of the details of her family dynamics and what her grandfather wanted and what she was protecting, but she had something her grandfather very much wanted.

"Then the animal park is a huge part of this trip," Kennedy said. "He must be proud of everything he does know. With the rescues and conservation efforts and everything."

Fiona grimaced. "He doesn't know about *everything*. He doesn't know about the protests or about the natural disasters. He thinks I run a sanctuary and talk to politicians about policies and laws."

"You do that too."

"Yes. But he'd be…concerned about the rest."

Kennedy lifted a brow. "He and Knox have that in common."

Fiona frowned at the mention of the man she was trying very hard to not think about. "Well, neither of them needs to be. I know what I'm doing and that work is important too."

But it was dangerous at times. At least more dangerous than sticking to her own fields and barns and meeting with politicians in their offices. All of that felt so clean and boring and... yes, safe. Didn't doing something that *mattered* mean taking a risk? Being willing to put yourself out there? Being willing to sacrifice?

She'd always thought so. If something didn't require her to get dirty and get her heart racing and potentially cost her something—time, reputation, health and safety, or actual money—it meant that she could push even harder. She didn't want to be a princess. Not literally or metaphorically. She wanted to give all she could to the causes that mattered to her.

But her grandfather was asking her to pull back. To think. To take something bigger into consideration and she had agreed.

That was another reason she was here in Autre now. To slow down and to bring more people into her causes so it wasn't always *her* taking the risks. She was going to pull back and not just go charging into every situation. She was going to let some other people take the lead once in a while. Or even often.

She already hated it.

"Anyway," Fiona went on. "My grandfather needs to see that I am serious about choosing a good place to live. Not just a place that's safe, but one that has other essential elements. Tradition and customs and family history are incredibly important to him. That's one of the reasons that he wants to keep Cara the way it is. He wants our family to be secure and have a rich history that we can always trace back." She was ready to acknowledge that she had more to consider than just what *she* wanted and needed. She had to meet the king part way if she wanted to get him to listen to her. "I want him to understand that can happen in other places too and Autre is perfect for that. He can come here and listen to *your* family stories and see your heritage and history reflected in everything you do and how it's made your lives and this town vibrant and meaningful."

All three of the members of the Landry clan she was sitting with gave her big smiles. The Landrys were a noisy, rowdy, meddling family, but they loved fiercely and fully and gladly welcomed others into their fold. Fiona had felt more sense of family and friendship, love and support, in Autre than she had in Cara growing up.

"Okay so your grandfather wants to know about the safety of Autre," Charlie said, looking at her cousins, then to Fiona. "And you want to introduce him to the Landrys and impress him with our animal park."

Fiona nodded. "That's it. We don't need a big fancy feast or red carpets or any kind of ceremonial anything. Honestly, my grandfather won't want to call attention to Autre and the fact that we're here now."

"So he's not going to roll into town in a big black stretch limo with eighty members of his entourage, wearing his robes and crown?" Kennedy teased.

Fiona chuckled. "Not at all. In fact, I'm about ninety percent sure that he's going to rent a red sports car at the airport and will show up in blue jeans."

Charlie laughed. "No way. The king?"

Fiona laughed. "Yep. There will only be a couple of guys with him for security and they'll hang back enough you might not even know they're there. But they're good. They're some of the best trained soldiers in the world. The only guy who will be with him the whole time will be his best friend and advisor, Oisin. And he's great. He'll love Ellie's. It'll remind him of his favorite pub back home. He'll be the first to hop on a swamp boat tour."

"We can definitely make that happen," Kennedy said with a grin. "So we should tell everyone he's just your grandfather and not actually a king, right?"

"Please. Except for maybe a very tight inner circle."

"Well, you know, our inner circle is very tight but it's kind of big," Charlie said. "Still, this is the town where Naomi LeClaire lived for years with no one from the outside world knowing. The town just had a pact that we'd protect her identity because everyone loved her."

"And no one wanted a bunch of crazy fans and paparazzi hanging around," Zander said.

Kennedy nodded. "She was able to be incognito for over a decade."

Fiona knew all about Naomi being a famous child TV star who'd retired at age fourteen and come home to Autre. She was definitely no longer incognito though.

She and her fiancé, wildlife rescue and rehab specialist Donovan Foster—who had been famous for a reality TV show and YouTube series himself—now had a reality show that they produced themselves and filmed right here in Autre. It was hugely popular not only because of the action and adventure and cute animals, but because of the love story between the two stars that played out right on camera. Naomi and Donovan couldn't hide their chemistry if they tried. And they didn't try.

"Yeah, if we can keep Naomi hidden, we can easily hide a sort-of-not-really-princess," Kennedy said. She knew a lot about privacy and security herself. She was in politics. Not only was she mayor of Autre, but her husband, Bennett, was the president of a non-profit foundation and had just won a state senate seat.

Fiona gave her a grin. "Okay, yeah, let's tell a few people so they know what's up. But we can generally just tell everyone that my grandfather is a suave older European gentleman who wants to see where his granddaughter is going to be living."

"Perfect." Kennedy clapped her hands together. "Let's head over to Ellie's. We can fill Tori and Maddie and Juliet in."

"And Jordan and Jill and Naomi are going to want to know," Charlie said. "Oh, and Caroline. Maybe it will help your grandfather feel better if he knows that you're really good friends with an FBI agent."

Fiona sighed. The "inner circle" in the Landry family was actually huge.

Zander must've read something in her expression because he said, "Relax, Princess. We've got your back."

She sent him a little smile. She knew they did. And honestly, she wasn't sure even King Diarmuid of Cara would be able to hold his own against the entire Landry clan.

"Well, we *are* engaged. I mean, everyone refers to her as my fiancée. Even me."

The sound of several otters squeaking in response to that made Knox's mouth curl at one corner in spite of his generally pissed-off-at-everyone-and-everything-but-especially-a-hot-brunette-princess mood.

"Yeah, I *know* I haven't officially asked her. But we talk about the future all the time."

More squeaking.

"I know I need to buy a ring. Why does everyone bring that up as if I don't know that? I'm not a total dumbass."

Clearly Griffin hadn't seen Knox approaching the otter enclosure. When Griffin thought he was alone, he talked to the otters. It was one of Knox's favorite things to walk up on. It was one of *everyone's* favorite things to walk up on. And it wasn't really that hard to do.

Griffin Foster was grumpy and stoic and loved only one human more than he loved animals. Charlotte Landry, his... okay, he was right, she was his fiancée. Everyone knew they were going to get married. But he hadn't officially proposed and she wasn't wearing a diamond on her left hand now that Knox thought about it...now that Griffin and the otters were "discussing" it.

Obviously it was on Griffin's mind.

Knox came around the edge of the enclosure and the big rock formations that blocked the area where Griffin was sitting on the manmade riverbank with Gus, Gertie, and their kids. The first batch they'd had in the enclosure had been named after candy: Snickers, Rolo, Skittles, Hershey, and Baby Ruth. The second litter had cookie names. Oreo, Biscotti, and Snickerdoodle were just as cute, rambunctious, and loud, and were, at the moment, climbing all over Griffin's lap as they informed him that Charlie was their *favorite* and he should definitely marry her right away.

At least, that's what Knox assumed they were saying. Why would they be saying anything else? Charlie was the best. And, specifically, the best for Griffin.

Knox cleared his throat.

Griffin looked up. He didn't even bother to look chagrined at being caught talking to the animals. At this point it had happened so often there was no point.

"Hey, Knox," he greeted, stroking a hand down Biscotti's back.

"Hey. How's it going?"

"Never ask otters for advice about engagement rings."

Knox tucked a hand in his front pocket. "No surprise they're bad at that. They're suckers for pretty girls. They think bigger is better in all things...slides, treats, fish. I'm assuming diamonds too?"

Griffin laughed. "I almost forgot that you know all of that firsthand."

Yeah. Knox had otters of his own. Thanks to Fiona. She'd brought him three newborn otters at Christmastime, told him she needed him to keep them for her just until she came back to town, and then disappeared for three months.

And now they thought Knox was their dad.

He was stuck with them.

What was he supposed to do? Just dump them out in the bayou?

That was exactly what he'd been tempted to do, as a matter of fact. For about a day. Okay, maybe five hours. Not that he'd admit to her that they'd won him over that quickly. But Basil, Cilantro, and Parsley were now very much a part of his home.

Yeah, he'd tried to name them after things he didn't really like. But, he actually liked the little fur balls. He did not, however, talk to them like Griffin did. Oh sure, he might say *hey guys how's it going?* Or *I suppose you're hungry?* But he didn't ask them for advice. He knew very well they would be big fans of Fiona's if they got to know her.

The fact that they didn't know her, actually made him feel a flash of irritation. She'd dumped them in his office and disappeared. That was on her. And it turned out that they didn't need her.

Maybe he didn't either.

"So what's up?" Griffin asked as Snickerdoodle climbed up his arm to his neck.

"Actually, I'm looking for Mitch," Knox answered. Parsley did the same thing to him when he watched TV and fell asleep on Knox's shoulder almost every night. She liked to hide under his hair.

"He's up at the big pasture with Drew working on extending the fences."

"Got it. So when are you going ring shopping?" Knox was

surprised he asked. It was not only none of his business, but it was really not at all the kind of question he generally asked. Griffin's raised eyebrow indicated that he knew that. But he said, "I've already got the ring. Just need to figure out how to ask her."

"You want it to be some big elaborate thing?" Charlotte Landry was a little bit more girly and sophisticated than a lot of the Landry girls, but Knox knew that however Griffin asked, the answer would be yes.

Griffin shook his head. "Nah. It would just be nice to surprise her. That woman knows me too well. I'd like to do something she wasn't expecting for a change."

Knox shook his head. "But you're sure you want to do it, right?"

Griffin grinned. "Can't imagine my life without her, and figure nobody will believe that she puts up with me on a daily basis over the next fifty years if I don't have a ring on her finger."

Knox laughed. "Not a bad point."

Ten minutes later, he found Mitch Landry and Drew Ryan at the north end of the pasture where the camels, donkeys, and zebra lived. All had been rescued from various abuse and neglect situations. Knox shook his head as he got out of his truck. There were actual zebras practically in his backyard. Sure, he had to walk a couple blocks, but he lived in a tiny town in Louisiana. He never would've guessed he would have zebras roaming just down the street.

He approached where Mitch and Drew were working, growing puzzled as he drew near. It didn't look like they were repairing fences or expanding the area behind the fences. They were building up the *height* of the fences.

"What the hell are you doing?" he asked as he got close.

Mitch looked over as Drew lifted a hand in greeting.

Mitch was a general handyman around Autre. He kept his

49

family's many businesses going—repairing the boats and docks for the Boys of the Bayou swamp boat tour business, keeping his grandmother's bar and restaurant going with plumbing, electrical, and air-conditioning work and any other maintenance she needed, and working on anything and everything else the family needed from leaky roofs to building otter enclosures at the petting zoo.

Zeke and Mitch together could build almost anything. But it was Mitch's imagination and enthusiasm for the animal enclosures that had resulted in general designs that included everything the animals needed, but still made the pens and paddocks look natural.

Drew Ryan was a farmer from Iowa. But he had a knack for caring for anything with hooves and he'd been excited to extend his experience with cows, horses, and alpacas to more unusual animals like camels and zebras. He'd become one of the primary caretakers in the animal park after falling in love with Rory—the owner of I'm Gonna Dye, the local hair salon—when he'd brought his reindeer to town to help out at Autre's Santa's Village.

"Hey," Mitch greeted. "What are you doing out here?"

"Need to talk about a project on Main Street. Kennedy thinks we need to do some general cleanup to impress some bigwigs."

Mitch laughed. "Yeah, Kennedy texted. I'm supposed to ignore your general attitude about it all."

Knox had come up with his plan after walking out of Kennedy's office. And he was sure Kennedy and Fiona both knew what it was. He wasn't surprised Kennedy had already texted Mitch.

"My attitude is that our citizens deserve to have working sewer lines and that we shouldn't be pushing back major projects just because we're getting some fancy visitors."

"She didn't mention the sewer lines to me," Mitch said. "She did say we'll be needing to do some painting and repaving."

Knox shrugged. "Nothing vital."

Mitch turned and climbed down his ladder. "We've been discussing this project for a while. A few storefronts need repainting. Kennedy wants new awnings, the whole sidewalk on both sides redone, and something about flowerpots." He shrugged.

Flowerpots? Like big flowerpots filled with...

Knox shook his head. He did *not* care about fucking flowerpots.

"We don't have funding for all of that," Knox said simply.

That wasn't untrue.

At one point, businesses had been in charge of maintaining their own storefronts. If something needed repaired, they did it at their own expense. Then about a year into his tenure as city manager, Knox had proposed having the city pay for those things. It relieved the burden on the business owners, which attracted more businesses to the empty buildings on Main Street rather than them heading out closer to the highway. It allowed the city to hire locals to do the work rather than the business owners hiring whoever was cheapest and the town could then also put stipulations on what those buildings looked like.

Was Knox stupidly picky about things? Yes. Did he care if most of the buildings were painted neutral colors, but one was bright orange and stuck out and looked ridiculous? Also, yes. Did he care if people thought he should be worried about bigger, more important things in town? No. He was capable of worrying about everything at once.

"Kennedy said that there was private funding behind it now," Mitch informed him as he moved toward his truck for another section of fencing. "And she said the four city council members she'd talked to were in favor."

Knox scowled. Kennedy hadn't mentioned the private funding or that she'd already talked to some of the council. Of course, those four had probably been in her grandma's bar for breakfast that morning and she'd run it past them casually. Still, he couldn't deny that it made his plan to block the whole thing more difficult.

And, dammit, the painting and repairs needed to be done. Main Street was looking shabby. Yes, it had been driving him nuts.

Flowerpots would definitely look nice. What kind of flowers should they plant? He'd have to ask his mother what would look nice with the awnings...

Knox rolled his eyes. He did *not* care what flowers they planted along Main Street. He did *not*. Much. Because that was ridiculous. He'd bet most of the guys who drove down Main Street didn't even notice that the awnings were tattered, not to mention tightening their hands on the steering wheel when they saw the *hole* in the awning over the post office.

He was a perfectionist. So what? It made him a great city manager. He knew and appreciated building codes and city ordinances and the like. He didn't like tacky, messy, or dilapidated. He liked rules and he had no qualms about making sure people followed them, and, most of all, he didn't mind being considered an asshole by people who didn't like rules.

"Who are the private donors?" Knox asked.

He'd headed out here to find Mitch first thing to make sure the other man told Kennedy he was too busy to take all of this on, but maybe Knox could head this off by stalling the donors' actual deposits.

If King What's-His-Name from the Island-of-Wherever thought Autre was just a little too weathered and worn and other-side-of-the-tracks for his granddaughter, then that was just too bad.

They could fix all the cracks and holes later. And add those flowerpots. Because yeah, those actually would look nice. Maybe with hibiscus. He really liked those. He'd definitely have to call his mom...

Dammit.

Knox stepped forward and helped Mitch lift the next huge piece of metal fencing from the truck bed and carry it to where Drew was waiting.

"Not sure. But I could take a guess," Mitch said, pointing to where he needed Knox to fit the piece.

Knox lifted the section into place and Drew started attaching it. "Yeah?"

Mitch gave him a look. "And so could you."

Knox sighed. Kennedy's husband. Bennett Baxter was a millionaire and was wrapped around Kennedy's little finger. "She shouldn't be coercing her husband into paying."

Mitch laughed. "I'm not sure asking Bennett for money that Autre needs is coercing him exactly. She and Bennett would be donating money to Autre for various projects even if she wasn't the mayor." Mitch started attaching his end of the piece of fencing. "And it's not like it's millions. Though she did mention wanting to put in new streetlamps. The photo she sent me is really cool. They look like gas lanterns from the French Quarter, but they're electric."

Knox's heart skipped a beat.

God, he was a nerd.

But cool streetlamps instead of the tall, boring streetlights they had now? Well, he couldn't help it. That was kind of exciting.

"But anyway, it's not Bennett," Mitch said, pulling his drill out and securing his end of the fencing.

Knox knew the answer by the time the whining of the drill stopped. "Fiona?"

"Yep. Girl's got money."

"I would expect so, yes." If she didn't, the royal family of Wherever-the-Fuck was doing something wrong.

Okay, so he knew the name of her country. Cara. That wasn't hard. Just like it wasn't that difficult to wrap his head around her being a fucking princess.

"So, Kennedy took her up on the offer. Because seriously, some of it does *need* to get done," Mitch said. "We have to fix that section of sidewalk in front of the flea market, for instance. Wouldn't want the king to trip and fall and break his arm."

"You think the *king* is going to the *flea market*?" Knox asked. "Think he might be looking for some dishes or to add to his vinyl collection?"

Mitch chuckled. "You never know. Besides Ellie's, it's the best place to get a taste of life here in Autre."

It was a building full of crap that people had either dug out of their attics and were trying to sell or had made and were trying to sell. But Mitch had a point. There was no better place to really get a look at the pieces of everyday life in Autre and along the Louisiana bayou.

But now Knox was even more irritated. That section of sidewalk needed fixed regardless of whether a king was coming to town, dammit. The flea market was only open two days a week and was hardly the busiest place in town, but Knox didn't want *anyone* tripping and breaking their arm. And dammit, he'd care if it was Fiona's grandfather regardless of whether the man wore a crown.

Did he actually wear a crown? That was...a very weird thing to be wondering about and the fact that he was made Knox even *more* annoyed at the entire situation. Because he knew he'd be Googling if the king of Cara wore a crown on a regular basis as soon as he got to a computer.

He would *not* do it on his phone.

Probably.

"You're not having any trouble believing all of this about

Fiona and her family?" he asked Mitch. "You don't seem shocked or anything."

Mitch met his gaze. "I don't know. I mean, maybe I was a little at first but...Fiona's got an air about her, you know? If somebody said, 'so a girl you know is actually a princess hiding out, who do you think it is?', she would've made my top three."

Yeah, that had kind of been Knox's general feel too. If anyone was going to be not just a princess but a run-away-from-home-because-she-didn't-like-the-whole-royal-thing princess, it would be Fiona. "Who would be the other two?" he couldn't help but ask.

Mitch grinned. "If I didn't know her, Charlie."

Knox laughed. Charlotte Landry *definitely* had a princess attitude about her when she needed it. "And?"

Caroline. He'd bet twenty bucks on Mitch saying Caroline. She was an heiress to millions, for one thing, and she'd shown up in town wearing a wedding dress that sparkled with jewels and a fucking tiara on her head. Plus she had a you-better-do-things-my-way-or-I'll-make-things-very-difficult-for-you attitude. But in a good way.

"Paige," Mitch said instead.

Knox blinked at him. "Really?" Paige was Mitch's girlfriend. She was essentially his fiancée, much like Charlie was Griffin's —everyone knew they'd eventually get married—but Paige had been proposed to five times before she'd met Mitch and she'd firmly told him that *she* would be the one to propose to *him* and he just needed to wait a damned minute. Or year. Or two.

Yeah, now that he thought about it...

"Okay, I see what you mean."

Mitch grinned, his expression full of affection. "Girl knows what she wants and that she's worth it and is strong enough to demand she get it. That's princess stuff, right?"

Knox had to nod. "That's princess stuff." And it fit Fiona to a T. He shook that off. "Okay. Let's get that part of the sidewalk done," Knox agreed. "But the painting and stuff can wait. You're busy here."

"Yeah, this is a big job. Drew and I aren't gonna be able to tackle downtown and I told Ken that. We've gotta get a lot done here. Zeke's gonna come help us, but everyone else will pitch in this weekend downtown."

Well, dammit. Knox gritted his teeth. His plan to have Mitch too busy to help was working out but the always-ready-to-help, *big* Landry family was going to come to the rescue. Of course. They could get anything done if they set their minds to it. And there really were a lot of them.

But who was he kidding? Knox wasn't going to be able to let that awning continue to have a big gaping hole in it much longer anyway. Even if they didn't have private funding for it, he'd probably been about forty-eight hours from digging into his own savings account. Now, knowing that they had the funds and the approval to get it done, there was no way he was going to block it.

He sighed. "Sounds like a lot will get done this weekend."

Mitch nodded. "Yep. Here and down on Main. Fiona didn't give us any warning on this but seems like she was planning for this a long time ago. We won't have to do much to the barn itself. When she gave us specs way back in the beginning, the measurements and design included the height and space we need now. We questioned it then, but she just said she wanted to be ready for anything."

Knox frowned at him, his heart rate kicking up. He just wasn't sure if it was actually irritation or anticipation. "Fiona brought more animals with her?"

But he knew the answer to that question. Of course she had.

Every time she showed up there was a new, unusual animal with her. And yes, he'd been irritated. He'd been dealing with calls from agencies making sure they had their paperwork in order, inspectors coming to town, and more and more visitors every month.

Which, of course, had been the goal of the Boys of the Bayou Gone Wild petting zoo and animal park. They were an attraction that relied, in part, on ticket sales.

But more visitors to town meant more traffic, which meant more traffic *problems*. Like back-ups at intersections and fender benders. And more wear and tear on the streets. And more noise and crowds and garbage.

Then there was the infighting amongst the Autre business owners. The convenience store closer to the highway had started selling more souvenirs and food items. The businesses downtown had complained that he was taking business from them. He'd said it was up to them to compete. They'd lobbied for better signage to direct visitors to Main Street. Some had wanted to extend business hours, others hadn't. Some had wanted to have sales and to give away samples and do other events on the weekends to draw people downtown, while others hadn't.

The town in general had demanded stop lights instead of just stop signs at multiple intersections to help with traffic flow. The general citizenry had complained about the difficulty getting around town to things like their kids' baseball practices and after-school activities and even just going out for dinner now that there were so many more people in town on the roads and dining and drinking in Autre.

There were a lot of good things the animal park had done for the town, but there were many not-so-good things.

And Knox got to hear about them all.

He was also tasked with solving them all.

And becoming completely fascinated by and attracted to the woman who was partially responsible for it hadn't helped.

Boys of the Bayou Gone Wild would have happened even without Fiona. Charlie Landry had been determined to turn the little petting zoo into something profitable and Charlie Landry always got her way. But Fiona was the reason they had endangered, exotic animals. She was the one who had recognized the big hearts, adventurous spirits, and bring-it-on attitudes of the Landrys and their friends and had decided to gently nudge them toward animal park and sanctuary status. She was the instigator, plain and simple.

He definitely blamed her.

"Of course Fiona brought animals with her," Mitch said with a laugh.

"I've only been here a few months and I even knew the answer to that," Drew added.

Drew had only met Fiona briefly at Christmastime when she'd stopped in, dropped off the baby otters, and disappeared. Still, Fiona was infamous in Autre.

"Yeah, okay," Knox acknowledged. And clearly it was something with hooves that needed a barn. "So what..." But the answer hit him before he finished the question. If Fiona was *moving* here, to stay, there was one animal that she'd be sure to bring.

And a second later, it was confirmed as one of the animals came ambling over the small rise in the distance.

"Of course."

There was a giraffe coming toward them.

4

"Pretty cool right?" Drew asked, grinning widely.

"Yeah...sure." It was. Of course. On one hand, there was a *giraffe* coming toward them. One of the most unique, interesting, and majestic animals on the planet. On the other hand, there was a *giraffe* coming toward them and there were *lots* of people who thought they were unique, interesting, and majestic. Which meant lots of people would be coming to Autre to see them.

There was suddenly a loud whistle and the animal's head swung toward the sound. As did Knox's.

On the west side of the huge paddock stood a little girl and her dad. They were leaning on the fence and the girl was holding out a handful of what looked like hay. The giraffe immediately started toward them.

Yeah, a giraffe—or *giraffes* because there was no way the feisty, make-his-life-messy princess had shown up with just one—would absolutely attract more visitors.

"Um, shouldn't someone be over here supervising our new arrivals?" Knox asked, straightening as he watched the giraffe head toward the girl.

"Nah, they're okay," Mitch said.

"They're okay? We're just letting people feed the giraffes already?"

This part of the animal park had restricted hours. They let people come and check out the zebra, camels, donkeys, and horses from a distance but because all of the animals had been rescued from traumatic situations, they limited the number of visitors and let the animals decide how close to the humans they got.

"We're gonna partition off part of the pasture," Drew said. "The giraffes are very used to visitors and are hand fed often, so Fiona wants people to be able to get close to them and allow the other animals to stay at a distance if they choose."

"But..." Knox watched the giraffe stop in front of the girl and lower its head. He didn't think it was fully grown yet. It wasn't nearly as tall as he'd expect. The giraffe took the hay from the girl and she ran a hand up and down his snout as if she was petting a dog.

"I'm gonna head over there."

What the fuck *he* was going to do with a giraffe he didn't know, but he'd feel better if there was someone nearby while the visitors interacted with the new-to-the-park animal. Hell, the fencing hadn't even been extended there. There wasn't really anything keeping the giraffe from stepping right over and heading down Bayou Road.

Again, he didn't know what *he'd* do if the big guy decided to take a tour of Autre but... Yes, he did. He'd be calling Fiona and telling her to get her sweet ass over here.

He'd probably even leave off the "sweet" part.

"So we'll talk about the sidewalks and awnings later then?" Mitch called as Knox strode toward his truck.

"And the streetlamps," Knox agreed. Then groaned. Dammit. He was supposed to be *stalling* the clean-up, not getting excited about of this. At least he hadn't said *and the flowerpots.*

But hibiscus really would look cool.

He drove the short distance to the west side of the pasture and parked. He approached the girl and her dad. And the giraffe. Jesus.

"Hey. How're you doing?" he greeted as he strode up next to them casually. Or he hoped he looked casual. And not like he was afraid they might be trampled to death right in front of him.

The man smiled. "Good."

"Welcome to Boys of the Bayou Gone Wild."

The little girl grinned at him as he moved to stand next to her at the fence. The giraffe looked at him, then decided to check him out. The animal extended his neck and sniffed Knox's head. Knox held perfectly still. He knew a bit about giraffes. They were Fiona's favorite so he *might* have looked a few things up.

The giraffe shifted his front legs closer to Knox, snuffling his snout along Knox's hair.

The girl giggled. "He likes you."

"You think so?" Knox asked, looking down at her without moving his head.

"For sure." She giggled again as Knox felt a slight tugging on his hair. "He's licking your hair. He does that to me too."

Knox jerked his head back, coming eye to eye with the big animal. It just blinked at him. Then swung his head back to the girl with the food.

"Don't worry, he didn't bite any of it off," the girl told him, laughing. "He only nuzzles people he thinks are trustworthy. It's because he's been bottle fed. He's spoiled." She ran her hand up and down his snout again.

Wow. They were already giving out a lot of facts about the new animal. "No kidding." Knox studied the animal. He could easily imagine Fiona bottle feeding the baby giraffe and he felt a warmth in his chest. Would that make him even more attracted to her?

Yes.

Fuck.

"So he must think you can be trusted," the girl said. "It's a huge compliment."

She was sweet. Probably about nine or ten. She probably had drawings of giraffes on her bedroom walls and stuffed giraffes all over her bed and giraffe socks and a giraffe backpack and a bunch of giraffe movies. Were there giraffe movies? Now he was going to have to look that up too probably.

"Are giraffes your favorite animal?" he asked.

"Oh, no." She shook her head.

Okay, well, he wasn't an expert in ten-year-old girls, after all.

"What is—"

"I like *wombats*," she told him enthusiastically before he'd even finished asking.

"Oh. Huh." He knew absolutely nothing about wombats.

"You know that wombats poop cube-shaped turds, right?" she asked.

He...did not. "That's a very interesting fact."

The man standing next to her hadn't said a word the entire time. He'd just stood there. Grinning. He was still leaning on the fence, watching the giraffe, listening, and still not saying anything.

"They're also marsupials."

Knox nodded. "Like possums." There, he knew a fact.

"And like kangaroos," she said. "And..." She looked up at him. "Do you know another?

"Koalas."

She beamed at him. "Yes. And wallabies, and Tasmanian devils."

"I did not know that about Tasmanian devils."

She looked proud. "And wombats are *super* endangered."

"They are?" Knox frowned. There were so damned many endangered animals he hadn't been aware of before Fiona. "That's too bad."

"Yeah. Really too bad. But I send five dollars a month to a group that's working to save them."

Knox looked down at the little girl. That made his heart warm too. "I think I want to do that too. What's the group called?"

"There are a few, but I send mine to Sleepy Burrows Wombat Sanctuary in Australia."

"Sleepy Burrows," Knox repeated. "Okay."

"Burrows because wombats dig burrows. Like tons of them."

He nodded. "Got it."

"But you should probably send ten dollars," she told him. "I mean, you're a grown-up. If a kid like me can send five, you can send ten, right?"

The man standing with her gave a soft chuckle.

"That's a pretty good point," Knox told her. And it was.

"Do you have a job?" the girl asked. "If you don't, I guess five dollars is okay."

Knox grinned at her. "I do. I can definitely do ten."

"Okay, good. Wombats eat a lot. One wombat can weigh as much as *three* koalas." She turned her attention back to the giraffe. Who had stood, just chewing and watching her. "I love giraffes too, of course," she said, holding out more hay.

Of course. He was glad they had the animals right here or she'd have him sending ten bucks to a giraffe sanctuary too. Hell, maybe he should be contributing money monthly to Boys of the Bayou Gone Wild. He hadn't ever given that any thought. But they probably had monthly donors. He was going to have to ask Charlie about that.

"You seem to know what you're doing," he said, watching her feed the giraffe, who seemed smitten with her, frankly.

She nodded and pulled more hay out of the bag that she was wearing. Wow. A hay bag. Who just had a hay bag? Maybe she'd been up at the petting zoo feeding the goats and alpacas. Knox didn't know for sure that giraffes ate the same things that alpacas ate, but he assumed it was similar.

"This guy just got to town. How did you find out he was here?" Knox asked

If this guy had come to town with Fiona last night that meant that he'd been here for just a little over twelve hours. If he'd showed up here with whoever else was coming up with Fiona then it was less than that.

Though he wouldn't put it past Charlie to have already put the word out. He supposed he could check the website. Or the Facebook page. Or the Twitter account. Or any number of other places that Charlie kept people in the loop about Boys of the Bayou Gone Wild.

The little girl giggled. "He came with me."

"Really?" He looked up at the man. He must work for Fiona. "I'm Knox. I'm the city manager here in Autre. "

"I'm Colin Daly." The man extended his hand. "I've heard all about you, Knox."

Surprise slammed into Knox. So this was Colin. And damned if the man didn't have an Irish fucking accent. And a very firm grip.

Knox shook his hand. "And I've heard a bit about you."

Colin gave him a smile that was knowing and just a bit smug. "I know."

Which meant Fiona had shared with Colin that Knox thought she and Colin were more than friends. And that until earlier today, Knox had not known that Colin was Princess Fiona's bodyguard.

Princess Fiona. Fuck. He supposed that made him the ogre

in this story. Appropriate that he lived by a swamp. And was generally pretty grumpy. And didn't like people all that much. And had donkeys living nearby.

"And who might you be?" Did Colin have a daughter?

"I'm Saoirse," she extended her hand. "Pleased to meet you."

"That's beautiful. How do you spell that?"

"S-A-O-I-R-S-E," she replied. "Most people don't know that it's pronounced Seer-Sha. Some don't know how to say it at all. Especially kids my age. It can be confusing for Americans."

Knox chuckled. "It's very unique."

"How do you spell your name?"

"K-N-O-X."

"Do you say it Knox?" she asked.

"Yep, that's right."

"Nice to meet you."

"You too. How old are you?" he asked.

"Nine."

"Going on forty," Colin added dryly.

"Fiona never mentioned you have a daughter."

"From my understanding, Fiona didn't mention a lot of things about me."

"She *made sure* to mention that you and she are just friends," Knox told him.

Colin didn't comment on that, but that damned smug grin tugged at his lips again. He did say, however, "Saoirse's not my daughter."

"No?" Knox looked down at the girl.

Saoirse giggled. "I'm his boss."

Colin reached out and tapped the end of her nose. "*You* listen to *me*."

"But still." She grinned and asked, "Can we tell him?"

"Yes. But asking in front of him isn't what we talked about." Colin met Knox's eyes again. "I understand you've been informed about Fiona's family. I'm Saoirse's bodyguard officially. Unofficially, I'm a friend, an uncle, her father... depending on what the situation calls for. We've done lots of pretending, haven't we, *a stór*?"

Saoirse nodded.

"Wait, you're *Saoirse's* bodyguard?" Knox asked.

"Yes. The king insists the princess be protected at all times." The smile Colin gave the girl was full of affection. "He's overprotective, but I certainly don't mind."

"The...princess..." Knox's mind was spinning.

And Colin clearly quickly picked up on the fact that there were two dots that hadn't been completely connected for Knox.

Colin put a protective hand on the back of Saoirse's neck and straightened. "Yes, Princess Saoirse is Fiona's daughter."

"You know who isn't going to stop a bunch of scumbags from transporting and selling tigers?" Charlie Landry asked the group of women seated the back of Ellie's bar. "A mom to infant twins who is also getting a bunch of Galápagos penguins pregnant." She said, pointing at Jill Landry. Then she pointed at Tori Landry. "Or a busy veterinarian who is also a mom to an active toddler." Then she pointed at Caroline Holland, one of the newest additions to the group. "Or the woman who is trying to get accepted into the FBI. You ladies can't end up in jail."

"There's no guarantee we'll end up in jail," Caroline protested. "We've got plenty of intel. And now we have Fiona here. She can tell us exactly what to do."

Fiona was sitting back in her chair, cradling a Mason jar on her stomach of the best sweet tea she'd ever tasted. And trying to stay out of this.

Which was one of the hardest things she'd ever done. This

group of women was one of the primary reasons she'd decided to move to Autre. For herself and her daughter and for her animals.

These women were bold, bright, passionate, and formidable individually. But put together, they were absolutely a force to be reckoned with. They were the kind of team that Fiona had always wanted to be a part of. Yes, she had a vast network of animal advocates and people she knew she could count on, but it was nothing like working with the Landrys and their friends.

The passion, trust, camaraderie, and sheer love for one another and the animals was like magic. This was what Fiona wanted in her advocacy life. And even if she wasn't going to be a part of it forever, she absolutely wanted this group to be doing this work for years and years to come.

These people were the types to inspire those around them as well. They had their community behind them as well as several outlets for reaching a wider audience, including their petting zoo, their educational programs that included outreach through their website, as well as the reality TV show that Naomi and Donovan produced. And there was a promising second generation coming up, Fiona thought, as she grinned at the beautiful little girl sitting on Tori Landry's lap.

She realized they were all looking at her and had been quiet for several moments, clearly waiting for her to respond. Well, crap.

"The problem with breeding and selling tigers in Texas is long standing," she said. "There are no state laws saying it's illegal. There are local laws in some places, but overall, in many of the small towns and rural areas, people can own tigers with no restrictions."

"But they can't cross state lines with them," Caroline said.

She was right. Kind of. Fiona nodded. "Certain licensed facilities can transfer tigers to other licensed facilities. But the

Endangered Species Act generally makes it illegal to sell a tiger to someone across state lines. However, the enforcement agency, U.S. Fish and Wildlife Service, interprets that to mean that it's okay to *give* a tiger to someone in another state. We— meaning wildlife advocacy groups—argue that even giving a tiger to a group that will make money off of it by exhibiting it or offering photo ops or a chance to hold and pet cubs, should also be considered illegal. But we haven't gotten very far in that fight."

There were many, many similar fights she and her colleagues took on every day and it often felt like banging her head against a wall.

"That's what's going on here," Caroline said. "These people say they're 'giving' these tigers to friends and then they get cash payments under the table or get overpaid for 'shipping expenses' or sell supplies that are marked up so high that it's laughable. Clearly, they're hiding the payment for the tigers in other things. But that's a loophole that hasn't been closed. And there simply aren't enough wildlife agents to investigate all of these guys."

"Or, like you found out, sometimes the local cops think everyone should mind their own business and they just look the other way," Naomi said with a frown.

Fiona felt her heart rate kick up and again had to take a deep breath and tell herself to calm down.

Caroline Holland had come waltzing into this very bar less than a year ago. She had not only turned Zander Landry's life upside down. She'd brought a fierce determination and sharp intellect that Fiona found exciting and promising. Caroline had spent much of her life gathering intel. The daughter of an incredibly wealthy and well-connected businessman in New Orleans, Caroline had been in the inner circle of the rich and powerful in Louisiana. She'd learned early on that if she played the part of the shallow socialite, people didn't think twice about talking business, even shady business, with her nearby. She'd passed a lot of interesting information along to her best friend, who just happened to be an award-winning journalist. They'd taken a few influential people down for corruption, tax evasion, and even personal scandal.

Caroline was now working as a consultant for the FBI in the area of white-collar crime and hoping to have her application to the agency accepted in another year or so.

"Well, I can definitely put you in touch with some people who can give you a lot of background information and can tell you how to get involved," Fiona said. "Kayla Wagner will be a good start. She's an advocate in east Texas. We met during the Hurricane Harvey clean up." They'd worked a few rescues together and Fiona knew Kayla would love Caroline and Naomi's energy.

Caroline narrowed her eyes. "But you'll come too, right?"

Fiona would so love to go to Texas with these women. She hated people who bred wild animals, especially exotic, endangered animals like tigers. These animals were not meant to be kept in private homes and almost across the board, these people had no idea how to properly care for them, not to mention the risk these animals posed to the humans as they grew.

She had been lobbying for changes to laws in the United States since she'd landed on U.S. soil. It was a frustrating, seemingly futile battle. It was actually one of the reasons that her grandfather had been able to get past her previous impenetrable resistance to the idea of coming home to Cara. At least in Cara the making and changing of laws was a more streamlined process. The only real problem there was they all had to go through her grandfather, who was a stubborn, controlling, know-it-all.

"With the move here and getting the animals settled, I can't head off to a new project for awhile," she hedged.

She noted the surprised expressions. Yeah, because that was completely out of character. She was always ready to jump in and head out to save whatever animal was in need. She had no trouble dropping her current responsibilities and priorities. Which her grandfather had been happy to point out to her. He didn't even know the full extent of all of the causes and projects she'd taken on over the years, but he did know that she was often gone, leaving Saoirse with Colin and Cian, and sometimes Torin.

Of course, her brothers also came with bodyguards, so her daughter had been with *three* private security operatives and, for all intents and purposes, five fun uncles any time Fiona was gone. Okay, Cian and Henry were fun. Torin, Colin, and Jonah more serious. But Saoirse was very well cared for. Colin was a fantastic cook. Torin was the best tutor any kid could ask for in any subject. Jonah had taught her self-defense, martial arts, archery, and how to shoot at least three different kinds of guns. And all of them read bedtime stories, indulged Saoirse's love for animals, and had had their nails—fingers and toes—painted at some point.

Fiona loved her daughter fiercely. She was on the path to becoming the ruler of an entire *country*. It was a small country that had very little influence in any global sense, but it was still kind of a big deal. And she was nine years away from being required, by Cara law, to return home to live on the island full-time.

Sure, Fiona had hoped that by now things would've changed and there would no longer be a throne for Saoirse to inherit, but that was not the case and there were no changes in process. Which meant Fiona had to at least start to prepare Saoirse for that eventuality. Saoirse knew about it. Her great-grandfather talked about it. Ad nauseum. And Fiona had never kept it from her daughter. Exactly. But it had always been far off in the future. Nothing to worry about *now*.

But the past nine years had gone by so fast. The next nine would too. She needed to help Saoirse prepare. She needed to focus on her daughter now. And while she was not apologetic about the animal advocacy and causes she had taken on over the past ten years while away from Cara, she realized that she now had to accept her responsibility and get more serious about something else.

And dammit, Knox obviously felt the same way.

Well, not about the motherhood thing—because he didn't know about that, which no doubt was going to bite her in the ass—but he thought her flying off into the aftermath of natural disasters and showing up on the doorsteps of animal abusers was reckless and irresponsible.

She might not ever admit this out loud to anyone but as her grandfather had lectured her in his office in Cara, she'd thought of Knox at the same time. He and his opinion had become more important to her than she'd realized and the fact that she knew he would agree with her grandfather irritated her. But she couldn't shake it.

So she was here in Autre for six months. That was long enough to settle her animals, teach the people here to care for the giraffes, hopefully see the birth of the giraffe calf she was ninety-percent certain was on the way, train these women in rescues and connect them to her network, and get Saoirse prepared for a permanent move to Cara. They'd get there in time for Saoirse to start the school year with new peers in a new system.

She hadn't told her grandfather—or anyone else, though she thought Colin probably suspected this move was temporary—about the timeframe. She wasn't ready to commit that firmly to her return to Cara just yet. And the king still needed to approve of her and Saoirse living in Autre, even if it was only for a few months. But mentally, she was preparing for all of this to be short-term.

And so she was soaking up as much of Autre as she could while she was here.

Another reason to be annoyed as hell with Knox. Spending every night of these months in his bed had sounded like a hell of a good plan.

She shook off the thoughts of the most irritating man she'd ever met.

"You guys will be great," Fiona went on before the other women could respond. They were obviously disappointed and surprised that she was not going with them to Texas. But this was part of why she was here. "I will put you in touch with my contacts, will get you the information and resources that you need, and you guys will be great. You're all kickass. You can do this."

Charlie looked around the table. "But that really just leaves me and Naomi. Maybe Maddie and Jordan. But the mayor can't go with us." She shot Kennedy a smile. "Probably more because of her senator husband than because Autre would care. But no one else can really risk the legal entanglements and a possible night or two in jail. "

"Well...not me either," Jordan said.

They all looked at the pretty blonde at the end of the table. Jordan was the educational director at the Boys of the Bayou Gone Wild. She had been a high school science teacher, but she loved her position at the animal park designing learning experiences, and leading hands-on interactions, and coordinating the virtual programs they did with kids around the country. She was married to Fletcher Landry, Zeke and Zander's older brother.

"Why not you?" Charlie asked. "You can take a couple days off. I'll talk to your boss." She gave Jordan a wink.

Jordan didn't really have a boss. Or, technically she had a *bunch* of bosses—Sawyer, Josh, Owen, and Maddie Landry, and

Bennett Baxter. But none of them really managed any part of the park. They left that up to Charlie and Jordan.

Jordan's cheeks got pink, but her smile was bright. "Because I'm pregnant. And I've been feeling kind of sick, and my blood pressure has been all over the place. I probably shouldn't be doing anything too exciting."

There was a beat of silence around the table and then all of the women gasped and squealed in unison. Everyone descended on Jordan with hugs and exclamations of, "oh my God!", "I'm so happy!", "I can't believe it!", and "Congratulations!"

Fiona sat watching, smiling goofily, feeling tears sting the back of her eyes.

This.

This was why she was here. This sense of friendship and family and community.

No one spent more than ten minutes with the Landry family without feeling like a part of them, and Fiona had been coming here and getting to know these people for almost two years. How could she not feel like this was where she belonged? How could she not want her daughter to be a part of this? How could she not feel like this was where her beloved animals needed to be if they couldn't be with her?

When they had all finally taken their seats again, with huge, silly grins in place and tears wiped away from their cheeks, Charlie turned to Fiona. "Are you sure it's just the move that's keeping you from coming with us? Nothing's wrong?"

Fiona looked at her in surprise. "Why would something be wrong?"

"Because I've known you for a long time now and Griffin's known you even longer. You have never shied away from an animal who needs you."

Fiona sucked in a quick breath. See, that was the one *problem* with coming here. These people were very insightful and their love for everyone around them made them pay special attention. And they were very willing to call the people they cared about out on their bullshit.

Finally she nodded. "There's a lot going on. But I'm not ready to talk about it all yet. I need to..." She took a breath, blew it out, and admitted, "There are some things I need to tell Knox before I tell anyone else."

No one looked shocked. Which kind of shocked Fiona.

"Is it something bad?" Naomi asked, looking concerned.

"No. Nothing bad exactly. Just something he'll be upset about."

Again, no looks of shock.

Fiona narrowed her eyes. "Why don't any of you seem surprised that I have some secret to tell Knox before the rest of you get to know about it?"

Charlie looked around the table, then met her eyes. "I'm sorry, are you under the impression that we don't know that something's going on between the two of you?"

Fiona sighed. "Has he said something?"

They all laughed. "Knox doesn't say things," Jordan answered.

Yeah, that had always been her impression too. "Then why do you think something's going on with us?"

"Because we've been around the two of you for the past two years," Tori said. "It's...really obvious."

Fiona opened her mouth, then shut it again. What was the point in arguing? They were right. Something was going on. Not that she had any way of defining it.

"Okay, anyway," she said. "I just need to talk to him first. So I can't go on this road trip with you."

Charlie and Naomi nodded and exchanged a look. "We've got this," Naomi said.

Charlie nodded her agreement. "Yep. Totally."

Fiona sighed. "Griffin and Donovan aren't going to try to stop you?"

Charlie laughed. "Nope."

The two women were going to be sisters-in-law. They were marrying the Foster brothers, two of the biggest animal activists Fiona had ever met. And that was saying something.

Those two men were another reason that Fiona couldn't imagine settling her animals anywhere else. Hell, all of the men and women here—whether they'd started as animal lovers or not—were now a part of something bigger and more amazing. And they knew it. Embraced it. Together.

"So, you said that Knox might be upset about whatever this is you need to tell him?"

Fiona looked at Kennedy. "Yeah. I'm about ninety-nine percent sure."

"Me too," the other woman said.

"What do you mean?"

"Judging from his expression, he already knows."

"What—" But Fiona followed Kennedy's gaze, turning in her chair as her heart kicked hard against her ribs.

Knox was coming straight for her.

5

Knox stopped right behind Fiona's chair, his gaze boring into hers. "We need to talk."

She rolled her eyes. "I've been telling you that since I got to town."

His jaw tightened. "Fiona."

That was it. Just her name. But his tone was full of frustration, and don't-mess-around. It was also absolutely not her nickname.

She glanced around the table. All of the other women were clearly reading the situation, accurately. No one was trying in any way to get Knox's attention.

She slid her chair back and stood. Might as well take *this* outside.

For just a moment she thought he was going to grab her arm. There had definitely been instances in the past where he had taken her arm and dragged her from the building. There had been another time where he'd literally picked her up and carried her out. Not without her consent, of course. Had she made even a squeak of protest she knew all of the Landrys in the building—male, female, young and old—would have moved to stop him. Though she was sure a firm *knock it off* would've sufficed. Knox was grumpy and opinionated and liked to have his way, but he wasn't angry, and he wasn't someone she would ever be afraid of physically.

Still, he kept his hands to himself as they walked out the door of Ellie's without speaking.

She followed him to his truck and climbed inside without saying a word.

She watched him round the front bumper trying to gauge his expression. But, as always, it was difficult. She considered herself exceptionally good at reading people. But Knox was difficult even for her. He didn't actually look angry, but he looked determined. He clearly wasn't happy. But he was here. They were going to be together in an enclosed space for at least a short period of time. She was glad about that.

She really did want a chance to tell him everything.

Yes, the men and women here in Autre who could help her care for the animals she already had and advocate for the animals that would need her in the future were a huge part of why she'd come to Autre.

The feeling of family and just the general love for life and how happy and appreciated she felt when she was here were a part of it as well.

And she would never leave Ellie Landry's gumbo or her crawfish potpie or her pecan pie off the list of reasons Autre was her number one pick.

But the man sitting to her left, stoically staring out the windshield as he drove, was also part of it.

She'd worried finding out about her wacky family, her you've-got-to-be-kidding-me past, and nearly unbelievable future, as well as her daughter, would probably ruin any chance of them being anything more serious than a fling. But there was something about Knox that made her want to count him among her friends. Or if not her friend, at least someone who respected her. Someone who would be happy to see her and someone she could continually flirt with. Someone who she'd grin about every time she thought of his reaction to the swearing parrots she'd added to the park.

Yes, she was more attracted to him than she had been to a man in longer than she liked to admit, but the idea of not being able to tease him and laugh with him and see that look of admiration on his face and have him ask her with genuine curiosity about her work was more of a heartbreak than anything.

"I'm surprised to see you," she finally said.

"Are you really?" He shot her a glance.

"Yes. After this morning, I thought maybe you'd be avoiding me."

His eyes were firmly back on the highway in front of them. She thought she knew where they were going. They were headed east out of town, which would lead them to the little town of Bad in about fifteen minutes. And the coffee shop there that served some of the best ice cream she'd ever had.

She'd only been there once. Over a year ago. With Knox.

She didn't know what to think of that. Was it an olive branch? Was it just a way to stay away from the prying eyes in Autre? That's what it had been the first time. He'd wanted to know more about her work, but he'd said he didn't want to give the town anything extra to gossip about. Apparently, Knox spending one-on-one, date-ish time with a woman would get a lot of attention.

She could understand that. It was a shock that this man was unattached. His long hair, his thick muscles and wide shoulders, his huge hands, the tanned skin that spoke of plenty of time outside, and the tattoos that just peeked from under the edges of his shirt sleeves were just the start. The grumpy demeanor, the fierce love for his town, his deep, long-term relationships with his friends, and his unwavering steadfastness in everything he believed in, made her certain that there was a list of eligible bachelorettes in and around Autre watching this man closely.

"I had intended to avoid you. Then I ran into a friend of yours," Knox said.

She didn't even have to ask who that was. "Crap," she muttered. "Really didn't intend for you to meet without me there."

"Are you talking about your daughter's bodyguard...or your daughter?"

Surprise slammed into her. Knox knew Colin's name. When she'd first started coming to Autre, he'd believed, as had everyone, that Colin was her boyfriend that she ran the giraffe ranch in Florida with. That was the story she and Colin used most often. It kept people from wondering why the two of them lived together. But she'd quickly informed everyone in Autre that she and Colin were just friends and she'd made sure Knox knew they were not romantically involved.

Still, there had always been a hint of jealousy from Knox when Colin's name came up and Fiona wasn't too proud to admit she kind of enjoyed that.

She'd known he was surprised to find out Colin was her bodyguard this morning. But on top of everything else, she figured, that was the least of the surprises.

Of course, Saoirse would be one of the bigger ones.

"You met Saoirse?"

"And one of the giraffes."

"I didn't know you would go out to the animal park. Or that they'd be there when you did."

"Well, if you'd kept any of them at your new house, I would've noticed too."

"Touché." She turned slightly on her seat and tucked her foot under her butt. "I came to town early to let everyone know what was going on. They came right behind and brought

Breccan because he's very dependent on us for his feeding. His mother wasn't very nurturing, and we had to do a lot of raising him by hand. He's particularly attached to Saoirse. But I didn't know they'd be here so early. Apparently, she couldn't sleep so Colin thought they might as well hit the road earlier than I'd expected." She paused and took a deep breath. "I really didn't plan for you to find out that way. But in my defense, you wouldn't let me tell you anything last night."

"You would've told me?"

"Of course."

He slammed a hand on the steering wheel. "There's no *of course* about it, Fiona." He looked over at her. "I've known you for almost two years and had no idea that you had a daughter."

She frowned at him, even as his gaze went back to the road. "No. And I had no intention of telling you for those almost-two-years, Knox. For the first few months that we knew each other, I was just a huge pain in your ass. Sure, we flirted. There was chemistry. But there was no reason for me to tell you anything personal. By the time we finally actually admitted there was something more going on and made a plan to do something about it, the plan was very clearly for it to be long-distance. I wasn't going to tell you about my daughter. You were just going to be some guy I saw once in a while."

His fists tightened around the steering wheel and his jaw clenched. He didn't say anything for several long seconds.

Finally, he nodded. "You're right."

"So why are you so pissed?"

"I don't know."

Well, she appreciated the honesty.

They pulled up in front of Bad Habit, and he shut off the truck, but they didn't immediately get out.

"Knox?"

"Yeah."

"Are we having ice cream?"

"I'm thinking about it."

"Isn't that why you brought me here?"

"Yeah. But now I'm wondering."

"Wondering about what?"

He finally looked over at her. "If I want you to ruin my favorite ice cream."

Her eyes widened. "Hey."

He shrugged. "I'm just saying. Depending on how this conversation goes, this might be something I think about every time I come here. And if it goes badly, it might ruin this place as my favorite ice cream."

"Wow."

For a second, she thought he was going to smile. He didn't. But it was close.

"Come on, me being kind of an ass is hardly a surprise," he said.

She lifted a brow. "You're right. But I thought we were kind of past that. You used to be an ass to me every time I was here. But then, we got a little...friendlier."

He held her gaze as he nodded once. "Yeah. We did."

It was strange, but that simple answer held a lot of meaning. And it made her regret so much.

Not getting even friendlier. Not getting to know him. Not letting him know that she wanted more. That he was the first time she hadn't just jumped in with both feet.

She always rushed ahead and followed her heart instead of her head. Until Knox. She'd let it go along slow and sweet with him. She'd enjoyed the flirting, the teasing, the butterflies in her stomach as she'd driven to Autre, winning him over slowly and going from growls to grins. She'd loved the slow realization that he was genuinely interested and appreciated what she did and that he even felt a little protective of her. It had definitely been a slow burn. She had not just forged ahead, consequences be damned. And now she regretted it.

"Well, maybe the conversation will turn out well. Like maybe I'll tell you there's a chance I won't be staying in Autre that long after all."

His brows pulled together in a scowl and instead of reaching for the handle on his door, he reached for the key in the ignition. He started his truck, backed out of the parking spot, and turned down the road.

"Hey," she protested, looking back at Bad Habit. "I wanted ice cream." It really was good ice cream.

"Too bad."

Two miles down the road they pulled over at a roadside stand that claimed to have the best beignets and pralines in the parish.

A few minutes later, Knox lowered the tailgate on his truck and they boosted themselves up, holding paper trays full of fried dough and powdered sugar.

"You're willing to let me ruin beignets for you?" She quickly lifted one to her lips before he could take it away from her. She had a definite weakness for beignets and she didn't want him to change his mind about this too.

"I like ice cream better than beignets."

Her eyes widened and she gave a little gasp, then started coughing as she sucked powdered sugar into her lungs. After she cleared her airway, she asked, "Are you allowed to live in Louisiana with that kind of opinion?"

"I don't let it be widely known."

She covered her heart with her hand. "You're telling me secrets?"

He frowned and nodded. "This is a good afternoon for that."

Right. Well, this was what she'd wanted. Even back at Christmastime when she'd stopped by before heading to Cara, she'd offered to tell him more. Like where she was going to spend the holiday. And with whom.

"Are you going to be telling me a lot more of *your* secrets?" she asked. "I still don't know your first name, come to think of it." Knox was actually his last name. His first initial was F. But he didn't tell anyone his first name and no one in Autre knew what it was. She'd been trying to guess since she'd met him. But honestly, she didn't really care. He was Knox to her and even if she did ever find out what the F stood for, he'd always be Knox.

"You know that's not what I meant," he said.

She licked her fingertips free of powdered sugar, then wiped them on her blue jeans. "If you remember, I showed up last night offering to tell you everything."

"You're right. So now, I want to know everything. I know you're a princess, for fuck's sake. And a mom. For double fuck's sake. Is there anything else?"

"There is. Stuff that's related to those things."

"There really is more?" He shook his head. "Of course there is." He almost said that to himself. He looked over at her. "You can't just be a simple girl. A hot woman who is mildly interesting and kind of funny who comes to town once in a while and takes her clothes off for me, right? There's just no way that could happen."

Stupidly, a shaft of heat shot through her belly. "No. I can't be that. I'm not simple, nothing about my life is simple. It never has been. But I really did intend to keep this thing between us simple."

He held her gaze for several beats. "I believe you."

She let out the breath she didn't realize she'd been holding. That mattered. She really wanted him to know that she had not let this get complicated on purpose, or that she'd been withholding information to try to somehow trick him.

He lifted one of the beignets from his tray to his mouth but paused before taking a bite. "Start talking."

"I don't get to eat beignets?"

"You can eat beignets after you stop being mysterious."

She gave a soft laugh. "Well, maybe I'll get to them sometime tomorrow." She set the tray to the side and brushed her palms together.

She braced her hands on the tailgate on either side of her thighs and focused on the dirt road in front of them. Tall grass and weeds swayed in the ditches beside the road and the buzz of insects filled the air around them. It was a sunny March Louisiana day. It wasn't nearly as hot and oppressive as it would be later in the summer, but there was still a wet warmth in the air.

"Okay. Stop me when you're bored."

He gave a soft grunt. "I can honestly say that's something I haven't been since I met you."

She shrugged. "I don't consider that an insult."

"I didn't expect you would."

"Okay, my grandfather is the king of Cara. My father died. So the next in line to take the throne would be my eldest brother. But Declan has no interest. He abdicated the throne when he turned eighteen and left Cara. He first went to England but then ended up in the U.S. He's made a ton of money, is a big CEO of some company, hasn't been home to Cara in a decade and no one here has any idea he's royalty."

Knox paused. "Wait. Declan Grady? The guy who owns a huge tech company, and a movie studio, and a football team, and hotels and stuff?"

She nodded. Yeah, her brother was *that* guy. So rich and handsome and headline-making that even people who didn't know him, knew him. "He buys and invests in things he's interested in and then is either stupid lucky or crazy smart. Or both." She shrugged. "We don't talk that much. But he's wildly successful, as you know, and wants nothing to do with Cara."

Knox shook his head. "Holy shit," he muttered.

She went on. "That left me and my other two brothers,

Torin and Cian. Torin is older than me by a year, Cian is younger than me by a year." She took a breath. "We were close growing up. Still are. And we were hellions. Very rebellious. Especially after our father died. I'm embarrassed to say that in our early teen years, we loved the fact that, as royalty, we could get away with a lot and we loved to push our boundaries. But we also thought we knew so much. Torin is brilliant. Loves to read and travel. Spent time studying in Ireland and England and touring around Europe. He probably should have become a professor or something. He got very interested in world politics and came to the conclusion that the monarchy was an archaic form of governing and that Cara should become a democracy. He wrote up a ten-year plan to transition Cara's government to an elected representative government and convinced me easily enough. And I've continued to hold that opinion actually."

Fiona glanced at Knox and found that he was simply staring straight ahead. He wasn't eating his beignets. He was paying full attention to her story. As he always did when he asked her about something with the animals or one of her rescue missions or, really, anything.

"Cian is just...kind of a lost soul. He goes along with whatever seems fun at the moment and, at the moment Torin was having this big revelation, Cian thought it sounded fun to piss off our grandfather." She sighed. "Anyway, long story short, the three of us went to our grandfather, presented Torin's plan, and told him that we thought Cara should do away with monarchy rule and hold an election. Torin was nineteen, I was eighteen, and Cian was seventeen. When our grandfather told us we were being ridiculous, as expected, we declared that we were abdicating the throne, packed our bags, and left."

Knox just closed his eyes and shook his head. But still said nothing.

"Of course, being stupid young adults, we thought that

would be enough of a statement that he'd change his mind, come after us, and agree to listen and change everything."

"Let me guess," Knox said dryly.

She nodded. "He didn't speak to us for about three years. Didn't send anyone after us. Didn't try to contact us. Nothing." She paused. "That's what we thought anyway. He did, of course, track us down. We just didn't know it. He kept tabs, but didn't actually reach out. Our mother and grandmother did. In fact, they came to the U.S. to visit us. But he never did. Not until Saoirse was three. After he'd had his first heart attack."

Finally Knox looked at her. "You had to have been pregnant when you left Cara."

She nodded. "I was. He didn't know. When my mother and grandmother came to visit, I was about eight months along. Obviously, they told him when they got back."

"And he still didn't reach out?"

"No. But Colin showed up two days later."

The muscle along Knox's jaw ticked. "Where's Saoirse's father?"

"Sean's in England. As you can imagine, there aren't a lot of jobs on Cara. He's a biochemist. Brilliant. Very successful. But Saoirse wasn't a part of his plan. We weren't in love. We weren't even seriously dating. We just messed up. He offered to help support us but—" She shrugged. "I'm an O'Grady. There's not much he could offer that I didn't already have."

"O'Grady?"

She nodded. "That's our family name. Declan had dropped the O when he came to the U.S. and so we all followed suit. Just another little rebellion." She rolled her eyes. "I was eighteen and full of myself and stupid, Knox."

He just gave a soft grunt. She assumed that meant he agreed.

"*Anyway*, Sean's not in the picture. Never has been. I haven't seen him since I left Cara. My grandfather made sure he signed over all parental rights and was compensated handsomely for it. He has no claim to her or any of her titles or anything to do with the kingdom or throne, of course. And he's never tried to contact us. Saoirse's only asked about him a couple of times and seems satisfied knowing that he was a boy I knew when I lived in Cara and that he lives in London now and that she might meet him someday, but might not." Fiona shrugged. "My daughter is very pragmatic. She's always had plenty of supportive male figures between Colin and Torin and Cian. Colin has been a steady presence. I don't think she feels any kind of missing piece."

Knox didn't reply and she looked at him again. He looked upset.

"Are you okay?" she asked.

He met her gaze. "I have no idea."

Well, that was...honest, she supposed.

"What do you think about what I've told you so far?" she asked.

He pulled in a breath. "I think that if anyone had told me about a woman who was set to inherit a kingdom but said, 'no thanks, I think I'll go see the world and save a bunch of animals instead', I would have said, 'no one would actually do that'." He paused. "Until I met you. And now that completely fits and I can't imagine you wearing a crown and attending elaborate balls and spending your time on an isolated island in a big old castle doing nothing."

Yeah, suddenly she didn't know how she was feeling either. That hadn't been what she'd expected him to say. "Thank you," she told him simply. "Though, there are never any balls and the crowns only come out on *very* special occasions and my grandfather actually does a lot and...I'm thinking maybe I need to...at least *consider* going back and doing some of it too."

His brows slammed together. "*What?*"

She lifted a shoulder. "With my father gone and all of us abdicating, Saoirse is the next in line."

Knox opened his mouth, then shut it again. His scowl deepened. "She's *nine*," he finally growled.

Fiona nodded. "My grandfather had his first heart attack when she was three. He, of course, realized she was the next in line as soon as he found out about her, but he got *very* interested when he realized his heart was bad. He had another when she was five. And then another just before Christmas last year." She pulled in a breath. "That's why we were there so long this time. Why I didn't get back here as soon as I'd planned. He, and everyone else, have realized that there really does need to be a solid plan of succession. And I..." She trailed off.

Knox reached over and hooked her chin with his finger, turning her face toward his. "You what?" he asked firmly.

"I realized that I'm probably not going to get my way. Even if Cara was to move toward a more democratic government, that kind of thing takes time. To an eighteen-year-old who wants to change the world, it looks a lot different than to a twenty-eight-year old who's been out in that world and sees how hard change can be and how long it can take. It doesn't mean it won't happen, but it's not going to be quick, even in a small country like mine. If the king becomes incapacitated or dies without a successor in place, or with a successor who's *nine* or even, I don't know, fifteen without having ever lived there or any experience in leading, what does that do to the country? Cara is small, but those people deserve to have stability. And...there are good things that...the queen could do."

"The queen," Knox repeated. "Meaning Saoirse. There are things Saoirse could do as queen that would be good."

She studied his shirt collar. "Of course. A democracy is the best way. The people being governed have more say in what happens then. But a *good* king or queen can do good things."

"So you think taking Saoirse back to Cara to get ready to

become queen is the right plan?" Knox asked. He tipped her face up again. "Or you think *you* getting ready to become queen is the right plan?"

Damn. Maybe she would have preferred a guy who didn't pay quite this close attention.

"I'm only staying in Autre for six months," she finally said quietly. "Just long enough to settle my animals, make sure everyone here can care for them, and train everyone in all the rescues and get them prepared to carry on that work. Then Saoirse and I will go to Cara."

Knox stared at her for several beats. Fiona felt them knocking against the inside of her chest.

"What would you do as queen that your grandfather hasn't done? Other than convert the whole thing to a democracy and give up power?" he asked.

See? That insight and ability to read her was kind of annoying. And kind of great.

She smiled. She loved her plan. "I've been trying to talk him into making half of the island a sanctuary for endangered animal species," she said.

He nodded. "Yeah."

She felt a warmth spread through her chest. That made sense to him. She could see it in his eyes. And that mattered to her. He understood.

"I left Cara determined to do something to make the *world* a better place. I hated how isolated Cara was. How we didn't connect with or interact with other countries. I was determined to go out and make connections and do something important."

"And you did."

"And I've worked my ass off, fought hard, and things have hardly changed."

Knox frowned.

She went on. "But Cara is perfect for what I want to do. We are isolated and self-governing. I wouldn't have to worry about lobbying to change laws. I would make the laws. The issues that I most disliked about my country before—the isolation and lack of cooperation with other countries—would be what I appreciate most."

"This doesn't sound like you."

"What do you mean? Wanting to make an entire *island* into a sanctuary? Wanting to have a safe place for *all* of the endangered species? Knox, we could actually save them all. They could propagate there. We could actually bring the numbers back. And *I* could make it happen. I'd be completely in charge."

He didn't say anything for a long moment. He sat just studying her. "So six months."

She nodded. "Six months. I also need to...practice."

"Practice?"

"Being more chill." She gave him a self-deprecating smile. "In case you haven't noticed, I'm not very good at just sitting back, taking in information, leading a team. I just jump in. And I've taught my daughter that. To go all in with her whole heart. But, we both need to be more..."

"Queenly?" he offered.

She grimaced. "Yeah. We have responsibilities."

"You realize when you say that word that your face scrunches up like you just smelled rotten eggs?"

She nodded, her face still scrunched. "I do."

"You might want to work on that too."

"Probably."

They were both quiet, just looking at one another.

Finally he said, "I knew the moment I met you that you were going to be trouble."

"You've mentioned that before."

"I'm right a lot."

"You've mentioned that before too."

"Anything else you need to tell me?"

"Besides that I'm a runaway princess, I have a nine-year-old daughter, I'm moving here to Autre for awhile and living right behind your house, I brought some giraffes with me, my grandfather, the king, is on his way here, and I might be going home to take over the throne eventually..." She thought about it. "I think that covers it."

"Okay, then, let's go." He stretched to his feet and carried his empty beignet tray to the trash barrel at the side of the road.

Fiona looked at her beignets. She'd have to take them with her. If Knox was done talking, she was done talking.

She jumped down from the tailgate. "Are we going to talk about us?" she asked as he came back to the truck.

He stopped in front of her. Not in touching distance. But there was sizzle in the air between them. "I can wait six months."

She blinked at him. "Wait? To talk about us?"

"I can wait six months to start our affair."

Her eyes widened as her mind spun. "We... you don't... we'll *wait*?"

He nodded. "We've waited this long."

"But...you still want it?"

"You mean *you*? Do I still want *you*?"

She pressed her lips together and nodded.

"More than I've ever wanted anyone."

Heat arrowed through her. Followed immediately by sharp annoyance. "Then why *wait*? I'm here. Right next door."

"Exactly. I don't date women who live within a one-hundred-mile radius of Autre."

She waited a second, expecting a smile. Or more information. Or...something. When nothing came, she lifted a brow. "Seriously?"

"Yes."

She put a hand on her hip. "How about fucking? Do you fuck women who live within a one-hundred-mile radius of Autre?"

He gave her a look that said I-know-you're-trying-to-push-my-buttons-but-it-won't-work. "I just told you that I don't."

"You said you don't *date* women within that radius."

"Same thing."

"It's not."

"They tend to think so."

She rolled her eyes. Though she believed him. Why wouldn't they? This guy *committed*. At least to his hometown, his job, his friends, his convictions, and the fucking *rules*. Why wouldn't the women who knew him think he'd be just as steadfast in his feelings about relationships with women?

He started for the driver's side of the truck, pausing only to open the passenger side door. He didn't wait to help her up, but it was semi-gentlemanly. She shook her head as she climbed up.

"Though Cara is far more than a hundred miles away," he said as he started the engine.

She looked over at him, emotions still swirling. She was outraged. And sort of relieved. And insulted. And stupidly turned on. And confused. At least she was pretty sure those were the things she was feeling. At least she was sure about the *confused*. "You sound happy about that."

He shifted into drive and pulled out onto the highway. "I would assume a princess...or a queen...would have a private jet. Am I wrong?"

Fiona frowned. "We do have a private jet." It was a pain in the ass getting anywhere from Cara via commercial air travel. It required flying from their one tiny airport to Dublin and then on to wherever. The royal family had had their own jets as long as she'd been alive. She and her brothers had even borrowed one to run away from home.

"And you're gonna miss the Landrys and your giraffes and stuff, I figure."

"So, you're thinking as long as I'm in town for other things, I can just stop over and we can have sex too?" she filled in.

He shrugged.

Nice. Really enthusiastic. Really into this. Really *committed.*

She worked to not give her irritation away. "And in the meantime? In this next six months...is there a Ms. One-Hundred-And-One-Miles-Away hanging around?"

"Not at the moment."

"But there *could* be?"

He shrugged again.

She wanted to punch him. That wasn't very queen-like, of course, but she was a royal work-in-progress. "Good thing I don't have any stupid rules like that, I guess. I had no idea the bayou grew 'em so nice. Though now I'm a little pissed I didn't convince Zander to use his handcuffs on me before Caroline showed up."

Knox didn't even squeeze the steering wheel tighter. "You never wanted Zander."

"No?"

"Not after you and I met."

He didn't even look over at her.

Wow. In the time they'd known each other it had always been *him* being annoyed as hell with *her.* Now it looked like it was going to be the other way around.

"This is how this is going to be?"

"How what is going to be?"

"You strutting around town, cocky and so sure that I'm dying to get into your bed, but you holding out because I live right next door now? Basically torturing me for moving here? And then the second I'm officially living elsewhere, you'll welcome me with open arms?"

He seemed to think that over. "Yeah, pretty much."

"So, when I'm *here*, you're gonna treat me like I have cooties.

93

But once I'm thousands of miles away, I'm your favorite person."

"I wouldn't put it *quite* that way," he said.

"How would you put it?"

"Well, you'll be my favorite person who visits occasionally, stays temporarily, and that I get to see naked."

Fiona ground her back teeth together. "Glad you made the insulting part super specific."

"Come on. It's not insulting. It's just giving this thing parameters. Everyone's happier when the expectations are clear."

It wasn't insulting that he only wanted to see her *occasionally* and *temporarily* and *naked*?

"Right." *You know that he never argued he wasn't an asshole.* "The queen of a country and single mom doesn't faze you a bit?"

He glanced over then. "I've been living in Autre, Louisiana, since I was fifteen."

"What's that got to do with it?"

"It means I've been dealing with crazy longer than I haven't. Single mom is really not that unusual and your daughter seems awesome. And queen of a country..." He shrugged. "I think deep down I was expectin' something like that from you."

She closed her eyes and counted to ten.

"Knox, that's stupid. I'm right here, now. Why can't we just—"

He cut her off. "The *plan* was a long-distance relationship. Not having a girlfriend who lived right next door."

Ah. She sighed. "I changed the rules."

"You're trying to," he agreed.

Of course he wouldn't like that.

"But in six months, things will go back to the way they were. So...I can wait."

"Not *exactly* the way they were," she pointed out.

He lifted a shoulder. "When you were in Florida, you came

to Autre about once a month. You had an animal sanctuary, a big job, a daughter. In Cara you'll have an animal sanctuary, a big job, a daughter. Colin will still be around to help. Your grandfather will be there still running things for awhile. It's not that different."

Fiona felt a throbbing start between her temples and sighed again.

Well, great. They'd switched roles. Knox was going to be the one with a plan, being completely...*vexing*—yes, that was a very good word for it—whenever she saw him, and *she* was going to be the grumpy one.

6

"Hi, can I come over?"

Knox turned to find Saoirse Grady standing on the property line between her backyard and his. Right on the line. As if someone had told her exactly where her yard ended and his started. He was sure that conversation had come from her mom and had gone something like, "don't you step one foot onto his side without permission". Behind her was Skylar Clark. Knox had gone to high school with Skylar's mom, Mandy.

"Looks like you're already over here," he said.

He had literally *just* stepped out of his backdoor to water the plants on his back deck. His mom had agreed that potted hibiscus trees would look great along Main and had given other suggestions for what to plant at the base of the trees, so he'd planned to take a look at his own flower beds and landscaping for ideas.

It seemed that the younger princess had been waiting for him.

Saoirse looked down at her shoes. "I'm on my side."

"You sure? I think your right big toe is on my side."

She shook her head. "I don't think so, but if you bring a tape measure over, we can check."

He chuckled. "Wow, you two must be *really* bored."

"It's *so* boring over here," she agreed. "They're working on the house so we can't be inside 'cuz it's so loud and there're guys *everywhere*. And outside there're guys *everywhere* and we're in the way. And they won't let us go to the petting zoo by ourselves. So we were thinking that we could play in *your* yard since it runs right into ours. It's like one big yard." She spread her arms out, encompassing the wide green space that really was one big continuous swath of grass.

How had he missed this was Fiona's child? Her big blue eyes and curly dark hair were a spitting image of her mother. Plus, the mischievous glint in her eye and the sassy tip of her mouth were Fiona through and through. Not to mention the dramatic flair.

Because you had no idea there was even a possibility there was a mini-Fiona walking around. Yeah, that.

"Where's Colin?" Knox asked, ignoring the punch to his gut that he didn't want to analyze.

"Over at my house. He's helping with the renovations."

"And I'm your next best option?" Fiona had clearly not told her kid that he was no fun at all.

"You just have the next yard over," Saoirse told him.

Not that Fiona thought he was *no* fun. She'd always had fun teasing him and flirting with him. And they'd had some fun in his office at Christmas. Though he absolutely regretted not letting that fun go further than it had.

But right now she was mad at him. He wasn't sure she'd talked about him to Saoirse at all and if she had, it probably hadn't been flattering over the last two days.

Unlike her previous visits to Autre, now she seemed to be staying out of his way. Yesterday was the first time they'd been at Ellie's at the same time since he'd taken her for beignets and she'd abruptly stood from her chair and left the building. Something absolutely every single person around that big back table had noticed. But his generally grumpy leave-me-the-fuck-alone attitude had served him well and no one had commented on it.

Until he'd laughed, pulled out a chair, sat down, and ordered lunch.

Then they'd all wanted to know who he was and what he'd done with Knox.

He'd just laughed at that as well and started talking about the new lampposts they were getting, asked Rory what color she wanted the front of I'm Gonna Dye to be, and told them the story of Tadhg O'Grady, Fiona's great-great-great-grandfather who, no shit, had saved the Danish king's life from pirates. It had taken some digging, but his father loved research and history and old legends so Knox had texted him and Jack had come through. It was a true story.

Everyone at the table had looked at him like he'd lost his mind.

Until he'd gotten to the part about the pirates.

Pirates were just cool.

He had been in a great fucking mood ever since he'd found out that Fiona was not staying in Autre indefinitely. And that he didn't have to be the asshole that ran her out. Her grandfather was going to take care of that. Her grandfather's health, and her love for animals, and a general sense of responsibility and inability to think there was anything outlandish about the idea of ruling a small island country were all combining to make Fiona think about donning her own crown.

And, frankly, if anyone should be a queen, it was Fiona Grady. Fiona *O'Grady.*

"Well," Knox told Saoirse. "It's not quite the same as a whole petting zoo, but I do have a project that I could use some help with and I have a feeling you might be just the girl. And you even have an assistant."

"Yeah, Skylar is my new best friend. I took her away from her other crappy ones."

Knox lifted a brow. He looked at Skylar. "Is that right?" He didn't know Skylar's whole history, but he did know that Saoirse was being raised by a very bossy woman and it was possible that Skylar had gotten in over her head with a someday queen. He could relate.

Skylar nodded. "Jacob was picking on me at recess and Saoirse told him to stop it and he said to mind her own business. She said it was her business if someone was doing something wrong."

Uh-huh, definitely Fiona's kid.

"Then she asked Katie why *she* didn't stop him and Katie said that Jacob was bigger than her and she couldn't."

Knox braced himself. "So what did Saoirse do?"

Saoirse was the new kid, he reminded himself. She was inserting herself into playground politics on her first couple of days.

"She told Katie that that was the *worst* reason to not stop someone from being a..." She turned to Saoirse. "What did you call him?"

"A gobshite."

Knox frowned. "A...what?"

"It's Irish," Saoirse told him. "It means someone who's kind of an ass. I learned it from Colin."

"Ah." Again, very Fiona-esque. "And then?"

"I stepped in between Skylar and Jacob and told him that some of the best people I know don't have dads. Like my uncles and my mom and me. And that if he'd like to tease someone about it, he could tease *me*."

"That's what he was teasing Skylar about?" Knox looked at the other girl. Her mom had raised her alone since birth. He had no idea that kids still cared, or teased one another, about stuff like that.

"They were talking about what kids without dads do on Father's Day. Skylar was sweet and just said, 'nothing', but I told them what my uncle Cian said one time," Saoirse said.

"And what was that?" Knox felt himself brace for her answer again. He didn't know Fiona's brother but...he was Fiona's brother. Surely his answer would be colorful.

"He said it was stupid there's a whole day dedicated to celebrating a bunch of blokes who just happened to get their sperm somewhere other than their hand for a change."

So, this was one of those times where laughing at something a kid said was not appropriate. He knew that. Still...

Knox coughed. "Then what did Jacob do?"

"What bullies always do when someone smarter than them challenges them and isn't afraid of them," Saoirse said. "He got even madder and he shoved me."

Knox groaned silently. *Never shove a girl, dude. And definitely not a girl with a bodyguard.* "And then?"

"I punched him."

Knox's eyebrows rose. "You did?"

Saoirse grinned. "No. I pulled my arm back though. Colin got there before I could swing."

"So Colin hangs out at school?"

She nodded. "He's the school safety officer now."

Uh-huh. They hadn't had a safety officer before. "What did he do to Jacob?"

Saoirse frowned. "Took him to the office. But he *grounded* me."

"Which is really why you can't go to the petting zoo, right?"

Giving him a *dammit I'm caught* look, she nodded. "Yeah. But he said I could come over and talk to you."

"I'm flattered."

"Do you have a dad?"

"I do. He lives in New Orleans. And he read all about your great-great-great-great-grandfather saving a bunch of people after a pirate sank his ship."

Saoirse's face brightened. "There's a statue of him in a town in Denmark and a matching one on Cara."

"Very cool," Knox agreed.

"But you have a project? For real? Because we really are *bored*. And we can go home and drive Colin crazy until he takes us to the zoo anyway, but if your project is fun then that could be better. It does take a while to wear Colin down."

God, she really, definitely belonged to Fiona. He would bet it didn't take all that long to wear Colin down actually, but the time probably felt long to a nine-year-old. Or to a female related to Fiona.

"Do you know anything about otters?" Knox asked.

Saoirse's eyes widened. "Mom got us some after she started coming to Autre. She brought two home with her one time. They went to live with Gus and Gertie when they got here."

So Fiona had taken animals from Louisiana to Florida with her sometimes too. Interesting. "Well, I have three. They live here with me. But when I got them, they were very tiny. They don't have a mom and dad. And, I've been waiting for...*someone* to come around and help me teach them how to swim. I know they have to be taught, but I'm not really sure how to go about it."

He'd been hoping that Fiona would be back in time and now knew that he was several weeks past the ideal start to the otter swimming lessons. He hoped that since these otters had been born off season because their parents had been kept indoors and their biological clocks had been a little screwed up, that maybe it wouldn't matter. He'd looked up some YouTube videos but hadn't quite gotten brave enough to try dunking the little fur balls himself.

Saoirse clapped her hands together. "I watched videos about this! Let's do it."

Well great, his assistant was nine and had watched the same videos he had. What could possibly go wrong?

But he did want to bond with this little girl. He wasn't going to pretend or call it anything other than it was. Saoirse was cool. And someday she was going to be a queen. And most of all, she was the daughter of the woman he was crazy about and planned to have a long-term affair with. That she was royalty and had a private jet were absolutely the sprinkles on top of the icing on top of this cake.

Yes, he had been strutting around for the past two days feeling very full of himself and like all the stars in the universe had suddenly aligned for him.

Fiona was pissed at him but she'd come around. She wanted him as much as he wanted her and she had been all-in on a long-distance affair at one time. She just had to get over being offended that the further away she was the majority of the time, the happier he was.

Okay, that sounded bad.

He liked her *a lot*. Too much to have her right next door. He respected her, enjoyed being around her, and thought she was pretty fucking amazing. He definitely considered her a friend. But if they were going to be involved on a deeper emotional level, he needed miles between them.

So he didn't fuck it up.

It wasn't her, it was him. And once he covered her in melted bourbon praline ice cream and licked her from head to toe, she'd see things his way.

And it sure wouldn't hurt if her daughter liked him.

"Okay, I need to get a baby swimming pool eventually, but I was thinking about starting them out in the bathtub," he told the girls.

Saoirse nodded. "Good idea. We can make sure the water

isn't too cold and we can start out where just their paws get wet and they can just kind of wade in it."

He nodded. "Right. So you need to let Colin know you're coming inside. And, Skylar, you need to ask your mom's permission too."

Skylar sighed. "I have to leave in five minutes. She's coming to pick me up."

"Oh, *no*," Saoirse said. "You have to stay. This is going to be so fun."

"I can't. I have a piano lesson."

"Let me talk to her," Saoirse said. "I'll tell her why this is more important. I can convince her, I know I can."

Mini-Fiona didn't like being told no any more than big Fiona did.

Knox put a hand on Saoirse's head. "Hey now, you gettin' involved with Jacob was the right thing, but you can't butt in with Skylar's mom. You need to know when to step in and when not to."

Saoirse looked up at him with wide eyes. He kind of looked at *himself* with wide eyes. What was *that*?

"But she can take a piano lesson anytime. When is she going to get to interact with otters and watch them learn to swim in person, herself, one-on-one? This is an important learning experience. And could help her turn into an advocate for animals and the environment."

Knox tipped his head. "Nice try, princess. You've learned from the best, I'll give you that. But I can resist even your mama."

Barely. And she's got even more practice with that charm and her big blue eyes do very powerful things to me. But even she hasn't totally gotten her way with me.

Saoirse sighed, realizing she had a worthy opponent in him. "Maybe Skylar can come over and play with the otters some other time with me though?"

He nodded. "Much better. And yes, definitely."

She looked at Skylar. "Ask your mom about tomorrow after school, okay?"

Knox chuckled. He supposed he should have been glad she hadn't told Skylar to ask for after dinner tonight.

Skylar nodded and started to turn away, then turned back, leaned in, and gave Saoirse a hug. "Thank you for being my friend today."

Saoirse hugged her back. "All the days," she said. "And remember, Jacob needs us."

Skylar frowned. "What do you mean?"

"We have to teach him how to treat people now so that he knows before he grows up and is a permanent gobshite."

Skylar grinned. "Okay."

She ran off toward the front of Saoirse's new house where her mom would, apparently, be picking her up.

Then Saoirse slipped her hand into Knox's and waved to Colin who came around the corner of the house. He lifted his hand in return.

"Okay, we're good."

"That's it?" Knox asked.

"Yeah. He knows where I am. And I'm with you."

"He doesn't need to inspect my house for booby traps or something?"

"I'm sure he already did. And he did a full background check on you before."

Knox studied the little girl. Colin had said she was nine going on forty. He knew another girl like that. Stella Trahan, the daughter of his friend Gabe, was bright and precocious and funny as well. And could probably rule a country and run a wildlife sanctuary all without batting an eye.

"You're sure he already checked my house out?"

"Probably while you were at work."

"That's called breaking and entering in *this* country. Does Cara not have rules like that?"

Saoirse shrugged. "I don't know all the rules yet. But maybe Colin just trusts you. I know he did the background check though when Mom started hanging out with you. She yelled at him about it."

"Did she?"

Saoirse nodded. "Told him he was paid to worry about me, not her."

Knox frowned. "Doesn't he protect you both?"

"I guess. When we're together. But his job is taking care of me."

Knox didn't like that. And he wasn't sure why that bugged him.

"Come on. I want to meet the otters." Saoirse started for his backdoor, tugging him with her.

Well, who was he to deny the future Queen of Cara when she wanted something?

"Inside, to the left, and up the stairs. Second door on the left."

He let Saoirse lead the way, even though it was his house. It just felt right.

"Did you know that a group of wombats is called a *wisdom*?" Saoirse asked.

"I did," Knox said. "And I know that they can kill predators with their *butts*."

Saoirse stopped and spun to face him, her mouth open and eyes wide. "You *know* about that?"

He grinned. He'd done some research today. Yes, he should have been calling people about rescheduling the sewer line project, but he'd taken twenty minutes to look up wombats.

Because he wanted *that* reaction from Saoirse.

"Yep. They have boney plates in their butts and hardly any

nerve endings there so if they get bitten or scratched there, they don't feel it."

"Yes! And they go head first into their burrows, leaving their butts at the opening," Saoirse said excitedly.

"Right. And then they flatten down a little, leaving some space between them and the side of the burrow."

"And *then* when the predator sticks their head in there, bam!" Saoirse said. "They smash their head with their butt!"

He laughed. Saoirse laughed. And he fell a little bit in love.

"I can't believe you know that," Saoirse said, wonder in her voice.

"I looked stuff up today when I was supposed to be working." He lowered his voice. "Don't tell my boss."

Saoirse giggled. "I don't even know your boss."

Maybe not. But she would. There was no way the Landrys weren't going to embrace this girl and make her one of their own.

She started up the stairs, her hand still in his. "Tomorrow, you need to look up echidnas. They're very cool. We'll talk about those tomorrow night."

Tomorrow night. She was going to come over again?

She stopped in the doorway of the otter room. "Oh...wow."

Yes, his otters had their own room. Of course they did. They'd needed somewhere to live, right? It had been *three months*. And, yes, he'd wanted to impress Fiona whenever she brought her sweet ass back to Autre and checked on his otter foster care.

Even before he'd known that he should be calling her Your Majesty.

"So you think she's got a couple months left then?" Drew asked Fiona as they headed out of the giraffe barn.

Fiona nodded. "I think so. Though we could be off by a month or so. We'll just have to keep an eye on her."

She'd introduced Drew to the giraffes today and gotten him up close and personal. It would be important that one person was familiar to the giraffes as their daily caretaker. They knew and trusted Fiona and she planned to have Drew with her as often as possible over the next several weeks so the giraffes would be comfortable with him as well.

Riona and Donal, her original pair, were the oldest of the giraffes and the most used to humans. Their oldest son, Niall, did reasonably well, but his girlfriend, Speir, had only been with Fiona for a little over a year and was young. She was still getting used to humans in her space. And she might never be completely okay with it. Giraffes had personalities just like people.

Speir was also pregnant, which made her behaviors unusual. She'd only been with Fiona for about a month before she'd gotten pregnant. She and Niall had hit it off right away.

"So we'll keep her in her stall on her own, let her out into the yard when the others are inside," Fiona said. "We should have some warning when she goes into labor, but the birth itself will happen fast, thirty to sixty minutes, and we don't want the males around when it does."

"Got it," Drew told her.

He pulled the door to Speir's stall shut behind them and they started across the outside yard. Breccan, the youngest of the giraffes, Niall's little brother, came ambling toward them. He was easily the friendliest. Riona had decided she was done with the whole mom-thing when he'd come along and Fiona and Saoirse had been hand-raising him ever since.

"Hey, big boy," Drew greeted as the giraffe came up next to

him and took the bill of Drew's cap between his big lips. He nuzzled Drew's head as Drew held his cap on and stroked the animal's neck.

"He thinks he's a dog, I swear," Fiona said with a laugh. She patted him on the other side.

The giraffe was completely comfortable with her and Saoirse, and Fiona was fine with her daughter being around the big animals. Saoirse knew how to handle herself around the giraffes. All animals really. She knew she was in a unique and privileged situation to get to hang out with wild animals, and she'd been raised to understand that they were not pets and could never be fully trusted to be calm and gentle at all times.

Fiona had always daydreamed about she and Saoirse rescuing animals together. She could already picture her daughter diving right into any and all situations with her enthusiasm and charm. But back on Cara things would be different...

"I've had cows and alpacas act like this," Drew said, completely unfazed. "Sometimes they just bond with us. It's strange and cool."

Fiona made herself focus on the conversation at hand. She ran her palm down the giraffe's neck. "Yeah, he's a big baby," she said affectionately.

One of the big babies she would miss intensely when she left Autre.

You can come back and visit him.

Yeah. Well, she maybe wasn't as into long-distance relationships as she'd thought she was just three months ago. She liked up close and personal and everyday more.

"So, this was a great first day," Drew told her, patting the giraffe and then starting across the yard again toward his truck. "I can't tell you how cool this is."

"I'm so glad to have you on board." She fell in step beside

him. Thank God for Drew Ryan. He had made her feel a million times better today about leaving her animals here.

She'd been hearing about the guy through texts and emails from the Boys of the Bayou Gone Wild ladies ever since Drew had come to town at Christmas with his reindeer and fallen in love with Rory. But they hadn't been exaggerating about how competent and hardworking and kind and funny he was. Or how good-looking.

Fiona barely knew Rory Robins, having only met the hairstylist a couple of times at Ellie's, but she was thrilled that the woman's new boyfriend was an experienced hoof stock farmer. Drew had worked with the usual horses, cows, pigs, and goats back in Iowa, but was particularly fond of alpacas and reindeer and was taking her instruction about the giraffes in stride. She was so relieved to have someone on board helping her with her gentle giants.

She would absolutely have giraffes in the wildlife sanctuary in Cara, but she couldn't imagine taking *these* animals with her. An ocean trip would be extremely difficult on the big animals as would any kind of air travel. Taking all five would be arduous and she couldn't break them up.

"Want a ride home?" he asked, as they stopped by his truck.

"Nah. I'll walk. It's a nice night." She looked back toward the animal park. If Saoirse was here, she knew her daughter would beg to walk the long way. Through the park. The path on the other side of the giraffe pasture would take them through the middle of the animal park and past all the main animal enclosures. She was always amazed that Saoirse never grew tired of the animals or took being around them for granted. She'd grown up in an animal park. She could walk into her backyard and see giraffes everyday. And she did. She loved them.

But Saoirse hadn't met her up here after school. Colin had texted to say she was grounded. Fiona needed to get home and hear what *that* was all about.

"'Kay. Night, Fiona." Drew climbed up into his truck.

"Goodnight. Thank you so much," Fiona returned.

"Tell Saoirse hi for me."

Fiona couldn't help her grin as she started across the grass toward her new house. Saoirse had only met Drew twice, but her daughter charmed people wherever she went. Especially male people. Fiona knew that she was probably going to have to look out when Saoirse got older. Then again, Saoirse had a bodyguard. Who adored her. And two very involved uncles who adored her. Who also had bodyguards who adored her.

Nah, Fiona wasn't going to have to worry one bit about Saoirse and boys and dating.

The poor girl probably wasn't going to date until she was forty.

She'll be Queen.

The thought almost stopped Fiona in her tracks. That was true.

She really could be by then. Of course, Fiona could live to be one hundred and Saoirse wouldn't have to worry about that until she was in her eighties but, even so...

Maybe Fiona would just arrange a marriage for her. Stranger things had happened. Her grandfather still had some deal with one of his closest friends—a billionaire from Denmark—that supposedly meant one of her brothers was going to marry one of that guy's granddaughters. Fiona didn't take the "contract" written up on the back of a playbill and with some of the words smudged by the whiskey that had been spilled on it very seriously. But her brothers did. They'd avoided getting anywhere near Linnea Olsen for more than a decade.

Before she knew it, she'd arrived on her new front porch.

Regardless of what Knox might think, she'd chosen the house because of its proximity to the animals. It wasn't any further than her house in Florida had been from her giraffe barn.

She breathed deep of the Louisiana air and appreciated the new sounds around her. In Florida, she hadn't had a bayou less than a mile away and she hadn't had a lion roaring in the distance. Okay, he wasn't really *roaring* yet. He was still a juvenile. But he made lots of sounds—growls and almost-roars and others. He'd get there. He'd been rescued from an illegal animal ring by Caroline less than a year ago and was doing extremely well at the sanctuary. Of course he was. These people were amazing.

Fiona also didn't have swearing parrots who said *you're a motherfucker* to each other at her park. Because she'd brought them to Autre. She couldn't hear them from here, but she knew they weren't too far away and even the thought of them made her grin. Because she knew Knox hated the things.

She did, however, hear the peacocks calling from where she was walking. That also made her laugh. Knox hated them too. She knew because he'd texted her about them. Peacocks were beautiful but they were damned noisy. And they pooped everywhere.

She'd also been texted by the grumpy city manager when one of them had been hit by a tourist's car. The town that had been inundating his emails and voice messages with complaints about peacocks had suddenly been all worked up over the fact that a tourist had killed one. She giggled at the memory. Not the memory of the dead peacock, but the guy who loved the town that drove him absolutely nuts.

He was so fun to mess with. He loved to put off that broody vibe when in truth he really just wanted everything to be perfect for everyone. She still hadn't figured out when she'd started finding nerdy perfectionism hot, but it'd probably been about the time the big guy had strode into Ellie's looking like a

Viking warrior and demanded to know if all of her paperwork was in order.

Too bad he'd ended up being *such* a jackass.

You'll be my favorite person who visits occasionally, stays temporarily, and that I get to see naked.

As she stepped through her new front door, she realized another thing she didn't have back in Florida. A house full of half-naked men at the end of the day.

Zeke Landry, Mitch Landry, Beau Hebert, Torin, Torin's bodyguard, Jonah, and Colin all turned to face her with *hey girl* bayou boy grins. Yes, even her longtime friend, Irishman, and pseudo-employee. Looked like the bayou had rubbed off. They were all shirtless, covered in sawdust and paint and sweat.

"I should be selling tickets over here rather than down at the petting zoo," she commented.

"We made a ton of progress today," Colin reported happily. "Should be done in another couple of days."

She focused on Mitch. "Everything looks good up at the giraffe barn. Thanks for all your work there."

He wiped his hands on the butt of his jeans and grinned. "Love doing it. Had a lot of help. It's awesome having Drew around."

She nodded her agreement. "He's been an amazing addition."

"Thank goodness the girls down here are as good at seducing Iowans as us boys."

Fiona laughed. "There are three Iowans here now, right? Tori, Paige, and now Drew?"

Mitch laughed. "Yep."

"But you haven't lost any Louisianians to Iowa yet?"

"Nope. But that Iowa connection is strong. Guess there's always a chance."

Zeke walked past his cousin, and clapped Mitch on the

shoulder. "It was close, though, Mitch was about to move to Iowa for Paige."

"True story," Mitch agreed.

"Good thing she came around. You would've frozen your nuts off up there in the winter," Zeke told him.

"Same could be said of you," Mitch said to his cousin. "Jill's from Kansas, for fuck's sake, and was taking care of her penguins in Omaha, *Nebraska*. If she hadn't ended up down here, you'd be teaching your twins how to make snowballs instead of boudin balls."

Zeke laughed. "Best thing is, we can do both. We go back and visit the grandparents and get the hell out of Kansas when we get too cold."

"Where're you from?" Mitch asked Jonah.

Jonah had been protecting Torin ever since the middle O'Grady son had come to the U.S., but Jonah was an American. Her grandfather had hired bodyguards for her brothers who were about their same ages and played the role of best friend, so no one realized they were being guarded. Or that they were important enough to need to be guarded.

"North Carolina," Jonah told him.

"So you don't know a lot about snow either," Zeke said with a nod.

Jonah laughed. "Well, we've spent some quality time on the ski slopes, but that's about it."

"Ah, but ski slopes mean ski lodges. And pretty girls who need to be warmed up by the fire."

They all looked over as Cian came sauntering into the room. He still had his shirt on. And was *not* covered in sawdust. And was carrying a plate and fork.

He grinned when he saw Fiona. "Holy shit, have you ever had bread pudding?"

She rolled her eyes. "Yes. Many times. Cora's is the best."

"I might never eat anything else ever again."

"You said that about the biscuits and gravy this morning," Henry, Cian's bodyguard and best friend, said as he came into the room. Also carrying a plate.

"I meant it then. But then I met bread pudding."

"Ah, much the way you handle your relationships with women," Torin said.

Cian just grinned.

"Do you have to eat any food he wants to try to be sure it's not poisoned?" Zeke asked Henry.

So apparently everyone here knew that Cian and Torin both had bodyguards. Fiona couldn't be upset though. Mitch, Zeke, Beau, and everyone else in the Landry inner circle were as loyal and trustworthy as they came.

"That's what I tell him," Henry said, scooping another bite of bread pudding into his mouth. "Drinks too."

"That's *not* a rule?" Cian asked.

"It's just common sense," Henry assured him.

Henry was British and was as close to Cian as anyone. Though he and Jonah were also good friends, having been trained in Cara by the king's own security team and having traveled together extensively over the past ten years.

"How about that 'rule' you put in place that says you should always dance with and spend a little alone time with the girls I'm interested in?" Cian asked. "Just to be sure they're not carrying any knives or guns or anything?" The corner of his mouth twitched.

Henry nodded solemnly. "Everything I do is for your safety and happiness, my liege." He even added a small bow, though was careful not to tip his plate.

Cian rolled his eyes but nodded. "Your loyalty is noted and shall be duly rewarded."

Henry snorted.

Fiona smiled, watching them all give each other trouble. Really, her brothers and their friends fit right in on the bayou.

Torin and Jonah and Colin were more serious generally, but they had solid friendships and did love to have a good time. Cian and Henry on the other hand... yeah, they were pretty much bayou boys with Irish and British accents.

Which she knew only made them even more tempting to many women.

Having them hang out in Autre too long could be trouble. The bayou boys themselves were all falling in love left and right. There weren't too many single ones left. The women around Autre would probably welcome some new audacious flirts.

All the guys in the room except for the O'Gradys and their friends were madly in love. And they had no trouble showing it. She knew all of their women were blissfully happy as well. Which of course made her think of Knox. Which she immediately forced herself *not* do.

Screw him and his I-only-like-you-if-you're-four-thousand-miles-away.

But the earlier talk about Zeke and his twins made Fiona ask Colin, "Where's Saoirse?"

"Oh, yeah, can you run and get her? I'll jump in the shower and then start dinner."

"Of course. Where is she?"

"Next door." He started for the stairs.

Fiona turned toward the front door then froze. She pivoted back. "*Where?*"

"Next door."

"Are there kids living next door that I don't know about?"

"I don't think so." Colin continued up the steps.

That could only mean one thing. Well, one *neighbor* anyway. "Colin," Fiona said firmly.

But he didn't stop. She stomped to the base of the staircase. "Colin!"

"She's over at Knox's."

That's what she'd been afraid he was going to say. "What is she doing at Knox's?"

"Oh, and she's grounded," Colin added.

Fiona frowned. "You mentioned that. For what?"

"Calling a kid a gobshite at recess."

Fiona rubbed the spot in the middle of her forehead.

"And almost punching that kid."

Fiona waited a second for him to go on. All she heard was his footsteps continuing across the upstairs floor.

"Colin!"

But he didn't answer. Fiona's heart was suddenly hammering. Her daughter was at Knox's? And she'd almost punched someone at school? Already? And how did being grounded mean she could go to Knox's?

She was at Knox's?

How had that happened? What were they doing? Was that okay? Knox didn't seem like the type to want to spend time with a nine-year-old girl. And she was over there alone? Colin never let Saoirse go anywhere alone.

Okay, that wasn't entirely true. She had friends in Florida. Who had been fully vetted and background checked, and whose houses had been fully checked out. When the family hadn't been home, of course. Which was legally a gray area and something Fiona chose to know as little about as possible. But not only had those play dates been rare and for short periods, Colin had always had a team staked out across the street from the house.

Fiona really didn't think that the half-naked men remodeling the interior of her house really qualified as a stakeout team. Henry and Jonah were both hired security, but at the moment, they were cracking open beers and talking about how to vet a whole boatload of women coming for a bachelorette swamp boat tour the next day. Cian was apparently helping Owen Landry with the tour.

"You think there's someone who just happens to be in town for her friend's bachelorette party who is also looking to assassinate a prince-in-hiding from a teeny tiny country no one's even heard of?" Beau asked.

"I'm just saying, I should probably meet with these ladies ahead of time to be *sure*," Henry said with a grin.

"Maybe we should just both go on the tour too," Jonah said. "You know, in case anything happens."

For Jonah, that was pretty playful. Maybe it was the Cajun food getting to him. Or the moonshine. Or the weather.

And if this was the new stakeout team, she and Colin were going to have to have a talk.

"Colin!"

But there was no answer.

She shoved a hand through her hair. The men Fiona got involved with never met Saoirse.

Of course, she wasn't really *involved* with Knox, was she?

Wasn't that the bottom line here? Wasn't that the entire point? Wasn't that why she was pissed at him and had been avoiding him for two days?

He wasn't put off by the fact that she was from another country, in line to potentially inherit the throne should she so choose, and moving back to that country in six months. For good. In fact, that had seemingly made everything perfect for him. Suddenly he thought everything would just revert back to their Christmas arrangement.

According to all reports—and in Autre there was no way to avoid getting all reports even if you wanted to—he'd been in a fantastic mood for the past two days. All of the women were astonished. They assumed she knew something about it and were asking her repeatedly what was going on with him.

Well, it seemed that Knox was just really fucking glad to be getting rid of her.

"Hey, Fiona?" Zeke asked from across the room.

"Yeah?"

"You want to know what Knox and Saoirse are doing over at his house, why don't you go over there and see?"

She crossed her arms. "Because I don't want to go over there."

Zeke chuckled. "Okay. Want a beer?"

She did not. "I'll give you two hundred dollars to go over and get Saoirse for me."

He laughed. "How mad would you be if I told you that it was worth more than two hundred to watch you stewing about it?"

She narrowed her eyes. "You should definitely not tell me that."

"Okay." Zeke tipped his beer bottle back, fighting a smile.

She looked at Henry and Jonah. "No one's concerned that a strange man has my daughter at his house by herself?"

Jonah rolled his eyes. "The same man that *you* went off with alone yesterday? That you text with all the time? That Colin did a full work-up on months ago?"

They knew she and Knox had gone for beignets? But she didn't ask. It was nice to know her grandfather was getting his money's worth, she supposed.

Fine. She wasn't worried about Saoirse being with Knox. Knox was a great guy. Two days ago, she would've been thrilled to think that he and her daughter were getting to know one another. Knox would love Saoirse. Her daughter was a very cool kid. And Saoirse would love Knox. She would probably wrap him around her little finger, make him smile, and tell him all about wombats.

Actually, there was a ninety-nine percent chance that right now Knox knew more about wombats than any other person in the town of Autre. Other than Saoirse and maybe Fiona and Colin.

"Hey, you guys work for me. One of you go get Saoirse," she told Henry and Jonah.

But they just laughed. She'd tried the you-work-for-me thing with them before. It never worked. Because they definitely did not work for her.

"Hey, Mitch—"

"Just go over there," Mitch told her. "Two of your favorite people are about a hundred yards away. Together. Just go be with them."

She frowned. "One of my favorite people and one of my *least* favorite people, you mean."

Mitch rolled his eyes. Which wouldn't be worth noting except that it was Mitch Landry. One of the nicest guys in the world. One of the most accommodating, considerate, do-anything-for-anyone people on the planet. *He'd* rolled his eyes at her.

"I'm mad at him," she said.

"Because you like him," Zeke said in a singsong voice more appropriate for playgrounds than a living room full of hot, sweaty men with beer.

Except maybe *this* group of hot, sweaty men with beer.

"I liked him before he turned into a jackass."

They all snorted.

"As far as I know, Knox's always been kind of a jackass," Beau said.

Which was fair enough.

"He's being a jackass about a specific thing," Fiona said.

"Yeah, well, maybe even princesses don't get their way all the time," Zeke said.

She gasped. She actually gasped. "This has nothing to do with me being a princess. Which I am not, by the way. And it has nothing to do with me getting my way. He's just being a jerk."

None of the men said anything to that.

She frowned. "Fine. I'm going over there but only because I need to get my daughter."

"You know I haven't met a lot of queens in my life. Do they all pout like that?" Beau asked Cian and Torin.

"Maybe not," Fiona said before her brothers could respond. "But do you know why they wear so many rings on their fingers?"

"Why?" He sounded amused.

She paused at the door and lifted her middle finger, with one of her favorite rings on it. "So it still looks pretty even when we do this." Then she exited in her best queenly flounce.

7

All the way across her backyard to Knox's front door, Fiona thought about why she was mad at him. The truth was, he was resisting her. And she didn't want him to be able to do that.

On every other trip to Autre, within ten minutes of her pulling her huge purple truck into town, Knox had showed up. Sure, he'd always acted put out and like he was there to find out what 'trouble' she'd brought with her. But she'd always liked to think it was because he wanted to see her. Even if they were bickering and teasing, she'd thought he liked all of that as much as she had. And that he instinctively couldn't stay away.

Now she knew better.

She was *right here* and she hadn't seen him in two days. Yes, she was avoiding him. Yes, she'd left Ellie's when he'd come in. But he could have come after her.

She'd wanted him to come after her, dammit.

He wasn't supposed to actually be able to stick with this I-can-wait-six-months thing when she was right here, every day, in his *backyard*.

But he was and it was *very* insulting.

Sure, it had only been two days, but she wanted to be I-can't-resist-you-for-even-an-hour-I-must-have-you-now-that-I've-finally-had-a-taste.

A little shiver danced down her spine. That's what he'd said to her at Christmas. That he'd needed to know how she tasted before she left Autre. God, she'd replayed that moment in her mind *so* many times since then.

Well, now he knew.

And he'd been resisting her for *two days*. When she was *right here*.

He was just so...Knox. She blew out a breath as her foot hit his front porch.

Just handle it. So this isn't going according to plan. You just need a new plan.

Right. A new plan. Like being Knox's...neighbor.

Whose daughter came over after school to play. Apparently.

She knocked on his front door and waited. But there was no sound from the other side and no lights shining on the first floor. It was still light enough outside that maybe they hadn't turned any lamps on, but they were clearly not in the yard. His truck was in the driveway, so as far she knew they were here unless they'd walked over to the petting zoo or Ellie's. She descended the steps of the porch and walked out into the yard, looking up at the house as she pulled her phone out and sent him a text.

There was no immediate response. It looked like there was a light on in one of the rooms upstairs though. She went back to the door and pounded a little harder. Then she tried the knob. It was unlocked. She opened the door and poked her head inside. "Hello? Knox! Saoirse!"

"Yeah! Up here!"

She followed the sound of Knox's voice up the stairs.

There was a light on in the second room on the left, but there was noise coming from the room at the end of the hall.

She glanced in the room as she passed and stopped in the doorway in surprise. Oh my God. It was an otter playroom. There was fencing across the doorway, but the rest of the room was set up for otters to run freely. There were little slides and tunnels and burrows. There was also a feeding and water station along with multiple levels for them to climb on. If she hadn't known better, she wouldn't have known if it was set up for guinea pigs or cats or what animal inhabited the space. But she did know. And her heart felt like it was swelling in her chest.

He'd kept the otters. At least that's what this looked like. If he had, she was officially going to fall in love with him.

She turned and headed for the room at the end of the hall, holding her breath. She half hoped that he'd kept the otters and half hoped that he hadn't. Being mad at him and getting over him was going to be a lot easier if he had pawned those otters off on someone else and now was fostering a dog. In a very strange bedroom setup.

She stepped into the doorway at the end of the hall to find a very hot, very big man in a wet t-shirt sitting on the edge of a wide, Jacuzzi bathtub with one leg in and one leg out. Her daughter knelt inside the tub, fully dressed, giggling, while a juvenile otter climbed up her arm to her shoulder.

Fiona wasn't sure if it was her heart or her ovaries that exploded, but something inside of her completely expanded and then popped open with what felt like rainbow confetti and hot bubbles of joy. The scene before her made her want to laugh and cry and take her clothes off and run all at the same time.

Fortunately, Saoirse was there, which ruled out taking her clothes off, crying, or running.

All of those things would've been way too hard to explain.

So, she laughed.

Knox and Saoirse both swung to look at her.

"Mom!" Saoirse exclaimed. "Baby otters!"

"I see that," she somehow managed.

Then her gaze collided with Knox's and the feeling of needing to be naked and crying intensified.

His brown eyes studied her. "Hey." His voice was strangely gruff.

"Hey."

"Mom, they're figuring out how to swim!" Saoirse's face was absolutely glowing.

Fiona focused fully on her daughter. "You're teaching them to swim?"

"Yeah, Knox was waiting for somebody to come help him. They're a little bit behind, but they're figuring it out fast. They've only been kind of playing in their water, so it's like they've just been waiting for this."

Fiona looked back at Knox. "You've been waiting for someone to help you?"

He'd been waiting for her. She'd dropped these otters off at Christmas and promised to be back.

"Yeah."

And she'd really intended to come back. She'd been testing him. She'd been honest about that. Even at the time. She'd needed to know that he would take in abandoned baby animals at the last minute and take care of them until someone else could come along. She told him then that she couldn't sleep with a man who wouldn't do that. And she'd meant that. Kind of.

Honestly, even in that moment she'd known that if Knox was not that man, she was going to be able to look past it. He was probably the only one she would ever make that exception for, but she'd wanted him enough even then to realize that he didn't have to share this passion with her.

But he'd kept the baby otters. Waiting for her.

She took a shaky breath. "I—"

"We've just been hanging out. I've been watching YouTube videos, but kind of wanted a second pair of hands when I first took them swimming. Then Saoirse showed up today and she seemed like the perfect helper. And I was right."

His gaze dropped to her daughter and again Fiona felt the incredibly confusing mix of warmth and hormones flood through her.

She wondered briefly if this was how Tori and Jill felt when they watched Josh and Zeke with their kids. Then realized that, of course it wasn't. They didn't feel the "oh shit" part at least. They *knew* and freely admitted they were in love with the guys who made their daughters light up and laugh like that.

And they were happy about being in love.

Fiona not so much. It was actually kind of a pain in the ass.

"So how have you been teaching them to swim?" Fiona asked, again trying to focus on her daughter rather than the big man who seemed to take up even more space than his chiseled body should.

"Well, first we just let them get in and get their paws wet," Saoirse said, jumping immediately into the explanation.

Her daughter's attention went back to the animals and Knox stretched a hand out toward Fiona. She frowned. He crooked his fingers in the *come here* gesture. She shook her head.

He tipped his head and then motioned again. "You need to come close to really see them."

Saoirse looked over her shoulder. "Seriously, Mom. Come here and look at them."

Fiona frowned at Knox. What was she going to do? Explain to Saoirse that being close to Knox made her heart hammer and her stomach swoop and other parts of her body do things that Saoirse didn't need to know about yet? Almost worse than having that talk with her daughter right now was letting *Knox* know all of those things.

But as Fiona took that step closer, she could see in his eyes that he already knew his effect on her. And enjoyed it.

Jerk. He was the one who didn't want to have an affair while she was here. He was the one who got excited about the idea of her living *across an ocean*.

"But then they were so brave and curious," Saoirse went on, oblivious to her mother's mix of emotions and hormones. "They'd dip their noses into the water and scamper around. So we made the water a little deeper and then they started really exploring. So then we made it even deeper and we kept our hands underneath them. And kind of helped them learn to dive!"

That did catch Fiona's attention. She was obviously not immune to interesting animal shenanigans, especially ones that happened with cute, furry animals. Especially ones that happened with cute, furry animals she had entrusted to the hot guy she wanted more than she wanted more of Cora's bread pudding. And especially when it involved him being sweet and patient with her daughter.

"You actually taught them to dive?"

Saoirse bobbed her head up and down excitedly. "Kind of like what their moms do when they hold onto their necks and take them under," Saoirse said. "We kept our hands under their bellies and just dipped underneath the water. And then pretty soon they were doing it by themselves!"

Fiona looked at Knox. "Wow."

He chuckled. "They're fast learners. And Saoirse is a great teacher."

"We thought they were getting kind of tired so we drained a bunch of the water just a little bit ago. You should've come over sooner and we would've showed you."

"Well, she can come over anytime. We can show her again some other time." Knox met her eyes.

Fiona waited for him to say something about her being

welcome in his big whirlpool tub anytime. But he didn't. Yeah, she thought. *Easy to flirt, but harder to hold back from following through when I'm right here in front of you and living right across your backyard, isn't it?* Maybe this wasn't so easy for him either.

"So how did you two get so wet? Did you dive under the water with them?" Fiona asked her daughter.

Saoirse giggled. "Not exactly."

"And you're just as wet as she is. She's *in* the tub. What'd you do?" Fiona asked Knox.

"The otters climb on him," Saoirse said with a giggle. "All the time. They love him. And they climbed on me some too. But he's their favorite."

I want to see that.

Fiona couldn't help it. She was an animal lover and she had, after all, brought these otters to this man specifically because she wanted to know if he would be good at fostering. So yeah, she wanted to see how he interacted with them. So what?

So, it was really fucking sexy.

There. She'd admitted it. The man was sitting on the edge of his bathtub with three baby otters, and her daughter, seemingly being patient and wonderful and kind. And it was an incredible turn-on.

"I guess that makes sense. You're warm and there's a lot of surface area there." She circled her hand in a gesture to encompass all of him.

He lifted a brow. "Are you saying that I'm hot and you'd like to climb on me?"

Well, yeah. But...she glanced at her daughter. The thing was, Saoirse was nine. And there were three otters to pay attention to. She didn't care what the grown-ups were talking about and certainly wouldn't pick up on any sexual innuendo.

So Fiona nodded. "I'm saying I understand their instincts."

He gave her one of those smirky, sexy half smiles. "Parsley

even falls asleep on my shoulder at night when I'm watching TV."

"You cuddle them at night on the couch," Fiona said.

He nodded. With a smug look on his face that told her he understood what that did to her.

Yep, *that* wasn't going to help her not be attracted to him.

Not that she thought anything would. Or that she was really trying that hard to fight it. Though it would make it easier to be mad at him if she didn't want to strip his clothes off every second she was with him in person.

"Parsley? Let me guess, you named them after things you're allergic to?"

He chuckled. "I named them for things I don't like. But I like how well you know me."

See, he was being sweet and flirty. That wasn't fair. He wanted her to get on an airplane and fly for several hours and then spend weeks there before she came back for a booty call. In fact, she wasn't even totally clear on how long she needed to stay away before she could come back and be invited into his bed.

She should probably ask for a printout of these "rules".

"The others are Basil and Cilantro," Saoirse said.

"Come here," Knox said.

His husky voice and the big hand he extended toward her again made her heart flip over in her chest.

Fiona shook her head. "I'm okay."

"Come on. Come here and really meet them. Again. It's been a while since you saw them up close."

She rolled her eyes. Yeah, yeah, okay. She'd left him here alone with the otters for longer than intended.

"Come *on*, Mom."

Fiona sighed and started to step forward without taking his hand, but he wrapped his big palm around her wrist and tugged her forward anyway.

But he didn't just mean to get her closer to the tub. He put his hands on her hips and brought her in to sit, settling her on the wide edge of the tub between his thighs.

Her brain scrambled and she didn't even think to protest as he leaned over, slipped off her right shoe, pulled up her right pant leg, then swung her foot over and into the tub with a little splash.

Saoirse giggled as he scooped up one of the otters and plopped it on Fiona's lap. She, of course, instinctively kept her hands around the animal as it nestled against her breasts, soaking her shirt, bra, and skin underneath.

"Thanks," she said through gritted teeth.

She felt his chuckle against her back. She was more or less cradled against him. There was room on the edge of the tub for them to sit separated, but it seemed that Knox didn't like that idea. His hands stayed on her hips, holding her against him, her butt right up against his fly with a now harder, thicker part of his body pressed against her lower back.

For maybe the first time in her life, she forgot for a few minutes that she was holding onto an animal. She absently stroked the otter, only half aware that her daughter and Knox were talking. His voice rumbled through her from behind, his hot breath danced over the skin of her neck, and the heat from his hands on her hips soaked through the denim and right into her bones.

She'd no idea how long she sat there just letting him hold onto her like that.

No matter how long it was, it was pathetic.

"Okay, maybe we should get them dried off and settled down. This has been a lot of excitement for today," Knox said.

Saoirse climbed out of the tub and wrapped a towel around her back before picking up one of the otters from the tub and cuddling him against her. Knox picked up the third otter and another towel. They dried the babies off, then Saoirse bounced up from the floor and headed out the door while Knox gripped Fiona's hips and lifted her up off the edge of the tub and set her on the bathmat next to them.

He handed her a towel.

Again he had that smug smirk on his lips. "You okay?"

"I'm not the one with all of the blood in my body diverted to one body part," she said, her eyes dropping to his fly. "Are *you* okay?"

He chuckled. "You sure I'm the only one with that problem?" His eyes dropped to *her* fly.

He was holding a baby otter in a fluffy yellow towel looking cocky and completely at ease, teasing her about turning her on simply by sitting behind her on the edge of a bathtub.

He was such a jerk.

"I'm not loving this new attitude of yours," she told him.

He grinned. A full-on grin. Which never failed to make her stomach flip because Knox grins were very rare. "You're not loving my new attitude?"

"Yeah. You think that you are calling all the shots between us. You think that you somehow have some upper hand. I can assure you that is not the case."

He stretched to his feet, his six-foot-four-inches towering above her five-foot-one-inch and stepped close, looking down at her. "So you're telling me that your daughter loving me, me keeping these three baby otters, me helping make this town absolutely shine for your grandfather's visit, and me running my hands all over your sweet body, aren't doin' anything to you?"

She sucked in a breath. "You're trying to get my daughter to like you to convince me to do this crazy long-distance affair thing?"

"I'm not *trying* to get your daughter to like me. Your daughter likes me. But I think that will all help you not be mad about the long-distance affair thing."

"That makes it sound like you think I'm going to do the long-distance affair thing whether I'm mad about it or not."

He lifted a hand and ran it through her hair. He stopped when his hand was cupping her face and ran his thumb over her bottom lip. "Oh, I think you're going to do the long-distance affair thing."

God, she loved him touching her. They had really not done enough of that yet. Still, she made her tone haughty and said, "I don't sleep with men I don't like."

"It's a good thing you like me then."

"You seem pretty sure of that."

The corner of his mouth tilted up. "Fi, you liked me long before any of this."

"I'm mad at you."

"Liking somebody and being mad at somebody are two different things."

"So you don't care that I'm mad at you?"

"I do care. That's why I'm getting your daughter on my side and being sweet with the otters in front of you."

She shook her head. "So you *are* intentionally being sweet with children and animals to win me over?"

"I am intentionally letting you *see me* being sweet with children and animals to win you over. But I'd do it whether you're here or not. I happen to think your kid is pretty cool and, in spite of my best efforts, I like these *noisy,* needy furballs."

She believed him. Dammit. "But you *are* intentionally manipulating my hormones."

He leaned in, putting his mouth right against her ear and then dragged his beard along her jaw until his lips were even with hers and said, "Oh, absolutely."

"Mom! I'm wet and freezing!"

She pulled in a deep breath and leaned back. "Why don't you run home? You can take your bath before dinner," she called to Saoirse.

"Are you coming?"

"In a little bit. I need to talk to Knox about something."

"Okay! Bye, Knox!"

"Bye, Princess," he called back with a grin, his eyes locked on Fiona's.

There was affection in his voice. And the return giggle from her daughter sealed Fiona's fate—she was definitely falling for him. The asshole.

"Tell Cian to share the bread pudding with you!" Fiona called.

"Cian?" Knox asked. "Your brother is here?"

"They both are."

"Should I meet—" He broke off. "Nope. Never mind."

Fiona sighed.

They stood just staring at one another as they listened to Saoirse's feet pounding down the stairs, then the sound of the back door opening, and closing again.

His gaze dropped to her mouth.

Fiona wet her lips. He was going to kiss her. And she was ready to give in. Definitely.

"We should probably get these otters into their pen," he said instead, plucking the otter from her fingers and wrapping it in the towel with its brother.

Fiona blinked. What?

Oh, right, otters. And it wasn't like they were being *quiet*. They were clearly hungry and...wanted Knox. The one she'd been holding quieted considerably once Knox was holding him.

She shook her head as she followed them down the hallway to their room.

Their room.

He'd kept them. And given them his guestroom. And was now teaching them to swim.

When she'd brought them to him to foster, her intention

had been to return within a couple of weeks. Three at the most. She hadn't even been one hundred percent sure he'd keep them that long. She'd known he'd give them to someone capable and competent, of course. But she'd hoped he'd at least try. She'd thought maybe him trying to keep up with three baby otters and failing would have been cute and funny and sweet.

But no. Of course he hadn't failed. He was a perfectionist and if he decided he was going to foster a trio of otters to get into her pants, then he was going to do it perfectly.

And he had.

But now, she realized he hadn't done this just to win her over. All of this was a very permanent part of his life now, obviously. At the point where her texts had gotten short and curt—because she couldn't tell him what was really going on and because she missed him so damned much that she'd hoped he'd stop texting—he could have put these babies back in the carrier she'd brought him and taken them to...well, any number of people. Most of whom were named Landry.

But he hadn't.

And she couldn't ignore how it made her feel.

Knox stepped over the barrier that kept the otters in the room and checked their food and water.

Damn, his ass looked great in those jeans. With an otter clinging to one leg and another climbing up his arm.

She scrubbed a finger up the middle of her forehead. She should have never given him those otters. She was done for.

Fiona figured this was the perfect chance to escape. "Okay, well I'm going to head home, then."

"Just hang on a minute."

"I think that's probably a bad idea."

He looked over at her from where he was crouching next to the otters' dishes. The otter now perched on his shoulder looked over at her as well. "You said you wanted to talk to me about something."

"I changed my mind."

"Chicken," he chided with that corner of his mouth pulling up.

She put a hand on her hip. "That's not going to work. You can't bait me into agreeing to have a long-distance affair with you. You don't get to call all the shots. You want me to just be your neighbor while I'm here in Autre, then fine. That's what I'll be. But that means I go home when we're both wearing wet t-shirts and you're being flirty and I'm feeling..."

"Pissed," he filled in when she trailed off.

"Horny," she said honestly.

She could see the heat flare in his eyes from across the room. His gaze tracked over the front of her shirt where the wet fabric clung to her breasts.

Fiona felt her belly swoop and her nipples tighten.

He cleared his throat. And went back to filling the food dish.

She should have left then.

But she didn't.

Maybe he didn't *want* to want to sleep with her while she was in Autre, but if she was going to be walking around turned on and unsatisfied for the next six months, then she wasn't going to be the only one.

Because if Knox thought he was bringing other women over here to scratch any itches while Fiona was just next door, she was going to *quickly* put that notion right out of his mind. She already had a few ideas about how she could interrupt and scare off any potential itch-scratchers. Given some time to really think about it—and at least two Irishmen and a Brit who loved a good prank—Knox was going to think bringing swearing parrots to Autre was the *least* of the annoying things she'd done.

He plucked the otter from his shoulder and the one from his thigh, putting them down and speaking to them softly.

Then he crossed the room, stepped over the barrier, and joined her in the hallway.

He stopped right in front of her. She had to tip her head back again to meet his eyes.

"I'm not trying to bait you into anything. I'm not trying to trick you or seduce you or manipulate you."

Yeah, well, he *was* seducing her. But that was happening just by him standing there and being *him*.

She moved her arms to cross them in front of her and took a breath. "Then what are you doing?"

"I want to explain why I want this with you."

"A long-distance affair? Isn't that pretty clear? Sex. With no strings. No commitment. No emotions."

"That's not what I'm asking for," Knox said, studying her intently. "I never said no strings or commitment."

Oh... God. She was going to hear him out.

She wanted him. And the logistics weren't her concern. The fucking emotions were. Dammit. It hit her in that moment that she wanted him to *like* her. Not just want her.

Well, fuck.

She intended to come back to Autre regularly. Sure, she might be running a country, but she was going to miss this place. She'd miss the animal park, the people, and hell, there had to be some perks to being Queen, right? If she couldn't just jet off for the weekend whenever the hell she felt like it, what was the point?

But, it was the no-emotions part of an affair that bothered her. That's what had changed during her three months away in Cara. She'd realized that she didn't just like the town and the Landrys. She *liked* Knox. Really liked him. More than liked him.

She just hadn't wanted to admit it.

But now, standing in his house, alone, with three baby otters just a few feet away—and okay, the wet t-shirt wasn't helping—she had to face the fact that she had already fallen for him. And she didn't want anyone else. She didn't want *him* to want anyone else. So, yes, she wanted to sleep with him. A lot. Regularly. But she also wanted more than that. She wanted to be his girlfriend. His only girlfriend. Which was pretty seventh-grade and she didn't really want to have to say that out loud.

But she also wanted *him* to want that.

Still, she knew that she was going to take him however she could get him.

She never knew what she was walking into when she went to a rescue either. And she always made it work. So...she'd be okay with however this played out.

"I just want you to know," she said after a long moment of just looking at each other. "You don't have to explain anything to me. I trust that you have a good reason."

He frowned slightly. "You trust that I have a good reason for the long-distance thing?"

She lifted a shoulder. "Yeah."

His frown deepened, but he was clearly puzzled. "Why?"

"Because you always have reasons for the things you do." It was true. This man did not do things spontaneously or without a very well thought out plan.

The crease between his brows eased, but he shook his head as if in wonder. "You would just accept this? Without really understanding why it's important to me? I thought you were mad."

She pulled in a deep breath. "I was. But then I realized that..." This was not the time to say *I'm in love with you*. So she fudged it with, "I know enough about you. I don't have to know every single detail. I know that I can trust you. That's what matters."

His eyes flickered with emotion and he moved closer. "Yeah. I get that. I didn't know every detail about you."

They both gave soft laughs at that understatement.

"And," he continued. "I was mad when I found out. At first.

But if someone had asked if I still felt like I *knew* you, and trusted you, I would have said yes."

That made her suck in a little breath as her heart squeezed hard. "Yeah?" she asked softly.

He nodded. "I might have *just* realized that now that we're talking about it, but yes. Definitely." His voice was a little husky.

She swallowed hard. That mattered. It really did.

"But I still really want to tell you my reasons," he said. "I *like* knowing your details, even if I didn't really *need* them to know who you are and that you're someone I want to be close to."

She wet her lips. Well, okay then. She did like him knowing all the things about her. She liked that he knew about Cara and what lay ahead in her future. She loved that he knew about Saoirse.

"Okay," she agreed. "But, there's something I need before we talk."

"Oh?"

"Yeah, lately whenever we talk, one of us ends up mad and walking out."

"I'm not going to be mad after this talk," he said with an almost-there smile.

"I feel like there's an eighty-percent chance I'm going to be though," she said. "And I'll probably get over that too, but I don't want to put this off any longer." She reached for the bottom of her shirt and pulled it up and over her head.

One of his brows rose.

"Your otter got my shirt wet and I'm cold."

"You can borrow one of my shirts." His voice was definitely a little rougher.

"Thanks." She reached behind her and unhooked her bra, pulling it off as well.

Knox's gaze darkened and heated. His jaw tightened.

He'd never seen her naked. He'd never even touched one of her breasts. But his eyes on her now made sparks of electricity dance across her skin and tighten her nipples as if his fingers were there plucking and squeezing.

"So *you're* seducing *me* then?" he asked dryly.

"Yes. Because dammit, the other night I should have just kept my mouth shut. So tonight, you're keeping yours shut until we do this."

"You shouldn't have told me you were my new neighbor?"

"I could have told you that *after*. I was trying to be noble. But fuck that. I'm *very* out of practice with anything having to do with nobility." She took a step closer to him. "I'm still mad at you. But I need an orgasm from you more than I need my next breath."

She watched his throat work as he swallowed and she noticed his fists were clenched at his sides, as if holding himself back from touching her. Her eyes intent on his, she flattened one palm on his abs.

"Please, Knox."

His hand came up and covered hers. "Well, it's gonna be hard to make you come with my tongue if I'm keeping my mouth shut."

"My God, that was the best thing you could have possibly said," she told him, running her hand from his abs to his chest. "You have my permission to open your mouth for any and all activities involving your lips, and tongue, and my various body parts."

Was he really not going to take this woman to bed? Knox knew better than to completely give in to Fiona Grady. This woman already had him twisted up and they had a lot to figure out. But if she needed an orgasm more than her next breath, he could help her out. And he sure as fuck wasn't gonna let anybody else help her with it.

Besides, she'd taken her top off. He was a very strong and stubborn man, but he had his limits. And half-naked Fiona was definitely one of them.

"Oh, I'm going to give you exactly what you need. But I'm getting what I need too," he told her, lifting a hand to cup the back of her head and curling his fingers to slightly grip her hair.

Her eyes widened and she wet her lips. "What do you need?"

What he needed was for her to understand that the things between them were going to be compromises. Was he completely wrapped around her little finger? Absolutely. No question. But he needed her to be wrapped around his as well. If they were to do this, whatever it was, and however it ended up looking in the end, they were *both* going to do it.

"I need to make you come," he said honestly. "If that's what you need, that's what I need. And then I need you to listen to me. We're not going to cuddle in bed, you're not going to spend the night, I'm not making pancakes in the morning. I'm going to finally fully taste you and touch every inch of you. And then we're going to *talk*. And then you're going to go home."

Fiona stared up at him and he knew she was surprised but he could see the heat in her eyes. And he didn't think it was just because of the words he said or what he promised to do. He didn't know her sexual history, nor did he want to. He didn't know what her dating life was like or what kind of guys normally got this close to her. But he would bet that most of them were very happy to keep their mouths busy on her silky skin and perfect nipples and sassy mouth and sweet pussy and didn't mind being told she didn't want to talk after.

"Fine, no cuddling after," she said, but her attempt at sass was completely erased by the breathlessness in her voice.

He tipped her head back and lowered his mouth for a kiss. He'd meant to simply taste her lips. But as soon as she sighed against his mouth and leaned into him, and he felt the hard points of her nipples pressing through the wet cotton of his own t-shirt, he tightened his grip on her hair and opened his mouth, sweeping his tongue into hers.

She gave a little whimper as her hands came up to fist the cotton at his back. She arched closer. But their height difference truly was a disadvantage at times. Like when it came to trying to align their bodies.

With a growl of frustration, his fingers went to the front button of her jeans. He quickly unfastened and unzipped them, pushing them down her legs, sliding the silk panties with them. She toed off her remaining shoe and kicked the panties and jeans free of her ankles. All without breaking contact with his mouth.

But of course, then she was naked. He lifted his head and stepped back for a look.

She was absolutely gorgeous. She practically brought him to his knees, which gave him the perfect idea for what was going to happen next.

"You're fucking perfect," he growled. He stepped close, running a fingertip over her tattoo, tracing the swirls of the letters and watching her nipples draw tighter.

Her breath caught. "Thanks," she said. "I'm assuming you are too. But I'd really like to see it for myself." She wiggled her finger up and down indicating that he was far too dressed.

He chuckled, loving that she didn't seem to mind standing there bare-assed naked in his upper hallway.

He grabbed his shirt between his shoulder blades and pulled it off over his head. But he wasn't going any further than that.

She ran her hand up his sides, making his stomach muscles tense and giving a tiny groan of approval. "Yeah, I definitely see why the otters like to climb on you."

He gave a soft chuckle. "And that is the last we're going to talk about the otters for a nice long time."

"But—"

He scooped her up under her ass before she could continue that sentence and carried her the four strides it took to get to the narrow decorative table that sat along the wall between the guest bathroom and the master bedroom. His mother had insisted it should go there. It looked nice, but Knox didn't really understand the purpose.

Until now.

It was going to be absolutely perfect. And they were definitely going to break the lamp that sat on the table.

He deposited Fiona on the top and she gave a little gasp, clutching the edge with both hands as the table rocked. "Knox!"

"Shhhh. When you keep talking then I have to talk back. We already made an agreement about how I'm going to be using my mouth."

With that, he knelt in front of her and spread her knees, running his hands up and down her smooth inner thighs.

She gasped again but this was definitely one of catch-her-breath desire rather than shock. "Oh my God, yes," she said softly.

Her pussy was perfect. Exactly as he'd expected. He'd dreamed about this pussy. And now it was right in front of him, all his, its owner wanting him to make her feel good.

Yes, ma'am.

He slid his hands toward the middle, running his thumbs over her outer lips.

She moaned and her head fell back against the wall behind her.

"Now be careful up there, the table's an antique."

Her eyes were closed but she huffed out a breath of laughter. "You've got an antique fucking table in your house?"

"I don't believe that's how it was advertised. Though they

probably could've charged double if they'd called it that. Never been used like this before."

Now that he had her here, he realized it was actually just about the right height to bend her over and take her from behind, too. He made a mental note.

"Well, I—"

He slid a finger up and down over her clit and she broke off with another little gasp.

"Yes?" he teased.

"Never mind. Just never mind."

He stroked her again and again, watching as her chest flushed and the pink crawled up her neck to her cheeks. She continued to grip the edge of the table, her knees apart, completely at his mercy.

Yes, he fucking loved this table.

He hooked a hand underneath the back of one of her knees and lifted her foot until he could set the heel on the edge of the table, spreading her open even further.

That got her eyes open.

"This is really not what I expected," she said.

"You complainin'?" He ran his middle finger over her clit again.

"No, I'm just thinking that I could really get used to people bowing in front of me, though."

That caught him by surprise, and it took him just a second to recover. He reached up and pinched her ass.

She laughed. "Don't like that attitude?"

"On the contrary, it's pretty fucking hot."

Then he slid a finger inside of her. He was finger fucking a future queen. Not just every guy got to say that.

Her eyes slid shut again and her head fell back. Her knuckles got white as she gripped the table and she gave out a long, low moan. "*Yes.*"

He continued, stroking in and out, just watching her face.

Then he added his thumb to her clit, circling slowly. God, giving this woman pleasure made him think that maybe he could get used to bowing, as a matter of fact. Paying homage like this couldn't be all bad.

Then she lifted a hand to a breast and started to play with one of her nipples.

Holy shit. Yeah, he was going to be worshiping this woman for a very long time.

He leaned in. "Here, let me." He fastened his mouth around the nipple and gave it a long, hard suck as he thrust a second finger inside of her with the first.

She arched her back and the table wobbled. Knox steadied her and the table with his unoccupied hand and felt a surge of satisfaction go through him.

He would enjoy every fucking minute of making this woman come apart. She was fierce and bold and smart and just *better* than about ninety-nine percent of the people he knew. And better than ninety-nine point five percent of the people walking the planet. The fact that she wanted anything to do with him was amazing and the fact that she would let him put his mouth and hands on her like this was truly a privilege.

"I've always said you were a handful," he said against her breast, switching to the other side, giving that nipple a hard suck and then a little flick with his tongue.

She reached up and grasped the back of his head, her fingers curling into his hair. "Good thing you have two hands then."

She had too much sass for this moment. She was supposed to be mindless and breathless.

He needed to do something about that.

He let her nipple go and kissed his way down her torso till he got to where his fingers were working in and out. He replaced his thumb with his tongue, swirling around her clit as he continued to thrust his fingers deep.

Her fingers gripped his hair tighter, and she spread her knees wider. The table tilted again and sure enough, the lamp wobbled with it.

But Knox was too busy to worry about stabilizing anything except Fiona. In fact, he didn't want to stabilize Fiona at all. He wanted to send her tipping and tumbling and careening over the edge of sanity.

Much as she had done to him.

He swirled his tongue again a few times, thrusting in and out, slowly increasing his speed as he felt her inner muscles tightening around him.

Then he curled his fingers against her G-spot and sucked on her clit.

"My God, yes. Knox. Please don't stop."

Not ever. He was never going to stop pleasuring this woman. Doing whatever she needed him to do.

A few minutes later, he gave her another hard suck and suddenly her body bowed and her pussy clenched around his fingers. The table tipped forward and the lamp went crashing to the floor as she came hard, calling his name.

The ripples of pleasure continued for a few moments and he lifted his head and slowed his strokes, watching her face and reading her body.

Eventually, she gave a long, happy sigh and slumped against the wall, and he eased his fingers from her. He lifted them to his lips and sucked them clean as her eyes fluttered open.

Her gaze was riveted on his mouth as he made sure to get every delicious drop.

Then he stood, leaned in, bracing his hands on the table on either side of her hips, and took her mouth in a long, sweet, deep kiss.

When he finally let her up for air, she blinked up at him. "Holy crap. That was good."

"Understatement," he agreed.

He felt more satisfied in that moment after making Fiona come like that, than he had in the last several times of coming himself. Even with other people. Though, those were a vague memory. He hadn't been with anyone else since he'd first met Fiona Grady in Ellie's bar.

They stayed like that, just looking into each other's eyes, both breathing hard for nearly another minute. Finally, she wiggled a little. "I didn't notice before, but this table is really better for the fucking, and not as comfortable for the blissful aftermath."

He chuckled, and scooped her up, setting her on her feet.

"Okay, let's go downstairs. We'll have a beer while we talk."

She froze. "Just like that? We're just gonna go talk now?"

"I think you need some clothes on. But, yeah, that's next on the agenda."

She looked at the table, then down at her naked body, then up at him. "Wow, I guess my seduction skills are a little rustier than I thought."

He lifted a hand and ran his thumb over her lower lip. "You got exactly what you said you needed. I think this worked out pretty well."

"And what about you?"

"Oh, I got exactly what I needed too."

Making her happy, finally tasting her like that, making her mindless, yet not completely losing his own mind.

He was feeling pretty good right now.

She stomped over to where her clothes were still rumpled on the floor. "Does the offer for borrowing a shirt still stand?"

"Sure. Help yourself to whatever you want. You know where the bedroom is."

She'd napped at his house on one of her trips to Autre after she'd been out all night on a rescue. She usually stayed with Charlie and Griffin but she'd asked if she could crash on his couch that day because "Landrys can't even take their shoes off quietly." He totally understood. But he'd insisted she take a bed. He'd meant the guestroom, of course. Pre-otter adoption. But he'd found her passed out in *his* bed when he'd gotten home from work.

"You're not going to come in there with me?" she asked, clutching her clothes to her naked body and turning so he could still see her very perfect, very enticing ass.

"Nope."

"Who's the chicken now?"

"You know how much I love an agenda and sticking to a routine. I said I'd give you an orgasm and then we were going to talk. We're right on schedule."

She blew out a breath. "Note to self, don't fall for a perfectionistic nerd ever again."

She turned on her heel and stomped toward his bedroom.

And only three thoughts rattled around in Knox's head. One, she was absolutely the most gorgeous woman he'd ever seen. With or without her clothes on. Two, she said she'd fallen for him. And three, she wasn't going to be falling for *anyone* else ever again, nerd or not, if he had anything to say about it.

8

Muttering under her breath about stubborn, nerdy, hot men while her body was still tingling and melty from the orgasm her favorite stubborn, nerdy, hot man had given her, Fiona stalked into Knox's bedroom.

He didn't want to have sex? Really? He could still resist after what he'd just done to her in the hallway? She kind of hated him right now.

But damn, just putting you up on that table and then kneeling on the floor like that?

Yeah, yeah. She'd *liked* that. It wasn't that she hadn't liked it. But she wanted more.

And he didn't? What. The. Hell.

She rummaged through his drawers, throwing the stuff that wouldn't work over her shoulder, letting it land on the floor and the edge of the bed. And leaving it there. That would drive him nuts.

Of course she also had to pick a *huge* guy who had ginormous shirts. And otters that got *her* clothes wet.

She felt herself smiling at the thought of his otters, and

firmly put a frown back in place. No. She was mad. And frustrated.

But not as frustrated as before, thanks to his tongue...

She slammed the drawer. Everything in the drawer smelled like him and her lady parts were not over his tongue and that smell was making them start asking *can we do that again? Like now? Like right now?*

She stomped to his closet and pulled the door open. A button-down shirt would be easier to wear. She pulled a light blue shirt from a hanger and slipped it on. She rolled the sleeves up, several times, until they were at her elbows and then buttoned it to the point where she had two long ends that she could tie up at her waist.

As she jerked the ends to make the knot, she admitted that she would probably never be over Knox's tongue. Dammit. She needed to get dressed and get downstairs and get whatever this *conversation* was going to be over with. Because she was not one-hundred percent sure that she would not beg him to put her up on his kitchen table, and any other table he had. If that was all he was going to do, then maybe they should just do that *a lot.*

She looked around for a place to hang her wet shirt and bra. The headboard of his bed looked perfect. And if that bugged him later when he went to bed and made him think dirty thoughts about her and regret not taking things further in the hallway, too bad.

And if it didn't...she was definitely doing something wrong.

"Okay, what are you asking for? Other than a great big, wide ocean between us?" she asked as she padded into his kitchen.

He was leaning against the counter with a beer in hand, reading on his phone.

He looked up. His gaze heated slightly at the sight of her in his shirt. He cleared his throat. "I have to tell you a story first. You willing to listen?"

"Is it something personal about you?"

"Yes."

Her eyes widened. "Wait, you're going to tell me something *personal?*"

"Yep."

"And not like your favorite color or what you like on your pizza or something dumb. Something actually personal that matters?"

"You don't care what I like on my pizza? That could cause problems."

"Knox."

He smiled. "Yes. Something personal that matters."

"Whoa."

"I know."

She laughed softly at his self-deprecating answer. "Okay, yes, I'll listen. But you realize this story better be good."

He nodded. "I realize. You want a beer?"

"I'm going to need alcohol?"

"Just tryin' to be a good host."

She studied his face. Yeah, she was going to need alcohol. "You got something better than beer?"

"No. But I have things *other* than beer. You need something more queenly than plain ol' beer?"

She rolled her eyes. "Yeah, something like that." She didn't like beer. But she and Knox had never had drinks together, so he wouldn't know that. They hadn't done a lot of things together. So how could she possibly be thinking about giving up a *throne* for him?

Wait. Was she thinking about giving up her throne *for him?* She'd already given the damned thing up ten years ago. Now she was planning to go back. But *now* she was re-thinking *that?* Since when? And because of Knox?

Of course you are. Remember the tongue?

But...it wasn't about his tongue.

She sighed. She really had zero experience being in love, but she supposed that's what this was. Still. Her crown really was pretty awesome. It had real emeralds in it.

"I don't have anything older than I am and nothing more expensive than about thirty bucks, sorry," Knox said.

She took a seat on a stool across the breakfast bar in his gigantic kitchen and watched as he moved around the space, pulling out two glasses and then a few bottles from a lower cupboard.

"What are you making me?"

"I'm gonna mix you something I think you'll like. Not too sweet, not too tart. A mix of a few interesting things that go pretty great together."

"Why do I think this is some kind of analogy?"

"Yeah, it's definitely not simple, but worth the work. A lot like you."

She shook her head. "I thought you weren't going to seduce me."

"This is seducing you?"

"Whenever you get sweet and flirty, it's a little seductive."

"I'll keep that in mind."

"As if you didn't know it."

"I can honestly tell you I don't give it a lot of thought. I guess the sweet and flirty just sort of happens when you're around." He started pouring from the various bottles.

She knew not many people saw him like this. Otherwise, there would be a line of women waiting to get permits for all kinds of things at city hall every damned day. He was pretty freaking irresistible when he let his guard down. And wasn't annoyed with her about something.

"Just like that. That totally sounds like a line, but from you, I'm not so sure it is. You definitely don't seem like the type of guy to bend over backwards to impress anyone. Especially a woman."

He didn't look up as he stirred the concoction. "What makes you say that?"

"Honestly? You don't seem like the type of guy who really wants a woman around. You don't like complications. Certainly in your work life, but I'm sure that extends to your personal life. And let's face it, even the most straightforward, low maintenance woman is a complication."

He crossed to the fridge and pulled out another beer. He twisted the cap off and poured it into a glass. Then he carried both glasses to where she sat. He placed the one with the pale yellow drink in front of her. She was far more intrigued than she wanted to be.

"People in general are complications." He lifted his beer and took a sip. "People come with expectations. They also come with emotions. Expectations and emotions don't always mix very well."

Fiona lifted her glass and took a little sip. It was sweet and tart with a definite lemon flavor and another that she couldn't quite place. "Wow," she nodded. "What is this?"

"Lemon vodka, lemon juice, and St. Germain."

"I love it."

"Told you."

She took another sip. "So this drink is actually an analogy. I had no expectations. So my reaction to it is fine either way. No emotions involved, right? I'm not disappointed, you're not offended."

He gave a soft chuckle. "Yeah, I guess so."

"Okay, so tell me the story. This explanation of why an affair between the two of us is best conducted over a great distance with lots of time in between seeing one another."

"Want to go back on the back patio?"

"So I can see the back of my new house?" She gave him a little smirk. "Or so my bodyguard can keep an eye on me?"

"Actually, he's Saoirse's bodyguard. And she's over there with him right now. I can probably do whatever I want to you."

A ribbon of heat twirled through her. She shifted on the stool and lifted a shoulder nonchalantly. "Technically that's true. Of course, he protects me whenever I'm with her."

Knox was actually frowning. "By default."

"Well, yes. But that's because she's important. She's the next queen of Cara."

"Until you take back your abdication. Plus, you're the king's granddaughter. That doesn't matter unless you're going to take the throne?"

"Well, it matters. On some level. But not as much as Saoirse." She tipped her head studying him. "Wait, you're bothered by this. You're bothered that I'm not actually protected? You realize that most people, probably every woman you've ever dated before, has not had a bodyguard."

"Nor have they had a reason to need one."

"But I don't have a reason to need one. I'm no longer in line for the throne. No one cares about me."

"I never even heard of Cara before the other day. Does anyone else really know about it? Are there other people out there who are trying to disrupt the line of succession to the throne?"

Fiona shrugged again. "I don't actually know. I think it's my grandfather being overprotective and a great excuse to keep tabs on me. There have never been any threats to Saoirse. But my grandfather says he has reason to believe that my father's death was not an accident."

Knox's scowled deepened. "What happened?"

"Car accident. Late one night on a quiet road. He went off the side of a mountain and wasn't discovered till the next day. It was ruled an accident but my grandfather either came up with the theory himself or had people give him the idea that there was foul play."

"You don't believe that?"

"I don't really have an opinion either way. It killed my father, whatever it was. That's what I care about. The throne and rule of Cara didn't matter to me at the time. I was about Saoirse's age, and honestly—" She paused.

She knew that a lot of people back home saw her as selfish and couldn't believe that she had turned her back on her kingdom, but she rarely talked about it or admitted her feelings out loud. She was sure that it would sound selfish and suddenly she didn't know if she wanted Knox's opinion about the whole thing. Mostly she went around not caring what people thought. Actually, mostly, she went around not thinking about Cara and her relationship to the throne at all. All of this had become a daily part of her thought process only in the past three months.

"What were you going to say?" Knox pressed.

She traced a finger around the top of her glass. "At the time and up to rather recently, I didn't really care if the throne turned over or the line of succession in my family ended. I told you that I've always kind of thought that Cara should be a democracy and have leadership that was elected by its people. I've been against the idea of the monarchy for years."

"You sound like you are possibly changing your mind about that."

She shook her head. She wasn't ready to go into this. She'd just started having some of these thoughts herself and was definitely not ready to articulate them. "No way, you got me to stay by telling me that *you* have a personal story for me. Let's hear it."

"Okay, front porch then."

"Why does the story need to be told outside?"

He gave her a grin and reached over to take her glass. "It's my experience that all stories are best when you're sitting outside listening to the frogs and the crickets and waiting for the stars to come out."

She couldn't help her soft chuckle as she slid off the stool and followed him to the front door. These small town boys. They were something. When she'd first met Knox, she would never have guessed that he was a front-porch-sitting-stargazing type. But again, these layers were getting to her.

He held the screen door open for her and she stepped out onto the wooden porch and headed for the swing. He settled next to her and handed her glass back. She took a long drink. Yeah, this was really good.

He started the swing swaying and stretched an arm across the back, resting it behind her, not touching her, but warming the air behind her upper back and neck and causing tingles to dance up her neck to her scalp.

"So there's some woman who ruined you for all other women? Or at least relationships?"

"Yep."

Her eyes got wide and she twisted on the seat. "You had a serious girlfriend and it ended badly enough that you don't want to have anymore?"

"That's not what I said. There was a serious relationship that taught me how my relationships should go. And what I should *not* do next time."

She tucked her foot up under her butt. "Well, I have to hear this. Not only are you telling me something personal, but you're actually admitting something went wrong and it was your fault?"

"Brat. Never said I was perfect." His tone was light though.

She knew he knew he was a perfectionist and that everyone around him knew it too.

"You're very aware that you come off as always thinking you're right, aren't you?"

"That's kind of the pot calling the kettle black."

She grimaced slightly. He was right, of course. Generally, she came off as very confident and prepared. Because, well, she usually was. But her self-esteem and assuredness had definitely taken a hit over the past three months. It was amazing what a grandfather could do. Of course, hers was a king. She liked to think that he came with a little extra pompousness and that his disapproving frowns were particularly effective and well-honed.

"Okay, spill," she told Knox, wanting a distraction from all of her own issues.

"Okay. Her name is Shannon."

He got a softer, affectionate smile on his face when he said her name and Fiona instantly hated the woman.

Ugh. This being crazy about Knox was really irritating.

"She was a local Autre girl," Knox went on. "Couple years behind me in high school so we didn't date until she'd gone away to college and came home. She's a baker. Amazing. She set up her own business out of her house and sold locally as well as online."

"And she was as sweet as her confections?" Fiona asked sarcastically.

"She is. She's kind and funny and everyone likes her. Figured we'd get married and stay right here in Autre."

"Is? She's still around."

"Yep." He lifted his beer.

Wow, Fiona had kind of expected the jab of jealousy but she had not planned on it being quite so sharp.

But of course Knox had gone ga-ga for a woman completely opposite of Fiona. She was sweet with lions, and tigers, and bears. Literally. And zebras and seals and giraffes and anything else with fur and four legs. But there were many humans who would laugh at the idea of someone calling her sweet. And they'd be right.

She also couldn't bake worth a shit.

"Did you propose to her?" Fiona asked, sounding pouty and hating it.

He lifted a big shoulder. "Didn't get to it, but I looked at rings."

Ugh. Well, at least he hadn't actually asked her.

Fiona rested her elbow on the back of the swing and started twirling her hair, feeling restless. "So you were in love with her?"

Knox slid her a glance. "I thought so at the time."

"And what do you think now?"

She couldn't say why exactly that was so important to her. Other than the fact that the idea that Knox had been in love really bugged her. Which was unfair. She hadn't known him back then and it wasn't like she had any claim to him. Even now they were just barely discussing having an affair. It wasn't like they were seriously committed or talking about a monogamous relationship that was going to end in marriage.

And that jab to her chest got even sharper.

She was being ridiculous. She had not come to Autre the first time, or *this* time, thinking about marriage. She had a lot of shit going on in her life. She'd always had a lot of shit going on in her life. Her life was full and busy and exciting and she didn't have time to devote to a relationship like that. She had never been serious about marriage and she had no right to be thinking about it now with everything with her life so up in the air.

She certainly couldn't be upset about Knox thinking about it with a girl years ago.

"Yeah, I was in love with her," he said. "But she wasn't in love with me. At least not enough to make it work."

"Yeah, tell me about the breakup," Fiona said grumpily. "I'd rather hear about that."

He gave her a knowing grin but continued the story. "She had a dream of opening a bakery. So I encouraged her. In fact, I sat down with her and drew up a business plan, ran numbers, got all the Is dotted and the Ts crossed. Even went and looked at buildings with her. She wanted to be in a little bigger area, of course, so looked at some buildings on the outskirts of New Orleans. But then I started worrying for her."

"Worrying for her? Like about her safety?"

"No, saying things like *new businesses often fail. And here's a list of all your competitors and how long they've been in business, and your specialty is whoopie pies but the survey that I conducted showed that most people go to bakeries for things like cupcakes and macarons.*"

"You did a survey for her?"

"Yeah, hired a company. Cost a ton too."

"Did she ask you to do that?"

"Nope."

Ah. "And how did she respond to all of this helpful criticism?"

"Poorly. She didn't think I was being very supportive."

Fiona nodded. "And then what?"

"I tried to pull back. But I'm a pretty intense guy." Knox blew out a breath and gave her another glance.

Fiona chuckled. "No kidding."

"I tend to be all in or all out on something. I did believe in her and her bakery. But once I knew about it and how important it was to her, I had a hard time just leaving it alone. I was constantly giving her advice, looking things up that she didn't ask me to, asking her how things were going, dropping by. Eventually it just got to be too much. *I* got to be too much. She wanted her business to be her business and she felt that I was too involved. And a know-it-all. We fought all the time. And eventually, we broke up."

Fiona thought about that. Knox *was* a very intense guy. When he believed in something, he did it with his whole heart. That was, in part, why Autre was such a great place.

His job as city manager of his beloved hometown was pretty much a perfect fit. He was a perfectionist so everything got done amazingly well, and he truly believed in the city and its people and making them the best they could be. His tendency to push people to do things better and bigger and to follow the rules worked here because it was his job, and he had the authority to do that. If he thought someone's yard needed to be cleaned up or a building needed to be painted, he could make that happen.

But with a girlfriend, she could see where that might be annoying. She supposed.

"Did Shannon ever tell you to back off?"

"Not in so many words. But I should have realized."

"She just bit her tongue."

"She realized I was trying to help. But eventually, I was just too much."

Fiona frowned. That sounded like bullshit. If the woman didn't want his input, she should have told him. "Were you brokenhearted?"

"I thought so. But I think maybe I was just more irritated that she didn't appreciate my input."

Fiona laughed. "Okay, and you're totally over her now?"

"Yeah. She opened the bakery and it's hugely successful in spite of the fact that she sells several different kinds of whoopie pies. In fact, she sends me a dozen of them every year on my birthday with a note that says, *Told you so.*"

Fiona laughed out loud at that. "I like *that* about her."

Knox nodded. "I'm happy for her. I've stopped by several times and I send people in there whenever they ask for bakery recommendations. We just obviously weren't a good fit in a long-term romantic relationship."

Well, thank God for that. Fiona didn't expect to ever try Shannon's whoopie pies, but it seemed that Knox really was over it all.

"So you've never been serious about anyone else since Shannon?"

"Once. Kendall."

"And what happened with Kendall?" Yes, Fiona wrinkled her nose when she said *Kendall*. She didn't care.

"She lived over an hour away. We kept it very superficial. Just fun. Didn't get involved in anything with her work or her personal life other than what we did together."

Ugh. Sounded exactly like what he wanted with her. "And?"

"She fell for me and moved to Autre to get more serious."

"Oh." She sipped from her drink. She knew the answer to her next question, but she finally asked, "How'd that go?"

"Lasted about four months. I held back for about a month, still not getting involved after I learned more about her work as a counselor with at risk teens."

Ew. A do-gooder. Fiona rolled her eyes and took another drink.

"But by week five I was planning a fundraiser to build a youth center here in Autre and had signed up for training to help on the crisis hotline."

Fiona's eyebrows rose. "Well, that's really nice..."

"Sure. Until we had a huge argument about how I always go overboard and think I know best."

She narrowed her eyes. "What did you do?"

"By month three, I'd agreed to let two foster kids stay with me and then I wanted to start adoption proceedings and I asked her to marry me. Married couples have an easier time adopting."

Fiona just stared at him.

Wow.

That was...a lot.

And totally in character.

He'd adopted three otters she'd asked him to simply look after temporarily. Yeah, he would have been all in on...anything a woman he cared about brought to him.

Fiona blew out a little breath. He definitely got involved.

"And then what?"

"She told me she couldn't handle me. She said she'd made a mistake coming to Autre, packed up, and moved."

"Back to where she'd been?"

"Farther actually. I think she's in Tennessee now. We...didn't stay in touch."

Fiona couldn't stand that. She reached out and put a hand on his arm. "So you think that things are only good when there's distance and time between you. When the woman is right there, all the time, in your everyday life, you get too involved."

"And end up overstepping and pushing her away by just being too much."

Fiona felt another jab in her chest, but this one wasn't jealousy. Or annoyance. This was a pain for Knox thinking that a woman he really cared about, maybe could have even loved, would get sick of him.

"So now you don't date at all?"

"Now I only date women who live far enough away that I don't see them regularly and who aren't...passionate."

Fiona frowned. "Who aren't passionate about their work?"

"Yes. That. And women who are laid-back and just go with the flow. About everything."

"That does *not* describe me."

"No. No, it doesn't."

He finished his beer and leaned to set the glass on the porch, then looked over at her.

"I love passionate women. I love that you're bold and ballsy. I can't resist you, Fi."

Her heart thumped hard at those words. And the look on his face. He was definitely an intense guy. But she loved that. She felt like his emotions were reaching out and drawing her in.

"And that's why this set-up with us is perfect. You have an

amazing job that you care about passionately. But not only will you be far away doing it, I am under *no* delusion that you want or need my input. You've made that very clear from day one. Even when everyone else in this town is calling me to solve problems, and assuming I'm in charge of all the paperwork and details, you've been on top of that before I even open my mouth." He reached for a strand of her hair, running it between his fingers. "And I think I've finally learned my lesson. I love strong, fearless women who don't actually need me. Who just want me. I can be your break from the stress. I can be the fun, the haven you escape to after you've been out kicking ass and saving the world. And I will leave your work the fuck alone."

Fiona just sat staring at him.

She had absolutely no idea what to say to that.

Of course she didn't *need* him. And yes, she definitely wanted him.

Coming to Autre as a break from everything, as an escape, as a haven was...well, what she'd been doing for nearly two years now. Sure, she'd been bringing them rescues and "helping" them build their animal park and sanctuary but when she was here, she hung out with some of the best people she knew. She laughed, and ate amazing food, and drank, and flirted, and basked in the knowledge that not only did these people *get* her, but she could depend on them and share her passion with them. And have a hell of a good time even in the midst of a hurricane clean-up or sitting in a jail cell.

And as of Christmas she'd thought she was going to add some screaming orgasms via their hot city manager to the agenda each time.

Yeah, haven was a pretty damned good word for it.

"So you *want* me to be queen?" she finally asked.

He gave a soft chuckle, twisting the strand of hair around his index finger. "What would you say if I came over to your new house and told you that you had to paint the shutters a certain color or that your grass was too long?"

"I'd probably tell you to fuck off."

"Exactly. I *need* to be with a queen. Someone who will tell me to back off. And not just call it quits."

The desire to grab him and hug him twisted through her. She hated that he felt like these women he'd cared about had given up on him because they hadn't cared about him enough in return.

But maybe that's what they'd done.

They hadn't told him that while they didn't need him helping with their business decisions, they still *wanted* him.

Those women were idiots.

"In Cara, you'll have your dream job with a wildlife sanctuary that will be run exactly the way you know it should be," he went on, making his case. "We'll see each other as often as we can. We'll text and Facetime in between."

"I'll be running *a country*. Not just a petting zoo, Knox."

He shrugged. "A small country."

She frowned.

He laughed. "I'm kidding. But you'll surround yourself with great people to help."

"It's a *nine* hour flight."

"It's ten hours from New York to Honolulu. People do those kinds of flights all the time."

"Every weekend?"

"We'll do every *third* then." He leaned in. "I really want this. I really want *you*."

And what was she supposed to say to that?

If only she hadn't experienced his magic tongue. That had been a really big miscalculation on her part.

But it wasn't his tongue—okay, it wasn't *just* his tongue. She really hated that he felt he was only good at relationships where he wasn't so *involved*.

She lifted a hand to his face. His beard was soft against her hand. "Well, I'm not going anywhere for a few months."

He nodded. "And your grandfather has to agree you can have the throne back, right?"

She sighed. "He and I have some talking to do. And yes, he has to agree to me abdicating my abdication or...whatever." She shook her head. "I really don't know how that would all work. He's been very focused on getting Saoirse back to Cara as soon as possible."

Even Knox was frowning. "Why?"

"Well, this might surprise you, but I was so pissed about the whole conversation that I walked out before I really got all the details," Fiona said dryly. "But I do know he wants her to go to school there. She needs to learn the local customs and the history of the island and all of that. And, frankly, to be queen, she should probably be *from* there."

"I guess all little girls want to be princesses right? How's Saoirse feel about it all?"

It seemed that Knox was trying for a lighter tone, but his expression gave away that he was actually concerned.

Fiona shrugged. "She's always known that in some far off distant future, she'll be Queen. She knows she's a princess. But...she's only *nine*. She wants to run around and play with her friends and teach baby otters to swim. She doesn't want to talk about politics and economics and international relations."

"Surely none of that would be a concern right now."

"She's the heir. My grandfather's heart isn't good. He's had three heart attacks. Whenever he is no longer able to rule, Saoirse is next in line."

"What if she's ten years old when that happens?"

"As crazy as it sounds, that's the way it's set up. She would actually take the throne. She would have a ton of advisors, of course. And my mother and grandmother—and I guess me and Colin—there to help her. My grandmother would possibly be queen by proxy or something weird like that. But that's the thing, she would have no idea what she was doing, nor would we."

"So that's another reason you're doing this. Taking back the throne," he said. "Not just for the animal sanctuary, but because you can't imagine Saoirse having to take on that responsibility."

"No, I can't. And I'm not sure I want her to ever have to take on that responsibility. She should have a *choice*. She should at least get to be a kid. Without knowing that all of this is looming in her future. Then when she's an adult, she can choose. If she feels compelled to take this on, and it interests her, then great. If it turns out that politics and foreign relations and all of that is her jam, then that's amazing. But if she wants to be a veterinarian or a schoolteacher or an astronaut, she should have that choice too. I hate the idea that her whole future would be decided for her like this."

Knox's jaw clenched under her palm, and she stroked her hand over his beard.

"There are a lot of reasons you should go." His voice was gruff. "You can have it all. You can help save the world. You can do it on your own terms. You can save your daughter from having to make these huge decisions. And you can still have Autre and me and whatever else you want."

He made it seem simple. So why were her guts all twisted up?

"Can I have you naked right now upstairs in your bedroom?"

His eyes flared with heat, and she felt that muscle jump under her palm again.

"I should be able to say no, but you know very well that you can get whatever you want from me."

"But you really don't want that right now."

"I do. Of course. It's just the closer we get while you're right here, right in my backyard, the more of a pain in the ass I'm going to be. I'm going to want to know everything about Cara. I'm going to get closer to Saoirse. And probably be overly protective of her. I'm going to want to help design your new animal preserve in Cara."

She wanted all of that. But he didn't.

Fiona gave a soft snort. "And all along you've been convincing everyone that *I* am the pain in *your* ass."

He nodded. "Pretty good trick, right?"

God, she really was in love with him. Dammit. She leaned in and pressed her lips against his. "Well, then I better get going." She handed him her glass and stood.

She started down the steps without looking back, knowing that was just easier.

"Hey, you're stealing my shirt?"

"Borrowing it."

"So I'll get it back?"

She wasn't so sure about that. Sleeping in this shirt every night seemed like a really great idea. But she called over her shoulder, "If you need it, I just live right over there." She pointed at her new, temporary house.

"Brat."

But she heard affection in his voice, and it made her stomach swoop. She made herself keep walking.

Some of this was really going to take some practice.

Like the queenly strut she was trying out.

And the walking away from Knox.

9

Three days later, Knox still did not have his shirt back. And he was quite certain he wasn't getting it back.

He didn't mind.

He still had Fiona's shirt and bra hanging on the headboard of his bedroom as well and he was happy to keep it there until she came back over the next time.

And there would be a next time.

He was going to try to hold out but he knew better than to think that he wouldn't have her back in his bed before she went to Cara. He'd been honest with her about his personality and his tendency to get completely wrapped up in whatever he was doing. Including dating a woman.

Fiona wouldn't tolerate that. She would hate having him all up in her business. So the longer he tried to resist, the better. Every day was a closer tick to her trip to Cara and moving four thousand miles away from him.

He realized that sounded idiotic. A man in love with a woman should want her not just right next door, but in his bed every single night wrapped in his arms.

And that would be fine. If he was okay with having her in

his life for only three to six months. But he wasn't. He wanted long term with this woman and the only way to do that was to limit his involvement in her life.

"Well, good morning to you," Elyse, the bubbly redhead who owned and operated Bad Habit, greeted as he came up to the counter.

"Mornin'." Knox gave her a grin. "My usual, please. Is Zander upstairs?"

"Are you okay? You sure you want your usual?"

"Why do you ask?"

"Either you've already had a lot of caffeine this morning or you're on some other major upper. You sure you want to add to whatever's coursing through your bloodstream?"

He narrowed his eyes but gave her a little smile. "I don't know what you're talking about."

"I've never seen you come in the door with a grin on your face. What are you on, Knox?"

Love. But he wasn't going to say that out loud. "I'm just in a good mood."

"Like I said, I've never seen *that* when you come in through that door. Maybe about half that on your way back out. But only after you've had a lemon scone and I don't have any of those this morning."

Knox laughed and shook his head. "Yes, the usual. A large. It'll be the first I've had this morning."

She braced her hands on the counter and leaned in. "Then it must be a girl."

Dammit. "Maybe I just got some good news."

"I see a lot of faces in and out of here. I see good news faces. I see I-just-got-laid faces. And I see I'm-in-love faces. I'd say yours is more the latter."

"Just pour the coffee, Elyse," Knox told her. She was no Ellie Landry, but maybe she was a little more insightful than he'd given her credit for.

Or he was more transparent than he'd realized.

Elyse turned away with a laugh. "Okay, but you might want to tamp that down a bit before you go upstairs. Zander's definitely not gonna let you off the hook that easy."

She had a point. Zander Landry was an investigator and interrogator for a living. He wasn't going to let Knox get away with *I got some good news*. Still, as Knox stirred his butterscotch latte, he couldn't dampen his smile. Dammit. He was just happy.

"Almost forgot. I have something for you."

Knox turned back toward the counter.

"Shannon left these especially for you." Elise held out a box.

Shannon. He was so glad he'd told Fiona about her the other night. Shannon supplied all the baked goods to Bad Habit thanks to Knox. When they'd opened and started offering pastries, he'd suggested they hook up with Shannon. As a local girl she'd given them a good discount, and it had turned into a wonderful partnership.

"Really? What is it?" Maybe she was trying out a new flavor of whoopie pie.

"She left a note."

He opened the box first. It was half a dozen macarons. He laughed and peeled open the note. *Bestseller. You were right.* Then she'd drawn a little heart and signed it with just an *S*.

His grin grew even bigger. He really did like being right. It happened a lot, but he enjoyed it every time.

Maybe Fiona needed to talk to Shannon. Shannon could absolutely attest to the fact that what he'd figured out about him and relationships was *right*.

He climbed the stairs to the loft with his coffee in one hand and the box under his arm. He found Zander at their usual table, tucked under the eaves at the back. Very few people came up to the upper level this time of day. He and

Zander had discovered the quiet out-of-the-way nook two years ago when their search for a place to sit and talk uninterrupted—and complaint-free—in Autre had come up empty.

There was no way Knox or Zander could go anywhere in Autre without being interrupted by complaints and people needing them. And certainly not if they were together. The city manager and town cop were always the ones people went to with every tiny problem and finding them together at the same time was a jackpot for the town whiners.

They'd each been to Bad Habit alone and one day Zander had suggested it as a perfect out-of-the-way meeting spot. No one in Bad cared that they were here and no one in Autre came to Bad for much other than an occasional stop at the restaurant on the edge of town for dinner and live music. The coffee shop was a great hide-out.

Zander watched Knox approach. "What the hell is with you?" Zander asked as soon as Knox was sitting.

"What do you mean?"

"What's with the big grin on your face?"

"What is with everybody hating people grinning?"

"It has nothing to do with grinning. It's about *you*. You never look like that. Especially this early in the morning. It's unnerving." Zander narrowed his eyes. "What's going on?"

"Nothing. Just in a good mood."

"Is it about the lampposts?"

Knox couldn't help that his grin grew. "They look pretty great, don't they?" The new lampposts had been put in two days ago, thanks to their "benefactor" paying more than double for the extra time and manpower it took.

"They do look great. Seriously. If you care about that kind of stuff," Zander said, clearly implying that most people didn't.

"People *think* they don't care about that kind of stuff," Knox said. "But they love when shit looks good and hate when it doesn't. It affects people's attitudes toward things. Even if they don't consciously notice."

Zander rolled his eyes. "I'll take your word for it."

"And you can't convince me that you didn't notice those hibiscus trees along Main."

Zander actually laughed at that. "Well, I'm naturally very observant."

"And they look great," Knox said, sitting back and propping an ankle on his opposite knee as he took a sip of his coffee. They did. He didn't need validation from Zander.

"They do look great. Just not sure they affect my entire *attitude*."

"They do," Knox told him confidently.

Zander chuckled and shook his head. "Well, most people don't lose sleep over that shit. Guess it's a good thing we have you."

"I didn't lose sleep over any of it."

"Tell me you didn't put in extra hours making sure all those lamps and trees and everything were delivered on time and that we had the right people to get them put in and planted."

"Well, sure, I might've worked a little overtime. That's not the same thing." He'd slept like a baby once those trees had been planted.

Zander nodded. "Exactly."

Knox just rolled his eyes. "That's why not everybody can be a city manager."

"That's a good point. After one day I would point my boat out to the Gulf and never come back."

Knox just flipped him off and took another sip of coffee. He didn't believe Zander for a second. Sure, not everyone was cut out to think about and manage tiny details. Or to take dozens of phone calls every day about petty gripes and complaints. Or to oversee all the moving parts to massive projects and manage budgets of hundreds of thousands of dollars. But Zander

Landry cared about their town just as much as Knox did. And he was willing to work overtime, lose sleep, and, in his own way, do whatever it took.

They were actually cut from the same cloth. They were guys who had grown up in a town they loved, and they wanted to give back. They had come home to use their strengths and talents to make their town the best it could be. They just had different strengths and talents.

City manager of Autre, Louisiana, was the perfect job for Knox. It allowed him to be a semi-obsessed perfectionist, boss people around, and make his hometown an amazing place to live.

"Did you notice the new awnings and the great paint job. And the very smooth and even sidewalk downtown as well?" Knox teased Zander as he passed the box of macarons to his friend.

Zander dug into the box and pulled one out. "I did not. Because I don't care about awnings or the fact that the storefronts are now a really nice pale yellow, with dark green accents that match the awnings and lampposts and the new planters that have gorgeous hibiscus trees growing in them." He popped the macaron into his mouth.

Knox gave him a grin. "Fair enough. I wouldn't expect a busy, macho guy like you to notice details like that."

Zander nodded.

"But so how are things going with the security detail for the king's arrival?" Knox asked, reaching for what looked like a lemon macaron. It wasn't a scone, but if Shannon had made it, it had to be just about as good.

"I've done about as much as I can do. Just waiting on my next meeting to fill in the details."

"Your next meeting? When's that? And with who?"

Zander's eyes moved from Knox's to something past Knox's shoulder. "About right now."

Knox stopped mid-chew and looked over his shoulder. Colin had just come up the steps. With four men behind him.

Knox turned back to Zander. "You're having a party? Thought this was our spot."

"Our spot? You brought Fiona here."

"You brought Caroline here first."

"First of all, Caroline and I got our coffee to go. Second of all, you had Fiona here before I had Caroline here. You two went out for ice cream a year ago."

"We also got the ice cream to go. I've never had anybody at this table but you."

Zander put a hand over his heart and nodded solemnly. "Me too, man. But this is important. And we couldn't meet in Autre or we would raise all kinds of eyebrows. But this doesn't mean anything. It's just a meeting."

Knox sighed. "Okay. You're just damn lucky that I believe that Colin and Fiona aren't sleeping together."

Zander gave him a smirk. "The fact that Fiona is in town now and that huge grin that you had coming up the stairs today..."

"Just a good mood, man."

"A good mood that started about the time Fiona got to town."

"Coincidence."

Zander snorted. "You know that you're not actually fooling anyone, right? You and she both know that we *all* know that something is going on with you guys, right?"

"Well, thank you," Knox told him.

"Thank me for what?"

"If something *wasn't* going on with me and her I'd be a fucking idiot, right? So thank you for not thinking that of me."

Zander chuckled as Colin pulled out the chair right next to Knox and sat. "Gentlemen," he greeted.

The other four men pulled another table and chairs up next

to theirs and settled in as if they'd been meeting and drinking coffee here with Zander and Knox for months.

Zander made the introductions. "Knox, this is Cian Grady, Fiona's younger brother."

Knox felt himself straighten slightly, and then tried to not look obvious. He coughed. "Nice to meet you."

"You too." Cian gave him a grin.

"And this is her other brother, Torin Grady," Zander said, tipping his head to the other man who looked a lot like Cian, minus the huge smile.

"I'm Knox."

"I know."

Right.

"And these guys are Jonah and Henry. They're Torin and Cian's bodyguards."

"As far as anyone knows, we're just their best mates," Henry said with a distinctly British accent. "But we stick close and try to keep them out of trouble."

"Of course, you know Colin," Zander said. "He's in charge of Fiona's security."

Knox frowned at the other man. "Well, kind of. If she's around Saoirse, right?"

Colin shook his head. "Still a little pissed about that?"

Knox narrowed his eyes. "Yeah. A little." More than a little.

"Okay," Zander said, clearly trying to take charge. "We're here to talk about the security concerns and plan for when King Diarmuid comes to town."

"The king's traveling with Oisin O'Connor, his best friend and main advisor," Colin said. "They'll be arriving on a private jet at the New Orleans airport because the king would like to see some of the city before driving down here. But, there are no official meetings planned while he's in the U.S., so for the most part, everything should seem like a grandfather coming to visit his grandchildren for a few days and nothing more. I think Jonah, Henry, and I can handle security for the most part."

"His wife doesn't travel with him?" Knox asked.

"No. The queen hates flying and also thinks it's ridiculous he feels the need to check up on his grown grandchildren," Colin said. He gave the two princes a smile. "Of course, King Diarmuid keeps a lot of his grandchildren's...shenanigans... from her so she doesn't realize that the need might be justified to some extent."

Cian laughed and Torin smiled, but neither denied it, or seemed to take offense.

"What about your mother?" Knox asked Fiona's brothers. "She didn't want to come visit?"

"Our grandfather is a pain in the ass," Torin said bluntly. "Mother spends as little time with him as possible. She certainly wouldn't take a nine hour one-way plane ride with him if she had the choice. She comes on her own."

Knox nodded. "Got it." He turned to Zander. "So you don't need to bring in any extra personnel?"

"I've asked Spencer and Wyatt to be available if we need anyone extra to come hang out. But Theo and Michael will be around to make sure we have some backup if needed."

"Who are they?" Jonah asked.

"Spencer is FBI. Wyatt is special forces with the Coast Guard. They're cousins of mine so can come to town and hang out without arousing any suspicion that anything unusual is going on. They're pretty handy to have around when you need someone watching your back," Zander said. "Theo is one of our game wardens and Michael is our fire chief. They are a part of our community so will be around anyway, but if we fill them in on our special guest, they'll certainly keep an extra eye out."

Colin, Jonah, and Henry shared a look.

"Can we trust them to keep it under wraps?" Colin asked.

"Absolutely," Knox said before Zander could respond.

This was Fiona they were talking about. He trusted all of those guys to do whatever was asked of them. If it came to protecting someone, they would do everything they could. But in addition to whatever Zander was going to tell them, Knox was going to make a special point to let them know that keeping Fiona and her family safe was the highest priority to *him*.

"Sounds like it will be fairly low-key while your grandfather is here," Zander summarized. "No grand balls or red carpets."

Cian laughed. "No, not because our grandfather doesn't like that stuff, but because he wouldn't want to throw a party for any of us."

Torin nodded. "Especially with me and Cian here. Actually witnessing us having a good time might kill him. And then we're all screwed."

"I mean we're already forsaking our country and our family's legacy," Cian agreed. "Can't actually be *enjoying it* too."

"So you're not excited to see your grandfather and he isn't that thrilled about seeing you?" Knox asked. "Why are you here?"

"We're here for Fiona," Torin said, meeting Knox's gaze directly.

Knox felt a little knock against his rib cage. "She asked you?"

Torin shook his head. "She wouldn't ask that of us. She knows how we feel about things. But we know she can use the moral support. He's..."

"A dick to her," Cian said.

Torin nodded. "And we want her to know that we have her back."

Knox liked that Fiona's brothers were offering moral support but something niggled at him. "Your grandfather just wants her and Saoirse back in Cara, right? Doesn't it make sense? Someone will have to take over when he's gone. Or if he is unable to do the job. Makes sense for them to be there. To know how things work. To show the people Saoirse and Fiona care. That all seems reasonable," Knox said.

The brothers exchanged another glance.

"Sure," Cian said. "But he's hard on her. Dismisses the things that are important to her. Makes her feel like she's done a poor job with Saoirse."

"Saoirse's great," Knox said with a frown. "What's his problem?"

"He's just trying to manipulate Fiona into going home," Torin said.

"Well, bringing *Saoirse* home," Cian interjected.

Torin nodded. "Right. He wants Saoirse as queen. Not Fiona."

"Why?" Knox asked, feeling his gut knot.

"Because Saoirse is more malleable and less opinionated. At least so far. Another reason he doesn't want her in the U.S. and away from his influence much longer. And because if Fiona takes the throne, she could easily hold it for another fifty, even sixty years. It's not like that's temporary. He knows what Fiona will do with her power."

"And what's that?"

"Reform. *Everything*."

Ah. Yes. He didn't even need to know specifics to know that was exactly what she would do.

"He thinks Saoirse will keep things his way?" Knox asked.

"He thinks his chances with Saoirse are better than with anyone else," Torin said with a lift of one shoulder.

Knox blew out a breath.

"Which is why we came to meet *you*," Cian added.

"Me? Why?"

"Because we were under the impression that you might want her and Saoirse to stay."

Knox's frown deepened. "Why would you think that?"

Zander gave a soft snort beside him. Knox ignored him.

"Because we know Colin was given reason to think he needed to do a background check on you months ago," Cian said. "Because we've seen her since we got here. Because Saoirse is crazy about you. Because you've been working to make the town look good to impress the king."

Okay, so maybe he and Fiona hadn't been as good at hiding their feelings from everyone as they'd thought. And maybe his heart thunked a little harder hearing that Saoirse was crazy about him. But no, he did not want her to stay. The opposite in fact.

"Fiona would be an amazing queen. There are a lot of things that she could do with Cara if she was in charge. Maybe all of that reform needs to happen."

"Well, yes, but—" Torin's gaze narrowed on Knox. "Wait. You want her to go?"

"I care about her," Knox said. "I know that Fiona is good at anything she does. If she's passionate about it, the way she'd lead Cara would be amazing."

"Exactly. *If* she's passionate about it."

Knox and Torin sat staring at one another for several beats.

Fuck.

Fuck, fuck, fuck.

She had to want to go. That was all he could think about. He wanted her to be passionate and happy and to have everything she wanted.

Being in charge—completely, totally in charge—seemed perfect for Fiona.

Didn't it?

"Well, dammit," Cian finally said. "We thought maybe you were going to step up and propose or something. Give Grandfather another reason not to pressure her to return home."

Knox felt his teeth grinding together and consciously

relaxed his jaw. "Her incredible work and her daughter and her *life* aren't enough for him?"

"Obviously not," Torin said dryly. "She's had all of that for a long time."

"I thought she *wanted* to go back."

"She's going back out of obligation. Someone has to do it. The king has health issues, Fiona doesn't want this to all fall in Saoirse's lap, she does want reform—"

"Why don't *you* fucking do it?" Knox broke in.

Torin lifted a brow. "Excuse me?"

"If you're so concerned about her and don't agree that she should be pressured to go back, why don't *you* do it? You don't have a job or a kid. And you're in line ahead of her, aren't you?"

"I am older than Fiona," Torin said. "But I do have things keeping me here. As does Cian. Things that Fiona doesn't want us to give up."

"Such as?"

"Torin can't complete his doctorate degree or do his research on Cara," Cian said. "We're a small, isolated country. Mostly self-sufficient. Our grandfather has preferred to keep us mostly cut off from the rest of the world. But Torin is doing work that fights famine and drought in the poorest areas of the world and works to *connect* countries and people—"

"It's okay," Torin interrupted his brother. He leveled his gaze on Knox. "I have work here. Cian has..." He looked at the younger prince. "Unfinished business here in the states that he wouldn't be able to complete if he returned to Cara. Certainly if he took the throne."

"And, of course, there's the issue of Linnea," Henry piped up. He was grinning in spite of the tension.

"Shut up, Henry," Torin muttered.

"What's a Linnea?" Zander asked.

"Linnea Olsen is the Danish heiress that one of the O'Grady

brothers has to marry if and when he returns to Cara and takes the throne," Jonah said, also grinning.

Cian groaned. "Seriously, shut up."

"Um...what?" Zander asked.

"Their grandfather lost them—"

"Henry," Torin tried to interrupt.

"—in a three-day long poker tournament," Henry went on.

"Seriously, man," Cian said over the top of his friend and bodyguard.

"—to one of his best friends," Henry said.

"When Torin was what? Four years old?" Jonah asked, adding to the story.

"Five, I think," Colin said. "Torin was five and Cian was three. So Declan would have been seven." He was laughing by now.

"Your grandfather *bet you* in a poker tournament?" Zander asked, seemingly needing clarification. "Like, he was out of money and said, 'you want one of my grandsons?'"

Cian and Torin just sighed.

But Colin nodded. "Pretty much. But they were at least open-minded enough to say that it just had to be one of them."

He, Henry, and Jonah all laughed.

Cian and Torin did not.

Despite...everything...Knox couldn't help but ask, "You don't like Linnea?"

"She's the worst," Cian said.

"Completely. And she hates us too," Torin said.

"Both of you?" Dammit if Knox didn't feel his lips twitching.

"All three of us," Torin clarified.

"How well do you know her?" Zander asked.

"Our grandfathers were friends so we spent time together growing up," Torin said.

Cian shuddered. "Lots of time."

"It's been ten years since either of them saw her," Jonah

made sure to point out. "They have no idea what adult Linnea is like."

"Doesn't matter. Arranged marriages are very last century," Cian informed him.

"So you'll just let your sister give up her entire life and go back to your country to rule instead?" Knox asked, jerking them all back to the original topic.

"I thought you didn't want her to stay. That you thought she'd make an amazing queen," Torin said.

Yeah, fuck. That was all true.

"Hey, if our grandfather had listened to Torin, none of this would even be an issue," Cian said. "Torin wrote up a whole plan about how to transition Cara to a partially representative government over ten years. When he laughed us out of the room was when we packed up to leave. It's been ten years right about now. Just think how different this all could have been if he'd just listened."

Well...fuck again.

This was complicated. Moreso than he'd thought.

He should have expected that. It had to do with Fiona. And his feelings for her. And trying to have a relationship.

Yeah, complicated seemed right on track.

Knox opened his mouth to respond again, but Zander's phone rang just then. He pulled it out and glanced down. "I gotta go." He looked up. "So security needs—do I need to get a hold of Spencer, Wyatt, Theo and the others?"

Colin nodded. "If Theo and Michael can hang out casually and no one will think it's strange and start asking questions, then it never hurts to have extra people here."

"What kind of threats are there exactly?" Knox asked. "Since you let Fiona go off by herself all the time, to rescue animals and wade through floodwaters and stomp around in earthquake rubble and wildfires, I'm just curious what kind of threats you're worried about here exactly."

Yes, now he was testy. Because now he had to wonder if going to Cara was the right call for Fiona. And if it wasn't, what that meant for them? Her giraffes were here now. She clearly loved Autre and the people here more than she had liked being in Florida. So if she didn't go to Cara, would she stay here? And if so...then what?

Yeah, he was definitely no longer in a good mood.

Colin rolled his eyes. "Not sure if you've ever tried to keep Fiona from doing something that she wanted to do, but that doesn't generally work out well for anyone. And those aren't exactly the kind of risks we're talking about here."

"That's why I'm asking," Knox said, frowning at the man. "None of you worry about Fiona's physical safety, it seems. I'm just curious why everyone's worried about Cian and Torin enough that they both need bodyguards."

"Listen, we don't make the rules," Cian said with a shrug. "It's a bloodline thing. All heirs have to be protected until they produce an heir. Fiona did that, so she's off the hook for having a twenty-four seven watchdog." He glanced at Henry. "No offense."

"That's one of the least offensive things you've said to me," Henry told him.

"Our older brother has security as well," Torin confirmed. "Even though he fires them on a regular basis. And they have to stay about hundred feet away from him at all times. But they're there."

"Seems that none of the rest of you should really matter with Saoirse around," Knox said.

Torin nodded. "That's what we were hoping. But apparently not."

"You're older than Fiona," Zander said. "Wouldn't you be first in line if your oldest brother says no?"

"We all abdicated," Torin said. "Saoirse is the only one who hasn't told our grandfather to go fuck himself."

"So *we're* the backups to Saoirse," Cian said. "She's first in line now. But if something happens to her, then one of us gets dragged back to Cara. I suppose they'd start with Declan, but the dude has enough money to have his own security who are very loyal to *him* and could make that a very difficult feat. Really, Torin is the one who's most in trouble if Saoirse wises up."

"You're pretty removed from the whole thing, huh?" Zander asked the youngest of the O'Gradys.

Cian sat back and linked his hands behind his head. "I'm also doing my absolute best to be sure that our grandfather would be *appalled* if the throne came to me. Just in case."

Torin rolled his eyes. Henry, the man in charge of keeping Cian alive and out of any lifelong prison sentences, sighed heavily.

"You know I could make you disappear," Jonah said to Torin.

"That sounds ominous." Torin gave his bodyguard a concerned look.

"I mean go into hiding. That'd be easy."

Henry nodded.

"You'd do that?" Torin asked. "Help me forsake my people?"

Jonah lifted his shoulder. "My loyalty is to you, not Cara."

"My grandfather would quit paying you."

Jonah grinned. "Your grandfather already doesn't pay me enough to put up with you. Since I've known you, I've been hungover more times, eaten more strange food, had more wounds need stitches, and been threatened in more languages than any man should in his lifetime."

Knox looked back and forth between the two men.

They definitely had the vibe of best friends who were practically like brothers. And they clearly had history. He supposed being assigned to be the bodyguard to a young, handsome, wealthy prince and sticking by his side no matter what for over ten years could've pretty easily turned into a real friendship.

"This is all very strange," Knox finally said. "I've been thinking about this like Fiona's been offered an amazing job overseeing a giant company. Like it's a promotion she should take."

But fuck, there was so much to all of this. This was damned messy for her family.

Colin shrugged. "There are some similarities."

"And I've been focused on things like Cara being safer for her," Knox added. "If she's there, fully in charge, there will be no poachers, no animal abusers, no law enforcement with questionable morals."

Colin nodded. "All true."

He thought about it. "What kind of weather does Cara get?"

"Pretty mild for the most part. Cool summers, mild winters. Cloudy a lot."

"You guys get wildfires?"

"Not really. It's pretty wet."

"Earthquakes?"

"No."

"Hurricanes?"

"Some kinda major ocean storms can come through. There are mudslides on occasion. Rockslides once in a while."

Knox nodded. He knew that there was no place on earth that didn't have *any* naturally occurring disasters or weather to deal with. But those all sounded pretty mild. Especially considering some of the things that Fiona had already faced.

She'd be safer in Cara. She'd be calling the shots. And she wouldn't be right in his backyard, where he would be constantly tempted to get all mixed up in everything. Even the little bit that her brothers had told him about her family and their history had fascinated him and made him want to delve into more.

"So what else do you need from me?" Knox asked Zander as the other man slid his chair back and stood.

"Well, now that we have those planters and lampposts in place, I think that we're doing pretty well," Zander said sarcastically.

Knox flipped him off.

Zander laughed. "Actually, I think we've got what we need."

"Well, I can give you one more piece of advice," Cian said.

Knox looked over at Fiona's younger brother. "Okay."

"Just keep her from fighting with him."

"Your grandfather?"

"Yeah. Just help her tone things down a bit. No major drama, nothing controversial, just keep things even keel while he's here."

"Funny coming from you," Henry said.

"I know," Cian agreed. "So you know it's especially important. I'll do my best to play the part of the spoiled playboy with a Peter Pan complex who likes to party, just to make her look better next to me, of course, but she could use a friend who can help her keep her cool."

All of the men who knew him snorted.

"Well, don't hurt yourself with that *acting* job," Jonah said.

"Thanks. I'll be okay," Cian told him. He looked at Knox again. "She just needs to make it through a few days without giving him any more reason to be on her ass and pressuring her to get home sooner. Fiona has a plan."

Knox felt his gut tighten. Fiona had definitely seemed less feisty since she'd been in Autre this time. But he figured that it had a lot to do with her being pissed at him. And the plan to move her animals to Autre and her daughter back to Cara.

"So just keep things cool while he's here. Just help as much as you can to keep a lid on anything that would make our grandfather think that Fiona doesn't have her priorities straight."

"Fiona's priorities are fine. Saoirse is a great kid," Knox said.

Cian held up a hand. "Dude, we're on the same page. We love that kid. She's amazing. And if she ever does end up being the queen, Cara will be super lucky. But our grandfather's old-fashioned and he hasn't spent a lot of time around her, and he's trying to guilt Fiona into coming home."

"And he's just kind of an asshole," Torin added.

Cian nodded. "And there's that."

"Okay," Knox said. "Even keel. No drama."

Sure. Even keel. No drama. Just nice and normal. Nothing strange or out of the ordinary.

In Autre, Louisiana.

They were probably pretty screwed.

10

S he knew everything about giraffes.

That was not something most women her age could say. She also knew a hell of a lot about lions and tigers, zebras, wombats—thanks to her daughter—otters, of course, and many other animals. But she knew *everything* about giraffes.

She could not, however, bake a decent batch of cookies. Apparently.

Fiona shook her head. She simply wanted to have milk and cookies waiting for her daughter when she got out of school. She wanted to sit at the fucking kitchen table and ask Saoirse how her day had been. She wanted to eat cookies and talk to her nine-year-old about normal nine-year-old things. And wombats.

Those might not be a typical nine-year-old topic, but they were interesting and made Saoirse light up. And if Fiona could be certain where the hell Saoirse would be living for the next several years, she could find a way to get her some. They were critically endangered but...that's what Fiona did. She helped endangered animals.

And hell, she might soon have half an island dedicated to

saving things like wombats. Cara would be the perfect sanctuary to partner with one of the wombat sanctuaries in Australia and Fiona could definitely impress whoever needed to be impressed with her experience and knowledge.

She could totally get Saoirse some of her favorite animals *and* help increase the number of wombats in the world.

After her daughter's trained-by-the-royal-security-forces bodyguard had made them both multi-grain waffles with raspberries and white chocolate sauce and then taken her daughter to school, Fiona had spent her day teaching an alpaca farmer how to tell if a giraffe's perineum was swelling, watching a lion play with his adopted German shepherd mom, helping a wildlife reality TV star round up a bunch of goats from the knitting club they'd crashed, and catching two parrots and separating them before a group of kindergartners came through the petting zoo and learned to say *you're an asshole* from the birds.

Just a typical day in the life of a working single mom.

Ha. She wasn't sure what the other moms at Autre Elementary would think of her.

She couldn't even pull off simple chocolate chip cookies.

Which was why she was walking toward Shannon's Sweets.

She'd managed to wait four days.

It had been *four days* since Knox had done his tongue-magic on her and she'd not only avoided *him*, but she'd avoided coming to his ex-girlfriend's bakery.

But now...well, she needed cookies. And they couldn't be grocery store cookies or Saoirse—and maybe more importantly, Colin—would know she hadn't baked them.

So this was the first bakery to come to mind. It wasn't like she knew all the bakeries in the area. Autre didn't have one and she was new to the area and she had it on good authority that this baker was amazing. Fiona rolled her eyes.

Sure it had been a twenty-eight mile drive, and yes, Cora

probably could've made her some pretty kickass cookies if she'd asked, but Colin and Saoirse had been eating Cora's food almost exclusively since coming to Autre. They might have recognized those cookies.

Besides, this seemed like a great way to show herself that she didn't care that Knox's ex was a phenomenal baker or that they were still friends.

Okay, that was a lie. She wanted to lay eyes on Shannon. For some reason, she really needed to see the woman who had broken Knox's heart.

She stepped into the bakery, which was, as much as she wanted to hate it, actually quite adorable. It also smelled like heaven.

There was a woman standing behind the counter. She was tall, thin, with big boobs, and blonde hair.

She was absolutely gorgeous.

And Fiona found herself praying that it was *not* Shannon.

The woman gave her a bright smile. "Hi. Welcome to Shannon's Sweets."

Fiona smiled back as she approached the counter. "Hi. I need some cookies. I know you specialize in whoopie pies, but I'm hoping you have some basics too?"

The woman laughed softly. "Of course. I wouldn't dare have a bakery without cookies."

"Great, then you're going to save my day. In fact, I probably need to take a few dozen and stick them in the freezer."

If she wanted to do this milk and cookies thing again anytime soon, she was going to need all the help she could get.

She just hoped that the burnt cookie smell was out of her house by the time Saoirse got home.

"I'm Shannon. I'm the owner here."

Fiona felt her smile die. Of course, the woman was beautiful. Knox wouldn't date someone who wasn't. The jerk. But she was also the exact opposite of Fiona in pretty much every way.

Not just the curves and the blonde hair and the six or seven extra inches of height, but the woman could bake.

"Hi. I'm Fiona."

"You're a new customer. Welcome."

"Yeah. I'm actually here on the recommendation of a friend. From Autre." She might as well be upfront about this.

Recognition flickered in Shannon's eyes. She gave a little nod. "Fiona isn't a real common name. Who's the friend?"

"Knox."

Shannon gave another little nod. "You're his new girlfriend."

Now it was Fiona's turn to be surprised. "Where did you hear that?"

"Well, Elyse over at the coffee shop in Bad said that Knox has been in an especially good mood lately. She thought maybe he was seeing someone. So she asked Regan, the physical therapist who works with kids at the petting zoo, who asked around, and your name came up."

Yep, that was pretty much how she would have expected the grapevine to work. She hadn't met Regan but she'd heard all about how the PT was using the alpacas and a few of the other animals in her therapy programs with kids. She and Jordan were friends, which meant she could have casually brought Knox up in conversation...

"And you're interested in who Knox is seeing?" Fiona asked.

"Of course. I want him to be happy."

Fiona studied the other woman. She seemed sincere. "Knox is a really good guy."

"He definitely is. And it sounds like maybe you're the type of woman to keep him on his toes."

"You got more information about me than just my name then."

"The woman who's been bringing wild animals to the tiny town in Louisiana? The girl who showed up with giraffes? Yeah, people are talking about more than just your name. Or even about you and Knox."

Fiona supposed that was fair. Giraffes showing up overnight in a tiny town that had previously—at least as of a couple years ago—been known for their swamp boat tours and alligator sightings probably got a little buzz.

"He keeps me on my toes too."

Shannon laughed. "Isn't that how it should be?"

Fiona didn't really want to talk about Knox with his ex-girlfriend, she realized. Things hadn't worked out between them. Shannon didn't seem threatened by her. Or like she was trying to give Fiona any trouble. Knox had actually seemed pretty well-adjusted except for the fact that his experience with Shannon had convinced him that he could only have long-distance relationships.

"So I'm looking for chocolate chip cookies. And anything else you recommend."

"Great. I can definitely do that. And might I suggest the whoopie pies? They're one of my best sellers."

Right. The item that Knox had been convinced would be a terrible idea. Was that a hint that Knox wasn't always right about everything? No matter how adamant he got?

Fiona met the other woman's eyes. And yes, she could read quite clearly that that was indeed exactly what Shannon was saying.

Fiona nodded. "I think I'd love a couple of those too."

"You *made* cookies?" Saoirse ran to the table and stared at the plate of cookies and glass of milk.

"Hi. Good to see you. And, you don't have to act like I split the atom or cured cancer," Fiona said.

Torin had followed Colin and Saoirse into the house, but

headed for the living room, while Colin went for the apartment they'd finished for him just two days ago.

Fiona knew her brothers were only hanging out in Autre until after their grandfather's visit, but she wondered what they'd both do after that. She suspected Cian might stay in Autre. At least until she and Saoirse and Colin headed to Cara.

Cian lived in Orlando because Fiona had lived in Orlando. Henry "took care" of him, in the strictest sense—Henry kept Cian from dying. Or being killed—but Henry didn't feed or clothe or even tell the prince "no" very often. But Cian liked to be around people. And if he wasn't getting that human interaction at Fiona's, where she, Saoirse, Colin, and lots of tourists were, then he looked for it at night clubs and parties and other places where he could more easily get in trouble. So her door was always open. Even when she wasn't home.

It had made it easy to convince people that Colin was one of her brothers, because he spent a lot of time with her actual brothers.

Torin was different. He didn't need people. He loved books and loved to travel. It wasn't uncommon for him to pack up and take off to some other country with less than twenty-four hours notice. Jonah was, fortunately, laid-back and had no problem packing up with no notice. Because, of course, Torin couldn't go alone. It was often just the two of them. At least until they got to their destination. Then it wasn't unusual for Torin to head to the dumpiest, most unassuming pub, restaurant, or café and sit down and start talking to the locals. He loved seedy bars, sketchy clubs, and rundown hotels.

It drove Jonah nuts. Fiona had heard him complain numerous times to Henry and Colin.

Cian was the one who was fun, outgoing, and most likely to lose all his money and his clothes in a spontaneous strip poker game and still declare it the best night of his life.

Torin was the one most likely to spend a month sleeping in

a shack on a farm in Argentina, learning to cook from the farmer's wife and to plant crops with the farmer and his son, then accidentally getting engaged to the farmer's daughter, and needing Jonah to sneak him out in the dead of night to avoid being married the next morning. But not before he left a huge pile of money for the family.

Her brothers both ended up in ridiculous situations. But for very different reasons.

She didn't envy either of their bodyguards.

"What is splitting the atom?" Saoirse asked as she climbed up on the chair next to Fiona.

That was a good question. And Fiona couldn't really tell her. "I just mean you don't have to act like it's such a big deal. They're just cookies."

She was glad Colin wasn't here. He'd know instantly she hadn't made these. It had taken her living with Colin Daly for only about a month for her to realize that she was going to get nothing past him and would never be able to lie to him. He was incredibly observant, never forgot anything, and had an extremely sensitive bullshit meter.

So she'd given up trying. She just did whatever she wanted and let Colin feel however he would about it.

It had definitely gotten better after Saoirse had been born. Considering his main focus had always been her daughter and not her, once Saoirse was detached from Fiona's body—at least most of the time—Colin had gotten far less irritable about Fiona and her activities and her attempts to keep him out of the loop. But man, those few months when he had been stuck to Fiona's side while she had still been carrying Saoirse had been awful. Colin was bossy as hell and really didn't care what anyone thought of him.

Except Saoirse. Her daughter had stolen his heart day one and the bond between them had never loosened.

He was firm with her and would do anything to keep her

safe, including piss her off and hurt her feelings. But for the most part they laughed and goofed around and he played and got silly with her in a way that was probably extremely sexy and swoony to any woman who didn't feel like he was just another brother and pain in her ass.

There had never been chemistry or sparks between Colin and Fiona, though over the years she had thought many times how much easier her life would be if there had been.

If only she and Colin could have fallen in love and he could have become Saoirse's stepfather, everything would've been so much simpler.

But no, in spite of his muscles and tattoos and beard and dark eyes and smirky grin, and the fact that he was wonderful with her daughter and could cook like a pro chef, Colin didn't do anything for Fiona.

And vice versa. In ten years of living together, they had, of course, had occasion to walk in on each other in various states of undress and see each other in intimate situations. But in spite of seeing her breasts at least three times that she could think of, Colin never seemed to have any kind of sexual feelings for her at all.

"These are really good, Mom," Saoirse told her, breaking into her thoughts.

They were *really* good. Fiona had of course sampled them on her drive back to Autre. Yes, Knox's ex was an absolutely amazing baker, just as reported.

Her whoopie pies in particular were amazing. He'd been really wrong about that.

"Thanks. How was your day?" she asked before Saoirse could ask more about the homemade cookies Fiona had *not* made.

"Good. We had to write about what we want to be when we grow up."

Fiona leaned in. "Oh. And how did that go?"

"Fine. I wrote about how I want to be President someday." Saoirse giggled.

"President, huh?"

"Well, I couldn't say Queen, but it's kind of the same thing."

They'd never kept Cara and the idea that Saoirse was meant to be the someday-queen from her. If nothing else, King Diarmuid himself had always made a point to talk to Saoirse about her future on the island and how important she was. So Saoirse had grown up knowing she was a princess, that someday she would be Queen, and that no one else could know about that.

"I guess it is kind of the same thing." *Except you're not elected, have no choice, and it's for life.* "Why not a veterinarian?"

It wasn't as if fourth grade was the first time this topic had come up. Saoirse always said she wanted to be a vet and work with giraffes and lions and elephants. Even *that* had seemed kind of out there. Imagine if she'd told them the truth about her future plans.

Except...being a wildlife vet really had been Saoirse's plans, at least until she'd turned eight and had thought that being a bodyguard might be cool—Fiona totally blamed Colin for that—and why the hell shouldn't she be able to pick one of those careers instead?

"I just was thinking about being Queen since Grandpa is coming," Saoirse said, reaching for another cookie. "But I knew I couldn't say that in school."

Fiona nodded. "Right. So what did the class say?"

"They laughed. They said nobody from Autre is ever going to be President."

Well, they hadn't met Bennett Baxter. "And what did you say?" Fiona asked.

"I just said, 'we'll see'. It'll be so funny when I have a crown and they have to bow when they see me." She giggled.

Fiona shook her head. "People don't bow for us, baby."

"They do on TV and movies."

"Yep. But that's not real life and none of *those* queens and kings are from Cara. We don't have rules like that."

"Oh." Saoirse thought about that for a minute. "Okay. But it *is* true that you can't tell me what my bedtime is or how much ice cream I can have when I'm Queen right?"

Fiona lifted a brow. "Who told you that?" But she knew.

"Uncle Cian."

"Uh-huh. Well, I'll still be your mom." She reached out and tickled Saoirse's side. She squealed and wiggled away. "And that means I'll always be looking out for you. Even when you're Queen."

Saoirse gave her a big smile. "I know. That's why I'll be so good at it."

Fiona felt her heart squeeze. "Yeah?"

"Uncle Cian said that too."

Huh.

"Oh, and I had a bloody nose after lunch."

Fiona frowned at the change of topic. "You had a bloody nose? Just all of a sudden?"

"All of a sudden after Jacob hit her," Colin said dryly as he strode back into the room, having changed into a pair of running shorts and a t-shirt.

"Jacob *hit* you?" Fiona asked her daughter. Then she looked at Colin, aghast.

"Listen to the rest of the story."

Colin dropped into a chair, looking unperturbed. No one was as protective of Saoirse as Colin.

Torin sauntered back into the room and reached for a cookie before taking the chair next to Saoirse. "What's going on?"

Fiona turned back to her daughter. "What happened?"

"Jacob was picking on Skylar again and I stepped in front of him."

"Was he trying to hit her?"

"Maybe," Saoirse said. "I didn't know what he was going to do. I just knew that someone had to be in front of her. He needed to know that I was going to protect her."

Saoirse was meeting her eyes but seemed completely unconcerned as she chewed.

"So you thought that Jacob was going to maybe hit Skylar, and you stepped in between them?" Fiona clarified.

Saoirse nodded. "And good thing. He did swing his arm and he hit me in the nose. If I hadn't been there, he would've hit Skylar."

"Then what happened?" Fiona asked. She glanced at Colin.

She knew at least part of what happened next. Colin had been instantly on high alert.

But she had to give her friend and daughter's bodyguard credit. Where he could certainly sweep in at any moment and defuse any situation, he often let Saoirse and the kids her age work through things. He would never let an adult threaten Saoirse, of course, but when it was one of her peers, he often let the situation play out. Saoirse needed to learn the ways of the world, and interactions and socialization with people her age were part of growing up.

Or so he told Fiona whenever she said, "What the hell, Colin?" about things like this.

She knew that Colin knew exactly how to take care of Saoirse. Fiona was always the one that Saoirse ran to first when she'd skinned her knee, or had a bad dream, or wanted to talk about wombats. But when she wasn't there, Saoirse, without hesitation, went to Colin.

"Well, the other kids came and stood there too then," Saoirse said.

"The other kids? More kids tried to come and hit you?"

Saoirse shook her head. "No. The other kids came and stood with me. Samuel and Sophia and Katie."

"I'm proud of you. It's always great to stand up for someone who needs help. I'm just...surprised."

"Why are you surprised, Mom?" Saoirse reached for another cookie.

Fiona plucked it from her fingers. "Three's enough."

Torin took the cookie from Fiona.

"I'm surprised," Fiona said to Saoirse as her brother settled back in his chair, also seemingly unperturbed by Saoirse getting hit. "Because it's a very brave thing to do when you're only nine. It's scary to have somebody trying to hit you."

"But it's what *you* do."

She looked at her daughter in surprise. "What's what I do?"

"You get between the bad people and the animals. The animals can't defend themselves, so you do. You're the one who protects them. And then other people come and stand with you."

Fiona felt her throat tighten and she looked over at Colin.

He gave her a little smile, but said nothing.

She swallowed hard. "How do you know I do that?" she asked Saoirse.

Saoirse rolled her eyes. "You've been doing it my whole life. Colin shows me the stuff online. He's always told me that's where you go when you're not at home. Skylar's a person so she can stand up for herself sometimes. But she's small and shy. So she sometimes needs somebody like me who's..." She looked at Colin. "What's the word you used?"

"Audacious."

Torin snorted.

Fiona looked at Colin with a little frown. "You told Saoirse she's audacious?"

He lifted a shoulder. "She is. She takes after her mom."

Fiona sighed. She wasn't going to get into the fact that there were a few not-so-complimentary synonyms for that word. He wasn't...wrong, exactly, in using it as an adjective for her. Or Saoirse.

"You're okay with her being the one who steps up like that?" Fiona asked Colin.

"It's okay, Mom," Saoirse said. "Somebody just has to be the first one. Then other people come."

Fiona focused on her daughter again. "That's easy for you to say. You've got a bodyguard. Not everyone has that. You're special. You can be brave because you know you have backup."

Saoirse nodded. "I know that. That's why I should be first."

Fiona thought about that. Maybe Saoirse should be first. She was right. Nothing bad would ever happen to her because Colin would always be there. If not Colin, then someone else. There'd been times when Colin had sent Cian and Henry, or Torin and Jonah. But Saoirse had never been alone. That did make her daughter special and maybe that meant she should be a leader.

That struck Fiona in the chest. It wasn't just the actual physical protection that Saoirse had. She had resources. She had a position that put her in a place where she could actually effect change.

Like you do.

"I want to be like you, Mom," Saoirse said. "I just want to do the right thing. You always have Colin and Cian and Torin and all your friends here. You have tons of people who will help you do good things. I think people who can do good things should. Because not everybody can."

It was getting harder to blink fast enough to keep her tears from falling as her daughter talked.

She looked at her brother. Torin seemed to have forgotten the cookie in his hand. He was looking at Saoirse as if she'd just hit *him*.

But Saoirse was right. About Saoirse, and Fiona, *and* Torin. Not everyone was given the same opportunities and resources and positions and power. So those who were, should use them. And they all had people who would stand beside them, or behind them, and help them.

"What about next time? What if you're not there and Skylar has to face Jacob by herself?" Fiona asked.

Saoirse nodded. "I was thinking about that. But don't you think that knowing that she had all of us there on her side today will help? Like next time, maybe she'll be a little braver because she knows that she's got friends and people who will support her."

Fiona smiled at her daughter. "Yeah. I think that will help a lot. I know how it feels when I go somewhere, and when I'm scared or nervous about what's going to happen. I think about all of the people who believe in what I'm doing and who think what I'm doing is right. It definitely helps."

"And I think it will help Jacob maybe not do it again," Saoirse said. "When someone knows that that many people don't agree with them and will stand up to them, that makes them think better the second time, doesn't it?"

Fiona sighed. It might work with nine-year-olds. She really hoped that it did. But it didn't seem to always work that way with grown-ups. Or if it made *one* of them think twice, there was always some other asshole waiting in the wings.

"Tell your mom the rest of the idea," Colin encouraged.

Saoirse nodded. "I think I should invite Jacob out to see the giraffes. And maybe have snow cones or something."

"You want to invite Jacob out to see the giraffes?" Fiona asked. ""Wouldn't you rather show them off to Skylar and your other friends?"

"Of course. Skylar and my other friends will get to see the giraffes a lot," Saoirse said. "But if I showed them to Jacob and tell him that if he keeps being a jerk, he never gets to see them again, that might matter. Maybe that'll make him try to be nicer. Because nice people get to do fun things."

Fiona looked at Colin. He was giving Saoirse a proud grin.

"You like that?" she asked.

"Good people get good things, bad people don't," Colin said.

"Seems like a pretty good lesson to teach a kid."

"You think it will make a difference?"

"I know that it puts the ball in his court. Then he's making the decision about how he behaves and is learning about the consequences. And it gives Saoirse a little bit of leverage." He grinned. "That's never a bad thing. And it teaches her how to use it in a positive way."

"Okay, well, if you invite Jacob over to see the giraffes, I think Skylar and all your other friends get to come too. And you have to be upfront with them that Jacob is going to be there and if Skylar doesn't want to be around him, you have to respect that and maybe give her a chance to come see the giraffes on her own. She shouldn't have to be around the boy who is treating her badly."

"I already decided that he has to apologize to her before he can come over," Saoirse said. "And then I thought I would have him come over by himself *after* everybody else gets to see the giraffes. He can come see them, but he doesn't get to have as much fun as everyone else. Until he's acting better."

Fiona nodded. "Sounds good."

"Can I go to Knox's and check on the otters?" Saoirse asked, sliding off her chair and already starting for the door.

"Wash your hands," Fiona said.

Her heart was hammering in her chest just from the mention of Knox. She so wanted to go over to see the otters with Saoirse, but she needed to stay away from him. "And you can only stay for a little bit. We have to talk about Cara and everything. Your grandfather will be here tomorrow."

Fiona had been giving Saoirse history lessons about their country and their family. Cian, Torin, and Colin had been helping. They'd been having dinner together for the past four nights and every night they talked about their relatives and what it had been like to grow up in Cara and had been quizzing Saoirse on facts about the country.

Saoirse groaned. "Why do I have to talk to you about it if I talk to Knox about it the whole time I'm over there?"

Fiona frowned. "What do you mean?"

"When I go over there, he talks to me about it too. He's been quizzing me the last three days."

Fiona sat up straighter. "Knox has been quizzing you about *Cara*?"

Saoirse sighed. "He looked up a whole bunch of stuff online and then he got a bunch of information from Uncle Cian and Uncle Torin. He even made flashcards."

Fiona stared at her daughter. Then she looked at her brother.

He popped another cookie into his mouth and shrugged.

"Is this true?"

He nodded.

"Why didn't you tell me that?"

"You never asked," he said around the cookie. He chewed and swallowed. "Figured the more quizzing, the better."

She didn't know exactly how to respond to that. Part of her wanted to laugh. That was a very Knox thing to do. At least if he really thought the nine-year-old should know every single tiny detail and fact about Cara. Flashcards were a very Knox thing. He was also very much the type to use Saoirse's love for the baby otters to get her to "study".

But Fiona also wanted to cry. He was so into Saoirse understanding everything about Cara so that her transition back to living in Cara and taking over the throne would be seamless.

Why was she madly in love with a man who couldn't wait to get rid of her?

Colin chuckled. "I can't help but like a guy who makes you speechless."

"Shut up," Fiona muttered.

"Can I go?" Saoirse asked with the backdoor already open.

Could she go hang out with a guy who made her smile and laugh and had baby otters and was quizzing her about the very information that Fiona wanted to cover with her tonight? What would possibly be a good reason to say no? Except that he was making *her* fall further in love with him at the same time.

"Yes, you can go." Then she glanced at the cookies. "Hey, wait a second." Fiona crossed to one of the cabinets and withdrew a plastic bag. She dumped the rest of the chocolate chip cookies inside, closed the top, and handed them to Saoirse.

"Hey!" Torin protested.

"Here, take these to him too," Fiona told Saoirse. "And tell him I got a history lesson today too."

Saoirse looked at her as if she was confused, but said, "Okay." Then she ran out the backdoor, across the yard, and up onto Knox's back porch.

Fiona stubbornly shut the door before she could see her hot neighbor when he answered.

11

F iona looked absolutely gorgeous. And miserable.

They were at Ellie's and the entire Landry clan had showed up to welcome her grandfather, King Diarmuid O'Grady, and his best friend and chief advisor, Oisin O'Connor, to Autre. Everything in town was done and looked amazing. Ellie's had even been cleaned up a bit and the Landry clan had...okay, not changed out of their typical denim and cotton attire, but had at least put clean jeans and boots on for the occasion.

Knox wondered if Fiona recognized the gesture.

He knew on most evenings, she would have, but she seemed nervous. Hell, he was too.

Diarmuid O'Grady, King of Cara, was an imposing figure. Even though he was wearing blue jeans and a button-down dress shirt. Much the way Knox dressed ninety-percent of the time. Still, there was something about the way the man carried himself, and looked at other people, and spoke that made it *seem* that he was dressed in...well, a fucking king's robe and crown. Maybe even with a scepter in his hand. Diarmuid had snow white hair and a beard and was 6'2" with a trim, athletic build and tanned skin that made him look easily ten years younger than he was.

He had flown into New Orleans, even though Bennett Baxter had offered them the use of his private airstrip. The one the millionaire used for *his* private jet. But Diarmuid had wanted to see a little of New Orleans and, it turned out, he'd wanted to rent and drive a cherry red Jag. It wasn't exactly understated. But it wasn't a limo and it wasn't a carriage pulled by white horses or something more "royal", Knox supposed.

The king was pleasant enough. Charming, even at times. But it was clear that rickety wooden tables, drinks served in Mason jars, and paper napkins were not his usual.

The Landrys, for their parts, were their usual friendly, jovial, loud selves. There were so many of them it was difficult for them not to be loud, but Knox noticed they'd all seemed to dial it back just a notch tonight.

He appreciated that. Even as it niggled a little at the back of his mind.

These were wonderful people. They were the reason that Fiona was in town. They, and their love for and passion for her animals and her causes, were what had made her think that Autre was a great place for her to settle.

They were her friends and her colleagues. She was especially close to Charlie and Naomi, who were the most outspoken animal advocates of all the women. And he expected her and Caroline to get very close as they spent more time together.

So while he appreciated the Landrys being on their best behavior, he hated that their usual might be perceived as too much for the king.

They had already covered all the pleasantries and introductions. King Diarmuid had complimented Kennedy on the town and she had introduced him to Knox. Charlie had been her usual charming self and had filled the king in on the family business, and how helpful and important Fiona had been to the overall enterprise. Ellie, Leo, and Cora, the older Landry generation and unofficial hosts of the evening, had kept the food and drink flowing.

So now they were on to more casual conversation and never one to truly appreciate a quiet moment, Owen Landry was telling them about his day with Cian as his co-pilot on the swamp boat tour with the bachelorette party.

"I'm givin' the guy a job, I swear," Owen declared. "The maid of honor was so hung over that she looked a little green before we even pulled away from the dock. She was wearin' this low-cut sundress and I knew she was gonna be puking before we were halfway to the first stop and I was afraid she was gonna pop right out of that dress as soon as she started heaving—"

Someone, probably his wife, Maddie, apparently elbowed him under the table, because he stopped, frowned, and then cleared his throat. "I thought she looked like she didn't feel very well and I was concerned that she would have some...trouble with her dress."

Cian laughed. "Oh, she was having all kinds of trouble."

"Well, she was *very* happy to sit next to you at the back of the boat," Owen said, giving Cian a grin. "Cian jumped in and appointed himself her personal babysitter. Talked her into buying a Boys of the Bayou t-shirt, cuddled up next to her on the seat, kept her near the edge so he could point her toward the water when she needed to pu...throw up, but kept her from pitching right overboard."

"He was out with the best mentor," Josh, Owen's cousin and business partner in the swamp boat tour company, said. "Owen's always been the one to volunteer first to go out with bachelorette parties."

Owen laughed. "I didn't even have to coach him. It's like he's a natural with pretty, skimpily dressed, drunk girls."

Henry and Jonah snorted.

Knox knew there were some very interesting stories in the young prince's past. But he also knew they weren't appropriate dinner conversation with Cian's grandfather.

"I might take you up on the job offer," Cian told Owen.

Owen's brow rose. "Yeah? 'Cuz, man, I'm serious. Not because of the pukey girl. You've got the right personality for it. Dealing with tourists all day takes being laid-back, and being able to laugh at just about anything, and charm just about anyone. But also bein' able to put your foot down when you're sick of someone's shit." He glanced at the king again and cleared his throat. "Stuff. Someone's stuff."

Cian seemed unconcerned about his grandfather. He leaned in. "Dude. I'm a spoiled, rich guy who was raised as a freakin' prince. Literally. Charm I can do, but I have no trouble telling people to piss off."

"It's true," Henry said. "Even when it's an absolutely terrible idea to do that."

Cian looked at his friend. "Your reflexes have gotten faster because of it though."

"Yeah, really sorry about that broken nose and the broken finger before I realized what a mouthy dumbass you were," Henry said dryly.

"Did those both happen at the same time or two different times?" Owen asked, grinning.

"Two times," Henry replied. "The finger was the second because *his* reflexes got better too and he got his hand up in front of his face."

There were several chuckles around the table.

"Ask him how many times *his* nose has been broken because of me," Cian said.

Knox noticed the king's clenched jaw and jumped in. "Are you thinking of staying here in Autre for a while?" he asked Cian. He hadn't known that was a possibility at all.

"I am," Cian said with a nod. "I can't live in Orlando alone."

Henry cleared his throat. "Thanks."

"You know what I mean," Cian told him. "I need at least four other people around to feel normal. But here—" He looked around the table. "It's *impossible* to be alone. I love it."

Again everyone laughed.

"So you're going to be a swamp boat captain."

Those were the first words King Diarmuid had spoken in several minutes.

Cian looked at his grandfather. "Yep. Dirty water, swamp critters, drunk pretty tourists. Sounds like my kind of thing, right?"

"Indeed." That did not sound complimentary. Or approving.

Cian seemed satisfied with that.

But hell, even if Cian was staying in Autre just to annoy his grandfather, he could still be helpful with the tour company. And if he had some fun, there was no harm in that.

But even if Cian didn't care that his grandfather clearly thought the job was beneath him, that bugged the shit out of Knox. The Landry family were some of the hardest working, biggest-hearted people he knew. They loved their business because it gave them a chance to show visitors their beloved Louisiana and the bayou. They told stories, gave history of the area, and introduced people to the culture down here that set southern Louisiana apart from everywhere else.

"Oh, Fiona, I wanted to talk to you about the trip to Texas," Naomi said.

Knox shot her a frown. But Naomi wasn't looking at him.

He supposed the other woman was trying to change the subject. And was diverting the conversation to the impressive work one of Diarmuid's grandchildren did. But he didn't know how Diarmuid felt about Fiona taking on these risky rescues.

Dammit, he was fighting the urge to take over the entire conversation.

Fiona shifted on her chair, sitting up a bit. She'd been very quiet as well. Knox wondered if she preferred Cian to be the center of attention—a role her younger brother clearly relished —because it kept Diarmuid's focus off of her. "Um, okay."

"We've been in contact with your friend, Kayla. She's hoping that we can drive down in a couple of days. Would you be able to go with us?"

Fiona glanced at her grandfather.

The king was watching her. "What's in Texas?" he asked.

"There's a guy who's breeding tigers and then selling them illegally."

"What does that have to do with you?"

"I'm just helping out."

"In what way?"

"Just offering advice. Resources."

"Oh, we were hoping you could come with us," Charlie broke in. "This will be our first one."

"Your first one?" Diarmuid repeated, turning toward Charlie.

"Our first rescue," she said brightly. "Once the guy is arrested, the tigers are going to need to be rehomed. We're going to be helping with that."

"I thought you were pulling back," Diarmuid said to Fiona.

"I am. I'm just giving them advice," Fiona shifted on her chair uncomfortably again.

Knox felt his gut tightening.

Charlie frowned. "Wait. You're pulling back? Does that mean that you want us to get to know Kayla so that we can help *her*? We're not going to be helping *you*?"

"We all help each other," Fiona said. She looked around the table. "This isn't really the right time for this. But yes, I want to connect you guys with my bigger network. I don't always need to be in the middle. Kayla can get in touch with you guys if she needs something. She can also bring new animals here when she has some that need a place. And if you have questions you can get a hold of her. She does what I do. And there are others."

"But we have you right here," Charlie said. "So we don't need to connect with Kayla."

Fiona took a deep breath and met her grandfather's eyes.

"Just in case there's ever a time when I'm not here. It's just good for you to have multiple resources."

Her grandfather's mouth pressed into a grim line but he didn't reply.

Charlie continued to look confused and concerned as she and Naomi shared a look. But she also didn't press.

Donovan, however, was not shy. "Why does that sound like you're leaving or dying or something?"

Fiona shook her head. "Not dying."

Donovan's eyebrows arched. "That doesn't mean you're not leaving."

Knox felt his jaw tighten. Fiona clearly didn't want to have this conversation right now in front of everyone. But this group was not great at dropping things.

He didn't know what her plan was for telling everyone she was going home to Cara. But certainly she didn't want to announce it in front of the entire group spontaneously like this. And she probably didn't want to do it in front of her grandfather.

Though it would be nice for him to see how upset everyone would be and how much they loved and would miss his grand-daughter.

Still, it was clear that in this moment, they needed to create a distraction.

"I think that—" he started.

Just then Ellie, Leo, and Cora all approached the table with dishes full of various desserts.

Ellie caught his eye and he realized she'd had the same thought.

God bless Ellie Landry.

But it was Cora Allain who actually caused the distraction.

She leaned over Oisin's shoulder to set bread pudding in front of him. And dropped it right into his lap.

"*Merde!*" she exclaimed.

The man looked up at her.

She immediately grabbed a napkin and reached for the spilled dessert, brushing the bread pudding from his pants onto the floor.

Knox couldn't see exactly where her hand was from across the table, but he could imagine.

The older man's face got red and he choked slightly as he started to stand. He grabbed Cora's wrist and the napkin. "It's fine. You didn't mean to."

"I just always get so clumsy around good-looking men. Your accent certainly doesn't help," Cora said, looking up at him. "And you certainly smell better than anything in my kitchen. I couldn't resist getting a little closer."

The entire table was quiet—which was in itself a feat—watching the interaction.

Oisin cleared his throat. "I'm sure I will survive a little bread pudding to the lap."

The man's accent was the thickest of any of the men from Cara. Diarmuid seemed to have toned his down some and Fiona's brothers could sound almost American, unless they wanted to turn their accent on. Colin's accent was obvious but not nearly as thick as Oisin's.

"Well, I shouldn't have taken my eyes off the plate. I probably shouldn't have been looking where I was looking in the first place," Cora said with a little self-deprecating smile.

There were actually a couple of gasps and at least two giggles around the table. Knox was definitely surprised, but when he thought about it, he knew he shouldn't have been.

Cora had been a bayou girl for seventy-some years. If the

younger girls who'd grown up in Autre were good at flirting, Cora was a pro.

"Well, I'm sure if the bread pudding is as good as everything else you've served, I'll enjoy it immensely. Even in my lap." Oisin told her.

They were still standing extremely close and Knox wondered if the other man remembered they had an audience.

"Well, it's going to be very difficult for you to taste it off of your *own* lap."

There were definitely some choking sounds around the table now. Even Oisin had to clear his throat.

If Knox didn't know Cora Allain, he would've thought that had accidentally come out sounding dirty. But he did know her. Cora was sweet, especially compared to Ellie, but she was sassy and she'd not only grown up on this bayou, she'd married a bayou boy of her own. And raised a couple. And had been helping Ellie keep *hers* in line all their lives. He'd seen her throw men twice her size out of the bar, throw pie, rolls, and more at Leo and his friends when they got mouthy, and throw an absolute *fit* when "her" Saints lost a game.

Yeah, the king's advisor had no idea who he was currently staring at like a smitten fool.

Knox quickly pulled his eyes away from Oisin and Cora to glance around the table. He was surrounded by intrigued and amused and delighted expressions.

Apparently, it had been a while since anyone had seen Cora flirting.

Knox caught Ellie's gaze again and she gave him a wink.

Yeah, this was very intentional. Still, he didn't think Cora was minding this a bit.

"Well, if you like her pudding, you should definitely try her pie," Ellie quipped as she finished setting dishes in front of her family.

Again, coughing commenced around the table.

Knox looked at Ellie. Of course *she'd* meant that exactly the way it sounded.

He looked at Fiona. She had her eyes closed and looked like she was trying to either keep from laughing or was counting to ten. Maybe both.

When they'd brought her grandfather here Knox hadn't realized that it was the older generation he was going to have to try to keep reined in.

Then Cian spoke up. "I mean, her pudding was my favorite until I got her pie in my mouth, O. Now I may never want any pie other than hers." Cian was grinning widely and shoveling a huge mouthful of said pie—bourbon pecan to be exact—into his mouth. "And we all know that's saying something."

Knox looked back to Fiona. This time she was definitely counting to ten.

"It's probably been a while since you've had any really good pie, though, right, O?" Torin, the *quiet* one, asked his grandfather's friend. "There's just no pie like this in Cara."

It was obvious that Oisin had been around long enough that he was more like an uncle to Fiona and her brothers than simply a colleague to their grandfather.

Fiona made a funny noise that he couldn't quite place and Knox had the urge to lean over and hug her.

He looked over at Diarmuid. He looked...resigned. Not pleased, but certainly not shocked. Though these people had a much different familial structure and background than the Landrys, they definitely had a similar feel with their teasing. Oisin, Henry, and Jonah had been a part of their lives for a very long time and seemed more like a part of the family than employees.

"Well, you need to be *very* careful with bayou pie," Ellie said, pointing at Cian with a spoon.

"And why is that?" Cian asked as he took one last huge bite of pie to clean his plate.

"It only takes one taste to get you proposing," she looked around the table. "Isn't that right, Bennett? Donovan? Griffin?"

Diarmuid looked at Charlie. "You bake?"

Charlie grinned and leaned closer to her fiancé. Yes, it was now official. She was wearing a big diamond on her left hand and everyone had been *loud* and thrilled when Charlie had announced that Griffin had finally, formally asked her to marry him a few days ago. "No. I don't bake."

Everyone around the table laughed.

The king nodded as if that had been the expected answer. He looked up at Ellie. "Oisin has been widowed for twenty years."

Ellie glanced at Cora and they all found that Cora and Oisin had moved slightly to the side and were now talking softly, unaware that the table was talking about them. Or, seemingly not caring.

"Cora too. You're okay with losing him?" Ellie asked.

King Diarmuid leaned back in his chair, the total picture of confidence. "Oh, Cora will have to learn the Cara ways."

Ellie chuckled. "You're not gonna make me call you Your Majesty when I argue with you, are ya?"

He lifted a brow. "Why wouldn't I?"

"Because I'm going to see you sloppy drunk later and that's first-name basis stuff, King D."

The corner of the king's mouth curled slightly, and Knox knew that if this was anyone other than Ellie Landry, he would've been surprised. But Ellie could charm a gator into climbing straight into her gumbo pot.

"You may call me Diarmuid."

"Perfect. Anyway, Cora's a bayou girl and can cook. Oisin's gonna be speakin' Cajun French by the end of this week."

"Care to make a wager?" Diarmuid asked.

And for just a second Knox thought that man might just have a sense of humor.

Ellie straightened. "Sure, you got an extra castle layin' around?"

"How about a gold coin from the pirate ship that my great-grandfather helped sink before he was given the island of Cara? Those coins are said to be full of the greatest luck an Irishman has ever had."

Ellie narrowed her eyes. "Deal. I've always considered myself quite lucky, but a girl can't turn down an offer like that."

"And what do you get?" Cian asked his grandfather.

"Ellie's gumbo recipe."

Everyone around the table turned wide eyes to Ellie. No one ever got Ellie's gumbo recipe. It had been a secret all their lives and Ellie claimed that she was going to take it to her grave. Literally. She was going to be buried with it. And if they wanted it, they were going to have to show up to the funeral and sweet talk the preacher into rolling her over in her casket.

"Deal," Ellie said.

A collective gasp went from around the table.

"Oh, relax. I'm not losing this bet. Y'all are too young to remember how crazy in love Danny Allain was with that woman. And he stole her from at least four other beaus. Oisin O'Connor is gonna be eatin' his shrimp and fish Cajun-style soon."

Diarmuid gave a little shudder and Knox could only assume the seafood in Cara had a lot less spice. But looking around the table, it was clear that everyone believed what Ellie was saying.

This whole impress-the-king-and-make-him-love-Autre wasn't really going according to plan. Knox sighed. But just as he was feeling defensive of the town and family he loved so much, he reminded himself that he didn't care how Diarmuid felt about Autre. He wanted the king to give Fiona her place back in line for the throne in Cara anyway.

The backdoor swung open just then, hitting the wall and announcing Saoirse's arrival.

"Hi!" Saoirse greeted everyone collectively.

Colin sauntered in behind her, closing the door, then taking a seat at the end of the table next to Jonah.

Saoirse ran to her mother, throwing her arms around Fiona's neck in a big hug. Fiona's face brightened as she held her daughter and Knox felt a pang in his chest. Damn, she was gorgeous when her eyes lit up like that.

"Hi, you're already done at the goat barn?" Fiona asked.

"Yeah, Jordan let us give the baby goats bottles!"

"You smell like it," Fiona said, giving her daughter another little squeeze.

Knox was surprised by the warmth that stirred in his gut. He was still getting used to Fiona as a mom, he supposed. He'd seen her gentle and nurturing with animals multiple times, encouraging in a you-can-do-it-you've-got-this way with their friends, and sweetly caring with Leo and Ellie and many others in their circle. But there was something different in the way Fiona looked at Saoirse that made his chest feel tight. It was a strange mix of affection and pride and desire that was as foreign to him as having a little girl just climb up into his lap as if she belonged there and had done it a million times before. As Saoirse did just then.

He froze.

She'd been over at his house every day since meeting the otters. She was comfortable around him, of course, and they'd laughed and talked. He knew every single fact there was to know about wombats. And echidnas. And platypuses. Including that platypuses was the plural of platypus. He'd also learned a lot about Cara, in order to quiz Saoirse.

He thought she was awesome. She could jabber non-stop about any number of topics. Many of them were animal related, but not all. She talked about her teacher and about math—

which he also loved—and the book she was currently reading and why she didn't like orange juice but loved apple juice and on and on and on.

And he never grew tired of it.

But she'd never sat on his lap. Of course, there hadn't really been an occasion. Now, however, he was seated at a table with a bunch of other people she knew, but with no empty seats. Everyone else was sitting forward, eating, drinking, and talking. He was the only one sitting back in his chair, with plenty of room on his thighs. Other than her great-grandfather.

She'd chosen him over Diarmuid.

Huh.

He supposed this was what he got for sitting back and just observing, as he so often did.

Saoirse got comfortable on his lap and he put one hand on her lower back to balance her. Then he met her mother's eyes.

There was surprise there, but her amusement was clear—she surely knew that he was as comfortable holding a little girl as he had been holding baby otters in the beginning. But there was also an unmistakable touch of heat.

Oh really. So watching him with Saoirse did funny things in her chest like what happened in his when watching her with her daughter?

Good to know.

"Have you seen the goats, Grandpa?" Saoirse asked Diarmuid.

"I have not."

"Have you seen the otters?"

The king shook his head. "I haven't seen any animals. I got a tour of the town and met with the mayor then was brought here for a...lovely meal."

Ellie gave a little snort, obviously noting his pause. Yeah, Diarmuid didn't like the spicy shrimp.

"Well, I'll introduce you to *all* of them," Saoirse said. "Even the ones at Knox's house. They are my favorites. But we can't tell Gus and Gertie."

Knox was shocked to feel his heart give a little flip. It was stupid that he was glad his otters were Saoirse's favorites. They were otters. They were all pretty much the same. Still, he liked to think that the favoritism Saoirse was showing his otters was more than just the animals themselves.

Which was also problematic.

He shouldn't get attached to this little girl. She was moving to another country. He would never see her once she was in Cara. Fiona would fly back and forth for their fling and to see the Landrys and to help with the animal park—maybe not in that order of priority, but still—but Saoirse would no doubt stay behind in Cara when she did.

And that made his heart twinge with an incredibly sharp pain.

"We'll see," Diarmuid told his great-granddaughter. "I have work tomorrow in the morning. Do you know what the time difference is between here and Cara?"

Saoirse nodded. "Six hours."

Diarmuid looked pleased. "Which means, when I wake up, my people at home will be in the middle of their day. I'll need to have a few meetings. Then I'll be visiting your school."

Saoirse wiggled on Knox's lap. "Really? Are you going to come for lunch? We're having chicken nuggets tomorrow."

"We'll see," he said again.

There was no way in hell the king of Cara was going to eat chicken nuggets and applesauce at school with Saoirse.

"Hey, doll," Ellie said to Saoirse as she set a dish of ice cream down in front of the girl.

"Ellie!" Saoirse pivoted on Knox's lap, almost knocking him in the nose with her head so she could hug Ellie. "Thank you."

"Of course, cher." Ellie put her hand on Saoirse's face with a soft smile. "You brighten my day, you know that?"

"You make my heart happier," Saoirse said sincerely. "And it was *really* happy because of the goats already."

Ellie laughed and patted her cheek. "The highest compliment."

"Ice cream for dinner?" Cian asked. "Must be nice to be a princess."

Saoirse giggled as she looked over at her uncle. "I had dinner before. This is dessert."

"No bread pudding or pecan pie?"

She shrugged. "Ice cream is my favorite."

And she and Knox had that in common too. Knox loved all of Ellie and Cora's desserts, but when he'd told Fiona that he liked ice cream better than beignets, he'd meant it. He met her eyes again and knew she was thinking about the same thing.

"Well, you sure ate the last of the bread pudding the other night without pause," Cian said. "Seemed to like it just fine then."

"I said ice cream is my *favorite*, not that I don't like the other stuff," Saoirse said. "Plus, you ate all my Butterfingers, so that was payback."

Cian laughed. "That was at Halloween. That was months ago."

Saoirse took a bite of ice cream and shrugged.

Grudges, revenge, and sass...she was going to fit right in as a bayou girl. But Knox quickly shut down that amusing thought that made him feel a strange sense of pride. Saoirse wasn't going to be a bayou girl. He ignored the sharp jab he felt near his heart too.

"Anyway," Saoirse said, turning her attention back to Diarmuid. "You can meet the otters at Knox's *after* school. That's when we do swimming lessons."

Diarmuid shifted his gaze to Knox's. "You have otters at your *house*?"

It was very clear from his tone how he felt about that. Knox was certain the king would think turning an entire guest room into an otter playroom was ridiculous. Because it was.

But it annoyed him that Saoirse's grandfather thought it was ridiculous when she was so obviously delighted by it. "I do." He met the man's gaze directly. "I've been raising them since they were practically newborn and abandoned at the petting zoo."

The other man looked bored. "I shouldn't be surprised."

"Meaning?" Knox asked.

"You obviously have some...relationship with my granddaughter." He looked at Fiona. "I know firsthand how uncooperative she can be if you don't appease her obsession with the animals."

Knox bristled. He didn't fucking like that at all. He wasn't sure if it was the clear implication that the king didn't think much of the relationship between him and Fiona, or that the king had not been such a sucker himself, or that the only reason Knox had the otters was because *he* was a sucker.

Or that he was right. About all of it.

But overall, it was the fact that the king was putting down both him and Fiona and his affection for the otters—and the fact that he'd just made Knox admit that he *had* affection for the otters.

"It's been my pleasure to care for the otters," Knox said. "I think whenever there is a chance to use our resources to make things better for someone or something else, we should. I feel like that's the true measure of a man's character. Surely, as the leader of an entire nation, you feel the same way."

The king narrowed his eyes. "I hardly think caring for otters and caring for an entire country of people can be compared."

Knox lifted a shoulder. "I don't know. One is on a much smaller scale than the other, of course. But the intention behind it is the same, right? You have the resources and power to care for and help your people. I have the resources and power to help the otters. I'm not sure the size of the action matters as much as the intention."

He moved his gaze to Fiona. Who was watching him with wide eyes. "And if you want to talk large scale, kickass, world-changing stuff, you don't have to go any further than your granddaughter." He swung his attention back to Diarmuid but was very aware of Fiona's eyes on him. "I'd be willing to wager that she's impacted as many lives, directly and indirectly, non-human and human, through education and as a role model, as you have, Your Highness."

He had no idea if *Your Highness* was a correct address for the king of Cara, but he was pretty sure the note of sarcasm in his tone when he said it meant it didn't matter anyway.

Diarmuid straightened in his seat. "I understand your point clearly."

And Knox thought that was probably true, since his *point* was that he was going to stand up for what Fiona was doing, whether it was raising her daughter, saving lions and tigers and bears, or convincing him to raise otter babies.

"Why is Oisin outside with Cora?" Saoirse asked, taking the conversation in a new, welcome direction.

Happy for the distraction, but also curious, as always, everyone at the table started looking around.

Sure enough, Oisin and Cora were missing.

Knox couldn't help but chuckle. Obviously the two had snuck out when no one was looking. Good for them.

"What were they doing out there?" Cian asked his niece.

His grandfather shot him a frown.

"Talking," Saoirse said. "But they were standing very close." She put her hands up in front of her face, the palms less than an inch apart. "Like Drew and Rory were doing after we saw them kissing in the barn."

Laughter and knowing looks erupted around the table.

Oisin and Cora were standing close like Drew had been standing with his fiancée. Interesting.

Fiona shifted on her chair and Knox looked over. She looked restless. Her expression was hard to read but he could tell she was uncomfortable. None of this was going according to plan. Her brothers had told him to keep this all calm and without any drama. He was supposed to show their grandfather that there was nothing for him to worry about with Fiona's decision-making or the way she parented Saoirse.

Instead, he'd just had an argument with the man.

Dammit.

His heart twinged again, but in a whole new way. He wanted to make this good for her. He wanted her grandfather to what? Love it here? Approve of her living here? Or put his foot down and demanded that she come back to Cara immediately?

Knox wasn't sure anymore.

The only thing he knew for certain was that he wanted Fiona happy.

Saoirse pivoted on his lap to look up at him. "Can I bring Grandpa over to your house tomorrow?"

It was then that Knox fully took in the girl for the first time.

His brows slammed together.

Saoirse had a black eye.

A fucking *black eye*.

The purple and blue bruise stood out starkly against her fair skin and the swollen lid and narrowed slit of her eye made rage tighten his chest, chasing away any twinges of softer emotion.

Knox took a deep breath and carefully took Saoirse's face in both of his hands. "What happened to your eye, Princess?"

She frowned, as if confused. "That happened after school yesterday."

He hadn't seen it at his house yesterday afternoon. He wracked his brain. Had he looked her directly in the face?

Surely he had. Maybe the bruising hadn't shown up by the time he'd seen her. He forced himself to take a deep breath. She'd been fine yesterday when he'd seen her. She was fine. "So it was an accident? Did you fall down?"

He willed his heart to slow. She was a kid. And she'd probably been playing. It was entirely possible she had run into something or someone had accidentally elbowed her during a game of tag. But the look of even accidental bruising on this little girl made his entire body tense with the need to make it okay.

She tried to shake her head, but he was holding her. "It happened when Jacob hit me."

Knox felt anger shoot through him, tightening all of his muscles.

"Jacob *hit* you? On purpose?"

He wasn't aware of anyone besides Saoirse. He was completely focused on her. So when Fiona's fingers wrapped around his wrist, and she said softly, "Knox," he found himself having to swallow and consciously release Saoirse's face. He hadn't been squeezing her, he simply didn't want to let go of her.

"It was kind of on purpose. He was trying to hit Skylar but I got in the way."

Rage burned in his gut. Knox had to remind himself that Jacob was only nine years old. But someone had hurt Saoirse. The bruising around her eye was because another human had hit her on purpose.

"Why was he trying to hit Skylar?"

"He was just being mean."

"And you got in the way?"

"Yes. On purpose," Saoirse said. "Like Mommy does."

Knox was aware that Fiona was still holding onto his wrist. He assumed that he also had an audience. The people at the table were probably listening and watching. Including Saoirse's great-grandfather. But he couldn't have taken his eyes off the little girl for anything. "What do you mean like your mom?"

"It's what Mommy does all the time. She gets between the bad guys and the animals that need her. That's what we're supposed to do. Like what you just said. When we're able to help someone or something that's in trouble, we should."

Her words in that sweet voice rattled around in his brain then slid through his chest and settled near his heart.

She was right. And she was learning that from the most amazing woman he'd ever met. The fact that Fiona did exactly what Saoirse had mimicked with Jacob and Skylar was why he was in love with her. Or at least was a part of it. And Saoirse was okay. He told himself that three times in a row. She was obviously physically okay. And, clearly, emotionally fine as well. And she had a bodyguard, for fuck's sake. Clearly Colin wasn't too upset.

Knox still felt himself rising from his chair. "I'm proud of you, Princess," he told Saoirse. "And you are absolutely right. We should always do something when we can."

He set her on her feet next to Fiona, shoved his chair out of the way, turned, and headed for the end of the bar. Where Jacob's father happened to be sitting with two of his buddies.

12

"Ted," Knox said, his voice firm and low.

Ted looked over at him. "Hey, Knox."

"Just wondering if you're aware that your kid is a fucking bully."

Ted's eyes widened and he swiveled on the bar stool to face Knox. "Excuse me?"

"Jacob. He's been picking on a girl at recess and her friend stood up for her yesterday and ended up with a black eye."

Ted glanced in the direction of the table where Saoirse and Fiona were still sitting. Saoirse not paying them any attention. Fiona watching them like a hawk.

"The school called. I know what happened," Ted said.

"Well, I want to know what happened when he got home."

"When he got home?"

"I want to know what you, his father, told him about what happened and what would happen the *next* time he did that," Knox said, his jaw tight.

"None of your fucking business," Ted said. He stood from his stool.

Knox had at least four inches on the other man, but Ted

worked on a huge fishing vessel and Knox would definitely feel it if the man took a swing and connected.

He didn't care.

"Just tell me that your kid isn't going to do it again," Knox said. "That's all I need to hear."

"You don't work for the school, and you're not that girl's parent, so this has nothing to do with you." Ted took a step forward.

Knox didn't budge. "I'm asking you a simple question."

"And my simple answer is, it's none of your business."

"Would you rather talk about it outside, where no one can hear?" Knox asked.

"If we go outside, we're not going to be talking," Ted told him.

"Fine with me," Knox said. The vision of the bruising around Saoirse's eye was seared into his brain and he would love nothing more than to have an outlet for the rage burning in his chest.

"Knox."

Knox looked over to find that Fiona had joined them.

"Fiona, just let me handle this. Ted and I have known each other a long time. Ted is simply going to explain to me how Jacob is going to act around the girls from now on. Or *I* will explain to *Ted* how Jacob is going to act."

"Oh, that's fine," she told him. "You have whatever conversation with Ted you want to."

Knox gave her a surprised look. But she was staring at Ted. And looked pissed.

Fiona went on. "I just overheard that Ted didn't feel comfortable talking to you about the situation because you weren't one of Saoirse's parents. But I am. So I thought I'd come over and make *him* more comfortable having this conversation. I mean, I wouldn't want *him* to feel upset or anxious. I definitely want *Ted* to feel at ease here."

Ted frowned at her.

"Well?" she asked. "This is your chance to explain to me what you've discussed with Jacob about this situation."

Ted glanced back at his friends. He definitely did *not* look comfortable. Knox crossed his arms and settled back on his heels, thoroughly enjoying it.

"I told him to knock it off," Ted finally said. "Told him to leave the girls alone. And I grounded him."

Fiona nodded. "Okay. Well, I hope that you'll still let him come over and see the giraffes with Saoirse. She's even asked me to get giraffe-shaped cookies from a bakery we just discovered. The animals love her and she's wonderful with them. She's patient and gentle and doesn't make them do anything they're not comfortable with. They know she respects them and they can trust her. Jacob will get to be right up close to them with her. He'll learn a lot."

Knox frowned. "Saoirse wants Jacob to come over to see the giraffes? And have cookies?" Yeah, he'd caught the reference to Shannon's bakery too.

Fiona was still looking at Ted. "She does. For some reason, she thinks that Jacob has some redeeming qualities and she wants to try to be his friend. She thinks maybe he's acting like this because he needs more attention or to know that someone really cares about him."

Knox looked at Ted. He believed everything Fiona was saying about Saoirse. But he was also fascinated by the idea that shaming Jacob's father was possibly even more effective than punching him.

"I, uh...will have to think about him coming over," Ted finally said.

"Fine," Fiona said. "I understand it's a little scary to think about your kid being somewhere that you worry might not be totally safe for him. How you might question the motives of the people around him. That you might be concerned about how they will treat him. I mean, after all, sometimes people are cruel to others who don't deserve it, for no good reason. But," she continued, "that will not be the case for Jacob at our animal park. Jacob can trust Saoirse and the rest of us to act completely appropriately."

Ted frowned at her, but he didn't say anything. He actually looked a little chagrined. Ted looked at his friends. "Come on, let's get out of here,"

"Don't forget to tip," Fiona said as the men stood and grabbed their caps.

They threw bills down on the bar top, then headed for the door.

Fiona watched them go. Then she looked up at Knox. "Is there somewhere we can go?"

"Go? You haven't said everything you need to say?"

"Oh no, I've definitely not said everything I need to say."

Great. Even though she had successfully chastened Ted and defended Saoirse herself, she was still pissed at Knox for starting this.

He glanced toward the back table. Sure enough, everyone back there was watching them. Including the king.

Except Saoirse. She was now standing next to Tori, leaning onto the table and talking animatedly to two-year-old Ella, telling her...who knew what. But Knox was sure it was charming as hell.

"Hey!" Fiona called, to no one in particular. "I have to show Knox something at the giraffe barn!"

Oh God, she was going to get him alone. In a barn. On the edge of town. Where there was lots of open area that would take the authorities a long time to search for a body.

Then again, she had a lion and a tiger in an enclosure not that far from the giraffe barn. That would be an even easier place to dispose of him.

"Bye, Mom!" Saoirse called. Completely unbothered by her mother leaving. Or the chance that Knox might not return.

"Is this a good idea?" he asked as Fiona grabbed his hand and started for the door.

"Probably not." She looked up at him. "But I've found that sometimes it's hard to tell what's a good idea or bad idea until afterwards. And then you just deal with the consequences."

He studied her face. There was a mix of emotions swirling in her eyes and all he could think was, he'd give her whatever she needed. She needed to leave right now? They were going to leave.

They stepped out into the night and she bee-lined for her big purple pickup.

Of course she was going to be in the driver's seat. Literally.

He sighed and climbed up on the passenger side.

Nothing in Autre was too far away from anything else in Autre so it didn't take them long to get to the giraffe barn. Fiona actually pulled around behind the building, away from the main road and even the small service roads they'd put in to get supplies to the barn.

She shut the truck off, killing the lights and leaving them with only the fading sunset to the west. The crickets and frogs were starting to come out and it wouldn't be long until fireflies started blinking in the field just beyond where they sat.

There was a line of trees about two hundred yards from them and the space was filled with long grass and marshy ground. They couldn't expand the animal park much further this direction. The ground started to get soft and swampy the closer they got to the bayou. They still had a little room to the west and south. But if the animal park continued to grow, they might have to put a portion of it in another section of town.

Fiona still hadn't said anything after another two minutes, and Knox was trying to decide if that was a good or a bad sign. He looked over at her, his hands braced on his thighs.

"Okay, I'm sorry."

She pulled her eyes from the scene in front of them and looked at him. "What for?"

"For embarrassing you in front of your grandfather. For failing to keep things calm and simple. For starting shit with Jacob's father. I know that I'm nothing to Saoirse and that I don't have—"

Fiona pivoted on her seat quickly. Her seatbelt jerked her back, and she swore, then stabbed her finger on the button to release it. Flipping the belt out of the way, she turned fully to face him.

"You are *absolutely* something to Saoirse. You've got nothing to apologize for, Knox. If anything, I'm embarrassed *about* my grandfather. I can't believe that he started shit with you about the otters. And honestly, the entire reason we're sitting here right now is because of the way that you defended the otters and Saoirse and me. If you hadn't gone up to Jacob's father, I wouldn't be sitting here right now. I might have been able to hold it together. I mean, I absolutely wanted to crawl in your lap after you said all of that to my grandfather, but my daughter was in my way."

She stopped and pressed her lips together, shaking her head. "She just crawled into your lap." Clearly, Fiona was struck by the wonder of that as well.

Knox nodded. "Yeah, she's never done that before."

"She's very demonstrative and loving and trusting. She's been raised around a whole bunch of different people. My brothers and their friends have been around her all her life, and Colin. Over the years, lots of my friends have crashed at our house after rescues and things. But I've never seen her take to someone the way she has to you. I've never introduced her to men before. Not men I...I've been...dating."

Knox didn't want her to elaborate on that. He understood, loud and clear.

"But there's clearly something about you that makes her just trust you. She's not climbing into Josh's or Owen's laps. She's not going over to their house at the end of the day."

"In their defense, they don't have baby otters learning to swim."

She gave him a little smile. "Josh has a ton of animals at his house."

It was true. Josh's wife, Tori, was a veterinarian and she had a tendency to collect special-needs animals. She didn't just have animals like cats and dogs and goats and pigs. She had a three-legged cat, and a dog that had a seeing-eye dog, and a cow that slept in their backyard with those dogs and refused to sleep with the other cows. And on and on. Since the petting zoo had opened, a lot of her animals were able to stay up at the barn with the other animals and they'd been incorporated into a program for educating kids about special needs and how to talk about and appreciate the physical differences in others. But Tori still had many at their house that she was hand feeding or that needed more hands-on care.

The bottom line was that there were any number of animal-crazy, bighearted people in this town that Saoirse could have gotten close to and had her fix of animals of all kinds. But she'd chosen Knox.

At that realization, he rubbed a hand over his heart where he felt that getting-familiar squeeze.

"She likes you. And I don't blame her," Fiona said. "I've tried to be mad at you ever since I got to town. But it never seems to last for very long. I mean, of course you'll probably say or do something soon that will remind me. But in the in-between times, it's really tough to remember that you're not this amazing guy that I've wanted ever since I first saw you."

Okay, this was sounding a lot less murderous than he'd expected. "So you didn't bring me out here because you're mad?"

"No. I thought I was going to be able to keep my clothes on, in spite of the way you defended me to my grandfather. Though I was debating about sneaking over for a kiss and make-out session later. But then you went up to Jacob's father. And it's not the tough-guy, willing to fight for her thing." She frowned, as if having a hard time explaining what she was trying say.

"I saw your face. You are..." She took a deep breath and met his eyes. "You are not detached. You are not trying to keep it all at a distance. You are...*wrapped up*. You're *involved*. You're emotional. All those things you told me you try to avoid in relationships. I know it's not the same kind of relationship but...it kind of is. You've looked up wombat facts. She told me you surprised her with facts about armadillos the other day. She was *thrilled*, Knox. You learned everything about Cara and helped teach her. And then you were ready to fight a guy you've known most of your life in a parking lot for her."

Knox felt his heart pounding.

She was right.

She was absolutely right.

Fiona shifted forward on her seat, leaning in close. "And, frankly, watching you fall in love with my daughter...I don't see how there's any way I'm going to be able to not get naked with you now."

His entire body reacted to that even before his mind really caught up with her words.

His breathing was ragged.

Even as he'd tried to hold himself back from getting involved in Fiona's work and what her life in Cara would be like, it wasn't just Saoirse he'd fallen in love with.

"Your grandfather is in town. I'm supposed to help you keep your cool around him. I'm not sure storming out of Ellie's and then fucking you in your truck behind a barn is exactly on plan."

"Storming out of a bar after starting a fight and getting

naked in a truck with the hot guy who just defended me is minor compared to what he's probably expecting while he's here."

Knox thought about that. In the past, he'd regretted opening his mouth, getting involved, making things messy.

Today he didn't. He'd do it again. In a heartbeat. And not just to get this woman naked. But that was a very nice side effect.

"I keep hearing the word naked," he finally said.

She nodded.

"But I'm not seeing a lot of it."

A smile curled her lips. She slid across the middle console and into his lap. She straddled his thighs, facing him. "And we can't really go back to your house, because obviously my daughter thinks she can come and go at her leisure there. And I don't have a house that doesn't have a million people in it. And honestly it just feels really right to be doing this in this pickup."

His hands gripped her hips and he squeezed. "This just feels really right no matter where we are."

Her eyes heated. "I agree."

"That could be a problem."

"Like I said, sometimes you just have to do something and decide later if it was a good or bad idea, and then just deal with the consequences."

He could handle that. After all, the idea of putting this off was getting stupider and stupider by the day.

They didn't really have anything else to talk about, he figured. He slid his hands up underneath the edge of her shirt, dragging the cotton with them, pulling it up and over her head. He tossed it on the floor. Then his hands went to the hooks of her bra, undoing them and pulling the silky pale pink cups away from her breasts. That also landed on the floor by his feet. By the time it hit the floor his hands were cupping her breasts, thumbs running over the stiff points.

"God, I love your hands on me," she moaned.

"Same. So much the same."

She reached between them and started working on the buttons of his shirt. He continued to tease her breasts and nipples, loving the little moans and breathless sighs it elicited. He leaned in and took one nipple in his mouth, causing a frustrated groan when she couldn't finish his buttons, that quickly turned into a long, happy sigh as he sucked.

He put a hand between her shoulder blades, causing her to arch her back, bringing her up against his mouth. He licked and sucked then switched sides. Her hands moved from his shirt to the back of his head, tangling in his hair as she gripped him closer.

"God, you could almost make me come like that."

She ground against him and the feel of her pussy rubbing against his cock, even behind denim, was heavenly hell.

"Please tell me I can have all of you tonight," she said. "Please. The other night was amazing, but I need you. All of you."

He couldn't hold anything back from this woman.

"Anything you want, Fi."

"This shirt off. Then your pants."

Bossy, as usual, but he was happy to comply. He leaned back and shrugged out of his shirt, popping the last button that she hadn't gotten undone.

"Oops," she said with a little laugh.

"I'll sew it back on."

"You can sew on buttons?" She shook her head. "Of course you can."

He gripped her hips, lifting her up and over the console again, tossing her gently into her seat.

"Hey!"

"Jeans and panties off. Now."

He started working on his button and zipper and her eyes

widened. Her fingers flew to the front of her jeans, and she quickly undid them, stripping them off and kicking them to the floor.

He shucked out of his as well, then lowered his boxers. She started to climb back towards him.

"Panties," he commanded softly.

"This is my first up close," she told him, her eyes riveted on his cock.

It throbbed and he had to wrap a hand around and give it a squeeze to ease some of the pressure.

She licked her lips and he wondered if she even realized she'd done it.

Okay, well, he didn't want her too distracted. He reached with his free hand, sliding his hand down her back and into the panties to cup her ass. He gave her a squeeze then continued to slide down the back of her thighs, taking the tiny scrap of silk down her legs as he went.

She gave a little wiggle, lifting one knee, then the other, so he could free them from her legs and then tossed the panties on the floor of the driver side.

"Okay, you want an up-close. Come here." He gently nudged her forward with his hand on her ass again, tipping her across the console 'til her nose was nearly in his lap.

She definitely took the hint. Her hand wrapped around his shaft and stroked twice before her mouth went to the tip. She swirled her tongue around his head, then gently pulled him into her mouth.

Knox's head fell back against the seat, and he let out a long groan. "Fuck, Fi."

"God, I love making you sound like that," she said, her voice breathless.

"I'm not gonna last long but give me some more of that sassy mouth," he told her as he moved his hand from her ass cheek to cup her pussy, his middle finger sliding along her center.

She moaned, the sound vibrating around his cock and they both groaned together.

He slipped a finger inside, finding her hot, tight, and very wet. She took him deeper as he pumped first one finger, then a second into her.

She had to use a hand, unable to take him fully in her mouth, but she gave it a valiant effort.

The cab of the truck filled with their sighs and moans along with the sexy sound of hands and mouths pleasuring one another.

"Need you," she finally said, pulling her mouth from his cock.

"Yes." He moved to grasp her waist, pulling her into his lap.

"Condom?" she asked.

Swearing under his breath, he reached for his jeans, pulling out his wallet and extracting a condom. Between the two of them, they got it rolled on in seconds.

She braced her knees on either side of his hips, then took his cock and positioned it. "I'm in charge?" she asked.

"As if anyone's had any question about that since day one," he said, teeth gritted. He needed to let her set the pace here, but he desperately needed *inside*.

She gave him a mischievous smile and then sank down onto his length.

They both moaned as she slowly took him. She was petite, so it took a little bit for her to take him fully, but it was an excruciatingly hot adjustment.

She started moving slowly but they soon found a rhythm. He helped guide her with his hands on her hips, but mostly let her set the pace, knowing that she needed to find the right angles and depths. Everything felt fucking amazing to him.

She had both hands braced on his shoulders as she rode

him, and he lifted his hands to play with her nipples.

Her head fell back and she gave out a lusty moan. "Yes, God, yes."

He pinched and tugged and felt the resulting squeeze of her pussy around his cock.

He leaned in, worshiping her nipples with his tongue, lips, and teeth as she tightened around him and picked up the pace.

They kept that up for several long minutes, just enjoying the ride. Her hands began to roam and settled on his abs as they contracted as he fucked up into her.

Eventually one of her hands found its way between her legs and she started to circle her clit.

"Okay, my turn," he told her.

"What—"

But he took her hips and turned her to face away from him. He pressed her forward until she crossed her arms on the dashboard and rested her cheek on them. He guided her hips back and down, thrusting up into her again.

"Oh my God," she groaned into her arm.

He grinned. "And it gets even better." His hand slid around her waist and down to her pussy. He pressed a middle finger over her clit and then circled.

She moaned and wiggled as if trying to get closer. But she was spread open on his lap and he had most of the leverage.

Thrusting up into her, with one hand stroking and circling her clit, and the other playing with a nipple, he felt her body tightening and listened to her breathing and her moans. Soon she was climbing toward the crest and he picked up his pace.

Then she did the most unexpected thing. She pushed back, straightening her elbows, bracing her hands on the dash, and looked down. "Oh, God," she groaned, watching where they were joined, where he was moving in and out of her body.

Knox felt his orgasm rushing at him as he imagined what she was seeing.

"Fuck," he ground out. "Fi."

She moved her hips with his. "Yes. So good. This is so good."

He gripped both of her hips, pounding up into her, and she cried out, clamping down around him, and Knox let go of his control, roaring her name, letting his orgasm wash over him.

As he came down from the high, he brought her back against him, nestling her against his chest and then using the lever on the side to recline the seat. He pulled his shirt up over the both of them, draping it across their bodies, and tucked her head under his chin.

Her breathing slowed and their bodies cooled.

Finally, she said. "Yeah, I'm thinking this was a good idea."

He laughed. "Endorphins. Give it a day. You might decide that make-out sessions in a pickup when you are supposed to be having dinner with your family does actually come with some consequences."

She sighed and ran a hand over his chest. "Yeah, well, my family dinners have all had consequences for the past several years. That is nothing new."

Knox felt his gut clench. He really wanted to fix every bit of that. Things were complicated with the O'Grady family.

Very complicated.

More complicated than opening a bakery business and selling whoopie pies to a populace that wanted macarons.

Even more complicated, in some ways, than working with at-risk kids.

With this one, he might start an international incident.

Why couldn't he have just kept this simple?

Impress her grandfather. Secure her dream job. Get her crown back. And then have sex in every room in his house when she came back to visit Autre. Occasionally. Temporarily.

It all made sense in his head.

Unfortunately, his head wasn't the only thing involved.

13

"Fiona."

Fiona turned to see Knox striding toward her across the grass that separated the service road from this end of the giraffe pens. Her heartrate quickened as she watched his long legs eat up the ground.

They'd had sex last night. Finally. For the first time. And not only had it *really* made her body happy, it had done things to her heart as well. She'd been thinking about him all day and finding herself drifting off into hot daydreams too often when she should have been working.

She'd been proud of herself for not calling or texting or going to find him for a repeat performance this morning. She'd made it this long without seeking him out and had told herself that she wouldn't go looking for him until three p.m. That way she wouldn't look *desperate* for him, but they'd have some time before Saoirse got out of school.

But it looked like he was coming to her.

She gave him a big grin as he stopped in front of her. "Hey."

He was frowning though. Frowning was not uncommon for

Knox, but she had kind of hoped that maybe the day after they finally had sex, he might have been giving her a smile or two.

"Donovan and Griffin are getting in the car to go to Texas to bail their girlfriends out of jail. Do you know anything about that?"

Oh.

Her stomach dropped.

Well fuck. She did. Kind of. At least she had a pretty good idea what this was about.

Kayla. Tigers. And a guy named Colby Sutton.

Fiona lifted a hand and ran it up and down the middle of her forehead. Maybe she should have let Kayla give her more information after all. But she'd been trying to be good and stay out of it.

"Naomi and Charlie are in jail?" She wasn't *shocked*. But that was...too bad.

"They were arrested trespassing on a ranch outside of Red Plains, Texas, around noon today. And I can tell by the look on your face that you do know what this is about." He sighed. "Dammit, Fi."

"Hey, *I* didn't throw them in jail. And I'm not sitting next to them. Shouldn't you be happy about *that* at least?"

"But if you were with them, the chances of them being in jail would be a lot slimmer, wouldn't it?"

Well, he had a point.

"In my defense, I didn't know they were going to Texas today. Also, I've spent more than a couple of nights in jail while learning the ropes. They'll be okay. And I have lawyer friends that I can get in contact with. And I'm sure that Kayla had planned for this contingency." She was working this all through as she said it out loud. All of those things were true. But she didn't love the idea of Naomi and Charlie in jail. Or how pissed Donovan and Griffin probably were. At *her*.

Knox folded his huge arms and frowned down at her with that look that she knew he meant to be intimidating, but that had always turned her on just a little. The same happened now.

He was mad, but she couldn't forget last night in her truck no matter what.

"You had *no idea* the girls were going to Texas today?"

"I knew it was a possibility. But I didn't know when for sure or what Kayla was going to have them do."

"You didn't train or prepare them for what was going to happen?"

"I'm trying to stay out of it!" she repeated. "I'm in Autre, in part, so that I don't always have to be the one leading the charge and sitting *my* ass in jail. I'm trying to be *chill* and trust others to be a part of the cause." She frowned. "Charlie and Naomi want to learn this, Knox. Jordan and Caroline too. And Jill, if she could pull herself away from the penguins. And hell, Griffin and Donovan have both done some of this shit themselves. They want this".

"They want to be arrested?"

"They knew it was a possibility. Probably." In truth, she didn't know what exactly Kayla had told them or prepared them for. But Kayla had been doing this for a long time. "Listen, I've known Kayla for years and we've done lots of rescues together. I wouldn't have trusted them to just anyone. She's teaching them how this all works. I'm sure that there's a plan."

"Why didn't *you* teach them?"

"Teach them to do the things you *hate* me doing?"

"Well someone has to do it!"

"Do they?" she challenged, planting her hands on her hips.

He hesitated, but finally said, "Yes."

"Uh-huh. Just not me."

"Well...maybe you."

She narrowed her eyes. "Uh-huh."

He shoved a hand through his hair. "Dammit, Fi. It's not that I don't think what you do is important. Of course it is. I just worry about you." He blew out a breath. "See? This is what I'm talking about. When I get involved, then I start stepping on toes and making the woman crazy."

"You've been making me crazy since we met, Knox. Even before we thought about getting involved."

"Think of how much worse it could be."

She shook her head. She really hated that he thought his caring and concern and interest in the women, hell, the *people*, he had in his life was a problem. "I like that you give a shit if I'm being eaten by a lion or falling into a volcano," she told him.

He frowned. "You've been on a volcano?"

She smiled. "Focus. Right now you're mad about Texas and Naomi and Charlie."

He sighed. "Right. But you've really stayed out of it?" he asked, looking like he believed her for the first time. And surprised. "You really don't know the plan?"

"I only know the very basics. They're trying to shut down a guy named Colby Sutton who breeds and sells tigers."

Knox frowned. Then his jaw tightened and his eyes narrowed. "So you're just going to wash your hands of this?"

"Wash my hands of it?" Ugh, this man was so exasperating. Now he was mad because she *wasn't* there? "Kayla was in charge of the rescue. Donovan and Griffin are on their way to get the girls. What would I be getting my hands dirty with exactly?" She glared up at him in return. "I would think you would be happy right now. I'm the one not in jail this time. I'm the one staying home and being good and not getting into trouble. I'm not leading this animal rescue. I thought that's what you wanted."

He looked taken aback. He blinked at her. "Why would you think that?"

"Because you think I always go running into these situations without thinking? Because you think I'm a troublemaker? Because you think I need to start acting more *queenly* so that I can take over the throne of Cara and lead my people and be classy and sophisticated and impress my grandfather?" She realized that her heart was pounding and she assumed that her cheeks were pink. "I mean come on, Knox. What would my grandfather think if, while he was here visiting, I got thrown in *jail*? That's not exactly what he's looking for in a future ruler. Nor is it fantastic parenting."

Knox just stared at her for several beats. Then he nodded. "Damn. You're absolutely right."

Of course she was. She frowned. "About which part?"

"All of it. Those were the things that drove me crazy at first. But they're also the things that make me crazy *about* you. Sitting back and letting other people take the fall is not your style. Sitting out a chance to save a bunch of animals that need you is not the Fiona I know." He stepped closer. "How much is it killing you right now that those girls are down in Texas and you don't know what's going on? And worse, that they're sitting in a jail cell without you?"

Fiona crossed her arms, pressing them against her body. Dammit. He knew her. She didn't hate *that*, but she worried that he did a little. Talk about being *involved*. Finally she nodded. "It's definitely killing me."

He nodded. "Yeah." Then he pivoted on his heel and started for his truck.

"Hey! Where are you going?"

"To get my stuff."

"What stuff?"

"Figure we might need a few supplies in Texas. And we'll definitely need snacks for the road trip."

Fiona felt her mouth drop open. "*We're* going to *Texas?*"

He turned back. "Tell me you weren't about to go straight to your house, grab a bag, and hit the road."

"Well, I..." Of course she had been. "Griffin and Donovan can get the girls," she said weakly.

Knox nodded. "Yeah. But someone still has to go help the tigers. And that should have been you all along."

She felt the air whoosh from her lungs. He made it to the truck before she was able to call, "And you're going with me?"

"It's far past time for you to have someone beside you on these trips."

He was at least twenty feet away from her and she still felt like he was stroking her hair or pulling her in for a hug. "I always have people once I get there. No matter where the rescue is."

He nodded. "But you're gonna have some calls to make. Way easier for me to drive while you do that. Plus I always worry when you do those long drives by yourself. Who are you playing road trip games with?"

She didn't know what else to say. He got into the truck and drove away.

Her heart didn't stop pounding the whole time.

She'd known that it bothered him that she went into dangerous rescue situations. She'd known that he thought she took a lot of risks for the animals she cared about. She'd realized since moving to Autre that he didn't like the fact that Saoirse and her brothers had bodyguards and she didn't specifically have one assigned to her.

She also knew that he understood that none of them really *needed* a bodyguard and that it was her grandfather overreacting and that most adult women didn't have bodyguards at all. But there was something about the protectiveness and the idea that he thought she'd been getting shortchanged that made her feel soft and squishy inside.

She also knew there were a lot of people who knew Knox

who wouldn't believe that soft and squishy had anything to do with him.

They'd be very wrong.

"I can't believe you brought me some of your ex-girlfriend's whoopie pies for this road trip," Fiona said, as she dug in the bag for the first of the snacks.

He started to pull the bag away. "Sorry. They're just really good. I don't really think about who makes them."

Fiona's hand shot out and she plucked the bag from his fingers. "I didn't say I wasn't going to eat them. They're *really* good."

Knox laughed. He loved this woman's confidence, and he supposed that had a lot to do with why he also hadn't thought much about Shannon and her whoopie pies. In a long time actually.

Fiona was not the type to be intimidated by another woman, especially one so far in his past. If he had occasionally thought about Shannon, and regretted how things had gone, and wondered if he should have tried to be a different man and give it another try, that had all ended two years ago when Fiona Grady had driven into Autre, in her bright purple pickup truck.

The bright purple pickup truck that he'd first made love to her in, and that was now heading west down the highway toward Red Plains, Texas.

He knew he was over Shannon.

What he didn't know, exactly, was what he was getting into with Fiona.

In general. And tonight in Texas.

He was sure it would be out of his comfort zone, a little chaotic—or a lot chaotic—and unlike anything he'd done before. And that at the end of it, he'd be a little more in love with her.

"Okay, so what's going on with this whole thing?" he asked.

He glanced at her as she licked the corner of her mouth, catching the crumb of chocolate there and swallowing before she answered. She'd gotten off a call with Kayla about ten minutes ago. He knew Fiona was not only fully up to speed at this point, but she was now in charge. As she should have been all along.

He sighed inwardly. Yes, she took risks. Yes, he was trying not to worry or lecture or get too involved. He'd looked *nothing* up about the laws surrounding tiger breeding or buying and selling in Texas and he was very proud of himself for that. But of course she should be in charge. This was what Fiona did. And he needed to know *this one time* because he was going with her. *This one time.*

"Kayla is a colleague. We've done several rescues before. She did call me about this one but, because I was trying to pull back and get the others more involved, I just put her in touch with Charlie and Naomi," Fiona started.

Knox just concentrated on the road.

"Kayla got a call from a woman named Jasmine about a month ago. Jasmine claimed that her boyfriend, Colby, was a tiger breeder. He has about twenty and he sells the cubs to private owners, roadside zoos, etc. Which, unfortunately, isn't illegal in Texas."

Knox tightened his hands around the wheel, then relaxed them. He knew a lot about the tiger trade because of Zander's girlfriend, Caroline.

"Well, Jasmine got upset when Colby apparently killed one of the tigers and called Kayla wanting to know what she could do."

Knox looked over at her quickly. "He *killed* one of the tigers?"

245

Fiona nodded. "Shot it. Told her he had to put it down because it was sick, but Jasmine didn't believe him. She'd overheard him talking to some guys about getting a new tiger. A young, pregnant one. He'd told the guys he'd love to have her, but he didn't have room and didn't have money to expand. So one of the guys told him to make room." Fiona sighed. "Obviously a tiger able to produce more tigers...with a baby on the way...is more valuable than an old male. So..."

"He made room."

Fiona looked pained when Knox glanced at her again.

"Yeah. That's what Jasmine thinks. He got the new tiger two days later."

"Okay, so she called Kayla for what though?"

"Kayla is part of an organization working to end private ownership of cats. Jasmine just wanted advice. Kayla, of course, wants Colby to go down."

Knox could see why Kayla and Fiona were friends.

"So Kayla came to the ranch and pretended to be an old friend of Jasmine's needing a place to stay for a couple of weeks. Colby went along with it and Kayla earned his trust. Then, last night, Jasmine was going to take him out for a big, sexy night out at a hotel since they hadn't had a chance to be alone in two weeks. While they were out, some friends were going to show up and help Kayla dig up the dead tiger. They were going to take photos and have proof to send to the authorities, who were standing by thanks to some contacts. With proof they could get a warrant and come out to search the ranch. Colby would be arrested and the other cats would be confiscated and rehomed to sanctuaries."

"He could be arrested for that?"

Fiona nodded. "If they could prove that he killed a healthy tiger. A veterinarian has to approve any euthanasia under the Endangered Species Act. So they would examine the body and determine if there was a reason to put the tiger down."

"And the friends that were going to help dig the tiger up were Naomi and Charlie?" Knox asked, his tone clearly full of disbelief. "Kayla doesn't have any other friends?"

"Actually, Seth, a guy we know, was going to do it, but he bailed at the last minute. But there was a miscommunication with Charlie and Naomi. Kayla wanted them there to see how it all worked, to help organize transferring the other animals, and to potentially take some smaller animals back to Autre. *They* thought she needed them at the ranch for the dig. They got there too early and were caught."

"There are other animals there?" Knox asked.

"I guess so. She didn't go into detail, but if Colby's in jail, all the animals will need homes."

Knox looked over at her. "Are we taking a tiger home tonight?"

She grinned at him. "No. We're not taking anything. We already have a tiger. Who's an old man who has always lived alone and probably wouldn't play very well with someone new."

"Oh." That was good. He should be in favor of that. "You won't want to take one home?"

"I always want to take them all home," she said. "But I know that's not practical, and I never go to a rescue expecting that."

That made sense. Still...tigers were really cool.

"So Naomi and Charlie were trespassing. How did Kayla think she'd get around that?"

"If she'd been there, she would have let them in, as a guest of the house. Not really trespassing. And *she's* not trespassing. Jasmine lives there and invited her to stay. She's been there for two weeks, with Colby's knowledge. It would be hard to make a case that *she's* trespassing. As for digging up his yard...well, it's not very good guest behavior but he'll be in enough trouble by then that I don't think it will really matter."

Knox shoved a hand through his hair. "So the communication with Naomi and Charlie wasn't great."

Fiona sighed. "I don't really know exactly what they were told. I seriously tried to stay out of it."

Yes, she'd said that before. And she was right that previously, he would've been thrilled that she wasn't part of this. But it just seemed wrong. She was the brains of all of these operations. He just knew it. He didn't know Kayla and he was sure that she was competent and passionate and all of those other things that all of the animal advocates and rescuers had to be. But he knew that if Fiona was there and in charge, things would always go smoother and everyone around her would feel more confident.

"I can't believe I'm saying this, but you need to be involved in the stuff. When something big like this is going down, you need to be in the middle of it."

She slid him a look. "Man, I wish I had a recording of that or had it in writing."

He gave a soft chuckle. "You don't need that. You know it better than I do. This is what you do, Fi. This is what you're meant to do. It's what you *want* to be doing. You can't let people hold you back." He paused for a moment and took a deep breath and blew it out. "Even me."

She gave a soft snort. "I know that was painful. Thank you."

"And for the record—" He paused so she would look over at him. With his eyes on hers, he finished, "I think rescuing wild, endangered, vulnerable animals from people who would exploit and abuse them is one of the most fucking queenly things you could possibly do."

She looked completely stunned.

Knox was grateful he had to pull his eyes back to the road a moment later. Otherwise, she would've seen all kinds of emotions in his expression, and he wasn't sure she was ready for any of them yet.

"Okay, what's the plan, Queen?"

They were parked at the end of the road that would lead them to Colby Sutton's ranch.

Fiona looked over at Knox. "I'm not queen of anything yet."

He shook his head. "Oh, that's not true. And you know it. And according to the really fucking dirty dream I had last night, my imagination sure knows it."

She lifted a brow. "Oh yeah?"

"Yep, you looked pretty damn great in that crown." He paused. Then gave her a sexy half-grin. "And nothing else."

"I was wearing a crown in bed?" Well, this was interesting.

"And riding me very regally."

She laughed. "My crown is really heavy. The thing would hurt if it fell off and hit you in the wrong place."

He turned on the seat. "You actually have a crown?"

"Of course. Last time I tried it on, it was a little big. But I've probably grown into it by now." She frowned. She was going to have to wear that damned thing. It wasn't an everyday accessory, of course, but for official functions she'd definitely have to have it on.

"It makes me a bad person to want to see that, doesn't it?" he asked.

A soft laugh bubbled up in spite of her thoughts about how she'd have to do some neck strengthening exercises if she'd be expected to wear the crown for more than an hour. "I don't think so. I like where your dirty dream was going anyway."

"Would you make me call you Your Majesty while you were fucking me?"

Heat shot through her with a surprising intensity. "I believe I would."

He let out a long breath. "And I don't think I would mind."

She could easily picture the scene, in great detail. Knox on his back, his huge body taking up most of her four-poster bed. Her in her crown—and nothing else—riding him cowgirl. Him doing whatever she told him to do and yet her still losing her mind with pleasure.

"You okay?" he asked.

"Huh?"

"You look like you zoned out there for a minute." His smile was knowing. And smug.

She shook her head. "Quit distracting me."

"Sorry. Tell me what we're doing now that we're here."

The four-hour drive had gone fast. She didn't mind road trips but with Knox it had definitely been more fun. They'd talked about this rescue and others. But they'd also talked about random stuff. And nothing. They'd sat and just listened to the radio for long stretches too. And yes, they'd played a couple of silly road trip games. She was really glad he'd come along.

"Colby has been picked up. Jasmine is on her way back to the ranch. Kayla and two others have the tiger uncovered and they're waiting for law enforcement." She glanced down at her phone. "We need to stay out here until we get the word they're ready for us."

They were parked on a backroad about a quarter of a mile from the ranch. Red Plains was just over the border from Louisiana and had taken no time to find. Kayla's directions to the ranch had been perfect.

"They found him, huh?" Knox asked. "The tiger?"

Something in his voice caused her to study him closer. He looked sad. "They did."

"So it was true."

"Yes. But we knew it would be. We trusted Jasmine."

"Maybe he did have a good reason."

Fiona stared at him. "You mean Colby? Are you hoping for that?"

Knox shrugged, the move calling her attention to just how freaking big his shoulders really were. "Yeah. I mean, animals get sick and need to be put down sometimes. That I can understand."

Oh boy. Fiona felt a familiar trepidation roll through her. But right with it was a stunned realization that she was feeling it in regards to *Knox*. The big tough guy who not only loved to boss people around but who seemed unaffected by things like, oh, baby otters, for instance. He'd totally taken those babies in because it was a way into her bed. She knew that. She knew that he knew that she knew that.

Then they'd stolen his heart.

He did not have climbing structures and a baby swimming pool because he was trying to get her panties off. He'd fallen for those otters. He was exactly the man she'd thought he was underneath the gruff, grumbly exterior. And she was thrilled.

Until she realized that his soft heart had now been uncovered and was going to get hurt.

The apprehension she was feeling now was the same way she felt when Saoirse asked her questions about why people did bad things to animals, or to other people. It was the same feeling she felt when she had new rescue volunteers working and they were first confronted with the true evil she and her colleagues so often saw in this line of work.

And she wanted to protect him. Just like she did Saoirse. She wanted to tell him that the bad things were super rare. That people who hurt and exploited animals were few and far between. And that she and her people and thousands like her were making a difference.

Of course, none of that was really true.

There were *lots* of horrible people being horrible every day. And she didn't know why. She couldn't explain it. And yes, she and the people like her were *trying* to make a difference and were fighting each battle they came across, but it sure as hell didn't feel like it was getting any better.

"Well," Fiona started carefully. "We can hope that he at least really *believed* he had a good reason and that—"

"Fi."

She looked over as Knox cut her off. "Yeah?"

"You don't have to do that."

"Do what?"

"Pull back. Sugarcoat it. You can lay it all out there. I'm a big boy."

She blew out a breath. "You sure? It can get pretty messy. This is your first rescue."

"Yeah. And...not everyone is cut out for this like you are. I get that. But I don't want you to tread lightly around me. I want you to be honest and I want you to be able to be real about this. I want to see what you see. And, if at the end of the day *you* need to scream or cry or rage about it...I want to be there."

She looked at him for a long moment, her heart hammering. "I *often* want to scream or cry or rage. My road trips home from rescues can be kind of ugly."

He gave a single nod. "Another good reason I'm along then. It's not safe to drive while you're crying and screaming."

She swallowed hard, feeling like she just might start crying right then and there.

"People like Colby get into this stuff for a lot of reasons. It sounds like he started out raising tigers with his mom because they thought raising them would help save them. But his mom died and he realized he could make good money at it. Money often corrupts people, even those who start out with a calling. What starts out as an innocent petting zoo of rabbits and goats turns into a money-maker where baby animals are taken from their moms and passed around like toys, adults are bred like cattle, and the older ones are discarded when they're of no use anymore."

"Fuckers," Knox muttered.

She nodded. "And you'll find all kinds on the rescue side. You'll find some that want to burn places like this down and are willing to do time for it. You'll find people like me, who are somewhere in the middle. And you'll find people like Kayla who think that these people can be reformed. Like she was."

"She was reformed? What does that mean?"

"A lot like Colby, she got into private ownership because she thought that was the way to really protect the animals. That the government didn't care and passionate private owners would do more for them. But then she got defiant and didn't do some paperwork"—Fiona gave him a grin—"and got mouthy with a judge and spent some time in jail where she had an epiphany. No living being should be locked up and at another's mercy. So now she works on the other side, totally against animals in captivity and especially private ownership."

Knox frowned. "Interesting."

"She is. So, she'll want to try to save Colby. She'll try to understand him. Try to reason with him. She always thinks everyone and everything is savable."

Knox was quiet for a few seconds. "Sounds a little like Saoirse."

Fiona thought about her daughter wanting to teach Jacob how to be kind instead of a bully. "I guess it does. But she's nine. Kayla is twenty-six. Surely, by the time Saoirse is twenty-six she'll learn that there are just some bad people who will always do bad things even given the choice and it's not our fault or our responsibility to change them."

Knox looked at her. "Goddammit."

"What?"

"I fucking hate the idea that Saoirse is going to have to learn that. And that something or someone is going to break her heart to teach it. That she'll become jaded. That she's not going to look at the world as this happy, hopeful place all the time."

Fiona had no words for him. He meant that. She could *feel* it in the way he'd said the words. He loved how her daughter was right now and he was going to mourn the hard lessons life was going to teach her.

That was a very...*parental* thing to feel.

In that moment, Fiona *really* wanted him around when Saoirse learned those things. She wanted Saoirse to have this big grumpy guy with the soft, sappy center to tell her that she was fucking badass and that fighting for the right thing was always the choice to make and that even if it sometimes hurt to do it, he believed in her. She didn't want her daughter across an ocean from him.

Unable to actually *say* any of that, instead, Fiona leaned in, grabbed the front of his shirt and pulled him close to kiss him slow and sweet.

His hand came up to cup the back of her head and he deepened the kiss but it stayed sweet somehow. It was a kiss full of emotion instead of heat and it sank into her very bones.

Finally, she let him go. "You're falling for my little girl," she said softly against his lips.

He sighed. "Yeah. You Grady women have a way of making even us grumpy bastards get all mushy inside."

She didn't say anything, just looked into those brown eyes that could make her feel hot and safe and beautiful and amazing and pissed off all in a blink.

Her phone buzzed, pulling her attention away from the man who was all kinds of dangerous for her heart...and her future plans. Which was probably for the best.

She sat back and looked at the screen. "It's Kayla. She says the cops are on scene. We need to go help coordinate getting all the animals new homes."

"I'm ready."

"You sure?"

That made him pause. "I will...do my best. Prepare me for what we're gonna do."

"I'll be the one directing which animals go where."

He smiled. "Not surprised."

She felt the surge of pride. She really was good at this. She knew all the players and was great at evaluating situations under pressure. "I'll be in touch with all of those people, working on getting the animals looked at and loaded up, and I'll be the contact person for the local authorities."

"Sounds good."

"So we'll be right in there with the animals. Counting, taking notes about them, trying to find paperwork, all of that. It's going to be a long night. We'll be here for the next twenty-four hours probably at least."

"I'm in."

God, she was definitely in love with him. She had no doubt that he'd be right there, for whatever she needed. Those muscles would definitely come in handy too. "Are you telling me that I finally got you past the eye-rolling and sighing over animal rescues?"

He leaned in, caught her chin between his thumb and fingers, and said, "I always did that just to poke you. Because you're hot when you're riled up."

She lifted a brow. "*Always?*"

"Okay, all the times after the first time. When I actually understood what you were doing. And how hot you are when you're riled up."

She grinned. "Well, Autre wouldn't have half the animals they do if you weren't hot when *you're* riled up, you know."

He narrowed his eyes. "I suspected."

"And I'm about to tell you something that's *really* going to turn you on."

"I'm listening."

"I could really use someone to be in charge of a bunch of

paperwork. Record the animals, tag numbers, where we're going to send them, keep track of phone numbers, names—"

"I'm your guy."

A shiver of emotion went through her. She *wanted* him to be her guy. But she grinned. "You're perfect for this."

"Though I didn't bring my clipboard."

God, he had a clipboard. Why was that hot?

"You'll have to improvise." She looked him up and down. "And you know that you're going to ruin those shoes, right? There's bound to be...mud. At least."

Knox looked down at his leather Oxford shoes. "Well...damn."

She laughed. "You said you were going home to get ready."

"Yes, and I was just thinking road trip. I really should've thought harder about what was on the other end."

She shrugged. "You'll learn."

But the quip fell a little flat.

Obviously, Knox wouldn't be going with her to rescue animals when she was back in Cara. It wouldn't matter what he'd learned. Or what new shoes he might buy to be prepared in the future. Because she had a feeling he was going to buy new shoes.

He might go along on other rescues with the Autre gang though. So he'd need those shoes. And that was...great.

But *she* wouldn't be doing any rescues. In Cara she'd be queen.

There would be no animals in captivity, no babies ripped away from their mothers, no one shooting endangered tigers because they were no longer "useful". She would fucking see to that. And she'd finally have that power.

Maybe her grandfather had been right to keep the power all along. A lot of humans couldn't be trusted to do the right thing a lot of the time. She'd left Cara to make a point, but nothing in Cara had changed. She'd come to the U.S. to make a difference, but not much had changed here either. Animals were still abused and neglected and unprotected by laws and species were still endangered.

As queen she could make things happen. No one could stop her. She could do almost everything she wanted to unilaterally. Hell, she could probably behead animal abusers in her country.

Well, maybe not that.

But...maybe.

She was going to think about that little bright spot when things got messy later on tonight anyway.

14

"Can I talk to you for a minute?" Knox asked Fiona. She was supervising the men loading a huge male tiger into one of the trucks for transport to...he checked the clipboard he'd pilfered from Colby Sutton's office...New Mexico.

She turned. "Sure. Everything okay?"

Was everything okay? Well, he'd seen a dead tiger. The animal had been shot in the head and buried in a guy's backyard. He'd seen sixteen other tigers cooped up in cages, some of them thin even to his untrained eye, and some of them obviously just babies. All of them had been wary of the humans. But not wary in the way an apex predator sizing up another apex predator should have been. Wary in the way an animal who had been in captivity all its life confronted with a crowd of new creatures that could do it harm would be.

No, he wasn't okay.

And at the moment, he was worried and a little annoyed.

"I think we have a problem, actually," he told her.

Fiona frowned. "Okay." She turned back to the men in the truck. "You guys good?"

"We've got it," one of them assured her.

Fiona started for the side door to the building where the office with the files—such that they were—and the cages with some of the smaller animals were housed. Once inside she faced him. "What's up?"

"I was looking into Steve."

She frowned again. "Okay."

Steve Athens was a new addition to the group of sanctuary owners. Fiona had only met him tonight. He was a friend of a friend of a friend and had been alerted that they needed sanctuaries for almost twenty tigers. Steve's property was in Oklahoma and he'd agreed to take two animals.

"I don't like him," Knox said simply.

Fiona sighed. He knew she was exhausted. And stressed. Seeing animals like this was hard enough for him. He was sure for an advocate like her, it really wore on her emotions. "What does that mean?"

"I met him and got a weird vibe. Everyone else was pitching in and clearly knew what they were doing. He's been hanging back. I went over to talk to him and he just..." Knox shrugged. "He seems detached."

"He's new to this," Fiona said. "He doesn't know any of us. He heard about this rescue through the grapevine."

"He's very new to this," Knox agreed. "His 'sanctuary' has one cat."

Fiona crossed her arms, her frown deepening. "Really? Did he tell you that?"

"No. Which is even more suspect. He says he's been doing this a long time. But the city manager there told me he moved to town only a year ago, has one tiger, and no one even knew about that until a UPS delivery guy stopped out there one day and happened to see it and then talked about it at the café."

Her mouth curled up. "You found out from the city manager?"

He lifted a brow. "You have your network. I have mine."

She laughed, but quickly sobered, her brows pulling together again. "Dammit. So he might not be experienced enough or even set up to do this."

"That's what I'm afraid of. I don't know that for sure, but he's been very closed lipped. And hasn't been jumping in to help. Which makes me think he's not comfortable and doesn't really know how rescues like this work."

She nodded. "I agree." She blew out a breath. "Crap. If we're not going to send tigers home with him we're going to have to find a home for two more."

"I know that's a pain in the ass, but we can't risk it. We need to check him out more fully before he gets involved here, right?"

She nodded. "So we need to recruit either two people to each take one more tiger or one person to take two more."

"Okay."

She studied him for a moment. "So go do that."

Knox looked at her in surprise. "Me?"

"You know what we need. I've got my hands full."

"Fine. I've got this."

She gave him a soft smile. "I know."

She started to turn away. But he stopped her.

"And I was thinking, just because he can't take cats this time, maybe we still need to talk with him," Knox said. "Arrange a chance for us to come up to his place and check it out. Maybe we can give him some tips about getting his place ready and invite him to another rescue, walk him through the whole thing. I'm not saying that he's not a potential future partner. Maybe he's just not ready yet."

She narrowed her eyes. "So work with him and get him ready? Give him a chance? Not just assume that he's a bad guy and doing something sketchy?"

Knox shrugged. "Yeah. It's always good to have as many people as possible on board, right?"

"That is a very Saoirse approach to this."

He grinned and tipped his head. "Thank you very much."

She started to turn away again, and Knox said quickly, "And just one more thing."

She turned back with a smile. "Yes?"

"Can we take one of those home?" He pointed to a cage across the room.

She lifted both brows this time. "Those are fennec foxes."

"Okay. Can we take one? They need a new home too, right?"

"Well, if you take one, you have to take all of them. They live in family units. That's probably a mom, dad, and their two babies."

Knox looked over at the four curled up animals. They were adorable. Right now they were sleeping, but he'd seen them awake earlier. They had pale tan and white fur, huge bushy tails, and enormous ears. They were small and one of the other volunteers had told him that they only got to be two to three pounds. "We can definitely have them at the zoo, right? The kids would love them."

Fiona put a hand on her hip, and he could tell she was fighting a smile. "If you take them home, you have to be responsible for them, young man."

"Okay."

"You already have three otters."

"I know. I'll take care of them. Wait, will these eat otters or something?"

She laughed. "I don't think so. For one, the otters will eventually be bigger than the foxes. Fennec foxes mostly eat insects and lizards. And eggs. And vegetation. But you're not going to keep these at your house with the otters anyway."

"I could."

"But you're not going to."

Had he turned into an animal lover? Maybe. Was it partly

because he knew that him being a big softy for cute little animals made her hot? Partly. But they really were cute.

And yes, he'd turned into an animal lover.

"You sure about that?"

She nodded. "Pretty sure."

"I kept the otters."

"You did."

"So I can keep these little foxes."

She lifted a shoulder. "We'll see."

H e needed to sneeze. But he could. Not. Sneeze.

He was going to die from trying not to sneeze.

But Heaven help him…he could not sneeze.

Because the four foxes were all asleep now and there were still two hours to get to Autre and he could *not* listen to four fennec foxes complain about this car trip for five more minutes.

Fennec foxes were very loud.

Four of them were *very* loud.

He also couldn't move so much as a finger for fear of waking one of them up.

Because of course the only way the foxes would sleep was curled up on his chest with his hands cupped around them, keeping them warm and making them feel protected.

So he was reclined in the passenger seat of Fiona's truck with a horrible cramp in his upper back and a crick in his neck, and his eyes watering from not sneezing.

Could a guy die from not sneezing?

He was glad when the foxes had finally fallen asleep, he'd already been looking at Fiona so his head was turned in that direction. He could at least watch her while he sat here in agony, afraid of four little fluff balls that weighed less than ten pounds all put together.

Fiona shot him a look. She was highly amused by this whole thing. "How are you doing?"

"Fine," he whispered. He really needed her to whisper too. She just snorted.

"If you wake them up, we have to trade places, and you have to hold them."

She shook her head, laughing louder. "This was your idea."

"You're telling me they're not cute?"

"Oh, they are adorable. Fennec foxes are also hyper, and loud. They'll also urinate to mark their territory. If they like you too much, they might pee right on you."

Instinctively he started to shift then froze. Could he withstand some fox pee to keep them quiet? Definitely.

"I'm kidding. Mostly," she said. "But I do think that we should eventually settle them at the petting zoo, rather than in your house."

"Okay." He looked down at them. "But this does make you more attracted to me, doesn't it?"

She sighed. "I'm not sure I could be any more attracted to you."

"I feel bad making you drive the whole way back."

She shook her head. "It's only two more hours. And I'm used to doing these trips completely alone. I like having a companion even if you're not driving."

His chest tightened a bit. This was the first time they'd done a rescue together and he regretted not having accompanied her before. He could've gone to Alabama to help her and the group with the hurricane cleanup last year. Several of the guys and Naomi and Ellie had all gone as part of the Cajun Navy. But he'd always thought he was better at doing the paperwork, like insurance forms, and talking to adjusters and helping people organize and make list of things they'd lost, rather than actually getting in and wading through floodwaters and getting his hands and shoes dirty.

He wiggled his toes. He couldn't see his shoes at the moment, but he knew they were done for. He had work boots, of course. He lived on the bayou. It wasn't like he never went outside and did manual labor. Hell, he went out and cut trees and moved debris and had done more than his share of pumping water and scooping mud when storms came through. It just wasn't what he felt he was best at. And maybe he wasn't. But being with Fiona...

Maybe *that's* what he was best at. He'd made sure she was drinking water, and handed her a sandwich at one point, insisted she drink a fruit smoothie at another, and had made her eat a granola bar and banana in front of him just a couple hours ago. He'd also pulled her in and hugged her at least four times. The woman was a dynamo. And it was clear that everyone around her in the rescue group was used to her taking charge and being the one they all looked to for direction. She took care of everyone. So no one thought to take care of her.

It had occurred to him that when she was in Autre, it was the same. Everyone let her lead the way and asked her for advice. They never overrode her decisions, never questioned her, and never insisted she stop, take a deep breath, sit down, and just rest.

He frowned and shifted oh-so-slowly so that none of his new furry friends would stir. He was the only person that he'd ever seen question her. When she'd first started coming to Autre, he'd been the one asking where the paperwork and permits were. And this time on the rescue, he'd been the only one to pull her aside and say that one of her decisions wasn't right.

He'd been the one to question her about Steve. If he hadn't butted in, those tigers would be on their way to Oklahoma. Which might've been fine. He didn't know for sure that Steve would be a problem. He just had some reservations. As he so often did. Being a perfectionist was like that. If things didn't line up in an absolutely straight line, he started to wonder if everything was wrong.

His questioning had resulted in a four-hour delay, and Steve being completely pissed off and leaving before they were able to assure him that they still wanted to work with him and offer a chance to come to Oklahoma and learn more about his operation. It had also added a burden to two other sanctuaries. One of them had needed to bring over another truck to transport the additional tiger.

Which was why he and Fiona were so late getting back to Autre. She'd refused to leave Texas until all of the animals were loaded and on their way to their new homes. So because of his question, Saoirse hadn't seen her mom for two days and King Diarmuid had been in Autre while Fiona had been in an entirely different state. She hadn't been at home convincing him that she could take over the throne and that he should allow her to rescind her abdication.

Dammit. He wasn't actually the only person to ever question Fiona, Knox realized. Her grandfather questioned her all the time.

By the time they pulled into Autre and Fiona parked at his house, Knox's stomach was knotted into a tight ball.

He'd inserted himself into a situation that Fiona had done a million times, very well. He'd been surrounded by people who did this on a regular basis and were led by a woman who not only knew what she was doing but had a passion and instinct for it that had caused him to fall in love with her. Still, he'd opened his big mouth.

And he hadn't been able to apologize or get into it with her in the truck for fear of waking the foxes.

Fiona rounded the truck and came to his side, opening the door. The sound and the night air seeped in, stirring the foxes, and suddenly the cab was filled with whining and chirping.

She laughed softly as she took two from him, gathering

them to her chest and talking to them softly about how they were just fine, and that they were making a big deal about nothing, and welcoming them to their new home.

Knox scooped the two remaining foxes up in his palms and followed her into the house.

"Where do you think we should put them?" he asked.

"I would say the laundry room. I think we can make the carrier into a den, make sure they have food and water, and then just leave them in there tonight. They'll feel safe and contained...and will be very far away from your bedroom so you won't hear them." Fiona was clearly amused as she spoke over the four foxes voicing their opinion about being awakened from their deep sleep in the truck.

He nodded. "Good call."

She always has good calls, dumbass. This is what she does. She's the expert. You should have let her lead the whole time.

He followed her into the laundry room and surrendered the foxes he held once she was sitting on the floor. He returned to the truck to gather supplies. He brought the pet carrier, blankets, and food in and went to bring their bags in while she set up the animals.

He detoured through the kitchen to grab a bowl of water and noticed a note on his kitchen counter. Picking it up, he felt his heart squeeze. He filled the bowl and returned to the laundry room, handing the piece of paper to Fiona.

"What's this?"

"Saoirse came over to take care of the otters while we were gone. Of course," he said.

She nodded. "This is not her artwork though."

The sketch of the three otters was incredibly good. "Look at the back."

Fiona flipped the page over. Her eyes and smile both widened. "Jacob?"

"I'm guessing Saoirse brought him with her to meet the otters. One of her attempts to soften his black heart."

"And I'm guessing this sketch of your otters means it worked a little?"

"Like I said, you Grady women have a way of softening up even us assholes."

She looked up at him from where she sat on the floor with tiny foxes crawling all over her. He had never seen a more gorgeous woman than this one in a rumpled t-shirt and blue jeans that she'd been wearing for two days, her hair tumbling out of the messy bun on top of her head, exhausted and emotionally drained, yet here *caring*. With her whole heart. About the animals, about the kids, even about him.

"I don't think you said asshole."

"We both know I am."

She frowned. She set a couple foxes to the side and scrambled to her feet. She crossed to where he stood and stopped right in front of him, tipping her head back to look up at him. "You're not. You try to be. And you have your moments when you annoy the shit out of me. But you're definitely not an asshole, Knox."

"I shouldn't have butted in."

She frowned. "What are you talking about?"

"I shouldn't have butted in with the tigers and Steve. We should have just let him take them. They needed a home, he was willing, and why not? So, he only has one tiger right now. Everybody probably started with one. It's probably *better* to start with one. You learn the ropes, you figure out what they need, and if you've got what it takes. If he has one and thinks he can take more on, who am I to judge? I know nothing about tigers. The people you work with do. It's their passion, part of their life's calling. But then I show up because I have the hots for their leader, and someone gave me a clipboard—" Okay, he had *taken* the clipboard. "And I suddenly think I know more than the people who called Steve in?"

"You looked everyone up, didn't you? You researched all of the sanctuaries." She nodded before he even started to answer. "And don't deny it. I know you. Even if I told you that they were legit and I knew them and I thought they were going to be great, you still would've looked them up for yourself."

He shoved a hand through his hair. "See? Asshole. Yes, I looked them all up. I called their city managers too."

"Why?"

"Because city managers know things. They know what's happening in and around their towns. They might not be in charge of actually doing certain inspections and issuing permits or enforcing the laws, but they know who has permits for what. And who doesn't. And who needs them and who doesn't. And more, they hear the gossip. They hear the complaints. They're out and about. And if they don't hear it directly, they know the people who run the businesses where the gossip happens. People might be hesitant to go to the cop about something like a tiger if they don't know the laws, but they're sure as hell gonna talk about it at the coffee shop."

Fiona nodded. "And they're going to know that someone is going to overhear and tell someone else and that eventually it will make it back to the right people if it's a problem."

"Yep."

"That makes sense."

Knox nodded. "And maybe it's not saving endangered animals, but city managers care about their towns and want to take care of the people in them."

She smiled. "So they don't mind being awakened in the middle of the night?"

He winced. "They don't mind if there's a fire or a natural disaster or, you know, an *emergency*. But..." He blew out a breath. "I probably didn't need to call them all and ask about their tiger sanctuaries." He was going to have to call them all back and apologize. God, this whole thing had gotten him wound up to the point that now he'd looked like an idiot to several of his colleagues. "My questions probably sounded ridiculous. And Steve probably really is just trying to change the world and make it a better place like you. But I had to throw up a red flag because something felt 'off' to me. Who do I think I am?"

Fiona just stared at him for several seconds before glancing back at the foxes, then she took his hand and pulled him out of the laundry room, shutting the door behind them.

The foxes started crying and Knox glanced back toward the door.

"They're going to be fine," she said, tugging him down the hall toward the front of the house. "The laundry room is also the best choice for them tonight because we're going to have to clean up fox pee and poop tomorrow. But otherwise this is going to be fine."

He let her lead him into the foyer, but that was where he stopped her. "You don't have to stay. I decided to bring them home with me so that's my responsibility. I didn't mean to pull you into that."

"Oh, I'm staying. For one thing, it's the middle of the night, and if I go home I might wake Saoirse and she definitely doesn't need to be up at two in the morning with school tomorrow. For another, we have some talking to do."

"I'm just sorry. I don't have anything else to say. I shouldn't have gotten involved. I know this about myself. I told *you* this. This is why I need to have the distance. I need a buffer. I get all wrapped up and start thinking I know best, and I need to back off, give you space, let you just be your amazing self."

"Don't you dare apologize for that."

He frowned. "What do you mean? I totally stepped all over your project."

"Maybe. Or maybe not. Maybe your call was totally right. Maybe Steve was the wrong choice. Or maybe you are wrong. If so, we'll fix it with Steve. But what you did, *for me*, was amazing. I don't want you to apologize for that."

"What I did for you? Making everything a bigger mess? Make you stay there longer? Keep you away from your kid and your family?"

"Look, my kid and family are great, because I've actually done a hell of a job in structuring it so that they can be. Saoirse is fine. She has a ton of people who love her and support her and she *knows* that. She also knows what I do for a living and believes in it and supports it. She's proud of me."

For a moment, Fiona paused. Then blinked. Then smiled. As if that moment, saying that out loud, was the first time it had really, truly sunk in that her daughter *did* understand and support what she did and *was* completely fine and proud of her.

Knox felt his chest tighten. Thank God Fiona understood that. Because she was right. Saoirse was very loved and very well adjusted and had an amazing mother.

"So when I'm off on rescues, I feel good about it," Fiona continued, confidence in her voice. "I don't worry about her, because she knows there are bigger things. And I need her to know that. I need her to live her life that way too. And she is." Fiona wiggled the piece of paper in her hand. "She understands that every small battle, every person and animal, has potential and is worth the time and energy. I'm doing a good job." She dropped her arm and stepped closer.

"So don't apologize about keeping me there longer. And don't apologize about getting involved in something that I love because you care about me. I love you getting all worked up this way. I love you throwing yourself into something that matters to me and finding out that it matters to you too." She took a deep breath, but her gaze on his never wavered. "I know that you feel like this guy inside of you is the problem, but Shannon and Kendall were idiots. *Please* be this guy for me. Please be this guy who gets involved in what I do and love. Who finds a passion for it too. Who will make mistakes because he cares so much about it. Please be this wrapped up in *me* and this passionate about *me*."

His heart was pounding and adrenaline was coursing through his body. He would've thought that it was frustration and maybe even anger that he'd done this again, messed this up *again*. But he quickly realized that it was passion and desire. For this woman. About this woman. Because of this woman. Not just physical passion, but a burning *enthusiasm* that he so often tamped down. She was giving him permission to be who he was naturally inclined to be. Someone who got involved and wanted to know everything and was too much for some people.

But he wasn't too much for her.

He didn't have any more words.

So instead, he reached up and cupped her face in both hands and lowered his mouth to hers.

The kiss was hot, deep, and sent searing need along with an intense relief flooding through him. He walked her back to the same wall that he'd pressed her against the night she'd showed up on his front porch and said she was going to tell him something that was going to change everything.

God, she'd been so right about that.

As soon as her back met the wall, his hands went to her ass and she instinctively lifted and wrapped her legs around him so he could hold her against the wall and press into her with his whole body. She immediately started working on the buttons of his shirt and he kissed her hungrily as he gripped her ass and let her feel his need.

He didn't have to hold himself back from her in this way either and it was incredibly freeing. And the biggest turn on of his life.

As soon as his shirt dropped to the floor, he leaned back. "Yours now."

She stripped her shirt off and quickly undid her bra as well. He lifted a hand to cup one breast, teasing the nipple as her head fell back against the wall.

"Right here or bedroom?" he asked, just as he had the first night.

"Anywhere. Both."

He grinned. "I like that. Tell me what you want and I'll give it to you."

A tiny shiver went through her. "I just want...you to give it to me."

He leaned in and ran his mouth up and down her neck, feeling the goosebumps trip down her arm and her nipples tighten. "Gladly," he said roughly.

"I..." She stopped and sucked in a breath. "Honestly?"

"Of course." When she didn't respond, he pulled back and looked into her eyes. "Fi. Yes. Honestly."

She tipped her head back and squeezed her eyes shut. "I haven't done this in almost two years. Well, until you the other night. And it's been...kind of a relief in some ways."

He frowned and reached up, grasping her chin. "Fiona," he said firmly.

Her eyes opened.

"Talk to me."

She wet her lips. "I'm just in charge so much. I have so much going on. So many people looking to me and asking me things and needing me that sometimes sex feels like just one more thing where I have to make decisions too. Where and when and what do I want and I appreciate that," she added quickly. "Of course. Consent is so important and people should be equal partners and people should *talk* about what they want. I believe that. But so...*not* doing it was often just so much easier. And after I met you and didn't really want anyone else, it was really easy to just...take matters into my own hands for orgasms and not do it with anyone else."

He stared at her, processing all of that. She hadn't been with anyone else since they'd met? She didn't want to make decisions like this? Was she saying...

"Do you not want this tonight?"

She quickly gripped his shoulders tighter. "I want this *so* much. And I want it with you. Not only because I'm crazy about you and I've never been this attracted to someone before but because I trust you to just take care of me, Knox. To just do things that will make me feel amazing and that will be so hot and that I don't have to..." She pressed her lips together.

He leaned in. "You know you have to finish that sentence," he said, his voice gruff. But he knew where this was going. And it was hotter than hell. She trusted him to take care of her. This amazing, kickass, didn't-need-anyone woman was going to trust *him* after he'd fucked up her rescue to take care of her in a way he wanted to so fucking bad it hurt.

"I don't have to make any decisions," she said softly. Then she pulled her bottom lip between her teeth.

They just stared at each other, breathing hard.

"I know that sounds bad," she finally said, her voice almost a whisper.

"No. That sounds like the best fucking thing you could have possibly said to me, Fi." His voice was more of a growl.

Her pupils dilated. She swallowed hard. "Really?"

"The chance to take care of you? To do something for you that I *absolutely* can deliver on?" He leaned closer. "To give the most amazing woman I've ever known more pleasure than she can even imagine? Fuck, yes. Bring it on."

She sucked in a quick breath. "Thank you."

He gave a low chuckle. "I haven't even started."

"Actually...you have."

Fuck. She was going to kill him. She was, supposedly, not

going to do anything, just let him be totally in charge, and she was still going to kill him.

He let her slide down his body. Once her feet were on the floor, he stepped back and studied her. Okay. This was Fiona. He'd been filling his time with sweet, submissive women who he kept things very vanilla with. Ever since he'd realized he liked bold, fiery women too much, he'd just trod carefully...in all things.

Fiona didn't need him to be careful. She'd tell him if he stepped over any lines or pushed too far.

He went to one knee and undid the laces on her boots, pulling them off and tossing them toward the door. Then he undid her jeans and slid them off, taking her panties down with them. She lifted one foot, then the other as he stripped her.

With her naked, he reached for her again, intending to carry her upstairs. But she stopped him.

"Oh, hang on. I have one thing for you."

He watched as she went to her bag where he'd dropped it at the bottom of the steps. She turned with something shiny in her hands. With a little grin, she pulled her hands apart, then lifted them to her head. Where she set a crown.

"What is that?"

She laughed. "I made it out of the wrappers from our burgers."

They'd hit a drive-thru on their way home and the burgers had come wrapped in shiny foil. That she'd folded into a paper crown.

15

Knox's heart thunked against his ribs so hard he actually had to take a breath before he said, "That's almost perfect."

"Almost?" She stuck one hip out and set a hand on it.

"Yeah. I'd really like that to stay on while I fuck you. But you're gonna need a couple bobby pins or clips or something to hold that on for what I have in store."

Her eyes widened, but she immediately straightened and then bent to dig in her bag again.

He strode toward her, swinging her up into his arms with a little, "Oooop!" before she found anything.

"I guess we can just keep puttin' it back on," he said, her hand holding the crown on as he carried her up the stairs.

She was smiling and he felt a surge of triumph. He wanted her hot and begging and so turned on she didn't know her own name. But he also wanted her happy. So damned happy that she never wanted to be anywhere else.

He almost tripped over his own feet as that thought hit him. Oh no.

He wanted to keep her.

He wanted to take care of her.

He wanted to rescue animals with her.

And then keep some of those animals.

Well, fuck.

"Knox?"

He looked down at her. "Yeah?"

"Why did you stop walking?"

He looked around. He'd stopped walking. Son of a bitch.

"I just got caught up in wondering where to start with you."

She wiggled and gave a little sigh. "I can't wait."

Focus. Just focus on tonight. Right now.

He headed for the bedroom and tossed her on the bed. The crown fell to the mattress and he grinned as she grabbed for it, putting it back on as he shucked out of his shoes and the rest of his clothes. "Gonna be hard to hold on to that."

"My hands are going to be full?" she asked, her expression coy.

"Something like that." He crawled up onto the bed with her. Then took her hands, held her wrists together in one hand, scooped his other hand under her butt, and slid her up to the top of the bed as she gasped.

The move knocked the crown askew, and he studied her tousled hair, her crooked crown, and her pink cheeks. Yeah, this he liked. A lot.

"It's kind of like your halo being just a bit bent. Makes me feel *a little* more worthy."

She laughed.

She was all stretched out for him and he couldn't resist leaning in and taking a nipple in his mouth. Her laughter turned to a deep, long moan as he licked and sucked. Her legs moved on the duvet restlessly.

"Okay, Queen, hang on." He could just feast on her all night but he had plans. Plans to make her let go. To really bask in letting him take over.

He rolled away and she gave a small groan of protest.

"Patience."

He crossed to his closet and pulled two neckties from the rack. He returned to the bed, sliding them across his palms as he walked.

"I've got you," he reminded her.

She simply nodded.

He knelt beside her on the mattress and leaned in. He first wrapped one tie—one of his favorites that he often wore into the office and would now forever remember from this moment —around her wrists, keeping them together.

The other he slid behind her head. He made sure she understood what was happening. "At any point you can stop me."

She nodded again. "I know."

He covered her eyes with the tie, fastening it loosely.

He studied her now, her wrists bound, eyes covered, that damn crown still sitting to the side on her dark hair.

Yeah, he definitely wanted to keep her. Forever.

Fiona had never been this turned on in her life.

She couldn't see him, couldn't touch him, yet her entire body was tingling and she felt as if she could feel him on every inch of her skin.

She had never been this vulnerable with another man. She would have never imagined being in a position like this. But with Knox this felt right. Thank God. She would've loved to just turn everything over in the past but had never met someone she could do that with. Not just because she never trusted someone like this, but also because she wasn't sure she'd ever met a man who would have fully embraced this. It wasn't because Knox was necessarily dominant or particularly into any kinky BDSM stuff but just because he really did like to take charge because he cared. It wasn't really a power trip for him. It truly was the way that he cared and loved.

It was strange for her to feel that way without any words from him. But this was the most loving he had maybe ever been toward her. And that included several other times where she'd felt a softness and a caring from him that she knew was unusual.

He'd been incredibly sweet with the animals, passionate about making sure the tigers were safe, take charge and incredibly helpful during the rescue. When he handed her a sandwich and then later a fruit smoothie, she'd melted. It was such a dumb thing to get emotional about. But while the volunteers on the rescue teams were wonderful about taking care of one another and making sure everyone was properly fed and hydrated and rested, it was rare for anyone to worry about *her*. She didn't mind. She'd never thought about it. Until Knox was there.

And now he was going to give her the most memorable night of her life. And it would've been even without him binding her wrists and covering her eyes with his freaking neckties.

She never dated guys who wore neckties and now the fact that he was using them in bed? Yes, this was freaking hot.

She felt his hands skimming down her body and she closed her eyes, even behind the blindfold.

She felt her body relaxing into the mattress and duvet underneath her. He had an amazing bed.

The sense of him surrounded her and the heat from his body enveloped her. She felt a strange mix of relaxation and pleasurable tension.

His big hands stroked over her, teasing her nipples, cupping her breasts, sliding over her belly and skimming over her mound before continuing down her legs. He continued the path several times, ratcheting up the general tension and need.

His mouth soon followed. He ran his lips and beard down her neck and over her breasts, pausing to suck on her nipples, giving them light nips that made electricity zip along her nerve endings. She arched closer and gave in to all the feelings that were pulsing through her as well as the urge to let go of all the delicious sounds she couldn't keep inside.

His mouth trailed down her stomach and kissed over her mound, giving her clit a little lick, before he continued over her hip bones and down her inner thigh. Then he parted her knees and licked his way back up to her pussy. He stayed there for a few moments licking and sucking until she was lifting off the bed trying to get closer and begging him to make her come.

Finally, he eased two fingers inside her, thrusting as he ate her. He said deliciously dirty things, telling her how amazing she tasted and how he would never get enough of her. He urged her closer to the summit, telling her how much he wanted to feel her lose control, and how much he wanted her taste on his tongue.

Eventually, she came apart, coming hard around his fingers.

"That's my girl," he told her. Then he shifted and when she thought that he would finally thrust inside her, instead she felt his hands around her hips and then felt her body being turned to her stomach.

Okay, well, this was fine too. She loved it from behind. But instead of putting her on hands and knees and thrusting, his big hands began working her sore muscles. He massaged across her shoulders and down her back, kneading his thumbs into her lower back and then down into her buttocks. She groaned into the duvet at the delicious combination of pain and pleasure as the knots slowly gave underneath his touch.

She was always sore after a rescue and his fingers seem to find each and every one of the tension points as if by magic. He worked up her spine and into her shoulder blades and then to the muscles over her shoulders and into her neck.

She had no idea how long she lay there letting him massage her whole body with his huge, hot hands, but she was a near puddle of relaxed pleasure when he finally grasped her hips and pulled her back, bringing her butt up into the air. He massaged her ass cheeks.

"So fucking gorgeous. Thank you." His voice was like gravel.

She laughed softly, unable to even gather enough power to give her voice any volume. "For what?" she practically whispered.

"For letting me do that. I want to take care of you so much. You have no idea what a turn on that is."

God, if this man wanted to take care of her like this, she was more than willing. She'd let him do this every fucking day. But she held that back. For some reason she knew that would bother him. Every fucking day wasn't on the table. He'd been very clear about that.

He ran his hands over her butt and down the back of her thighs. Then he brought his hand around and cupped between her legs, his middle finger teasing over her clit.

It'd been a few minutes since her orgasm but immediately her body lit up for him again.

She pressed back against his hand. "Yes, Knox."

"I want you so damn bad."

"Yes."

"You're so tight," he murmured as he slid a finger into her again. "So perfect."

She pressed against him, encouraging it.

"Fuck." He withdrew his finger and she heard the sound of a condom package ripping. Then a moment later she felt the tip of his cock against her opening.

"You good?" he asked.

Her head was resting on the mattress, her arms stretched above her, still bound.

"I'm so relaxed and turned on at the same time, you might have to hold me up, but I'm so okay."

He ran a big hand up her back. "Oh, I can hold on to you. I'd love nothing more."

Her breath caught in her chest for just a moment. Surely he didn't mean that the way it sounded—that he'd love to hold onto her for good, in any other way other than physical. He meant right now, at this moment, while he fucked her.

She wiggled her butt.

He took the hint. He pressed forward, sliding into her slowly, stretching, the friction and the heat and the pressure incredible.

She gave a long groan. "Yes, Knox."

"Damn." He sounded like he was speaking with his jaw clenched.

She could picture it. His face, that mouth in a grim line, though not because he was upset, but because he was trying to hold back.

She felt his fingers curl into her hips as he pulled her back. He sank deep and then held for just a moment as they both adjusted to him filling her completely.

Then he started to move. The friction and heat built quickly and soon he was thrusting hard and deep.

She knew that it was important that he could go with his urges and instincts. He trusted that she would tell him when it was too much, tell him what she couldn't handle or didn't want. Not that she could imagine a time when she would do that, when she would ever push him away, but she loved the fact that he knew he could trust her.

This was different than what they'd done in the truck. This was more intimate somehow. This was in his bedroom, with his ties, but it was also with their feelings laid bare. This was after he'd shared one of the most important things in her life with her with the rescue and after she had confessed to him that this was what she wanted, someone to take over and...take her. She had never said that to anyone before. She couldn't imagine saying it to anyone else.

This was definitely next level stuff for them.

That realization ratcheted up her emotions, even as the pleasure built deep inside her, and she felt herself spiraling toward her climax.

She couldn't reach her clit with her hands bound, but it seemed that Knox could sense exactly what she needed. He reached around and found her sweet spot, circling and pressing perfectly. She shot over the summit a moment later, crying out his name.

He thrust hard and fast, pounding into her, and was soon shouting her name as he came hard, his fingers digging into her hips.

He collapsed forward, taking her to the mattress with him and rolling to the side. He tucked her against his chest. Her arms rested in front of her, but they stayed bound. Neither of them moved to untie her or lift the blindfold and she was fine with that. It was sexy thinking that she looked like some kind of captive for this nerdy warrior. He had these two sides that never failed to make her shake her head with wonder.

After several long minutes of breathing heavily and not moving, Knox finally slid the blindfold up over her head and then pulled the tie around her wrists loose. He tossed both onto the duvet.

She turned to face him and looped her arm around his neck and pressed her body against his. She put her mouth to his, kissing him deeply, then pulled back. "Thank you."

"Ditto."

They just looked at each other for a long moment, both

acknowledging the moment, both acknowledging the thanks and what it meant.

Then he reached past her and the next thing she knew he was settling her very crumpled paper crown back on her head.

"Definitely a dream come true," he told her.

She looked into those brown eyes and couldn't agree more.

F iona was surprised that she wasn't sore when she woke up the next morning. Of course, the amazing massage she'd had the night before probably had a lot to do with that. She did, however, wake up extremely hot. She stretched and then rolled away from her own personal furnace. Lord, the man made her sweat. Literally.

Knox felt her move and stretched as well, his eyes sliding open.

She gave him a smile. "Good morning."

"'Morning, Your Majesty."

She laughed. "You really do like that, don't you?"

"That I got to tie up, blindfold, and fuck a *queen* last night? Are you kidding me? Hell yes, I do."

She rolled to her back and stretched again. "Not a queen of anything."

"Yet."

She felt him roll toward her and his big heavy hand settled on her belly. She rotated her head toward him.

She leaned over and kissed him. "We'll see."

"You should let me keep thinking that. Otherwise, I might have gotten your sweet ass up to help clean up fox pee and poop."

"Those are *your* foxes. I would have said, 'no thank you, but bring me coffee when you come back up' and rolled over and gone back to sleep."

He laughed, the sound low and rumbly, making her stomach swoop and ribbons of heat slip low between her legs. She slid closer. "But you got up early to go check on them?"

He ran his hand back and forth over her belly, dragging the sheet over her skin. "This may surprise you but I'm not really the type to sleep in."

"Yeah, huge shock."

"I was going to stay in bed and check on my emails and stuff, but I forgot my phone downstairs for some reason last night—" He gave her a sly smile. "And thought while I was up getting that, I'd look in on them. And check on the otters."

"Aw, you missed them."

He rolled his eyes, but he didn't deny it.

"And you were worried about the *new* additions to your menagerie."

He lifted a shoulder. "Anyway, everyone's fine. I came back to bed and was gonna wake you up for sex, but you looked exhausted and sweet, so I just climbed back in with you."

"Well, I'm awake now." She rolled to her side. "Is the morning sex still on the table?"

"Sex on the table is definitely doable. But not right now," he added as she arched closer.

"Why not?"

"Because I brought your phone up too and you've got a bunch of notifications for voicemail and texts."

She frowned. "Dammit."

"And I hate to admit it, but the idea of unread messages drives me a little crazy."

She laughed. "I'm shocked about that too."

"Your phone's right there on the table." He lifted his chin, indicating the table on her side of the bed.

Well, he was distracted now. If she put her hand down his pants, she *might* be able to get him focused back on her, but it would be just as easy to check her messages, tell him it was nothing, and *then* strip him out of the gray athletic shorts she really hoped he was wearing sans underwear.

She reached for her phone and swiped her thumb over the screen. But it only took her about a second to realize that she wasn't going to be having morning sex. "The voice message is from Kayla," she told Knox.

"Kayla from Texas?"

Fiona nodded. "And that's not a good sign. We don't usually talk this soon after rescue." She hit the replay button for the voicemail.

It was definitely not good news. She sighed and disconnected a minute later.

"What's going on?"

"I'm being sued."

"*Sued*?" Knox repeated. "For what?"

"Trespassing is in there, along with some other things, but basically it has to do with taking the tigers and other animals."

"But that wasn't just you, specifically. There were a bunch of people there and law enforcement was on scene."

"Yes, but I've been singled out. I was leading the group. And anyone can sue anyone else for anything. It probably won't actually go very far. But it becomes a hassle for me. And isn't great for my reputation. The ultimate goal is just to make trouble for me."

"Who's suing?"

"Colby Sutton."

Knox scowled. "How did he even know your name?"

She sighed. He was *not* going to like this part. "Steve told him."

"One Tiger Steve?"

"Yep."

"Dammit." Knox sat up, shoving a hand through his hair. "Because we didn't let him take a tiger? I never should've said anything."

Fiona's frowned at his back and sat forward. "Hey, this just goes to show that you were right. Steve is not a good guy. Even if initially his intentions were good, who goes behind the back of the rescue organizer and turns her over to the bad guy? Your instincts were spot on, Knox."

He looked over at her. "But I still got you in trouble. If I'd just kept my mouth shut—"

"You did the right thing. I will be fine. He's not going to get away with suing me. I didn't do anything wrong."

"But you have to deal with this. Pay an attorney. Hassle with it."

She nodded. "Well, that's the other side of all this rescue stuff. There are people fighting us. I've had to deal with calling my attorney several times. There aren't enough laws and regulations. Sometimes some of this falls in a gray area. A lot of times it's a case by case basis and depends on where we're working."

"I hate that it's such a battle for you. I don't know how you do it."

She put a hand on his back and rubbed it up and down. "I want you to think about those tigers last night. And those foxes downstairs."

He was quiet and pulled in a long breath.

"You do know how I do it," she said softly. "You get it."

"How can I help?"

She shrugged. "Right now, just keep telling me I'm amazing and that you think it's hot that I fight these battles."

He gave her a sexy grin. "I most definitely think it's hot that you fight these battles."

"That's all I need." And that wasn't untrue. Him believing in her and now having been there with her, mattered a lot. "Now let's see what my brothers need." She swiped over the text and read the messages from both Cian and Torin. "Well, apparently my grandfather wants to talk to all three of us. They noticed that my truck was back and are hoping that I can meet them up at Ellie's in a little bit. He's getting ready to go home in a day or so."

"Well, that works out, I'm starving." Knox threw the covers back and swung his legs over the side of the bed. "How about we take a rain check on the table sex and we take this to the shower?"

"I don't—"

But he was already around to her side of the bed and scooping her up into his arms. "That was rhetorical. I make the sex decisions. Remember?"

She hooked her arm around his neck and let him carry her into the bathroom happily. She did remember. And *I make the sex decisions* sounded damn bossy and like something that could, would, and probably already had, gone to this man's head.

It was seriously one of the best things she had going on.

They walked through the door at Ellie's about an hour later. Cian, Torin, Jonah, and Henry were seated at the back table with Diarmuid and Oisin. Fiona had let them know they were on their way, so they were expecting her. It looked as if they'd already finished eating and were sitting around casually chatting, but butterflies kicked up in her stomach for some reason.

This was her family. But unlike Knox and the Landrys and her other friends in Autre, she had a lot harder time reading the O'Gradys. She didn't know where they stood on a number of issues and she really didn't know what to expect from a family meeting like this.

She and Cian and Torin saw each other semi-regularly but never formally. They hung out, had dinner, laughed, caught up.

When she and Saoirse went back to Cara, occasionally one of her brothers would be there but the last time they'd all been there together had been this past Christmas. And it had been formal. But not so much a meeting where they all exchanged ideas and opinions, as it had been a chance for their grandfather to lay out all the ways the three of them had failed the family and all the problems they'd caused.

This felt like that. In spite of the lack of fine linen tablecloths, two-hundred-year-old china, and a mahogany table that kept her grandfather a healthy ten feet away from all of them.

"Hey, everyone," she greeted nonchalantly as Knox pulled out a chair for her next to Cian and then took the one on her other side.

Diarmuid gave him a look. "We will be meeting about issues having to do with Cara."

"He can stay," Fiona said firmly. "There's nothing about this that he can't hear." She met her grandfather's gaze directly.

Did that mean Knox was more to her than a friend? Yes, it did. What did *that* mean to Diarmuid? Well, that depended a lot on what came out of his mouth by the time she finished her praline-stuffed French toast.

She felt Knox's hand settle on the back of her chair in a protective and supportive gesture that she very much appreciated.

"Very well," her grandfather said in a distinctly disapproving tone.

"What do you need, honey?" Ellie asked, setting mugs down and pouring coffee for Fiona and Knox.

Fiona met Ellie's eyes and knew that the other woman meant what did she need for breakfast...and in *any* other way. She smiled. "Praline-stuffed French toast and bacon. For now."

Ellie winked at her then looked at Knox. "How 'bout you? I see our city manager's getting a late start."

"Rescued a bunch of tigers yesterday," Knox said proudly,

sitting back in his chair, but leaving his arm behind Fiona. "Brought some foxes back too. Late night."

Ellie nodded. "You got a permit for those foxes?"

"Well, I...yes. I mean, not yet. But..." He looked at Fiona. "Do I need a permit for the foxes?"

She grinned. "The animal park will have some paperwork to do, but hopefully once we explain the situation they were in and that we are providing an emergency refuge, we'll be okay."

He shifted uncomfortably. "You mean, we really might get in trouble?"

"It's illegal to own foxes in Louisiana," she told him, lifting her cup for a sip. "But if the authorities still say no, I have a friend in Arkansas who will take them in."

His face fell. "I might not be able to keep them?"

She reached over and squeezed his thigh. "It gets complicated."

"You were *rescuing tigers?*" Cian asked.

"Colin knew," Fiona said. "I was called out of town last minute."

"That was unfortunate while your grandfather was in town," Oisin said. "We had hoped you would stay while he was here."

She nodded. "That was the intention. But sometimes things don't go according to plan."

That was an understatement. Things like changing her mind about becoming a queen. Or falling in love with the guy she'd meant to only have a long-distance fling with. Just for instance. She stoically avoided looking at Knox.

"But your grandfather is rarely here and this is an important trip. We were under the impression you wanted him to reconsider your abdication," Oisin said.

"Fiona is the leader. She's the problem solver. When things went a little sideways, they needed her," Knox said.

Oisin nodded. "I understand."

Knox leaned in. "Do you? Do you *really*?" He looked around the table. "Fiona saved the lives of thirty animals last night. She led a group of volunteers, gave them direction, worked with law enforcement, and stayed until the very last animal was safely on its way to a new home. Every single person there looked to her for her leadership."

Fiona put a hand on his thigh, but she knew he'd understand it was a *thank you* rather than a *back off*.

Cian nodded. "I've been on rescues with her before. I agree it's impressive."

"How about you, Your Highness?" Knox asked, focusing on the king. "Have you ever seen your granddaughter in her element? Truly shining? Living out her calling?"

Fiona felt warmth blossom in her chest and her fingers tightened on his thigh. Wow. That was...maybe even hotter than the neckties last night.

"I have not," Diarmuid replied. "But that transitions us perfectly into the topic for conversation today. We might as well get right to it."

She could feel the tension in Knox's body. "And what's that?"

Her grandfather's attention shifted to her. "I've reviewed the proposal you left with me in January. And I've decided to approve it."

No one said anything, but Cian sat up straighter in his chair and Torin frowned.

It took several seconds but his words finally sank in.

The bastard.

Fiona leaned in, resting her forearms on the table. "Just like that?"

"Yes."

She'd given him the proposal for the animal sanctuary two years ago. She'd left it with him *again* in January when she'd been in Cara.

"*All* of it?"

"Yes."

She just watched him for a long moment. He met her gaze calmly. He knew how hard that would be for her to walk away from.

"Any stipulations?"

"No."

She didn't believe him. He'd want something in return, surely. It only took her a moment to realize what that something was. She took a deep breath. "Who will run it?"

"We'll take applications, of course."

Anger and jealousy stabbed her in the gut. It was her dream sanctuary, including every single detail she'd asked for, but someone else would get to run it. "I see."

"Of course, if *you* wanted to come home and run it, the job would be yours."

She blinked at him. Ah, there it was. "So," Fiona finally said after nearly half a minute of just watching her grandfather. "You're going to approve an animal sanctuary on Cara. To my specifications. Every detail. And I can run it. But if I *don't* come home, you'll still open it. And put someone else in charge."

"Well, someone will have to oversee it," Diarmuid said.

Of course someone would. And no one would do it better than Fiona. And it would make her crazy thinking of someone else doing it.

"What about the throne?" Knox asked. "If she comes back to Cara, will you put her back in line for the crown?"

Fiona looked at him with surprise. She hadn't even thought of that. She looked back at her grandfather.

Diarmuid was clearly annoyed that Knox had inserted himself into the conversation. Still, he answered, "There would be no better way for me to observe her leadership skills. I could see how she acclimates to living on Cara full-time. How she interacts with our people. See her communication and public relation skills in action."

Knox's jaw tightened, but he said nothing. Fiona also found herself without words. Because Diarmuid was right. She hadn't lived in Cara for ten years. Her grandfather had no idea if she would make a good queen. It was probably fair for him to want to see how it would go. Especially because he did have an option.

Saoirse.

The animal park was the perfect way to get Fiona home and thereby, get Saoirse to Cara. Young, still impressionable Saoirse whom he *could* still train and mold. He could drag this whole "audition" out for Fiona, never giving her the crown but keeping her in Cara because of the animal park.

No. If she was going to Cara and starting an animal park, she was going to do it as *Queen*. There would be no laws or regulations or paperwork or permits keeping her from doing exactly what needed done for the animals. No assholes like Colby keeping animals in their backyards. No one suing her for saving them.

And she would be so damned good at it, Diarmuid wouldn't be able to deny her the crown.

"I need a minute to think," Fiona said, suddenly shoving her chair back and standing.

Diarmuid tipped his head, as if he'd been expecting that answer. "Of course. I leave in..." He looked at his watch. "Thirty-three and a half hours."

Fiona opened her mouth as if to reply, then closed it, and swallowed hard. "Fine." Then she turned and stomped out the backdoor of Ellie's.

Knox stood and turned to follow her.

He needed to stay the fuck out of...whatever this was. Fiona had assured him that stepping in last night had been fine. Good even. But she didn't *need* him. Certainly not in regards to her work. He didn't know what to say or do anyway.

But he couldn't just let her go.

He nearly ran into Ellie, carrying their plates of breakfast. "I um...think we'll need those to go."

"Come back later. There's nowhere to eat French toast by the giraffes."

"You know she's heading to the giraffes?"

"Don't *you* know she's heading to the giraffes?"

He nodded. Of course, she was.

"And hell, later on, she might need somethin' stronger than French toast," Ellie said. "Cora's shrimp creole will be perfect."

"That helps with big decisions?" Knox asked. "I've never heard that rumor."

"Nah, it helps clear out stuffy noses after hard cryin' though."

He nodded. "Got it." Then he sighed. "I don't want her crying."

"Well, that's too bad. She's got a heart for loving and a soul made to try to fix a lot of hurt. That guarantees cryin' sometimes." Ellie narrowed her eyes and focused on the table behind him. "Not to mention a prick for a grandfather."

Knox had always considered Ellie and Leo adopted grandparents of his own, as did many in Autre. He leaned in over the plates she held and kissed the top of her head. "Not everyone can be Landry lucky."

She smiled up at him. "Well, we've got room at our table for a few O'Gradys, so if you want to convince her to stick around, I'd be okay with that."

That jabbed him in the chest. "I...don't know if that's my place."

Ellie rolled her eyes. "You're gonna go fuck this up then, huh?" She sighed. "Okay. Come back in a few days when you're miserable and I'll give you some wise words that will make it all make sense and *then* you can fix it." She moved off muttering something about the men on the bayou being dumber than the gators.

He *almost* stopped her.

But Fiona was up with the giraffes. And probably crying. And suddenly he had to get to her.

He found her, as expected, with the giraffes. He approached, knowing that she knew he was there. He moved to stand at the fence next to her without a word. He leaned in on the top slat, linking his fingers.

They both just watched the giraffes for a few minutes. Finally, she sniffed.

He looked over at her. Her bottom lashes were wet, but it didn't look like she had actually been sobbing.

"You okay?"

"No. I'm really going to miss..."

"The giraffes," he supplied.

He wasn't sure if they were to the point where they would talk about how much they would miss each other. Things between them last night and with the tiger rescue had *just* happened. Things had *just* shifted between them.

It was too soon to tell her he was madly in love with her. It was definitely too soon to expect the same from her. Even if they both thought it, that was the kind of thing that people spent months testing and considering even after they said it.

She nodded. "Yeah. The giraffes. Speir is probably about three months away from giving birth."

"So you come back when she's close. You don't have to miss things here." He clasped his hands together, squeezing hard.

"You can be here for the big, fun moments. You'll be back and forth. You'll see Jordan's baby. You'll do other rescues with the girls. You'll come home for Charlie and Griffin's wedding. All of that."

Finally, she looked over at him. "Yeah. That's true. That's what we talked about from the beginning, right? Me going back and forth between Cara and here."

"Yeah. Exactly what we talked about."

This did not *feel* like what they'd talked about at all. This was a hell of a lot more than they'd talked about. Breccan wandered over and immediately nuzzled against Knox's head, then chewed a little on his hair. Laughing, Knox pushed the giraffe's snout out of the way and gave his nose a rub.

"So you think I should go?"

Knox took a breath. Well, there was the question. He'd been expecting her to ask him, but he wasn't sure he had an answer. Or if the answer he had was the right one. "He's manipulating you. We both know that. But…"

"But?"

"He's giving you the sanctuary. Right now. You thought you'd have to wait. We thought you'd have to be in charge to get it or that you'd have to wait for *Saoirse* to do it. But he's willing to do it now. Sure, he wants something in return but it's…a compromise."

She squinted off into the distance, watching the older giraffes back by the barn. "It's a carrot. Dangled to get me where he wants me to go."

"Yes. But it also shows this is important to him. He's listening. He's heard what you want and he's willing to give in."

"So you do think I should go?"

He shifted, turning to face her, leaning an elbow on the fence. "You *deserve* to go. To have this sanctuary your way. To not have to answer to anyone. To save tigers and so much more." He took a deep breath. "Fi, you can save hundreds of animals. Without anyone in your way. No laws and regulations —or lack thereof—telling you what you can do or can't do. No fighting, no arguing, no paperwork. It's your dream job."

She nodded. "Yeah. It is."

"And you can show him how damned queenly you are. You shouldn't have to, but you definitely can. It'll take him about ten minutes to see it if he's really watching."

She made a sound that was half a snort of disbelief and half a laugh. "You know a lot about queens and how they act?"

He'd been thinking about this for a few days. He nodded. "As a matter of fact, I've been living amongst them most of my life."

Now she turned to face him. She swallowed hard.

He stepped closer. "What *really* makes a woman a queen, Fi? She's someone who knows herself. Who has the respect of others and leads by example. Who doesn't just wish things were better or just talk about changing things, but actually puts herself out there and makes changes happen. She's fierce and bold and full of grace and love." He took a deep breath. "My mom, for instance. She's a prosecutor. She fights for justice. She takes on some of the worst of our society and makes sure they can't hurt other people.

"And Ellie Landry," he said with a small laugh. "She's the ultimate queen. She loves with her whole heart. No matter how people come to her, she sees them and their potential and their intentions and brings that all out.

"Cora Allain lost her husband and her grandson. Her son is in prison. But she still loves and laughs and takes care of people.

"Rosalie LeClaire not only loves and remembers her culture and traditions, but she helps us all know and love them just by the way she *lives* them.

"And then there's Charlie and Jordan and Jill and Naomi and Caroline, who turned a simple petting zoo into a place for people to learn about and interact with animals. To get closer to them and fall in love with them and become inspired to protect them. They've been willing to mess up and learn along the way, but they never quit."

He took another breath. "They're all queens. And you are right there in the middle of it all. Encouraging them. Teaching them. Supporting them. You *are* a queen, Fi. Make your grandfather see that."

Fiona stood just staring at him. A tear slipped down her cheek and Knox lifted a hand to wipe it away.

He knew that he had stunned her with that little speech. Hell, he'd stunned himself. But he'd seen it all in action. He'd sensed it in her the very first time he'd met her, but she had continued to prove it to him over and over again. And he was grateful. Not just for what he'd learned about her, but that she'd really made him appreciate all the other women too.

Finally, she said. "And I can still have you, right? You still want the long-distance thing at least?"

"You have me whether you want me or not. Whether I ever see you again or not. You have me, Fi."

She pulled in a shaky breath, and then stepped forward and wrapped her arms around him. He hugged her tightly and felt his whole world tilt again, because of this woman.

All great changes are preceded by chaos.

Damn. He'd thought that was a warning label.

Instead, it had been a promise.

16

It turned out that pretty streetlamps and hibiscus trees along Main Street did not actually make everything better. That did surprise him just a little.

What didn't surprise him, however, was that only texting, calling, and the occasional video chat with Fiona were not enough.

Fiona and Saoirse left Autre with Diarmuid and Oisin thirty-three and a half hours after the family meeting. Exactly as the king had said.

Typically Knox appreciated punctuality. In that case, he'd hated having one more thing in common with Fiona's grandfather.

Two weeks later, he was miserable.

He missed them. So much it hurt. Literally.

He'd become Drew Ryan's right-hand man in the giraffe barn in an attempt to feel closer to his girls and he'd gotten stepped on by Breccan.

Thank God, he was the smallest of all the giraffes and Knox's left foot was only badly bruised. If it had been the fully grown bull, Donal, Knox would have been in a cast. As it was, he was walking with a distinct limp and was pretty fucking crabby about the whole thing.

The sore foot was the only thing that had kept him from going along to the rescue that Naomi and Charlie had done two days ago. He pretended not to notice that Charlie and Naomi had seemed more than a little relieved when he'd said he was staying in Autre.

They hadn't ended up in jail and everything had apparently gone smoothly, and still, he found himself peppering them with questions at Ellie's before Donovan had asked, "What the hell is with you?"

What was with him was that he was a newly impassioned and enthusiastic animal rescuer. It was like a drug. Or maybe that was just Fiona. Either way he was addicted, and he knew there was no cure.

He was also in love with a woman and her daughter who now lived in another country and whom he would see only occasionally and temporarily.

All of which was slowly but surely turning him into an even bigger asshole than he had been before.

Or maybe not so slowly.

That was why he was eating his dinner at the bar today, rather than at the table with the rest of the Landrys. He knew he'd been hard to be around for the past two weeks. And while he was damned tired of their knowing looks and innuendo about the topic, they'd now graduated to blunt input like, "Can you just move to Cara?" and "You were the dumbass that told her to leave, remember?" and he was definitely sick of that.

Of course, he remembered. And as miserable as he was, he still maintained it was the right decision.

Ellie set his plate of food down in front of him and refilled his tea glass. Then she leaned in on the bar. "I can only assume you're sitting up here because you want to talk to me."

"I'm sitting up here because I'm sick of your family."

She rolled her eyes. "You get sick of my family every other day and twice on holidays. You still sit with them anyway."

"Can you remind me why again?"

"Because they're your people. And they're pretty fucking entertaining."

He ran his fork through his etouffee. "They're my people? You sure about that?"

"Very sure. You never heard that quote?"

"What quote?"

"The one that says, *you're going to be too much for some people, but those aren't your people.*"

He lifted his head and looked at her. "And you think that applies to me?"

"You don't?" She actually seemed surprised by the idea that he might not.

"You're telling me that the *Landrys* are the only people who can tolerate me?"

Ellie chuckled. "Well, there's lots of ways to be too much. I'll give you that my family can be too much in the volume department. Certainly in the meddling department. Absolutely in the inappropriate humor department at times. For some people we're too much in the loving-you-whether-you-want-to-be-loved-or-not department. But we can all be too much in our own way."

"And in what way am I too much?"

"You're too much in the I-love-you-and-that-means-I-want-to-know-everything-that's-going-on-in-your-life-and-get-involved-with-it-and-make-it-absolutely-as-fucking-great-as-it-can-be department."

He just stared at her. "You think so?"

"*I* don't think so. I think you do all of that exactly right. Never too much." She shrugged. "But I'm one of your people, so of course I like that. I subscribe to much of the same philosophy, in fact. But some people might find that too much. Like maybe Shannon. Or Kendall, for instance."

He continued just to watch her. "But that's how you see me?"

"That's who you are. And I'm very good at seeing people for who they are. Knox, you don't get involved in people's stuff because you're a perfectionist, or because you can't stand to see something go wrong, or because you think other people can't handle it or will do a bad job. You're an over-involved know-it-all because you care. Now, can it seem intense and a little heavy-handed? Sure, maybe to some people. But like I said, those just aren't your people."

"Well, then I guess I'm where I need to be. In Autre, taking care of stuff here for people I care about."

Ellie tipped her head. "As opposed to where? Someplace like Cara? With Fiona?"

Knox shook his head. Of course Ellie was going to go there. He wasn't sure anyone could be a big enough jerk to actually scare this woman off. That was one of those queenly things he admired about her. "Yeah, okay?"

"Well, I'm not really sure I would say it's okay. You ran off one of my favorite people."

"Ran off? I didn't run her off. She wanted to go. It's her dream job."

"I will guarantee if you'd asked her to stay, she would have."

"How could I've done that? Cara is perfect for her. She can have a huge animal sanctuary and she can do whatever she wants with it. Please tell me where I messed up by giving the woman I love her dream opportunity."

"Do you really think that was her dream opportunity?"

"Don't you?" Knox's heart was hammering in his chest. That had to be her dream. Otherwise, being apart from her was going to be even more torturous.

Ellie filled a couple of beer glasses from the tap and passed them over to the men sitting two stools down from Knox. Then she returned to him and their conversation. "I absolutely love the sanctuary here in Autre."

Knox nodded. "It's amazing. They've done a great job with it. But Fiona can save so many more animals in Cara. There is just so much red tape here."

Ellie nodded. "I understand that. But I don't love it because of the animals."

He frowned. "What do you mean?"

"Boys of the Bayou Gone Wild has been a sanctuary for the women running it as much as for the animals," Ellie said. "I love the critters, but those women have my heart. Seeing them come here and be set free to find their passions, to escape the cages they were in—whether it was a job, or a relationship, or an idea of who they were supposed to be—and find a place where they could be free to be their true selves and make the life they wanted to live, has been one of the great joys of my life. And I've had a lot of joy, Knox." She gave him a sincere, heartfelt smile. "That place has been a sanctuary for *people* more than anything. Some of my boys have found their true loves because that place has brought those loves here or has opened those loves up to their true passions and possibilities."

Knox felt like a band had wrapped around his chest, keeping his lungs from fully expanding.

"And now Fiona has a place like that. Where she has endless possibilities and can fully live out her passion."

Ellie nodded. "A place where everything is easy, where *you* don't have to worry about anyone giving her a hard time, or her making any bad decisions, or anyone giving her any trouble, because she's fully in charge. So unlike Shannon and her bakery or Kendall and the kids, or even Fiona's work here in the states, with her in Cara, *you* have no worries. There is literally nothing that can go wrong for her."

Knox simply nodded. Ellie Landry was right. As always.

"So, you should be feeling great. You should be thrilled."

"I should be."

"And are you?"

He blew out a breath. Ellie would know if he was lying. "I feel like I do when I forget to cc someone on an email. Or when I miss filling in a line on the form."

Ellie laughed. "Exactly. Because you thought you dotted all these Is and crossed all these Ts, but something in your gut is telling you that you missed something."

He swallowed. "What did I miss with Fiona?"

Ellie leaned further onto the bar and Knox knew she was on tiptoe on the stool she used behind the bar to reach over the top. She put her hands over his.

"You're not getting the fact that an easy animal sanctuary in Cara is like a cage to her."

Knox felt like she'd just punched him in the chest.

"Now I'm not saying there shouldn't be a sanctuary there," Ellie went on. "But Fiona needs to be fighting and educating and inspiring *people*. She needs to get her hands dirty and have sore muscles at the end of the day. She needs to feel like she's part of a team. Not the untouchable queen all alone in her tower waving her magic wand.

"She wants to be a warrior, out making things happen with her own hands and head and heart. She doesn't want it to be easy, Knox. And she doesn't want to do it alone. Anyone could run a sanctuary in Cara where there are no limitations. But not just anyone can do what she does *here*. *Real* queens do the hard stuff. They lead and make tough decisions and put themselves out there."

And just like that, the fist around his heart loosened slightly and he could finally take a deep breath.

He'd said the same thing. He'd told her what made a woman a queen. She was someone who led, who inspired, who made things happen. And Ellie was right...a *real* queen was someone who did the hard stuff that no one else wanted to do, the unglamorous stuff, the stuff that involved dirt and mud and shit—literal and metaphorical—and that didn't always turn out the way she'd hoped, but that was still worth the fight.

"Autre was her sanctuary too. The place where she could live the life she wanted, with the people she loved most, where she felt the most understood."

Ellie nodded. "Yep. And then you sent her off to the place where she's *least* understood."

"Okay. I got it." He sighed. "Cara *looked* perfect." He paused. "On paper."

Ellie gave him a smile full of understanding and affection. "Real life very rarely fills in all the lines and checks all the boxes perfectly, Knox."

"Since I'm the one who said she should go and I'm the one who thinks it makes so much sense, I should probably be the one to get her, huh?"

Ellie squeezed his hands. "Yes. And," she added. "I swear to God if it takes you more than ten minutes to pack, I'll kick your ass myself. You don't need to perfectly fold a thing, got it?"

He laughed. "Got it." He was eager enough to get to Fiona to possibly even forget to pack his toothbrush. Something that had never happened before. He had a checklist, after all.

"You want my gold coin from Cara for luck?" Ellie asked, pulling the coin from her pocket that had actually been pirate gold, not Cara gold. Of course she'd won the bet. Oisin was smitten with Cora. They were talking every day and even though he wasn't living in Autre—yet—he already had plans to fly back to Louisiana next week.

"I don't think I need a coin for luck," Knox said, suddenly feeling a surge of optimism. "But, I could definitely use a friend calling in a favor with a guy who has access to a private jet."

"Well, I think I can help you out with that too," Ellie said with a wink.

Yeah, he should definitely take advantage of Oisin's crush on Cora.

He might not have another chance to ride on King Diarmuid's jet after he talked the future queen into spending her life on the bayou with a commoner.

W ow, this was the dream.

Fiona stood at her office window in O'Grady Castle. The room was the size of three rooms in her house in Autre and had floor to ceiling windows on this side that overlooked a flower garden so gorgeous the Queen of Denmark came every year for the Bloom Festival.

There was a carefully manicured hedge that was laid out in a maze that, alongside a bright white stone pathway, wove through a multitude of flower beds bursting with every color in the rainbow. There were stone benches and fountains and sculptures dotted here and there and it was truly a spectacular scene.

Beyond the main flower garden was an herb garden, then an enormous vegetable garden, and off in the distance, the orchard where they had apple, lemon, and plum trees. To the west were the greenhouses where they grew everything they wanted year-round. They even had beehives and their own honeybees.

Fiona had to admit it was all impressive. She hadn't appreciated it as a kid, but not only did the castle have everything anyone could want, they also employed a huge staff to provide it.

She knew the people who worked for O'Grady castle were also free to take home whatever they wanted from the gardens, greenhouses, and the small farm that supplied the castle. That included meat, eggs, milk and cheese from the dairy, as well as wine, whiskey and beer from the distillery, and bread and pastries from the kitchen. The production of those goods had all been modernized over the years, however, the recipes and techniques for making everything from the cheese to the whiskey to the pies had been refined over generations of seeking the very best for the royal family. No one could get better food anywhere.

And now there would be an animal sanctuary sponsored by the royal family.

Just having the O'Grady name attached meant that they would have an influx of applications from the very best people, not only from Cara, but from other countries as well. Fiona would have unmatched, unlimited resources and supplies. This would be a world-renowned sanctuary within a year. Maybe sooner.

She had half an island worth of land. Only about a third of Cara was actually settled. There were some mountainous areas that wouldn't be usable for the sanctuary, but she still had nearly four hundred thousand acres to work with.

She could import any animal she wanted. There were no laws here restricting that. Even if there were, her grandfather could change them with a swipe of his pen.

She had enough money to not only ship the animals here but supply anything they needed.

She already had exotic animal veterinarians interested in the job. Of course she did. A multitude of species with unlimited resources to care for them? This was a dream job for them as well.

She had a pile of applications for jobs ranging from keepers to trackers to administrative assistants lying to the side of her desk. On top of saving animals, she was going to be creating jobs for her country's economy.

Her network of animal rescuers and advocates were thrilled. Of course, they'd been more than a little surprised to hear her whole story and find out that she had the power and resources she did. But once they'd recovered from that shock, they'd been excited and supportive.

She'd even been in touch with a few universities and wildlife groups that were working on propagation programs for some of the most critically endangered animals on the planet. They were equally excited to partner with her.

And she'd done all of that in two weeks.

It was absolutely amazing what you could get accomplished when there were no regulations or waiting periods. Or forms to fill out.

Of course, every time she thought of forms—and felt weird about not filling anything out—she thought of Knox. She didn't miss forms at all, but she desperately missed the nerdy, form-loving, perfectionistic bayou boy.

Texts, phone calls, and video chats weren't enough. They almost made the missing him worse.

Plus...she was bored.

When she'd lived in Florida she'd been busy all the time, so missing him hadn't been so bad.

And, of course, back then they hadn't slept together. And he hadn't been amazing with her daughter. Or stood up for her to her grandfather. Or shown her how sweet he was with the otter babies. Or the fennec foxes. Or accompanied her on a rescue.

"Argh!" Fiona shoved both hands through her hair. How was she going to make this work? Could she fly to Autre every weekend? Yes. Technically. Though wow, what a waste of jet fuel.

But she was already going stir crazy here. Her animal sanctuary was coming together without a hitch. There were no rescues to organize, no protests to plan, no meetings with Congress to prepare for. She was just...sitting here. In charge.

She turned with a sigh and looked around the room. This had been the room that her father had used as his office. She barely remembered it. She'd been young when he'd worked here, and she hadn't visited him in here much, seeing him more often in their residential rooms in the west wing of the castle.

But the floor to ceiling bookcases across from the windows were impressive and she knew the chandelier hanging in the center of the thirty-foot ceiling was as old as the castle itself. This was the original castle, built by the King of Denmark, Frederick the seventh, for her great-great-great-grandfather, Tadhg O'Grady. The desk she was sitting behind had belonged to Tadhg's grandson.

Everything around her was impressive and historic and had a story behind it.

And she loved that, on some level.

But it was nothing like the plethora of photos and memorabilia on the north wall of Ellie's bar. There were dozens of framed photographs of her family throughout the years at various events and on various occasions. Most of them were simple day-to-day things—fishing and crawfish boils and just laughing together at the bar or downtown Autre or on the docks—that had been captured because of the moment. The wall also held cut out newspaper articles, and posters, and sports team banners. It was an eclectic collection of special mementos and memories from the Landry family's life and it meant more to them than all the portraits of the O'Grady ancestors, the artwork that cost more than Ellie's bar would probably appraise for, and the tapestries that could be traced back to Tadhg O'Grady himself meant to Fiona's family.

Tapestries. Who still hung tapestries anyway?

Her phone buzzed with an incoming text message and she lunged for it on her desk. It was three p.m. for her which made it only nine a.m. in Autre. Hoping for a message from Knox, she was just as happy to see it was from Naomi. She and Charlie had gone to western Louisiana yesterday to help Kayla with a pickup at a site where law enforcement had found over forty animals being kept in one house. They had been asked to come help rehome and transport the collection of dogs, cats, and even a few rabbits and two snakes.

Naomi: *We're home. Everything went smoothly. Mostly.*

Fiona smiled. She was so glad the girls had been willing to go back out already with the way things had turned out in Red Plains with the tigers. But when she'd said that, Naomi had just laughed and said, "I just think What Would Fiona Do? And you wouldn't let a few hours in a jail cell slow you down."

That had meant the world to her.

Fiona: *I'm glad. What's 'mostly' mean?*

Naomi: *Had some guys meet us on the road and try to stop us. But we figured it out.*

Fiona's eyes widened. *Who tried to stop you?*

Naomi: *Just some guys. But Charlie turned on the charm and thanked them for the help with the transport and started loading animals into their trucks. Started with the dog that was having diarrhea and then the skunk and then the snakes.*

Fiona read that twice and started laughing. *That's perfect. I love you girls.*

Naomi: *We learned from the best. Miss you.*

Unexpectedly Fiona's eyes welled with tears. *Ditto. I'll be back soon.*

"Mommy!" Saoirse came running in just then.

Fiona sniffed and tucked her phone into her pocket, smiling and turning toward her daughter.

Saoirse wasn't happy about the move to Cara, but she was enjoying being with her grandfather and horseback riding and being spoiled by an entire staff of people to whom she was literally a princess. Fiona was grateful for the fact that Saoirse generally took everything in stride. She didn't know if it was because Saoirse had spent her life with a group of men who were the epitome of laid-back or if it was because she was simply wired to take things as they came. Either way, it'd been a blessing when she'd told her daughter that they were moving again. In twenty-four hours.

"Hey, pretty girl, what's going on?"

"Jacob went with Skylar to the petting zoo."

Fiona studied her daughter's face. Okay, Saoirse didn't look happy or laid-back at the moment. She looked genuinely upset.

"Jacob and Skylar from Autre?"

Of course, it was Skylar and Jacob from Autre. Saoirse hadn't been in Cara long enough to make new friends. She'd spent the first week at the castle with her grandfather. The tutor had come in to evaluate where she was in her studies and to implement an appropriate program for her until Fiona had put her foot down and insisted Saoirse was going to go to the public school. She'd started on Monday and had, for the most part, been fine, but she was definitely not close to anyone yet.

"They went and looked at the alpacas and the goats together yesterday." Saoirse held up her phone. "They texted me."

Fiona looked at the picture of Skylar and Jacob, grinning together as they held the goat between them.

Fiona frowned. "Are you...jealous? Did you have a crush on Jacob or something?" Well, she hadn't seen that coming. She supposed Saoirse wasn't too young to develop romantic feelings for a boy.

Saoirse frowned as if totally confused. "What? Ew. No. I didn't have feelings for Jacob like *that*. He's my friend."

"So why are you upset about him being with Skylar?"

"Because he's being nice to Skylar."

Fiona frowned. "Isn't that what you wanted? You should be so thrilled. You got through to him, Saoirse. You showed him what it's like to be a friend instead of bullying her. This is wonderful."

"I know. I am happy. But...I just wanted to be there when he did it."

"When he did what?"

"Jacob told me that he wanted to invite Skylar to the petting zoo as a way of saying he was sorry for being mean to her. I just wanted to see how happy she was in person and I wanted to tell him I was proud of him."

Fiona's heart swelled. Yeah, she got that. She understood very well how amazing it was to see a plan come together. She loved watching people figure out that they could do things they didn't think they could do and that they were braver and capable of bigger things than they ever thought they were.

Fiona gathered her daughter in for a hug. "I understand. I'm really sorry you couldn't stay and see that." She turned the phone so they were both looking at the photo of Jacob and Skylar. "But look. You can see it in her smile. And you can video chat with them later tonight, when they're out of school."

Saoirse gave a little sigh and nodded. "I know. But it's not the same."

Fiona's heart squeezed. No. It really, really wasn't.

Fiona's phone dinged with another text. Again, she reached for it quickly, *Knox* the only thing in her mind.

It wasn't him. Again.

This time it was Mark. An animal rescue volunteer she knew from Florida.

Hey, did you see the news out of the USVI?

There was always a lot of earthquake activity in and around the U.S. Virgin Islands, the British Virgin Islands, and Puerto Rico but a particularly large one had hit the Virgin Islands three days ago and there was significant damage.

Yes. You there? she texted back.

Mark had been the one to take her to her first post-disaster rescue. It had been a wildfire out in California. Then he'd taken her to Houston after Hurricane Harvey. When Hurricane Maria hit the Caribbean shortly after, she was ready and had headed there immediately.

On St. Thomas, Mark replied a moment later. *When will you be here?*

She smiled. She liked that people just assumed she'd be at these sites. She liked that that was her reputation. But she sighed a moment later. *I'm kind of in the middle of something.*

We need you.

Her heart broke. She'd seen the photos on the news. She *wanted* to be there. Instead she was sitting in an office with *tapestries* doing...nothing. For two weeks. At most, she'd been making phone calls and doing basic paperwork. Okay, she'd been taking notes in her notebook—Knox would never allow that to qualify as actual paperwork. While there were people digging through rubble and taking supplies in and trying to find displaced animals in an area hit by an earthquake.

Not to mention that people all around the globe who were fighting poachers, confronting abusers, arguing with lawmakers, literally lifting animals out of horrible situations and into new homes, bandaging wounds, or just holding the animals and keeping them warm while they slept.

Fiona felt her eyes stinging.

"What's wrong, Mommy?"

She looked up at Saoirse. And really thought about her daughter's question.

There were a lot of things wrong. But she could help fix some of them.

Yes, a sanctuary was a dream come true. It was the ultimate haven for so many animals. But...it was the happily ever after. There was a lot of stuff that came before that. And she wanted to be a part of the journey to that happily ever after.

"I'm just missing some things, and some people, too," she said.

Saoirse wanted to be a part of making happily ever afters happen too. And she deserved to see her patience and how putting her heart out there paid off.

Naomi and the other girls in Autre—and the guys too—wanted to be a part of that journey as well. They could have just stayed a petting zoo that took tickets and sold snow cones and enjoyed having little kids come play with the goats and pet the alpacas, but they hadn't stopped there.

They'd developed a program for kids with emotional issues to come work with therapists and comfort animals. They had an entire colony of endangered penguins that were reproducing and thriving. They were producing an online reality show about how to protect wildlife and their habitats. They had already taken in numerous animals that needed new homes, from dogs and cats to a harbor seal and a lion.

Yes, there was definitely some happily ever after there—a lot of it actually—but they were on the journey and Fiona knew it was for the long haul.

She wanted to be there with them.

And with Kayla, and Mark, and all the other people she'd met along the way.

She wouldn't even mind the paperwork.

No, that wasn't true. She didn't want to do paperwork. But she knew the right guy for that part of the job too.

"I have an idea," Fiona said, giving Saoirse a hug.

"What idea?"

"I think we need to head back to Autre."

Saoirse tipped her head back, her eyes wide. "Really? To visit?"

"Really. But to stay. Why don't you go pack?"

Saoirse grinned broadly. "Okay!"

"I'm going to go talk to Grandpa."

Saoirse went running out the door toward the residential wing. Fiona took a deep breath and headed for her grandfather's office.

Her heart was hammering by the time she approached his secretary's desk. "I need to speak with him, Mary. Is he in?"

"He is. He's finishing a call."

Fiona nodded. "I'll wait."

"I'll take you in. He's nearly finished."

Fiona followed the woman into the king's inner office. It was twice as big and three times as impressive as hers. No one ever saw the interior of the office she was using. Not so with the king's.

She walked around the room, studying the portraits she'd seen dozens of times but had never really looked at. She was, of course, aware that they were all the past kings, but this was the first time it really hit her that these were the Ellies and Leos of her life.

But she didn't feel the warm connection to them that she knew the Landrys felt when they looked at photos of their family.

That made her sad.

She wandered the room, not listening to what her grandfather said, just vaguely aware of his voice in the background.

The shelves that lined the office were filled with books and statues and vases and various other knickknacks. She wondered if they all had meaning. Or if *any* of them had meaning. She wondered if there were stories here like there were behind everything displayed at Ellie's. She'd heard many of those.

If there were stories about the items in her grandfather's office, she'd never heard them. Even as a kid. She'd rarely been invited into this office either. If her grandfather had brought her here and sat her on his lap and told her about their history himself, pointed out why the statues and pieces of art mattered, would it have made a difference? Would she have felt more connected to it all? More a part of Cara?

She traced her finger over the bottom of the frame that surrounded the charter giving Cara to the O'Gradys.

"Fiona."

She turned as her grandfather greeted her.

"I came to tell you that Saoirse and I are leaving within the hour. I'm needed in St. Thomas."

Her grandfather frowned. "St. Thomas? What for?"

"There was an earthquake. I'm sure you're aware."

"Yes."

Fiona sighed. Unlike Mark, who had just assumed Fiona would be on her way, her grandfather wasn't making this connection at all. "There are rescue efforts going on and I've been asked to come. I will be sending Saoirse on to Louisiana with Colin."

"That's ridiculous," Diarmuid said. "Even if you were to go to St. Thomas, which of course you will not, Saoirse and Colin will be staying here."

"No. My daughter will be with me wherever I am."

"If you'll be in St. Thomas, she may as well stay here."

"I will be going to Louisiana when I'm finished in St. Thomas."

Diarmuid sighed heavily and came around to the front of his desk. "You only lasted two weeks. I really thought you could handle at least a month."

"What does that mean?"

"It means that you can only be responsible and pretend to behave like a queen for two weeks."

"Actually, that's not true at all." Fiona straightened her spine, but she didn't cross her arms or put her hands on her hips. In fact, she wasn't feeling all that defensive. She was confident in what she was about to tell him and felt it deep down in her soul. If he didn't understand what she was about to say, that was on him. But she knew she was right. And she was proud of it.

"I'm going to St. Thomas to help a group of volunteers with a rescue mission for displaced animals, to coordinate supplies, recruit additional volunteers, and help with cleanup efforts, and that is extreme queen behavior. As is taking my daughter back to a place where she can be surrounded by people who do that same exact thing every single day. Staying here on this isolated island, where everything is easy, where I can just order things to be done, where I don't have to be accountable to anyone, where I can spend all of my time looking at gorgeous gardens and having people bring me things and trusting that other people are doing all the hard work, is the *least* queenly thing I could do.

"For the past ten years I have been working and educating and inspiring people, making connections, making a difference, and being so queen-like that my daughter has absorbed it just by being around me and watching. I have taught her through action and by modeling the behavior."

Fiona stopped and took a deep breath. Conviction coursed through her and she said firmly, "So, Grandfather, regardless of how you feel about it, I am leaving today with my daughter to go be the best queen I know how to be, in the debris and despair in St. Thomas. And then I'm going to go *home*. To the family I found and created and who loves me for who I am and who I want to be rather than for who they think I should be."

"So you're just going to walk away from all of this? Give this all up?"

"Yes. Because that is the best thing for me, my daughter, our future, Cara quite honestly, and the world."

"I agree completely."

Fiona spun quickly toward the deep male voice behind her. Her mouth dropped open and her eyes widened as she saw one of the last men she ever expected to see standing in her grandfather's office doorway.

17

"Torin?" Fiona gaped at her brother. "What are you doing here?"

Torin strode into the room. He was dressed in blue jeans, a blue button-down shirt that was untucked, with rolled-up sleeves, and stupid Oxford leather shoes that reminded her of Knox so suddenly that she felt her breath catch in her throat.

Her brother looked the epitome of the laid-back, casual businessman. His hair was windblown and he had a pair of sunglasses in his hands as if he'd gotten out of the car and come straight to the office.

"I am here to take my rightful place as the next King of Cara."

There was dead silence in the office.

Her grandfather and Torin just stared at each other. Diarmuid's eyes were narrowed. Torin simply met his gaze, unblinking.

Finally Fiona spoke. "What are you talking about?"

"Everything you said just now is true," Torin told her, though he didn't look away from their grandfather. "You have been out there for the past ten years making a difference.

You've become an amazing woman and you have been doing work that really matters. There are a ton of people who are missing you right now. You being here on Cara in that office doing—whatever you've been doing—is a waste of your time and your talents and your heart. But Cara needs a new ruler in line.

"Say what you will about Declan," Torin went on. "He's sinfully rich and a total asshole, but he's made a life. And he at least gives some of that money to good causes. So it falls to me as the next son. I have work to be done, but as the king of Cara, I'll have the resources and power to see it through."

Finally, Torin met her eyes. "You and Saoirse should not have to give up your life. And whatever the future for Cara holds, however we change the way this country works, it's not going to happen overnight and it's not going to happen without a new leader making those changes. So I'm here."

Fiona was staring at her brother. She had never seen Torin step up like this. She'd never seen him take charge. He was brilliant. He cared. He wasn't a jerk or a flake. But he'd been...restless. She might've argued with him that he was ready for this, but she'd never seen him look so confident.

Besides, there was time for Torin to try this on and see if this was the choice he really wanted to make. Diarmuid's heart wasn't great—and at the moment he looked angry enough that it was possible he was going to have a stroke—but Torin didn't have to take the throne over tomorrow.

"Thank you," she finally said, at a loss for any other words. "That's amazing."

"Well, coming from you, that word means a lot. You've done some pretty amazing things yourself. And I know you're there to help me if I need it with this whole thing."

She laughed softly. Only her brother would refer to ruling an entire country as *this whole thing*.

She stepped forward and pulled Torin into a big hug. "I'm proud of you."

It was maybe strange for a younger sister to tell her older brother that, but she didn't think anyone, including Torin and Cian, would deny that they both had a little growing up to do.

"You're forgetting one thing," Diarmuid broke in.

Fiona pulled back and turned to face her grandfather. "And what's that?"

"I have to agree to rescind Torin's abdication of the throne as well."

"Which I assume means keeping me here, teaching me, quizzing me, making sure that I'm up to the task," Torin said.

The king nodded. "At least."

Torin spread his arms. "Bring it on."

"There's also the matter of a betrothal to a certain Danish heiress," Diarmuid added. "We'll have to have the Olsens over for dinner."

Torin sighed. "I'll be sure to wear my nut cup and hide my baseball bats."

Fiona wasn't sure what *that* was all about—and she really wanted that story—or what had gotten into her brother in general and she almost wished she could stay just to watch this whole thing play out.

Almost.

"Holy shit. It's really an actual castle."

Cian laughed. "You thought we were kidding? What else do kings and queens live in?"

Okay, that was a decent point. Knox hadn't given it a lot of thought.

The town car pulled up in front of the...yeah, castle. That was really the best word for the building, house, whatever.

"You didn't look it up?" Cian asked. "I thought you knew everything about Cara."

"I—" He hadn't. This was the one thing he hadn't looked up about Cara. He supposed he had been picturing just a huge house. He wasn't sure Fiona had ever used the word castle. Or if she had, he'd thought she was being dramatic. But this thing was huge. It had tall stone walls, multiple turrets and spires. And a moat. It didn't have a drawbridge, however. The moat only ran around three-fourths of the castle with a wide paved drive leading up to the front gate.

"Does a footman or someone have to come greet us?"

Cian pushed his door open and jumped out. The prince looked like any other guy his age coming home for a visit. He wore blue jeans and a t-shirt with a jacket, a baseball cap, and sunglasses. He was also wearing tennis shoes.

"Naw. Come on. We can just go in. Callum might meet us. He probably saw the car drive up."

"Who's Callum?"

"The butler."

Knox sighed. There was a butler. Of course there was a butler.

"What about the bags?"

Cian glanced back. Then frowned. "Uh. I don't know. Someone will get them."

"You sure?"

Cian shrugged. "Yeah. My bags always end up in my room and I never take them there."

Knox rolled his eyes.

Cian just laughed. "Hey, I carry my own bag in the U.S. Henry would kick my ass if I left it behind and thought he'd carry it."

"And you know this because you did that once, and he told you that."

"Yep. And then I told him I'd fire him for talking to me like that."

"And?"

"I tried. He ended up getting a raise."

Henry, who always traveled with Cian, came up next to Knox. "I love when he fires me. I always get a raise."

"How many times has that happened in the ten years?" Knox asked.

"Eight."

"Wow. You've had eight raises?"

"Oh no. I've had fourteen raises. Just eight for being 'fired'. There are plenty of other reasons to deserve raises in this job."

Knox lifted a brow. "The King is generous."

"The raises come from Oisin." Henry grinned. "He understands very well what it's like to spend so much time with an O'Grady."

He clapped Knox on the shoulder and started after Cian, who was already halfway to the front door.

Yeah, he had his own O'Grady that he wanted to spend his full time with and she was right inside this castle.

Knox followed the other men.

He had no idea what was going to happen from here but he was happy to have Cian and Henry here.

Hell, Torin and Jonah were here too. They'd left an hour before Knox had announced to everyone at Ellie's that he was heading to Cara. He'd fully intended to get a hold of Oisin to ask about a seat on the private jet, but Cian had been at Ellie's and had immediately wanted to come along to see Knox's big gesture.

And the king's reaction to it.

When they'd discovered Torin had already taken off for Cara, for reasons unknown, Cian had been even more determined to get to the island and when the O'Grady private jet had been unavailable, he'd called in a favor from a friend. The son of a billionaire who happened to have *two* private jets.

You need to lead with you were wrong to think that she belonged anywhere but Autre.

No, you need to lead with I love you.

You were wrong is better. She knows you love her.

Maybe you need to offer to stay there with her. Just tell her you want to be together.

But she needs to be in Autre.

The front door swung open before Cian even touched the handle.

"Prince Cian," an older man greeted with a short bow.

"Hey, Callum," Cian greeted. "Hope I'm in time for lunch."

"Anything you want, Your Majesty," the butler said. "I'll inform the kitchen."

"Excellent answer." Cian turned to Knox. "Callum, this is Knox. He's here for Princess Fiona."

Callum lifted a brow. "I see. She's upstairs."

"Great. Want a steak? Or a sandwich? Or an omelet?" Cian asked Knox. "I don't even know what time it's supposed to be."

They'd left Louisiana at two a.m. Which was eight a.m. Cara time. Which meant it was just after eleven a.m. in Autre. But five p.m. in Cara. Yeah, Knox didn't know either.

"No. I just want to see Fiona."

"Very good." Callum turned on his heel and started down the hallway.

Knox looked around the foyer. At least Knox was telling himself it was a foyer. He wasn't sure if there were certain terms for the rooms in the castle.

Of course, this "foyer" could fit all of Ellie's and probably Autre City Hall inside it. The ceiling spiraled upward at least a hundred feet and the white marble floor gleamed brightly, the inlaid ribbons of gold sparkly in the sun from the skylight overhead. It looked like a museum. There were windows everywhere, artwork adorned the walls, and he felt the need to whisper.

Cian did not seem to have that same instinct.

"Hello! Banished prince home to visit!"

"Banished?" Knox asked.

"Sounds better than runaway. More wounded. More, it's-them-not-me," Cian told him.

Knox laughed. "It also sounds inaccurate."

Cian gave him a self-deprecating grin. "Fortunately, the good people of Cara, especially the ones who work in this castle, think I'm charming."

"Or are they paid to pretend they think you're charming?"

"Potato-potahto."

Knox chuckled.

"Well, while I wait for dinner, let's go find my sister." Cian started across the foyer toward the staircase at the far end. Knox had only taken a single step to follow him when he heard, "Knox?"

He stopped and looked up at the sound of a young girl's voice.

Saoirse stood at the top of the stairs, staring down at him.

"Hey, Princess."

"Oh my gosh!" She came running down the stairs toward him.

They met at the bottom and he scooped her up into his arms, squeezing her tightly.

"I can't believe you're here!"

Cian coughed. "Uh, hello? Favorite uncle, right here."

Saoirse giggled and turned her head to look at Cian, resting her cheek on Knox's shoulder. "I never said you were my favorite."

"No way is Torin your favorite."

"He helps me beat you in water gun fights."

323

"He only does that because he can't beat me without *your* help," Cian told her.

She laughed again, then pulled back to look at Knox "Who's taking care of the otters?"

He laughed. He loved that that was her first concern. "Skylar and Jacob, actually."

"That's nice." She smiled. "I'm glad Jacob turned out to be good."

"I'm glad that you helped him believe that he was good."

Suddenly Knox's throat felt tight and he squeezed her again.

"We're coming home! Did you come to keep us company on the plane?"

Knox set her down, but crouched in front of her. "What do you mean?"

"I was just packing. Mommy says we're coming home to Autre."

Her words made his chest ache. He loved that Saoirse considered Autre home. And that Fiona might refer to it that way. But he didn't want to get his hopes up. "You mean you're coming to Autre to visit?"

But she shook her head. "No, *moving* back."

"Princess, I would love that. But I think your mom meant you were coming for a visit."

"No, she meant moving back. For good."

He lifted his eyes at the sound of a woman's voice.

But not just any woman. *The* woman. His woman.

Fiona stood halfway up the staircase watching him with Saoirse.

His throat tightened and he had to swallow hard. Before he could say, "Really?"

She nodded, continuing down the stairs, her gaze locked on his. "It's where I belong. It's where Saoirse and I both belong. I just informed my grandfather. We're leaving today." She came to stand right in front of him.

"Well, damn. That's too bad."

She lifted her brows. "It is?"

"You ruined my whole rescue. I was going to barge in here, sweep you off your feet, explain to you that you might be too much for some people, like your grandfather, but he's just not your people—"

"I love that quote," she said softly.

He nodded. "And then I was going to take you home, to your people, and save you from this"—he looked around, then back at her with a half-grin—"dismal existence."

She gave him a small smile. "Cages come in lots of shapes and sizes."

That made his heart clench hard and he stepped close, lifting a hand to cup her face. "You have to know though, if you come home, I'm not letting you go again."

"Thank God."

Then she gave a little jump and he caught her in his arms. She wrapped her arms around his neck and buried her face in his neck. He just held her like that, squeezing tight, her hugging him, both of them just breathing, soaking each other in.

He looked at Saoirse. This wasn't how he'd planned to do this, but the moment felt right. "Saoirse, I was wondering if you might be okay with me marrying your mom?"

Her face broke into the biggest grin he'd seen on the girl yet. And that was saying something. Especially considering she'd taught baby otters to swim.

"Yes! Yes! Mom, you have to say yes! That means I get to live with the otters and the foxes!"

Knox felt Fiona shaking in his arms and he pulled back slightly to find her laughing even as tears streamed down her face. She looked down at her daughter. "You act like you haven't grown up around cool animals your whole life."

"But I've never shared my bedroom with otters!"

"You think you're going to have the otters *in* your bedroom?"

"Oh, I'm putting my bed in the otter room," Saoirse informed them both. "And we have a very long flight home for me to convince you of all the reasons that's a good idea."

Knox and Fiona looked at one another.

"Looks like we can take the girl out of the castle, but I don't think we can fully take the princess out of the girl," Knox said.

Fiona laughed. "Some things are just in her blood."

"So what do you say?" He squeezed her ass. "Marry me? I promise to do all of your paperwork and forms from now on."

"Yes. Even without the forms and paperwork. Though that will definitely get you some..." She glanced at Saoirse then back to Knox, clearly censoring what she was about to say. "... extra credit."

"This might shock you, but I *always* go for the extra credit."

She laughed. "No, my hot, nerdy bayou boy, that doesn't surprise me a bit."

The next kiss didn't get quite as deep and heated as it could have, considering they had two kids watching—one who looked like a nine-year-old girl and one who looked like a twenty-seven-year-old man—but it was enough, for the moment.

"Okay, let's go home," Knox told her, turning and starting for the door.

"Just one thing."

Knox stopped and looked at her.

"Did you get new shoes?"

They both looked down at his feet. He was wearing new leather Oxfords. "Yes. But I also have boots in my bag. I'm learning."

She took his face in her hands and kissed him. "Awesome.

We have to take a detour on our way back to Louisiana. There was an earthquake."

"In St. Thomas." He'd heard about it. And wondered if it was bugging her not to be there.

She nodded.

He looked at her for a long moment. He was going to have to get used to this. But instead of exasperation, he only felt excitement. "I don't consider that a detour, Fi."

"No?"

"Nope. That's a regular road on this journey we're on. And I'm right here beside you."

She gave him a dazzling smile, then leaned in to kiss him again before saying, "You have no idea what a perfect thing that was to say."

EPILOGUE

Two months later...

"Giraffe baby!"
Everyone in Ellie's pivoted to look at Saoirse.

"Really?" Naomi was the first one on her feet.

"Really! Come on! It's happening!"

"Saoirse, Princess, hold the phone still. I'm getting motion sick," Knox told his soon-to-be stepdaughter.

Saoirse lifted the phone in front of her face. "Sorry. I keep forgetting."

Fiona had tossed the phone—and video chat with Knox—to Saoirse when she'd gone into the barn to check on Speir. She'd been intending to scoop more hay into the expectant mother's stall for the pending birth but had found front hooves showing, indicating the baby was literally on its way. In her excitement, Saoirse had taken Knox and the phone with her as she'd run from the barn to Ellie's bar to tell everyone. The bouncing scenery on the way had him nauseous.

"Let's go!" Griffin said, leading the way out of Ellie's.

Someone swooped Saoirse up and put her on their back

328

piggyback. Saoirse and the phone bumped along as the group headed back to the barn.

Knox just closed his eyes and waited for them to get there.

A few minutes later, everyone was gathered around and Fiona had taken the phone back from Saoirse. "Oh my God, Knox. This is exciting,"

She'd turned the phone so that he could see the giraffe pacing around her stall. Sure enough, there were two front hooves showing and he'd watched enough YouTube videos with Saoirse to know that as soon as there was a snout showing everything else would go quickly.

"I wish I could be there," he said.

Fiona turned the phone to look at him. "It is your own fault that you're sitting in a jail cell instead of here to watch this."

He sighed and looked to his right, meeting Donovan Foster's eyes. He was watching the same scene on his phone via a video call with Naomi.

"Yeah, well, it didn't go quite according to plan."

Fiona laughed. "I swear I thought keeping Griffin home this time would mean this rescue would go smoothly and no one would get into trouble."

The last time the three guys had gone on a rescue without the girls, Griffin had punched a guy and ended up needing four stitches himself.

"When did Zander say he was going to be here?" Knox asked.

"He left an hour ago, so I think you just have to sit tight for a bit."

The guys had headed out to help some friends load the animals from a puppy mill that had been broken up about three hours north of New Orleans. Fiona had wanted to go along but hadn't felt she could leave her very pregnant and likely-in-labor giraffe. That had been a good call.

The contact that had tipped them off to the puppy mill had

also been right when he'd informed the rescue group that the owner would be pissed and not surrender the animals easily.

Knox and Donovan had showed up before law enforcement and the puppy mill owner had gotten very mouthy and Donovan had taken offense at being called a fucking bleeding heart bastard. But they hadn't thrown any punches until the guy had picked up a puppy by the neck and tossed it to the side.

"You can keep me live for this whole birth?" Knox asked.

"You want to watch the whole thing, right?"

"Absolutely. But I can get on the live stream that Charlie's doing. If that's easier for you."

"Oh! That's true," Fiona turned the phone back to face her. "Do you mind? I want to share this with you. But I do want to make sure that we're ready for once he or she is born."

"Yeah, no problem. I'll just get on Charlie's feed."

"Okay. I love you. Um... hurry home." She smirked.

"This is all your fault, you know," he told her. "You O'Grady girls made me all mushy inside and sappy about animals and now I'm sitting in jail."

"It's weird how not sorry I am."

They disconnected and Knox pulled up the Boys of the Bayou Gone Wild live feed on their website. There were over a hundred thousand people watching the giraffe give birth with him.

He shook his head. "This is amazing," he said to Donovan. "Thinking back to where we started with all of this."

Donovan nodded. "I know. The whole thing was just a petting zoo when I came to visit Griffin that first time. Couldn't believe how easily he'd gotten sucked in. Suddenly, my big, tough, wildlife vet brother was all gaga over a bunch of goats and otters." He laughed. "Of course, then I met the Landrys and totally understood."

Knox nodded. "Takes about ten minutes."

"Probably more like five for me."

They sat just grinning and watching a giraffe walk around her stall for a few minutes.

Then Donovan asked, "So your first name is really actually just the F?"

When they'd been booked the cops had, of course, needed Knox's first name. He'd produced his driver's license and showed the photo of his birth certificate that he kept on his phone for just such occasions. It didn't come up much, but it was very hard to convince people that his real first name was just a single letter, so he'd learned it was simply easier to have that with him. Donovan had, of course, overheard.

"Yep. Just the letter F. Believe it or not, it's legal."

"How'd that happen?"

"My dad's father's name is Franklin and my mom's dad's name was Frederick and they were trying to decide between the two and couldn't. So when it came time at the hospital, they just filled in the first letter and told everybody that they'd make a decision within a few days after they got me home. And they never got around to it. So it's always just been F."

Donovan shook his head. "So when you were like, four they were just calling you F?"

"No." Knox laughed. "When we were with my dad's side of the family, they called me Frankie. When we were with my mom's side, the family called me Freddie. I answered to both. When were at home, they just called me kiddo or sweetie. It wasn't an issue until I started school. They realized then it was going to be a headache, so they registered me officially with my first name, but then told everyone just call me Knox." He chuckled. "It was really never a big deal, but it sure has been fun making people wonder."

"Fun? Hell, I lost fifty bucks."

"Fifty? What did you bet it was?" He was sure that's what Donovan meant. He was certain the whole Landry clan had a pool going on what his real first name was.

"Fort."

Knox snorted. "Thank God my parents actually like me."

"Fletcher bet it was Fletcher."

Knox laughed.

"The best was Sawyer's guess. He figured it was probably Fionn and you couldn't admit it because that's so close to Fiona."

Knox groaned. "No."

Donovan laughed. "I actually love that the answer has been right there in front of everyone all along. Everyone's actually always known your first name."

Knox shrugged. "I've enjoyed my own inside joke, I'll admit."

"Okay, so how much is it worth to you for me to keep the secret?"

"What you want?"

"Can it just be an open IOU?" Donovan asked.

Knox had a feeling that was very dangerous. But he didn't really have a choice. "Okay." He narrowed his eyes. "Use it wisely."

"And does that include keeping this secret from Fiona? Or does she know?"

"Well, we're gonna have to go get our marriage license pretty soon, so I suppose she'll find out then." He grinned. "But I have ways of keeping her quiet."

Donovan chuckled. "Nice."

"Okay guys, you're free to go," the sheriff's deputy announced, unlocking the cell door and pulling it open. "Your bill's been paid and there are a couple guys waiting outside to help you load up the wolves."

"Wolves?" Knox asked. "What wolves?"

"Apparently there were some wolves mixed in with the dogs and someone told the rescue group that you were the best ones to take them."

Knox and Donovan looked at one another. "Fiona," they said at the same time.

Donovan slapped his thighs and stood. "Okay. Let's go."

Knox got up a little slower but followed Donovan out of the cell and down the hallway to where Zander was waiting for them.

So they were going to go load up some wolves. And take them back to Autre where there would probably be a new baby giraffe by the time they got back. And then he was going to go home to three otters and the four fennec foxes that had ended up staying at his house after all. Though it had taken *a lot* of paperwork.

And then he would welcome the love of his life home after she fed her zebra and the tiger and lion, and checked in on the harbor seal, the red pandas, and the sloths, and then met her daughter at the enclosure where the wombats lived.

Knox grinned. He couldn't believe how wild his life had gotten.

Or how damned much he loved it that way.

ᘯ

Thank you for reading Knox and Fiona's story! I hope you loved it!

But wait... it's not all over just yet!

What about Griffin's proposal? You want to see that don't you? Email Erin at Erin@ErinNicholas.com to request the link!

And what if I told you I had a whole SECOND EPILOGUE?!

Now this is only for SUPER fans of the series! Everyone shows up in this... I mean everyone! So if you haven't read all the bayou books, you might be a little lost!

But if you have... you can get a second epilogue from ELLIE'S point of view! (including a WEDDING and some baby announcements!!)

AND, some extra goodies! Like that bonus scene where Josh and Tori had their baby! And the Hot Bayou bonus scenes from last summer! And a full character guide to the series! And more! All in one place!

Just head to the book page on ErinNicholas.com and find OTTER CHAOS for how to buy!

WHAT'S NEXT?

Sad the Boys of the Bayou Gone Wild series is over?

**Well, get ready for the
Badges of the Bayou!**

*The next series from NYT bestselling romance author, Erin
Nicholas!*

It's got everything you love about Erin's books set on the
Louisiana bayou– the small town of Autre, friends that are
more like family, laugh-out-loud hijinks, tough, sexy, blue-
collar men, and the feisty women who tame them, and heat
that'll have you searching for a spot to skinny dip to cool off!

And now Erin's added a touch of intrigue and, of course, the
sexy, protective men who wear badges and keep all the
shenanigans under control. Or try to anyway!

Gotta Be Bayou, book one

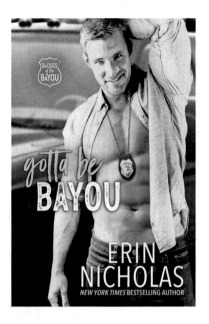

Sleeping, unwelcome, on the couch of the woman most likely to cut him up and feed him to a gator probably isn't the best idea.

Even if he deserves it.

Even if it's for her own good.

Even if she makes him hotter than a Louisiana summer night.

Sexy, broody, FBI agent **Spencer Landry** is not leaving that couch until he knows that fiery investigative journalist Max Keller is safe.

Unless she lets him into her *bed* ... again.

Bayou With Benefits, book two

What's next?

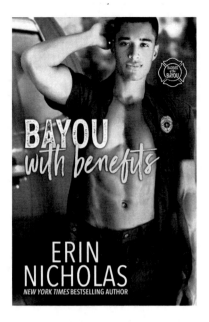

Firefighter and single dad **Michael LeClaire** needs a nanny.

Ex-beauty queen Amelia Landry is perfect for the job.
Well, at least, he's willing to give the family friend the job.

But now that she's working for him, *living with him*, and even more important to his young son, his friend's little sister is even more off-limits.

Of course they're friends too. But there can't be any extra "benefits" in this relationship. Even if she is sleeping just down the hall...

Rocked Bayou, book three

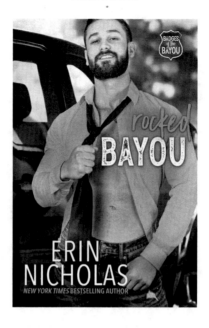

Ex-bodyguard Colin Daly needs three things:
To figure out how to have a real job after his longtime client no longer needs him.
To find some really good Irish whiskey in the land of homemade moonshine.
To stop having dirty dreams every time he hears young, beautiful, recently-discovered-thanks-to-social-media music sensation, Hayden Ross, sing. Which seems to be every time he freaking turns around lately.

But now the new-to-the-spotlight sweetheart has a stalker and needs 24/7 protection. And Colin will be damned if he's going to let anyone else take this job. No matter how much being her temporary, very protective roommate is going to rock his world.

IF YOU LOVE AUTRE AND THE LANDRYS...

If you love the Boys of the Bayou Gone Wild, you can't miss the Boys of the Bayou series! *All available now!*

My Best Friend's Mardi Gras Wedding (Josh & Tori)

Sweet Home Louisiana (Owen & Maddie)

Beauty and the Bayou (Sawyer & Juliet)

Crazy Rich Cajuns (Bennett & Kennedy)

Must Love Alligators (Chase & Bailey)

Four Weddings and a Swamp Boat Tour (Mitch & Paige)

And be sure to check out the connected series, Boys of the Big Easy!

Easy Going (prequel novella)-Gabe & Addison

Going Down Easy- Gabe & Addison

Taking It Easy - Logan & Dana

Eggnog Makes Her Easy - Matt & Lindsey

Nice and Easy - Caleb & Lexi

Getting Off Easy - James & Harper

If you're looking for more sexy, small town rom com fun, check out the

The Hot Cakes Series

One small Iowa town.

Two rival baking companies.

A three-generation old family feud.

And six guys who are going to be heating up a lot more than the kitchen.

Sugar Rush (prequel)

Sugarcoated

Forking Around

Making Whoopie

Semi-Sweet On You

Oh, Fudge

Gimme S'more

———

And much more—

including my printable booklist— at

ErinNicholas.com